Nobody writes characters like Joyce Magnin, and Harriet Beamer does not disappoint. A story that's all heart; you'll be cheering Harriet on with every page.

> JENNY B. JONES, award-winning author
> of *Save the Date* and *There You'll Find Me*

Absolutely delightful! There's surely a bit of Harriet Beamer in all of us — that mixture of trepidation but desire for adventure, and a relishing of God's pleasure in becoming all He's created us to be. I'd barely swiped away my tears before breaking into new peals of laughter. *Harriet Beamer Takes the Bus* is Joyce Magnin's best yet.

> CATHY GOHLKE, award-winning author
> of *Promise Me This*

If *you* want to feel God's pleasure, take this delightfully unpredictable journey with Harriet Beamer and the unrivalled Queen of Quirk, Joyce Magnin. I know of no other author who can bring the truth of the Gospel so close to earth and yet lift the reader so high. Ya gotta get on this bus.

> NANCY RUE, Christy Award-winning author
> of *The Reluctant Prophet*

You'll love Joyce Magnin's tale of a grandmother's unconventional cross-country trip toward family togetherness.

> RICHARD L. MABRY, MD, author of the Prescription
> for Trouble Series

Grab your toothbrush and pack extra jammies — you're in for quite a ride! Harriet Beamer rocks.

> REBECCA PRICE JANNEY, author of nineteen books,
> including *On a Steed of Iron*

Harriet Beamer's adventure sparks that longing in all of us to who, as Thoreau said, when it's time to die, don't want to discover that we have never truly lived. I fell in love with Harriet when she decided that money, a cell phone, and God were all she needed for her journey. And what she comes to learn in her travels is a lesson for life — that being who God intended us to be can bless others beyond measure.

> CHRISTA ALLAN, author of *Love Finds You in New
> Orleans*, *Edge of Grace*, and *Walking on Broken Glass*

Also by Joyce Magnin

Carrying Mason

HARRIET BEAMER

Takes the Bus

a novel by
JOYCE MAGNIN

ZONDERVAN®

ZONDERVAN.com/
AUTHOR**TRACKER**
follow your favorite authors

ZONDERVAN

Harriet Beamer Takes the Bus
Copyright © 2012 by Joyce Magnin

This title is also available as a Zondervan ebook.
Visit www.zondervan.com/ebooks.

This title is also available in a Zondervan audio edition.
Visit www.zondervan.fm.

Requests for information should be addressed to:
Zondervan, *Grand Rapids, Michigan 49530*

Library of Congress Cataloging-in-Publication Data

Magnin, Joyce.
    Harriet Beamer takes the bus / Joyce Magnin.
       p. cm.
    ISBN 978-0-310-33355-5 (pbk.)
    I. Title.
  PS3601.L447H37 2011
  813'.6—dc23   2011036018

Cover design: Anderson Design Group
Cover photography: iStockphoto®, Shutterstock®
Interior design: Beth Shagene

Printed in the United States of America

12 13 14 15 16 17 18 /DCI/ 21 20 19 18 17 16 15 14 13 12 11 10 9 8 7 6 5 4 3 2 1

For Rebecca
Fellow traveler

HARRIET BEAMER

Takes the Bus

Chapter 1

HARRIET BEAMER NEVER LOST A BET IN HER LIFE. NOT THAT she did much gambling, and she never bet more than a few dollars, but still, she could honestly say she'd never lost a bet. Not until her daughter-in-law, Prudence, enticed her to wager not just a few dollars, but her entire house.

Harriet lost what she later learned was a sucker's bet. Not wanting to be known for the rest of her life as a welsher, she did the only thing a woman in her station in life could do: she honored the bet. In accordance with the conditions of the wager she sold her house and agreed to move to Grass Valley, California, even though she had been mostly happy living with Humphrey, her basset hound, in suburban Philadelphia.

Here's what happened.

Christmas came around, as it did every year, with just the right amount of fanfare. Harriet loved Advent — going to church and watching the children recite verses and light candles in preparation for Jesus' birth. She enjoyed shopping for gifts, attending the Sunday school Christmas pageant, and baking cookies. She had become famous for her butter spritz cookies, which she lovingly decorated with green and red sugar and candied cherries. Nearly every home in the neighborhood and every family at the Willow Street Church received a tin filled to the brim with her one-of-a-kind fudge and a generous sampling of the buttery cookie delights. Last year she counted the number of cookies she had baked, sprinkled, and given away. The grand total was 1,032. She did the math and calculated that if she placed them end-to-end, she had baked 129 feet of butter spritz cookies.

Christmas gave her great joy. But the busyness of the season caused frequent bouts of distress and, at times, copious amounts of indigestion. And Christmas had taken on a new patina after Max died—her husband of twenty-eight years. He had loved Christmas—every last bit of it from the lights on the trees to the mall Santas. He loved the wrapping and the giving and especially the old Perry Como and Andy Williams Christmas specials on VHS, which he watched almost continuously for the entire week leading up to Christmas Eve. Missing Max was a wound not easily healed.

So when he died suddenly on Christmas Eve fifteen years ago, Harriet was left to face Christmases yet to come with sadness and regret. Sadness because she missed Max so much that it hurt, and regret because of what their son, Henry, did—and with her blessings to boot!

* * *

Henry called from the airport to let Harriet know they would be arriving soon. They just needed to grab their bags, procure a rental car, and make it out to her Bryn Mawr home in rush-hour traffic.

"You might be better off taking the back roads," Harriet said. "Just find Bartram Avenue and then jog over to Lansdowne, you know, past the big Catholic church, and then over that sweet little bridge, past the high school, and—"

"No, no," Henry interrupted. "Prudence has her GPS programmed, and the expressway's our surest bet."

"That's nice, dear," Harriet said. "Prudence always has things figured out. I'll be waiting with cookies. And please be careful. It snowed earlier and the roads might be slippery still."

"Okay, Mom, see you soon."

Harriet pushed the End button on her phone and sat at the kitchen table. A GPS, she knew, was a gadget that helped people find their way, but since when did Henry need a GPS to find his way home? She folded her hands in front of her and pondered as Humphrey nestled at her feet.

"How about that, Humphrey," Harriet said, "I know the initials stand for Global Positioning ... something or other, but in this case I say they stand for Grumpy Prudence System. Prudence sounded a little grumpy the last time I spoke to her. Probably that super-duper lawyering job of hers, which is probably why Henry is coming home her way."

Humphrey let go one of his long, loud howls.

"You're right," Harriet said. "If they would just settle down and have a baby ... or two."

Harriet reached down and scratched behind Humphrey's long, loppy left ear. "I still don't know how you get around with these things."

For the next thirty minutes Harriet waited for their arrival. She kept going to the front window and looking out, hoping to see them drive up to the curb. She rearranged all of the snowmen salt and pepper shakers on the mantel, the Christmas tree shakers on the end table, and the elf-shaped shakers that she always liked to line up along the window sill in the living room so they could look out. Harriet owned an extensive novelty shaker collection spanning more than fifty years.

She had been a proud member of the Shake It Up novelty salt-and-pepper-shaker club for fifteen years and attended their biannual meeting held at the Knights of Columbus. She had a preference for bench-sitter shakers and was proud of her Indian chief and Indian maiden set her friend Martha found in an antique store in Connecticut. A man named Darby offered her sixty-seven dollars for it last year. But she couldn't part with it. Of course her one dream was that someday she could visit the Salt and Pepper

Shaker Museum in Gatlinburg, Tennessee. But that didn't seem likely.

After fiddling with the shakers, Harriet checked the water in the Christmas tree. The tree twinkled with multicolored lights. She had planned to wait for Henry and Prudence before hanging any ornaments. She wanted that to be a family thing, with Christmas carols playing in the background and maybe even a fire blazing in the fireplace. But she couldn't contain herself any longer and opened the Christmas box. She pulled out a couple of glass balls — red and silver — and hung them on the tree. Then she dug around for her favorite — an antique ornament of a little boy and girl wearing Lederhosen on a swing. The boy once had a feather in his cap but that was long gone. The ornament had been made over a hundred years ago in the Black Forest of Germany. She let it dangle from her fingers and looked at it from all angles. She could almost hear Max in the background. "Go on, honey, hang it on a good branch, where everyone will see it."

Max had given it to Harriet on their first Christmas as husband and wife. It was considered an antique even back then and was ever so delicate. Harriet loved it from that moment on. She grabbed a dining room chair and placed it near the tree.

Humphrey whimpered and looked up.

Harriet stood on the chair to make it easier to reach one of the higher branches. Unfortunately, Harriet didn't realize she had set the chair on the wadded-up piece of newspaper used to wrap the ornament, and the chair wobbled. Harriet lost her balance and crashed to the floor.

She sat there, pain radiating from her foot to her brain and wishing that she had gotten one of those "I've fallen and I can't get up" buttons. Humphrey toddled over to check on things. He howled. Harriet howled back.

"I don't think it's broken," Harriet said. "My ankle. I felt it twist and well ... I did hear a snap, but that was probably only a tree branch. Did you hear a snap, Humphrey?" She looked at the tree. Her ornament dangled from a branch — secure but not secure enough. "Good, my ornament isn't broken either."

Harriet tried to get up, but as she did the pain went from tolerable to mind-numbing. For a second she thought she saw a circus elephant sitting on her foot. Humphrey tramped next to her and sat. He rested his head on her thigh. She patted his head as a tear slipped down her cheek. "Humphrey. I'm so glad you're here."

He whimpered and looked up over his wiry eyebrows and let go a solemn doggy sigh.

"It's okay," she managed as another blast of pain shot through her foot. "Don't fret. They'll be here soon."

As she waited, images of her and Humphrey crossed her mind like picture postcards. She remembered how she had rescued him from certain death at the pound. The way his ears perked the moment they made eye contact. There was no doubt that they were meant to be the best of friends, and a bond between woman and dog was forged that seemed to transcend the ordinary.

She attempted to get up again, but Humphrey held her in place. "Fine. I guess you know best."

The doorbell rang.

"It's them."

Humphrey trotted to the door.

"Oh dear. It's locked," Harriet said. "I hope Henry remembered his key." Tears streamed down her face.

The bell rang again, followed by three sharp knocks.

Humphrey danced on the linoleum-floored foyer, his toenails clicked on the floor. Then he scratched at the door and yowled.

"Come in," Harriet called as loud as she could, hoping they would hear, "but only if it's you, Henry? Please come in." Harriet managed to remove the fuzzy slipper from her injured foot. The pain felt so intense she could hardly raise her voice. It seemed like her whole leg had caught fire and a gazillion fire ants were crawling all over it. "Come in," she called again as she watched her foot turn the color of a plum left in the refrigerator crisper drawer too long.

The knocks came harder until Harriet finally heard the key in the door.

Humphrey toddled back to Harriet.

"Henry," Harriet called the instant the door opened.

"Mom! What are you doing on the floor?"

That was when Prudence pushed her way in, dropped a leather briefcase on the floor, and said, "Isn't it obvious, Henry. Your mother's had an accident. I was worried this would happen." Prudence was a pretty woman, tall — maybe an inch taller than Henry. She always dressed fashionably and wore her hair in what Harriet said looked like tossed salad, but it was attractive, especially with the mahogany streaks.

"Mom," Henry said. "Are you all right? What happened?"

Henry lifted his mother up and carried her to the couch. She wasn't what you would call a slight woman, and Henry was not the biggest man on the block. She stood about five feet four inches tall and weighed just over 170 pounds. She had a bit of a tummy paunch, which probably contributed to her high blood pressure and weak ankles. But at age seventy-two, Harriet Beamer had plenty of energy. She just didn't know what to do with it sometimes.

"I was hanging the little girl-and-boy ornament and fell off the chair. It's nothing, really; just a sprain. I'll be . . . fine." She tried to hide her discomfort.

Harriet caught a definite look pass between Henry and Prudence. She knew they'd been talking about her living alone and how they thought it would be safer if she moved to Grass Valley and lived with them in their big sprawling house. The house still without children or a dog or the aroma of chocolate chip cookies baking in the oven.

"You should really put some ice on that Hari — er, I mean Mother," Prudence said. Harriet had suggested that maybe if Prudence called her Mom or Mother it might help them bond. So far it

14

had only been uncomfortable for Prudence—something Harriet could not understand.

"Ice is a good idea," Henry said. "Then I think I should take you to the hospital."

"Oh, it's just a sprain," Harriet said. "Like your Gramma always said, nothing to do but keep it till it gets better."

Prudence smoothed the back of her skirt and sat on the sofa near Harriet. "From the looks of it," she said brushing dog hairs from her lap, "I'd say it's broken."

"Ah, fiddlesticks," Harriet said. "Your degree is in law, not medicine. It's merely sprained." Harriet heard the words leave her lips and felt bad for jumping down Prudence's throat. "I'm sorry. I didn't mean—"

"I can tell a broken ankle when I see one, Mother," Prudence said. "It's misshapen, purple, swollen, and whether you'll admit it or not, you are in incredible pain. I can see it written all over your face."

"That's just wrinkles, dear. Can't read anything into them."

Harriet winced again and Humphrey ambled near. He licked her hand.

"Look," Prudence said, "even Humphrey knows it's serious."

Henry returned from the kitchen with a Ziploc bag filled with half-moon-shaped ice cubes.

"Henry," Harriet said. "That reminds me. Do we still call them cubes even if they're not shaped like that anymore?"

Prudence chuckled. "Of course, Mother."

"Oh, well, that's good to know," Harriet said. "May I have the ice *cubes*, dear."

Harriet gently placed the bag on the sorest part of her ankle. "Look at that. I'd say it's the color of DMC embroidery floss number 797." She grimaced.

"Please, Mother," Henry said. "Let's get you to the hospital. What can it hurt?"

15

"Just her pride," Prudence said. "She'll never admit it's fractured now."

"Fractured?" Harriet said. "I bet it's only a sprain. A bad one, but still just a sprain." Harriet winced again. "Falling just that little way off a kitchen chair won't break a perfectly good bone."

"How much would you care to wager?" Prudence asked.

"Mom," Henry said, "don't do this. Let's just get you to the ER before it gets worse."

"Fiddlesticks." Harriet looked Prudence square in the eyes. "I'll take that action, Counselor. What's the stakes?"

Prudence raised her eyebrows, stood, and then paced three times across the living room like she was in court. "Okay, let's say if it is broken you come live with us in Grass Valley, where you won't be alone should anything like this happ—"

"Hold on a second," Henry said. "Let's think this through. You know how seriously she takes these silly little wagers."

"Yes," Harriet said with a wince. "That would mean selling my house. The house your father built with his own two hands."

"Don't start, Mom, not now," Henry said.

"I'm not starting." Tears dripped down her cheeks.

"Yes, you are. Just another opportunity to bring up Dad's construction business and—"

"Henry," Prudence said. "This isn't the time."

Harriet moaned. "Well, you did quit the business and then talked me into selling the company and then—" she snapped her fingers—"just like that you moved to California to become a . . . a writer."

"It's what I wanted, Mom. It's what Pru wanted. She had a great opportunity, and I needed to see if I could make it as a writer—something I wanted to do since I was a kid."

Prudence touched Harriet's knee. "He's happy."

Harriet's stomach went wobbly as the pain grew steadily worse. The ice did not appear to be working at all as her ankle was now the size of a canoe.

"Okay, so back to the bet. If I win then—"

"Then you get to stay in the house until you . . . well until—"

"I die. You can say it. I know I'm going to die one day, same as you."

"Well, no one is dying today," Henry said. "Let's get you to the hospital."

Henry helped his mother off the couch. She hopped toward the front door with Henry's help. Harriet reached out her hand to Prudence. "It's a bet, Your Honor."

"It's a bet," said Prudence, shaking Harriet's hand.

* * *

Three painful hours and four X-rays later, Harriet learned she had lost the bet. Four months after the orthopedist declared her ankle fully mended, Harriet sold her pretty little custom-built Cape Cod and met her obligation. Her bank account grew to a size she had never thought she would see again, and she phoned Henry and Prudence to tell them she was on her way.

"I'm so glad, Mother," Prudence said. "It really is for the better. You'll see."

Humphrey rested his head on the sofa as close to Harriet as possible.

"It's going to be all right, boy. We'll be just fine in California."

Harriet looked out her bay front window. Spring was definitely on the fringes. "I hope so anyway. I hope."

Chapter 2

THOSE FOUR MONTHS WERE, TO SAY THE LEAST, A WHIRLWIND —to say the most, heart-wrenching. Harriet's house sold quickly, being in a fine neighborhood with a good public school district and, of course, the Saint Denis Parish. She didn't even need a lawn sign—she preferred not to inform the entire neighborhood of her plans anyway. People clamored to be in Saint Denis. So Harriet was mostly pleased when she sold the house to a young couple with four school-age children.

A month before settlement day, Harriet invited her best church friend for pie and coffee. She decided it would probably be a good idea to let Martha know—she didn't want to simply up and leave. People might think she had died or been kidnapped or something.

Martha arrived early as usual. Although she was the same age as Harriet—two months older, in fact—Harriet always thought of her as younger. Martha possessed such a free spirit and was as spry and youthful as any forty-year-old. She wore what Harriet called bohemian clothes—colorful skirts, bandanas, sandals in summer, and sneakers all winter—and made a living creating stained glass windows. Harriet never told her, but she sometimes wished she had even an ounce of Martha's artistic talent. Harriet, who wore flowered dresses and sensible shoes and concerned herself with keeping a neat house, serving nursery duty, returning her library books on time, and keeping her weekly date down at Saint Frank's for bingo, never did anything unexpected or out of the ordinary.

"Martha," Harriet said as she opened the door, "you're early —again."

Martha laughed. "You know me. I'll probably die early."

"Oh, don't say such a thing. Come on in. I was about to set the table."

"Set the table? You must have something mighty important in that brain of yours if you're setting a table for us."

"I do," Harriet said. She followed Martha into the living room. "But it can wait a few minutes."

"Then at least let me set the table while you get the goodies ready. You made pie, of course."

That was nice and neighborly and all, but Harriet wanted to set the table herself. Martha had a way of making even the most mundane things prettier and better. Most of the time it was a welcome set of skills, especially at a church supper, but that day, with such an important announcement to make, Harriet wanted to be in charge. Still, since Martha had already started folding the cloth napkins into swans or parrots or something equally exotic, Harriet let her continue.

"You have your good crystal out and china—my, my, what a pretty pattern." Martha peered into a French Haviland pie plate. "Now you've got me guessing. What in the world could be so terribly important as to warrant good china and your favorite salt and pepper shakers—oh, let me guess, Prudence is preggers. How marvelous."

Preggers. Harriet swallowed. "No, no, Prudence is not . . . preggers . . . she's too busy with her lawyer job, and you know Henry, still writing his books."

"Well, I wish for your sake she'd change her mind. The old bio clock is ticking." She moved her index finger back and forth like a pendulum.

Harriet placed a deep-dish apple pie with a golden crust on the table. "Look who's talking. Weren't you forty-two when Wyatt came along?"

"Yeah, well. I already had three others, and he was kind of ... well, Wyatt was definitely God's idea. Jack and I were not planning. He's our 'You said it would be all right' baby. 'Course he's all grown up now, but he still keeps me young."

Harriet set out the good silver and watched Martha rearrange the cut flowers in the vase on the table. She magically made them look better than Harriet's best effort only thirty minutes previous. Harriet sighed. How can they be the same daffodils? Then again, Martha could scrape a dead raccoon off the street and turn it into a lovely centerpiece.

"Oh, where's your pooch?" Martha looked around. "He usually greets me."

"He's out back. I'm not ready for him to hear my announcement yet."

Martha smiled and moved toward the glass sliders leading to the backyard and looked out toward Humphrey's doghouse. "Honestly, Harriet, sometimes I think you believe that hound is human."

"I never claimed he was human, but I'm fairly certain he understands me. He's picked up quite a bit of English."

"As opposed to dog speak."

"Yes, and please don't call him a hound. He's sensitive."

"Well, that's what he is. A basset *hound*."

"But it's derogatory."

Harriet poured herself a cup of coffee and stirred cream into it. She had been thinking about the best way to tell Martha her plan and thought she had come up with the perfect segue. "I've been enjoying Pastor Daniel's messages these last few weeks — all about purpose and destiny and such, finding our place in the grand scheme of things. The center of God's will and all that, even though I'm not certain I know how that feels or if I will ever understand predestination." She glanced at Martha over the tops of her glasses.

"Oh, oh, I know what he means." Martha chimed in as she set a slice of pie on her plate. "When I'm working with the glass I feel something extraordinary. It's like the line in that old movie about the missionary, about feeling God's pleasure when he runs. I feel God's pleasure when I work with the glass. It's like I know God made me an artist and I really have no choice but to do it."

Harriet stirred her coffee. "You mean *Chariots of Fire*. Eric Liddell." Harriet stared into her coffee. Nothing fancy. No hazelnut or coconut flavors—plain old coffee—the same brand she had been drinking for over twenty years. Ordinary—that's how Harriet had been feeling, she just didn't know it. She could not remember the last time she felt God's pleasure.

"I'm in a rut," Harriet said after a moment. "I wake up the same time every day, make coffee the same time every morning, drink it from the same mug, sit in the same pew, attend the same bingo game every Thursday—never win more than $47.50. And then I give it to the church." She looked away from Martha. "My life is boring. I don't want to believe I was predestined to live out my days baking cookies. I just never had the gumption to try anything different." She looked away and then back at Martha. "I never had the courage."

Martha tapped Harriet's hand. "Oh, for heaven's sake, Harriet, what are you trying to tell me? You must have something heavy on your heart. Does it have anything to do with Daniel's sermons? Did you get a bad test result?"

Harriet sipped her coffee. She considered forgetting the whole thing, thinking it couldn't possibly be as exciting as making art or getting a bad test result. "Oh, it's nothing really. I'm just . . . moving. That's all." She looked straight at Martha. "I'm moving —soon."

Martha swallowed a bite of pie without chewing. "Moving?

21

You mean into one of those fancy assisted-living places? Or the Presbyterian home?"

"Presby Home? No." She looked away from Martha again. The Presbyterian Home was a fine alternative for someone in Harriet's station of life, and after being a faithful member of the Presbyterian Church (even though she played bingo at St. Frank's), she certainly qualified for a bed.

"California," Harriet said.

"California? Well, what in the world?" Martha looked away and then back at Harriet. "Oh, I get it. Isn't that where Henry and Prudence live?"

Harriet nodded. "Yes. And ... you can't talk me out of it. I already sold the house."

Martha shook her head. "Harriet Beamer. I never thought this would happen. You love this house."

"I do, but ... well, I'm getting older and —"

"Oh so what? You're not ancient. Did you lose a bet or something?"

Harriet pushed gooey apple slices around on her plate. "Yes. It was a stupid bet."

"I knew it," Martha said. "I told you one of these days that your gambling ways would get you into trouble. Not everything in life is a sure bet."

"Well, good for you, Nostradamus," Harriet said. "Your prediction came true. But it really is all because of that broken ankle I had at Christmas. Henry and Prudence are worried I can't take care of myself anymore."

"Oh, that's preposterous," Martha said. "You fell off one chair — so what. You are far from a doddering old woman."

"I suppose." Harriet nodded and sipped her coffee, lost in thought. "Maybe it's not such a bad thing. I know I can still take care of myself. But I'm not getting younger. What do I have left? Ten decent years?" Harriet swallowed a bite of pie. "Remember how long ten years was when we were younger, and now —" she snapped her fingers—"it could go in a flash. I mean, really, what can I do now? My life is practically over."

"Don't be morbid. Ten years is plenty of time. You can do whatever you want. Go wherever you want. I keep saying I'll teach you to work with the stained glass. You can take a class in Russian literature, anything. You don't need to sell your house and move clear across the country." Martha seemed to swipe a tear away.

"Maybe I do," Harriet said. "Maybe the kids are right. Maybe I've used up my usefulness here, and now it's time for my children to take care of me."

Martha shook her head. She sipped coffee and looked around the kitchen. "There must be more to this."

"No. Not much more." Harriet stirred her coffee again. "Although I guess there is a part of me that figures when—or should I say *if?*—they decide to have a baby, I'll be there. I'd want to be part of the baby's life. And that trumps any assisted-living home. Come to think of it, it would be assisted living in reverse. I'll get to assist them." Harriet smiled at her realization.

"That is one way to look at it. But to sell your house and move so far—" Martha sniffed. "I'm going to miss you."

Harriet was glad when Martha left. But as she was washing the dishes and packing the china into a sturdy box marked "good dishes," a melancholy crept into her bones. Martha still had purpose. That was certain. She felt God's pleasure when she arranged the colorful cut glass into gorgeous pictures. For Harriet that day, it seemed God had finished with her, that he had no more purpose for her life than she did with the tiny bits of leftover apple pie she pushed down the Insinkerator.

* * *

When settlement day, June 2, finally arrived, Harriet slipped into her favorite cotton dress with the purple flowers and lace on the collar. She most always wore dresses. She never felt comfortable in blue jeans, although she did wear clam diggers in the warmer weather and when she visited the shore. But that day she slipped into her most familiar clothes. Signing the house over to Barry and Samantha Fredrickson was a bit more serious than a trip to the shore. A fact that struck her as she sat across the table from the young couple. When it came time to sign the papers, her hand shook, and as a result, her signature was wobbly. But she walked away with a happy, fat check. Max had seen to it that the house would be paid off in the event of his premature demise, so she owed only taxes. She deposited the check on her way home to tell Humphrey the news. The new owners said it would be fine with them if she remained in the house an extra day or two to get things settled. They charged her rent, of course, but Harriet didn't mind.

Harriet stopped at Larry's Deli and purchased four glazed donuts and a can of sardines in a bright red wrapper.

"Humphrey," she called when she opened the front door. "Mommy has treats for you."

Humphrey scrambled from his 2:00 p.m. resting spot in the sun.

Harriet plunked the sardines into Humphrey's bowl. She only gave him sardines when she had a good reason. A smidgen of guilt crept into Harriet's heart as she wiped sardine juice from the floor. He probably still remembered eating sardines the day before she took him for a trip to the vet, which turned into something a little more than routine. Let's just say Humphrey came home a little lighter the next day.

Humphrey lapped the fishies up faster than flies find a warm pile of poop in July. Harriet knew he was a little worried and wondered if she should even tell him. But that wasn't fair. She couldn't just spring it on him at the very last minute. Besides he had been watching her pack and must have known something was up.

"Humphrey," she said just as he swallowed the last morsel. "I got something to tell you." She sat at the kitchen table and opened the donut bag. Humphrey scooted toward her. He had learned to do this on his butt, not that standing up and walking was so hard, but why waste the energy? His eyes brightened as she jiggled the donut bag.

Harriet figured Humphrey had come to know her pretty well. Sometimes a dog can know things without words; a simple look on a human's face can be enough to spell impending disaster or even unspeakable joy like a fresh warm donut from Larry's.

Harriet knew Humphrey knew. She scratched behind his ears and smiled into his impossibly sad, bloodshot eyes. "We're taking a little trip, you and me." She tried to sound as upbeat as possible and fed him part of the donut, which he wolfed down in no time.

Humphrey perked up. The dog wagged his tail and performed his version of the happy dance, which was little more than a few tail chases. Harriet loved that.

"Good boy, Humphrey. You are going to have so much fun on that airplane." She patted his head.

Humphrey yawned. Walked away. Did a double take and whimpered.

"I don't care what anyone says. I know you can understand me. But don't worry, you're going to love the plane."

* * *

Harriet spent the rest of the day packing, unpacking, and repacking. It was difficult to decide what to keep, what to donate, and what to throw away. It had taken her nearly three years to rid the house of Max's clothes and belongings. But as she went through closets and drawers she came across other Max memorabilia and had a tough time keeping tears at bay.

"Oh, Max," she said, holding an old wristwatch. "You never did get this fixed. But that was just like you. Say one thing, do another."

By dinnertime she had grown so weary of crying over Max she set about packing her salt-and-pepper collection. She had gone to the U-Haul store and purchased nice sturdy boxes, strapping tape, and a large black Sharpie.

"I'm going to ship my collection to Grass Valley, Humphrey."
Humphrey barked.

"Well I'm glad you agree."

Most of the shakers were on shelves in Henry's old room. Henry helped install the shelving and even painted the room a sweet robin's egg blue. Harriet loved the way the color looked with all her multicolor shakers. It was like walking into a rainbow every day.

She pulled the shakers off the shelf one by one and wrapped them in newspaper. Martha, an absolutely rabid recycler, had given Harriet stacks of newspapers that Martha had been saving ever since Harriet informed her about the big move.

"Look, Humphrey, this is the set Maggie and Joe sent me from Guatemala. Imagine that, all the way from there." She wrapped the boy-and-girl-shaped shakers and lovingly set them in a box. Next she wrapped a set shaped like apples. Pepper had a blue bow and salt had a pink bow, but they both were wide-eyed and happy. "These came from Washington State. I think Jolene Farber brought them back from her visit with her mother."

Harriet couldn't help but entertain the flood of memories and feelings that surfaced with each set of shakers. But it was the set from Ocean City, New Jersey, in the shape of saltwater taffy that brought the deepest reaction.

"I bought these. We went to the shore every summer — the first week of August. For twenty-eight years, well except the year Henry was born. I was so pregnant that August I could hardly move."

Humphrey rolled onto his back. His tongue lolled out. "No belly rub now, boy. I have to get these packed."

Harriet held the saltwater-taffy shakers. A tear welled in her eye. "Now what's going on here? I have no reason to cry." She sniffed.

"What is wrong with me, Humphrey?"

She glanced around the small room. For a moment she felt a

bit . . . flustered. "Look at all these shakers. They're from all over the world—most of them were given to me as gifts or I traded for them at conventions. But these taffy shakers are the only ones I actually got on a trip of my own."

Humphrey scrambled to his feet after a brief struggle to upright himself. He barked. Twice.

"I just realized something. Max and I never went anywhere—except the Jersey Shore. Just about the whole world is represented in this room, and I've seen none of it—not really. Max never liked to travel. He was such a homebody."

And that was when a lightbulb bright enough to light up Tokyo came on in Harriet's mind.

She dropped the taffy shakers into the box and raced down the steps, nearly tripping over her own feet on the way. Humphrey followed quickly behind.

Harriet grabbed the kitchen phone and tapped Martha's speed-dial number. One.

"Hey, Harriet, what's up? How goes the packing? Need help?"

"Martha. You need to come over here right this blessed minute." Harriet was so excited that her heart pounded like a trip hammer.

"Why? What's wrong? Is everything okay?"

"Just come over. Please."

"Okay. Hold on to your shakers. I'll be over in a flash. Just have to slip my shoes on."

Harriet clicked the phone off. "Humphrey," she said, "I have a scathingly brilliant idea."

Chapter 3

HARRIET PULLED OPEN THE FRONT DOOR. MARTHA STOOD there in bright pink crop pants, a blue denim jacket, a purple tie-dyed shirt, dangling earrings, and green hands. "What's so important? I was in the middle of painting—"

"Come in. Come in, I've got something to tell you."

"You changed your mind," Martha said as she walked into the living room.

"Nope. Not that. I'm going."

"Oh, yeah, I can tell by the boxes. I wish you'd let me help."

"Maybe later. But now hold on to your hat. I've made a decision. I'm going to take the bus."

Martha burst out laughing. "The bus? You mean like Greyhound?"

Humphrey howled.

Harriet sat in her wingback chair. "No, maybe, I don't know. It's possible. Any bus, maybe a lot of buses or trains."

"Okay, now you're just being obtuse. Tell me what's going on."

"I've decided to take the scenic route. Whatever that entails, local buses, trains, a hot-air balloon if I have too. Whatever. But I'm going to start on the local bus."

Harriet could see that Martha was having a difficult time containing her hilarity. "You're not serious. Harriet, you're seventy-two years old. You have a little arthritis, high blood pressure, and let's face it — not the keenest sense of direction."

"Okay, so I get lost in the supermarket. This is different. Buses and such have schedules and — " Harriet leaned toward Martha — "I want to see the country before I die. I want to do something courageous and unexpected."

"You're a nut. You know that? What brought this on? I figured you and Humphrey would fly."

"I was packing my collection, you know, to send on ahead to Henry, and that's when it hit me. I have all these shakers from all over the world. Places I've never seen. Sent to me by friends and missionaries. It made me think that Max — God love him — never took me anywhere."

"Jersey shore."

"Doesn't count. But if I take the slow way to Grass Valley I'm sure I'll see some sights, starting with the Salt and Pepper Shaker Museum in Gatlinburg, Tennessee — oh, Martha, I've been wanting to see the museum for eons now."

"Have you told the kids?"

Harriet looked away from Martha. "I think I'll wait until I'm on the way. They'll get all worried and frantic — especially Henry. And I don't want them to talk me out of it."

Martha clicked her tongue. "You're a card, Harriet Beamer. A real card. But what about Humphrey. You can't take him on the bus."

"I know. I'll have to send him on the plane. He's going to hate it but what can I do?"

* * *

The day before Harriet's scheduled departure, she brought Humphrey to the airport. It was a terrible thing to push him into a crate, but there was no other way to get a sixty-two-pound basset hound to California. She placed a brand-new rawhide bone and his

29

favorite chew toy, a red rubber hydrant, into the cage. She also put a blue towel and note to Henry inside.

"Now don't you worry," Harriet said when she locked the crate door. "You'll be fine. I'm sorry they wouldn't let me buy you a regular seat, but airlines have their rules."

Humphrey's head drooped.

"I know you must be scared." She reached two fingers into the metal crate and touched Humphrey's ear. "I love you so much." Harriet's heart broke into several pieces.

The dog closed his eyes and opened them as though signaling that he understood.

Harriet sniffed back tears. "Now Henry and Prudence will get you at the airport in Sacramento. I'll get there as soon as I can but . . . but." She turned her head away.

Humphrey whimpered.

"Oh dear, maybe . . . maybe I shouldn't do this."

She wiped tears on her sleeve.

"Excuse me, ma'am," said a worker, "but I need to take the dog."

"Okay, but . . . but I can't . . ."

"Ma'am?"

Harriet touched Humphrey's snout. "I'll see you soon. And please don't worry about me."

Humphrey yowled but only a little.

* * *

When she returned home that morning, Harriet phoned Henry to tell him when to expect Humphrey.

"Okay, Mom," Henry said. "Flight 1411 at 6:30. We'll be there. And Mom, it will be good to see you."

"Oh, you won't be seeing me," Harriet said. "Not yet."

"But why? We'll just pick you up at baggage claim and then go to wherever the animals—"

"But I won't be there, dear. I'm taking the bus."

There was a long pause until Henry finally said, "The bus? But . . . why?"

"Because I want to see the country, dear."

"But Mom, that's ridiculous. You can't travel all that distance alone."

"I can too. I . . . just think that if I must come to California so you and Prudence can put me out to pasture—" she sniffed tears back. "Then fine, but I'm doing it my way. I'll let you know when I get there."

"But . . . but which bus? When? And we're not putting you out to pasture."

"Then what? I'm an old lady who can't take care of herself any-more and . . . and has outlived her purpose, like an old plow horse."

"Mother, I'm sorry you feel that way, but—"

"But I want to do this, Henry. Now, I'm not sure when I'll get to Sleepy Valley—"

"Grass Valley," Henry said.

"Whatever. Still sounds like a rest home. But I am going to take my time."

"You're being silly, mother."

"I am not. Now I got to go. I'll call you when I'm on my way."

Harriet ended her call, and a swarm of butterflies invaded her stomach. "Oh dear, I know he's upset, but . . . but I just have to do it my way."

* * *

Later that evening Henry and Prudence arrived at the airport to get Humphrey. It was apparent to them that the plane ride had not been a pleasant one for Humphrey.

"Look at him," Henry said. "I didn't think it was possible for that hound to look any more put-out, but just look at him."

Prudence looked at the dog. "He's pitiful. Let's get him home. I'm sure he'll settle in quickly. I just hope Sandra Day will accept him."

31

"Oh, your cat will get over it." Henry unlatched the crate. Humphrey barely moved.

"That must be his leash." Prudence pointed to the coiled canvas lead in the crate.

"Okay, just a second, old man," Henry said. He reached inside and grabbed the hydrant and rawhide bone. He dropped them into a plastic Ziploc bag he pulled out of his pants pocket and handed it to Prudence. She held the Ziploc like she was holding plutonium. "Dog slobber. I hate dog slobber. And please leave the towel — Lord knows what he did on that."

"You'd slobber too," Henry said, "if you just traveled 2,500 miles in the cargo hold of a jet with no windows and — " he looked at the crate next to Humphrey's — "a snooty-looking show dog."

Humphrey perked up.

"Look at that," Henry said. "I think he understands me. My mother said he had an uncanny ability to understand things."

"He's a dog, Henry."

Humphrey didn't respond.

Henry grabbed the leash, and when he did a piece of yellow paper floated to the floor.

"What's that?" Prudence asked.

"I don't know." Henry picked up the sheet and unfolded it. "A note. From my mother."

"Oh, geeze, leave it to your mother to hide a note in his cage."

" 'Dearest Henry and Prudence,' " Henry read.

I know you will take good care of Humphrey. I will see you soon. Please be sure to scratch behind his ears. He likes sardines and glazed donuts, but make sure they're fresh.

Love,
Mother

P.S. Please don't worry about me. I'll be fine.

Henry repeated the P.S.: "Don't worry about me. I'll be fine."

He looked at Prudence. "I am going to worry about her. I still can't figure out what made her want to take the bus."

"I know. I know," Prudence said. "I just wish she had told you which bus. And when. All we can do is assume she's taking Greyhound."

Humphrey yowled.

Henry clicked the leash onto Humphrey's collar. "Maybe she got nervous about flying. She's never flown that I know of."

"Really? How is that possible?"

"She and my dad never traveled much — just to the Jersey shore every summer, and that's only an hour and a half car ride."

Humphrey walked next to Henry.

When they made their way out of the terminal Prudence spotted a grassy area near the parking lot. "Maybe you should let him . . . relieve himself. Over there." She pointed.

"Yeah, his bladder must be as big as a football by now."

Humphrey lifted his leg near a light pole but was forced to stop midstream when a security guard approached. Humphrey never liked uniforms. He let go a very loud bark.

"Hey, you can't let your dog do that here. Get him out of the airport first."

"It's just—"

The guard interrupted Prudence. "I don't care if it's Chardonnay, you can't let your dog pee on airport grounds."

"Fine," she said. "Come on, Henry."

They walked a little farther before Henry signaled his car. The red SUV beeped and the lights flashed a second or two.

"I love remote entry," Henry said. "Makes it easier to find your car in a crowded parking lot."

"You say that every time," Prudence said.

"It's true. The wonders of technology. My dad would have loved this. He was forever forgetting where he parked his car." Henry opened the lift gate.

"Come on, boy, hop in."

Humphrey tried. He made three or four concerted efforts to jump into the vehicle, but his short legs belied his good efforts. He gave Henry a look.

"Pick him up, Henry," Prudence said. "My goodness, his legs are the size of link sausages."

Henry reached under the dog and gently lifted him into the car. Humphrey gave him an appreciative lick on the cheek, which Henry promptly wiped.

"Ewww," Prudence said, "dog kisses."

Humphrey stretched out in the back on an old blanket and whimpered.

"Well, what should we do, Henry?" Prudence asked once they were out of the airport and onto the highway. She cracked a window and let the early spring air into the car.

"About what?"

"Your mother. Should we check the bus schedules? I suspect she'll be taking Greyhound. We could go online and see if a bus from Philadelphia is arriving today."

"Oh, not today. It will take longer than a day to travel clear across the country."

Prudence made one of her noises. "Oh, that's right," she said. "I didn't even think about that. Who knows when she'll be arriving?"

Henry reached over and squeezed Prudence's shoulder. "Look, we'll check the Greyhound website when we get home. If she left today after Humphrey's flight, she'll be arriving here in a couple of days I would imagine."

"I hope so, Henry. You know how much I love your mother, but I've got the election coming up and this big case. I don't need the distraction."

Henry sighed. "Leave it to my mother to do something so harebrained as this."

"Whoa," Prudence said. "I didn't say that. Harebrained? Okay, okay, the bus might not have been her smartest move, but I

34

bet she thought long and hard about this. She sold her house and most of the furniture all by herself, not to mention shipping what needed shipping — including her entire salt-and-pepper-shaker collection."

"How do you know that?"

"She called yesterday and said the FedEx driver just picked up the boxes."

"Oh. I didn't know."

"And don't forget she arranged for storage for everything else and got Humphrey on an airplane. Harriet Beamer is not a hare-brain. Just . . . unconventional."

"All right, all right. You made your point."

Prudence smiled and touched his cheek. "I'm sorry, honey. I'm just worried and . . . and stressed. Running for the council and — "

"I know," Henry said, "but who has the best legal mind in this car or any of those cars out there?"

She kissed his cheek on the same spot Humphrey licked. "Dog germs."

"Everything will work out. Mom will get here unscathed, Sandra Day will grow to love Humphrey, and you will be elected to the city council and then who knows — the Supreme Court. Unless of course you'd rather start thinking about having — "

"Oh, not the baby discussion. I'm . . . just not ready. My career is — "

"I know, honey. I know."

Prudence stared out the window. The trees whizzed past at seventy miles an hour. "I hope Harriet knows what she's doing."

Humphrey whimpered and closed his eyes.

Chapter 4

HARRIET LOOKED AT THE CLOCK ON THE KITCHEN WALL — she was leaving it behind for the new owners. "Two o'clock. Humphrey must have landed by now." She sighed. "I hope he's okay."

She finished wiping down the counters and made certain the refrigerator was clean and smelled fresh. As excited as she felt about her decision to take the scenic route and see the country, she also felt nervous, scared to death at times about traveling alone. But she wasn't about to admit that to anyone, including Martha. God knew her anxieties and that was enough.

"Ah, fiddlesticks," she said to the clock. "Maybe I should just get on an airplane. I mean what the heck. So I'll never see the country — what's so great about a salt-and-pepper-shaker museum anyway?"

She flopped onto the kitchen chair just as her cell phone chimed.

"Henry," she said. "Did you get Humphrey? How is he? Is he terribly nervous?"

"Yes, Mom. He's here. He's fine. But I wish you had come with him."

"I'll be there soon. I — "

"Listen, Mom," Henry said. "Just take the plane. Taking the bus is crazy. It's nonsense."

Harriet felt her eyebrows arch like a gothic cathedral. "Nonsense? Crazy? It's not nonsense. And I am not crazy." Harriet felt a twinge of courage resurface. "I . . . I want to see the country before I die."

"But Mom, alone? Why not wait until next summer, and we'll all take a trip."

Harriet sucked a deep breath and let it out slowly. "No, I . . . I want to do it myself. Now. And I know you mean well, dear, but you and Prudence will never find the time, and I'm not getting any younger."

"But mom, it's ridiculous."

"Sorry. But that's my plan. Kiss Humphrey on the nose for me and buy him a glazed donut. He deserves it after such a long trip." She could hardly believe it was her speaking.

"But, Mom, when—"

Harriet closed her phone. She had never hung up on Henry —or anyone—before. She didn't like the way it felt, but she suddenly needed to take a stand.

She slapped the kitchen table. "I'm doing it. Starting tomorrow morning. Harriet Beamer is taking the bus, and no one can stop me."

* * *

That evening Harriet packed her rolling suitcase. It was purple with silver zippers. She packed only a few articles of clothing— two dresses, two pairs of capris and coordinating tops, her toothbrush, deodorant, things of that nature. She knew she would have to pack light. "I can always buy anything else I might need on the road," she said as though Humphrey was still right next to her. She even looked down once or twice expecting to see him. She already made sure she had a full month's supply of her blood-pressure medication, and while she was at the CVS she even purchased a rain poncho in a plastic package. She packed all her other clothes in boxes that Martha said she would ship later. She cried once when

37

she found one of Max's shirts stuffed in the back of a drawer. It still smelled like him, well, just a smidgen.

Even after a long day of packing Harriet didn't sleep well. She took an Excedrin PM. It didn't help. Not much. She dozed and woke. Dozed and woke. The butterflies in her stomach had morphed into something that felt more like hopping toads. Her last night at home did not pass quickly, but it did pass. As the sun broke, Harriet's mood rose along with it.

"Okay, Lord," she said as she dressed. "If I'm doing this, you're coming with me." She smiled. "I know, like you'd ever let me go alone."

Harriet moved her suitcase and tote to the entryway and took one final look at her now nearly empty house. She sniffed back tears and sighed deeply. "Good-bye, house. Good-bye Max. We had a great run."

After locking the front door for the last time, Harriet met up with Martha. She handed her the key. "Thanks for coming to the bus stop with me."

"You sure you have everything you need?" Martha asked.

"I have my tote bag filled as full as I can with stuff that I might need to get to easily — you know, my cell phone, a book, my wallet, tissues, pictures of Humphrey and Max, stuff like that. And I packed everything else in this suitcase."

"Okay, but promise to call me and send me some postcards."

Harriet hugged Martha. "I will. And you can call me, you know."

"I will."

The bus to West Chester pulled up right on time, 7:10 a.m. Harriet froze the instant the door opened.

"Go on," Martha said.

"I ... I can't. Oh my goodness. Am I really doing this?"

"Yes." Martha gave Harriet a slight nudge. "You're really doing this."

"Are you coming, lady?" said the driver. "I got a schedule to keep."

Harriet couldn't move. Her nerves tingled all over. "I ... I don't—"

"You're going," Martha said, and she gave Harriet another nudge.

Harriet stepped into the bus. She had her tote over her shoulder and used both hands to lug her suitcase up the three small steps. She cringed at each bump.

"Cash or card?" the driver said.

Harriet put two one-dollar bills into the bill acceptor and headed down the aisle. She dropped into the first seat she saw—a window seat. The bus pulled away. Harriet waved to Martha as a big tear slid down her cheek.

* * *

At the next stop a large bald man with scary tattoos on both arms and his neck sat next to her.

She smiled at him, hoping he wouldn't eat her.

"Hello," Harriet said.

The man only grunted.

"I'm going to California, well, eventually. First I'm going to Gatlinburg, Tennessee. How about you?" Harriet sniffled. She knew she had to be brave and thought small talk would help hide her anxiety.

The bus driver pulled against the curb. The large tattooed man got up. "Don't think this bus will get you that far," he said. And then laughed.

"Well, no not this bus but a lot of buses."

Then a woman wearing a pink hat and tight white pants sat next to her.

"Hello," Harriet said. "Do you know how far this bus goes?"

"Just to the university. West Chester University, I think." The woman's breath smacked of cheddar cheese.

"Oh, the university. I've never seen the university, as long as I've lived here I've never seen it. Oh, I've driven close by it but never actually saw it."

"That's nice," the woman said. She had turned her attention to the other side of the bus. That was when the thought struck. There must be millions of buses in the country. But I wonder if it's even possible to make so many connections.

She tapped the woman in the pink hat. "Excuse me, but do you think it's possible to take public transportation all the way to California?"

The woman laughed. "Are you serious?"

"I am," Harriet said. "As serious as a root canal."

Pink Hat Lady winced. "Well, I don't know for sure, but I sort of doubt it. I know SEPTA doesn't go that far. You'd have to take a lot of buses."

Harriet smiled. "That's what is so exciting. I'm going to see the country."

Two stops later, Pink Hat Lady got off, and a woman in a striped skirt, holding the hand of a small child, got on. She and the little boy sat next to Harriet. From the looks of the woman's tired eyes and the boy's mussed hair, Harriet figured they were having a bad day and didn't say a word, although the little boy smiled and made Harriet remember Henry at that age—they had similar haircuts. Harriet and Striped Skirt Lady rode together to the university stop.

"This must be it," Harriet said. "The end of the line for this bus, anyway."

Striped Skirt Woman ignored Harriet and hauled her little boy off the bus in a huff.

"Excuse me," Harriet said to the driver.

"Can I help you?" she said.

"I was wondering. How can I take the bus to Tennessee?"

The driver laughed. "Are you nuts, lady? You can't take public transportation to Tennessee. You need to go Greyhound or an airplane or even Amtrak."

Harriet shook her head. "Or all three, I suppose."

Just as she stepped off the bus her phone jingled.

"Hello?"

It was Henry.

"Mom, are you okay? You haven't answered your phone."

"I know, I'm sorry. I wanted to get a head start before I called you."

"Where are you?"

"At West Chester University."

Henry was silent a moment. But Harriet did hear Humphrey's distinctive woof in the background.

"Oh, Henry, please tell Humphrey I miss him and give him a good ear scratch for me and maybe a donut. Glazed. Never jelly."

"I don't understand, Mom."

"It's simple, dear. Just reach down and scratch behind his ears and give him a kiss on the nose. Then go buy him a glazed donut."

"No, Mother, that's not what I mean. Why are you at West Chester?"

"I wanted to see it, the university. Like I told you. I want to see things, Henry. It's a big, beautiful country. And I've seen none of it."

"The Jersey shore."

"Oh, big deal. I want to see more. I have money, a cell phone, and God. I'm going to do this." The words left Harriet's mouth even though her knees felt a little wobbly.

After a quick walking tour of the campus, which she found both exhilarating and daunting, Harriet found a restaurant called Penn's Table on Gay Street. It was small and comfy and not very crowded. She ordered a cup of coffee, a grilled cheese sandwich with tomato, and a vanilla milk shake.

The waitress was young, maybe nineteen or twenty years old, and wore a green polo shirt with the name Penn's Table embroidered in white above the breast pocket. Tall and skinny with long brown hair pulled into a ponytail, the girl introduced herself as Lacy. She wore the tightest-fitting jeans Harriet had ever seen, although she couldn't say they were lewd or obscene, just tight and made Lacy's legs look thin as chopsticks. The jeans might as well have been painted on.

Lacy refilled Harriet's coffee cup just as Harriet swallowed the last bite of her sandwich. The day's activities made her develop the appetite of a lumberjack.

"Thank you," Harriet said. "May I ask you a question?"

"Sure," Lacy said. She smiled.

"Do you think I can get to California on buses? And not Greyhound. I mean regular door-to-door type buses, unless of course I can't, and then I suppose Greyhound or the train."

Lacy stared at Harriet for a few long seconds, possibly trying to decide if Harriet had slipped a few gears.

"I'm not crazy, if that's what you're trying to figure out, young lady—"

"Oh, no, I'm—"

"It's okay, dear. I would think the same thing in your shoes. Funny old woman comes in and orders grilled cheese and tomato with a vanilla milk shake and coffee and then asks if she can take the bus to California. Guess it does sound outlandish, but you see—"

Lacy looked at the clock.

"Oh, I'm sorry, dear, am I keeping you from your other patrons?"

"Oh, no," Lacy said. "My shift ended ten minutes ago."

"Then you better be going," Harriet said. "I won't be keeping you."

Lacy sat down across from Harriet in the booth. "Are you really talking about taking public transportation all the way to California?"

"I am," Harriet said. She noticed how Lacy's bright blue eyes lit up. "Gonna do it too. Somehow. Oh, I'm sure I'll need to take a train and maybe even a Greyhound. But first, well, it's going to sound silly, but I want to go to Gatlinburg, Tennessee, because that is where the only salt-and-pepper-shaker museum in the world is."

Lacy laughed. "There really is a museum for salt and pepper shakers?"

"Sure is. It's my hobby. Collecting them. I have hundreds — they're already in Grass Valley. I sent them ahead. Well, they should be getting there soon."

"Imagine that," Lacy said.

"So do you think I can do it? Get clear across the country on buses?"

"I imagine anything's possible. Especially if you got a GPS."

"GPS?" Harriet said. "Of course. My son and daughter-in-law use one of those. Do you know where I can get one? It's not that I don't like to keep current. I just never saw the need, and if there's no need, why bother?"

"I can understand that," Lacy said. "RadioShack or Best Buy might be the best place, but you might already have one in your phone."

"Really?" Harriet pulled her phone from her tote. "In this little thing?"

Lacy shook her head. "Not so sure about that model. Let me see it." Lacy opened Harriet's phone and pushed some buttons. "Nah, you don't have it, but you could get it. Or just buy a Droid, depending on your carrier."

"A what, dear? Droid?"

"Sure, it's the name of a phone. Then you'd have a GPS right in your phone. Should do the trick. Who's your carrier?"

"Verizon. That's my ..." Harriet's brow rose. She pushed her glasses into her face ... "carrier."

Lacy smiled. "Okay, there's a Verizon store down the street actually. I'll take you there. Sounds like fun."

"You mean it? Can you help me buy a Droid?"

"I can try, I mean I never bought one before. But . . . why? You running away from home or something?"

Harriet laughed. "Let's just say I'm taking the scenic route home."

Harriet and Lacy walked down High Street until they came to the Verizon store.

Close to an hour later Harriet emerged the proud owner of a spanking new Droid with touch screen technology and a GPS.

Harriet discovered a never-before-tapped interest in gadgets and devices. "I think this phone will do everything but cook my lunch," Harriet told Lacy.

"No, but it will tell you where you can buy lunch. Just keep it charged."

"Now did I hear that fella correctly?" Harriet said. "All I have to do is start walking and this little phone will adjust the directions and get me to Grass Valley."

"That's right," Lacy said. "The satellite will always know where you are."

Harriet looked into the darkening sky. "Wow. From way up there?"

"Yep," Lacy said.

As Harriet and Lacy strolled down the street, a stationery store caught Harriet's eye. "Oh, look there. Maybe I should stop inside. I would like to purchase a notebook — you know, to record my . . . my thoughts along the way."

Lacy stopped walking. "That's a great idea, Harriet. You should get a Moleskine."

"A what? A Moleskine."

"Oh, yes, they're just the best notebooks. And they're kind of famous."

"How can a notebook be famous?"

"The story goes that Hemingway and Van Gogh and Picasso and, well, just droves of famous artists used them. They would never use an ordinary notebook."

44

Lacy pulled open the door to the stationery shop. "Come on. This is where I buy mine."

"Moleskine? Are they made from real mole skin?"

"No. And some folks call them Mole-*skeen*."

"Still don't know what moles have to do with it, but I'll take a look."

Harriet fell instantly in love with the notebooks. She especially appreciated the feel of the paper, so smooth.

"And gel pens," Lacy said. "You need to write with gel pens on these."

"Okeydokey," Harriet said, now completely enthralled with the notion of using a notebook that Hemingway used. "Who knows, maybe my story will become famous."

Harriet paid for a package of three Moleskines and two gel pens — black — and a package of three of the famous notebooks for Lacy.

"You don't have to do that," Lacy said.

"Of course I do. You helped me so much."

The new friends left the store. Harriet reached into her tote bag, found her wallet, and pulled out a twenty-dollar bill. She gave it to Lacy.

Lacy shook her head. "Oh, that's okay. I think what you're doing rocks. Glad to help."

"Take it," Harriet said. "I'm sure you can use it, and truthfully, honey, I didn't leave you a big enough tip."

Lacy pocketed the cash. "So where to?"

"The next stop," Harriet said, "Gatlinburg, Tennessee. The home of the only salt-and-pepper-shaker museum in the world."

Chapter 5

"What do you suppose got into my mother?" Henry asked Prudence over morning coffee. "Why in the world would she do this? Now? At her age?"

Prudence sat at the kitchen table and poured a few drops of skim milk into her coffee. "I don't know. Maybe she just wants a last chance to do something. Didn't you tell me your dad was always so busy with work and church business he never wanted to travel, only to the shore for one week every August?"

Henry chuckled. "Yeah. His idea of a vacation was sitting in the backyard watching burgers burn on the grill."

"So she's just doing a lifetime of vacationing in one fell swoop." Prudence sipped her coffee. "And speaking of work . . ."

"We weren't speaking of work."

"In any case I need to get to Sacramento for a meeting, and you need to get back to that novel. Help take your mind off your mom."

Henry shrugged. "I hope so. I'm not making much progress."

Prudence kissed Henry's cheek. "The words will come. They always do."

"So I guess you'll be late tonight?"

"Yes. And that gives you more time to write. But give her a call if you're worried."

* * *

Harriet had just boarded the Acela Express train toward Washington, D.C., even though she was stopping at Baltimore, when she heard her phone jingle. She thought she had tucked it into the mesh compartment on her tote bag like Lacy suggested. "Easy access," Lacy had said.

But it wasn't there. "Oh dear, where did I put you?" Harriet unzipped the main pocket and rooted around inside.

"Oh, don't stop chiming," Harriet said. "I'll find you."

No phone. "Oh dear, where in the heck are you?" The phone jingled once more and then stopped before she found it tucked into her dress pocket. Lacy had also suggested that Harriet might be more comfortable traveling in jeans than dresses. But Harriet had still not stopped to shop for them, or for comfortable shoes.

She opened her phone. "Henry called," she said aloud just as a large woman wearing an orange suit slid next to her with a thud.

Harriet fiddled with the phone. It was different from her old one. For one thing it didn't have a flip lid. She pressed the button that locked the screen.

"Hello," she said to Orange Woman.

The woman in orange looked at Harriet. "Afternoon."

Harriet sighed and unlocked her phone. She tapped Henry's name, thankful that the nice man at the Verizon store was able to transfer her contacts and waited for him to answer.

"Mom. Where are you?"

"I'm on my way, dear."

"But where are you?"

"The train."

There was a long silence as Harriet glanced at the Orange Woman. "I'm on my way to California."

The woman harrumphed and looked away.

"The train?" Henry said. "I thought you were taking the bus."

"I am."

47

"Then why are you on a train?"

"It's a strange thing, Henry. You can't always get a bus from here to there."

"So are you taking the train the whole way to California? When will you arrive? Which station?"

"Oh no. I have no idea when I'll get clear to California. It's a long way, you know. I'm stopping at Baltimore first, and then I absolutely must stop in Tennessee to see the Salt and Pepper Shaker Museum."

"Salt and Pepper Museum? Mom, are you nuts?"

"No, dear. I've always wanted to see it and—"

"Then take a plane to . . . what did you say, Tennessee?"

Harriet took a breath and glanced at Orange Woman who seemed to be eavesdropping.

"I already told you. Because I want to travel, see the country."

"Travel?" Harriet heard a distinct annoyance in Henry's voice. "Are you doing this because you're still mad at me?"

"Mad at you. What in the world for?" The train jostled. Harriet liked the sensation and smiled at Orange Woman who still appeared to be listening in.

"For selling Dad's business and—"

"No, Henry. I'm doing this because . . . well, just because."

There was another uncomfortable pause until Henry said, "Okay, call me when you get to the museum or someplace in between."

"I will, dear."

"Which reminds me," Henry said. "Your boxes arrived this morning—early."

"Oh, good. I hope none of them broke. I packed as carefully as I could."

"Want me to check?"

"No, no. Just leave them packed."

There was a bit of silence until Henry asked, "Are you okay?"

"Sure, dear. I'm fine. I kind of like traveling. 'Course lugging my rolling suitcase up and down steps is a bit of a nuisance. But thank goodness you are more or less expected to carry luggage onto a train. People look at me funny when I lug it up the steps on the bus."

"Listen, Mom," Henry said. "I just had a good thought. Do you want me to come? To you? We'll travel together?"

"What? Really?" Harriet slipped her feet out of her shoes and wiggled her toes. She smiled at the relief.

"I haven't even mentioned the idea to Prudence. I just thought of it a second ago but—"

"No. I ... I appreciate the thought but ... no, Henry. I think this is a journey I need to take alone. This could very well be my last chance to see the country and ..."

"And what?"

"Now I'm not so sure I know, and what ... something."

"Well, now you're just being cryptic, which worries me even more. You have no plan, no schedule—"

"I know that. That's the adventure part."

Harriet heard Henry make a noise. The same snorty noise Max used to make when he was getting a little peeved. "Are you sure you don't want me to meet you?"

"Yes, I'm sure I don't want you to meet me. And I think I would like to hang up now. I want to see the scenery."

"I just don't know why you think you can do this—travel such a long way by yourself. You have no experience and—"

"That's right, Henry. I have no experience."

"But you can have the same experience if we travel together."

Harriet laughed. "I don't think so, Son. Now please. Let me do this—my way."

"I'm sorry, but I'm going to worry."

"Oh, oh, I almost forgot," Harriet said just before she clicked off. "How's Humphrey? Does he miss me?"

"He's fine. And I think he does miss you."

"Tell him I'll see him soon."

Harriet locked her screen and looked through the window. Was it possible she was still angry at Henry? She smiled at her seatmate. Orange Woman smiled back and said, "California, huh. It's a long way."

"That's what I'm counting on."

Orange Woman, who was clutching a large green handbag on her lap, smiled and then said, "My name is Mauve. Mauve Riggins, and I admire your style."

Harriet grinned ear to ear. "And I admire your . . . orange suit."

So for the next fifty minutes — give or take, Harriet and Mauve enjoyed each other's company, swapping daughter-in-law stories. And Mauve, who was a businesswoman — in sales — even showed Harriet a few tricks for her Droid. Harriet especially liked the alarm. Now maybe she'll always remember to take her blood-pressure medicine. But the conversation always managed to get back around to children.

"My son," Mauve said, "married that woman without even telling me. It was like I didn't exist. All I got was a phone call two days after. By then it was too late for me to have any say."

Harriet clicked her tongue. "Oh dear, I'm sorry to hear that. Henry and Prudence had the good sense to give me a church wedding to attend. But I must say that it wasn't what you would call a traditional wedding. She wore a very strange white outfit — more like a wedding pants suit than a gown. It was ugly, but I would never tell her that."

"Now I got to say, I do love my grandbabies," Mauve said. "Three of the cutest little boys you ever set eyes on. How about you? Got any grandbabies?"

Harriet adjusted her tote between her feet. "No, not yet. Prudence is busy with her career — she's an important lawyer, and Henry is writing books."

"Books? Really. Well, that's pretty impressive."

"I know but—"

Mauve laughed. "Look out that window, Harriet. The world is flashing by a hundred miles an hour, and in every one of those miles there's a million stories like ours—imagine that. Mothers. We get none of the breaks. But we also get most of the blessings. You wait, there'll be grandkids."

"I would like that." Harriet glanced out the window. "But right now, it looks like . . ." She sighed. ". . . rain."

"Well, it is still spring, and spring means rain," Mauve said. "Now how come you let your daughter-in-law talk you into selling your house and moving clear across the country when you didn't really want to."

Harriet swallowed and looked at her reflection in the train window. Then she turned to Mauve. "I lost the bet, and I am no welsher."

Now it was Mauve's turn to click her tongue and shake her head. "Uhm, uhm, uhm. Girl, that ain't the reason; that's an excuse. People don't move almost three thousand miles unless they want to. You got to figure out why you wanted to."

"I lost the bet."

"Harriet," Mauve said. "When my children tell me it's time to put me out to pasture like some sorry-butt mule, I'm going your way—the long way. I will not go gently into that good night. But I will tell you this much. It will be because I'm ready, not because I broke my ankle hanging an ornament on some lame Christmas tree."

"One word of advice," Harriet said. "Get a GPS."

"You bet I will. Now you have a safe journey. And Harriet, maybe you should program your GPS to help you find what you're really looking for." Mauve smiled, exposing the whitest set of teeth Harriet had ever seen.

And with that Mauve was gone from Harriet's life but not her memory. She pulled her brand-new Moleskine notebook from her bag. She opened it across her lap, closed her eyes, and sighed. Now she not only missed Humphrey, but from out of the blue, thoughts of Max percolated in her mind. Grief and missing someone was like that — sneaky, hits you all of a sudden when you weren't expecting it. Harriet allowed herself to miss Max for a bit, wishing he could be along for the ride — but then again, Max might not have been too keen on the idea of a multistate, multicity trip on mass transit. Harriet felt a smile build deep down inside her gut. She liked to believe that now that he was in heaven helping build all those mansions he might be watching from way up high and could see the whole trip already planned out like a giant patchwork quilt. She clicked the top of her brand-new black gel pen and wrote:

Dear Max:

Now hang on to your halo. You might already know this; in fact I'm hoping you do. Of course, I don't know for certain how things work in heaven. I'm on my way across the country to go live with Henry and Prudence. I'm taking the long way because I got to thinking the day I was packing my collection. You never took me anywhere. There, I said it; so now I'm going — everywhere.

My fancy new Droid phone informs me that I will be traveling 2,748 miles, give or take on account of making a side trip here and there. I know you must think I'm nuts — what's new, right? But I'm doing it. Been on five different buses already and now a train bound for Baltimore, Maryland. I have in mind to visit the Salt and Pepper Shaker Museum in Gatlinburg, Tennessee. Don't laugh. It's a real place. Today I met Mauve Riggins. Isn't that a lovely name — Mauve — only she wore orange. She was a pleasant woman; well, I found out later she was pleasant. When she first sat next to me in that awful orange suit I cringed. She barely spoke a word until she heard me talking to Henry. Mauve told me she was going to follow in my path when it came her time. Imagine that, honey — me — an inspiration. I miss you every single day. Humphrey is already in California. I hope he's not too upset with me. He's not just a dog. I hope you aren't too upset with me either, Max. But I know I have to do this.

Harriet closed her notebook and brushed her fingertips across the smooth cover. She leaned her head back in the seat and closed her eyes. It had been a tiring day, and it wasn't even suppertime.

Chapter 6

HENRY LEANED BACK IN HIS DESK CHAIR AND YAWNED. HUMphrey ambled close. He sat on his haunches and stared up at Henry through his bloodshot eyes.

Henry leaned down and patted his head. "It's no use, old man; I can't write. It's like I have completely forgotten how."

Humphrey let go a howl. Then he whimpered.

"You need to go out?"

Humphrey barked.

"Okay, okay. I can use the break." Henry glanced at the time on his laptop. "Geeze, I've only been working for an hour . . . feels like longer."

Henry clicked the lead onto Humphrey's collar. "Come on. Let's go see the outdoors. It's a beautiful day. Sun is shining, my wife is interrogating witnesses, my mother is taking some harebrained trip across the country, and I lost all my talent. Still, it's a beautiful day."

Humphrey finished his business and looked up at Henry.

"Oh, all right. Once around the block."

Henry and Prudence lived on a lovely cul-de-sac. The houses were mostly split-levels with two-car garages and yards with maple and laurel trees. They still hadn't met all of the neighbors, but from what Henry could tell the neighborhood was nice and quiet.

"I guess I'm a little nervous about her moving here, Humphrey," Henry said. "I mean, I know it's best for her, but . . . well it's the dad thing. The business. I don't know if she ever really forgave me for not following in my old man's footsteps."

Humphrey stopped, sat on his haunches, and looked up at Henry.

"But I couldn't do it anymore." Henry tugged the leash. "I am a lousy businessman and an even worse builder." He made a noise through his nose. "Heck. I can't even write anymore. And Prudence is not ready to try and have a baby. Maybe she doesn't have any confidence in me; maybe that's why. Things are not going so well."

* * *

Harriet's train pulled into Baltimore's Penn Station at exactly 2:10 p.m. She waited in the cushy comfortable seat a little while as most of the other passengers grabbed their overhead luggage and briefcases. Harriet was able to keep her tote on the floor between her feet. But she had to pack her bag in the overhead. She liked watching the people move around. They said little as they went about their business. It was hard not to notice that some folks looked sad, others glad, and still others just plain frustrated—perhaps because they had business in Baltimore they weren't looking forward to.

When she saw an opening, Harriet squeezed into the aisle, pulled her bag from the bin, and thought she might have broken her foot when it came crashing down onto the same foot with the busted ankle. "Oh my!" she said. Instinct told her to reach down and rub it, or at least look, but there were too many people in the aisle. So she pulled up the handle on her suitcase and set off down the aisle . . . limping and thinking, this is a grand way to start my trip.

Once she was on the concrete platform, Harriet found a bench and looked at her foot. No apparent damage. But her instep hurt. "I'll just have to favor this foot awhile," she said.

Unprepared for the hustle and bustle of the passersby, Harriet's head spun and she felt a tad disoriented and maybe a little too conspicuous. But the truth was that no one paid her any attention. Harriet felt a pang of fear wriggle through her body. She had never been so far from home—alone. Max had always been with her. Max always made her feel safe, and if the truth be known, Harriet never had to figure things out when Max was alive, not that she couldn't. She often deferred to Max because it made him feel good. And even after he died, she relied on Henry or the folks at church to help her with home repairs and finances. But now, so far from home, she found herself needing to make decisions and choices she had absolutely no experience with—particularly when it came to trains and buses, motels and restaurants. It was going to be a long ride clear across the country to Grass Valley, but so far, Harriet was doing okay, making her way—even if her feet felt like they had been encased in cement. She made a mental note to check into purchasing a pair of Dr. Scholl's footpads, considering that the people in the TV ads didn't look so old. And she most definitely needed a pair of sneakers and some jeans. This she decided after noticing a greasy blotch on her dress. Traveling was dirty business.

Harriet took a deep breath and grabbed her suitcase by the handle. She stepped through the doors into the station. She had never seen anything so grand. She couldn't help but wonder what it was about trains that made people want to design such elaborate stations. It was more like a museum. She passed through huge, tall rounded archways into the middle of the station.

She first noticed the gorgeous skylights above her. Round stained glass windows with patterns in green and blue and yellow. The ornate glass made her think about—and miss—Martha.

"Martha would love those," she whispered. "I wonder how they got them all the way up there without breaking."

She looked around for a ladies room and quickly found one. It was not as nice as the rest of the place. The smell was pretty terrible; two of the stalls were out of order, and the only one available was out of toilet paper. No problem, though; Harriet never left home without a small pack of tissues. She washed her hands, looked at herself in the mirror, and decided that she really didn't look too bad. After pulling a comb through her hair and adjusting her bra, she set out for her next destination, a place to stay for the night.

Harriet checked her GPS and saw that Amelia had rerouted her onto Charles Street just outside Penn Station. She decided to name her GPS Amelia because it sounded nicer. And besides, the phone could speak, so it seemed only reasonable. She chose the name Amelia in honor of Amelia Earhart. Before she ventured out of the station she thought it might be prudent to ask at customer service about a nice place to eat and maybe to spend the night. A blond man in a blue uniform greeted her at a counter.

"Can I help you, ma'am?" he asked.

"Yes, young man, I was wondering if you could tell me where I could find a nice hotel around here. Not far. Some place I can get to on the bus."

The young man smiled and pointed toward the station doors. "Inner Harbor has some nice places, like the Hyatt Regency."

"Can I get there by bus?"

"Sure. Just head out to North Charles Street and wait for the bus. The driver will be able to tell you."

Inner Harbor. Harriet liked the sound of it.

The sky had turned overcast and dreary for a spring day. But that was okay. Harriet would rather shiver from cold than sweat from heat.

Yellow taxicabs lined the street like a wide yellow river. Gray flower boxes with pretty purple flowers lined the sidewalk. But it was the giant aluminum man, or was it a woman, that caught her off guard. Right there, smack in the middle of everything, stood a giant figure of a human being. There was no obvious way to discern if it was a man or a woman, and she figured it was probably meant to represent both sexes. A notion she didn't understand the need for. She rather appreciated the notion that there was both men and women in the world. She never did go in for that whole unisex craze that struck way back in the early seventies when the Sit and Curl Beauty Parlor started serving men also and became a salon.

Harriet stared up at the thing for a few minutes until a bus pulled into the square. The driver stopped when Harriet waved. The door opened.

"Hello," Harriet said. "Does this bus take me to the Hyatt Regency Hotel in Inner Harbor?"

The driver, who seemed a bit surly, wrinkled his brow. "No, lady. You need the 64. It'll be along in a few minutes."

"Thank you," Harriet said.

She waited, still staring at the strange sculpture and wondering if a cab ride might be the better choice. "No," she said aloud, "I said I was taking the bus and I am going to take the bus."

Ten minutes later the 64 pulled up.

"I need to get off at the Hyatt Regency in Inner Harbor," Harriet told the driver. "Could you be a dear and not let me miss my stop."

The driver, a woman in her mid thirties or so, nodded. "It's about five minutes."

"Thank you," Harriet said as she lugged her suitcase up the steps.

She found a seat toward the middle even though she would rather have stayed as close to the driver as possible. After all, she was traveling in what amounted to a foreign country to her, and she did not want to get lost. Even though Lacy had assured her that Amelia would get her where she needed to go. As long as she kept the battery charged. But she figured that was true not only of her Droid but her body as well.

Harriet sat down with a bit of a thud on account of the driver took off quickly, jarring Harriet into her seat.

"Goodness gracious," she said as she sat back.

A man about the size of a redwood tree occupied the seat next to her. Harriet smiled but he looked away. She resisted the urge to tell him she was traveling clear across the country. He did not look the type to care about her travels.

The driver was right on schedule; five minutes or so later the bus pulled up to the curb. Harriet saw the driver glance in the rearview mirror. "Must be my stop," she said to Redwood Tree. He promptly grunted.

"Now how do I get to the hotel?" Harriet asked the driver.

"It's a short walk down Light Street. You can't miss it. Just look for the tall ships."

Harriet stood on the corner as she watched the bus take off. She looked in different directions until she had the good fortune to spot a woman about her age walking toward her.

"Excuse me," Harriet said, "but can you tell me how to get to the Hyatt?"

The woman stopped and pointed a finger. "It's just over there. Just keep walking. You can't miss it."

"Thank you," Harriet said. She pulled her suitcase behind her and set off toward a building with more glass than she had ever seen in her life.

"My goodness," she said out loud. "This is quite the fancy place." She could see the overcast day, with its dark clouds, reflected in the glass like a watercolor painting. "I am so glad that is not sunlight," she said. "It could likely blind a person."

She headed into the hotel and was immediately struck with its grandeur. She walked in a circle, taking in the sight. All the glass on the outside provided natural lighting for the spacious lobby. She saw several customer service windows with young folks in uniform helping other customers.

She stood third in line and waited patiently.

"I'd like a room for the night," she told the young man behind the counter.

He eyed her up and down, making Harriet feel like she had asked for something terribly impossible.

"Do you have a reservation?"

"No," Harriet said. If she had a reservation she would have said so first.

The man looked at his computer screen. "Will you need a single or a double? Or would you prefer a suite?"

"A suite?" Harriet said. "Oh, goodness gracious no, young man. I just need a room to rest my wearies. I need to get back on the road in the morning. I am on my way to California."

"I have a room with two queen beds."

"Two? But I only need one."

"That's how the rooms come."

"Well, okay. It sounds nice." She liked the notion of sleeping on a queen bed.

A few minutes later a bellman approached.

Harriet thought her room was spectacular. In the middle sat two large beds with three pretty blue pillows stacked against the headboards.

The bellman placed her suitcase on a small folding table. Then he pulled open the heavy draperies. The view of what she assumed was the Inner Harbor made her feel a little dizzy at first.

"Oh, gracious, but we're high up."

"The bathroom is right through there," the bellman explained. "And this is your climate control."

"Thank you," Harriet said. She dug down deep into her tote bag, found her wallet, and tipped the young man five dollars.

Harriet decided she would sleep in the bed closest to the bathroom. She sat on the edge of the bed. She bounced twice, then three times, then four. "Comfy." That was when she noticed the large television on the credenza-dresser. It was bigger than any television Harriet had ever seen. "And I bet it gets a million channels of nothing."

A short trip to the bathroom held more interest for Harriet.

"Oh my," she said, "even the bathroom is ritzy."

She admired the colorful tile, including a sky-blue stripe that went completely around the room, except, of course, for the doorway. The showerhead was big enough for an elephant, and a fluffy white robe hung on a peg near the shower door.

"A bath would be nice . . . a little later." She rubbed her aching neck.

And after washing her hands and rinsing her face with cool water, Harriet went back to the spectacular view. She could see boats and sailing ships in the harbor and buildings that seemed to go on forever. She had heard about the National Aquarium and wondered if it might be the large blue-and-glass building on her left. She consulted the complimentary city guide on the desk. "Yep, that's the aquarium all right." She glanced at the alarm clock on the bedside table. "It's going on three o'clock. Maybe I'll visit tomorrow."

Harriet pulled her phone from her tote and set it on the bedside table. There was still some green in the teeny-tiny picture of a battery. Lacy had showed her how to read the icon, and Harriet checked it often. Then she slipped off her shoes and rubbed her tired feet. Traveling was a tough business no matter how you went.

Her phone jingled.

"Martha," Harriet said, "I'm so glad you called. I'm in Baltimore, Maryland. I'm fifteen floors up in a big hotel. It's like . . . well, it's like being in the sky, way up high like I climbed Jack's beanstalk . . . you know what I mean, Martha. I can see so far. I had no idea the world was so big."

"I am so proud of you, Harriet. What's your next stop?"

"Well I'm definitely going to the Salt and Pepper Shaker Museum. But before that? I don't know. I guess wherever Amelia sends me."

"Amelia?"

Harriet laughed. "My new Droid phone GPS brainiac. She is so smart."

"Oh, oh, I am so glad you got one of those. That will be a big help. Help you find hotels and restaurants too."

"I miss you already, Martha."

"I miss you too. But I'm sure I'll see you soon. Did you tell Henry your plan?"

Harriet laughed. "Yes. He's not so happy. He wanted to come meet me and travel along. I told him no. I am quite capable of traveling cross-country all by myself."

"Good for you," Martha said.

Harriet clicked off her phone after they said their good-byes and set it on the table. She noticed she had only a tiny bit of battery left. The phone salesman told her she would need to give it a full charge once she got settled somewhere. She rooted through her tote bag, looking for her charger. She dumped the contents out and sorted through, but no charger. Panic wriggled through her body.

"Oh dear, where is it?" She checked her dress pockets, her tote bag. Nothing.

Harriet felt tears begin to well up at the corners of her eyes. She swiped them away. "I will not cry because of a lost phone charger."

She sighed. "Some traveler I am."

Chapter 7

AFTER CHECKING THROUGH ALL OF HER BELONGINGS ONE more time Harriet decided to call the main desk.

"I . . . I don't know if you can help me, but I seem to have lost my cell-phone charger. I must have left it on the train or at the train station, and I only have a tiny bit of the green left." She looked at her phone. "Make that less than tiny."

"That's not a big problem," said the sweet voice on the other end of the connection. "I'm sure there's a store around here where you can get a replacement."

Relief filled Harriet's chest and stomach. "Really? You mean I can just go right into a store and buy one. It doesn't have to be—"

"That's right, as a matter of fact, ma'am, if you like I can check with the concierge. We might be able to have one brought to your room."

Well, this news just about floored Harriet. As a matter of fact, she had to steady her shaking knees. "No kidding, really? You people will do that for me? It has been a terribly long day, and I have never been in Baltimore before."

"Let me check," said the voice. "Solomon will have the answer."

"Thank you," Harriet said. "Should I wait here?"

"Yes, you hang tight, and I'll call your room the moment I have an answer. Now what kind of phone do you have?"

* * *

After sitting at his desk for nearly three hours—checking email, googling stupid stuff, playing a few rousing games of Solitaire, and writing a little, Henry decided it was time for lunch. Humphrey must have heard Henry's stomach growl because he scrambled to his feet with a terribly excited expression. Henry patted his head. "Don't tell Prudence, old man, but I much prefer you over that hairy cat of hers."

Humphrey rolled over onto his back and let his tongue loll out as Henry rubbed his belly. "Are you hungry, boy? Do you like tuna sandwiches?"

A few minutes later Henry sat at the kitchen table with Humphrey at his feet. They were both enjoying tuna. "So what do you think?" Henry said, looking down at the dog. "What bug bit Mom that made her decide to travel clear across the country on a bus or . . . or whatever. I mean, what is she trying to prove? Her last chance, she said."

Humphrey simply stared at Henry.

Henry's stomach wobbled. He swallowed. "Is she okay? You don't suppose she's . . . she's sick or something and this trip—"

Humphrey barked.

"Nah, you're right. She wouldn't have kept that from us. Would she?"

* * *

Harriet yawned and kicked off her shoes.

"Next order of business," she said, "buy a pair of sneakers." Harriet wore leather shoes, and they were beginning to bite back. She lay down on the bed, a queen-size beauty, and closed her eyes. She had only been traveling for a few hours, and already it felt more like a few days.

"I miss Humphrey," she said out loud. "At least I could talk to him."

She yawned. Then the next thing she knew she was awakened by a knock on her room door. She saw five-thirty on the clock. *Goodness. I was tired.*

She scrambled to her feet, checked herself in the mirror on her way to the door, and was just about to open when she thought to ask, "Who is it?"

"Bellman. I have your charger."

Harriet thought from his tone that he had been standing there for a few minutes, knocking and calling. Harriet was a sound sleeper. She pulled open the door. The same young man who showed her to her room stood there holding a package.

"Your phone charger, ma'am."

Harriet grabbed the young man by the hand and practically pulled him into the room. "Oh, thank you," she said. "That was quick."

"You're welcome."

He stood a moment staring at Harriet. She stared back and then realized he was waiting for a tip. "Oh, oh, dear me, I'm sorry. Let me get my purse. Should I pay you for the charger?"

"No, ma'am, it will show up on the credit card you presented at check-in."

"Now, isn't that nice and convenient?" She opened her wallet and discovered she only had two twenties, a ten, and a five. "Oh dear." But having a new charger without needing to go to the store herself was worth a good tip. She handed the young man another five-dollar tip thinking he would be pleased. But he simply smiled and said, "Thank you."

She opened the package and plugged in her phone. A huge wave of relief washed over her as she saw the tiny little lightning bolt flash on her phone. She decided it would be prudent to map out the next leg of her journey, so she spent the better part of an hour with Amelia, and much to her delight, Baltimore and Washington, D.C., had an incredible array of public transportation routes available. It was almost too much for her to decide. She could have taken the train clear to Winston-Salem, but where was the fun in that?

She saw the room-service guide sitting on the credenza and perused the hotel offerings but decided against them. This evening Harriet wanted to go out. So after a refreshing shower and changing into clean clothes, Harriet made her way to the hotel lobby. It seemed even bigger than when she first arrived. Bigger and busier. She spied the concierge desk, and since he was so kind as to get her a phone charger she thought he might be able to suggest a nice restaurant. Nothing too nice, but nice enough.

"You could try our own Bistro 300," he said with a smile. "It's on level three."

"Level three." Harriet said. "The Bistro. It sounds delightful, young man."

"I'm certain you will enjoy it." He smiled again.

The restaurant was nice, and Harriet had to wait only a few minutes before a table was ready. She had to admit that she felt odd sitting at a table alone and even odder when the server attempted to remove the place setting meant for a companion.

"I was wondering," Harriet said, "would it be such a bother if you left all of that there?"

"Oh, I'm sorry," the server said. "Are you expecting—"

"No. No, it just makes me feel . . . not so alone."

"I understand."

Harriet figured the only thing he really understood was that Harriet was off her noodle and was entertaining an invisible guest, a pukka of sorts like Harvey. And so, after thinking about it for another minute and before she could even open the menu, she decided to allow the server to remove the place setting. And besides, the notion struck her that others might think she had been stood up. And that was worse than dining alone, even for a woman her age.

She caught her server's eye, and he returned to the table. "I'm sorry. I changed my mind. You can take the extra plates and water glass and . . . and stuff away."

He looked at her kind of funny. "Are you certain?"

"Yes, I am. Please."

And so Harriet enjoyed what she thought was her official first meal on the road. First real meal, now that she was out of Pennsylvania, totally committed and ready for adventure.

* * *

Harriet finished her meal around seven o'clock. Dessert was scrumptious. She always did have a soft spot for cheesecake. And the hotel's cheesecake was something special, made with pecans, chocolate, and caramel. The server asked her to sign the bill. "You mean, no money. Just sign?"

The server smiled, although Harriet thought it might have been a kind of smirky smile. "Yes, ma'am, it will be added to your hotel bill."

"Oh, that's fine." She took the pen and signed her name. *Harriet Beamer.* She thought about adding the word *Adventurer* after her name but figured that would cause trouble. But she did cross her *t* with a flourish she never knew she had.

Chapter 8

THE NEXT MORNING HARRIET JOINED THE EARLIEST TOUR group at the National Aquarium. Fortunately, she was able to check her suitcase at the coatroom inside the museum. She especially enjoyed the stingrays and sharks. She had hoped the souvenir shop would have jellyfish shakers, but she had to settle on a blue dolphin pair with the words Baltimore Inner Harbor on them. She tucked them safely into her tote bag, and set off to find a FedEx or UPS office so she could send the shakers. Harriet worried that toting brand-new souvenir shakers around could become not only a heavy ordeal but a dangerous one — they could break. Amelia helped her locate a FedEx a couple of blocks from the aquarium and Harriet overnighted the dolphins to California.

Then Harriet made her way to the first bus stop of the day just in time to catch the 1:07. The Baltimore bus was attractive: green along the bottom and then white with the usual advertisements splayed across the wide sides like traveling billboards. The destination display of the bus she boarded read: Johns Hopkins Hospital.

Harriet climbed aboard and smiled at the driver. "The bus station, please."

The driver, a young man this time, said nothing, which made Harriet feel a little put off. So far, all of the drivers had been quite cordial. She chose a seat toward the middle and sat next to a woman who appeared to be about her age.

"Hello," Harriet said.

The woman looked out the window, obviously not wanting to be bothered. Harriet didn't press it. The ride to the station was only a few minutes long, not enough time to form a real connection anyway.

Six minutes later Harriet's stop came up. She wasn't the only one getting off, and in some odd way that made her feel as though she was part of a group.

Harriet checked with Amelia one final time. Amelia still said that Winston-Salem, North Carolina, would be her next destination by way of Greensboro, with many little towns in between. If she saw something that tickled her fancy along the route, then she'd stop. She had all the time in the world to explore—the entire rest of the spring if she wanted.

Harriet bused clear to Bowie, Maryland, a lovely suburb of Baltimore. From there it seemed a little more difficult to find connecting buses. So, after several frustrating moments she stopped at a small coffee shop for pie and coffee and asked the waitress if she knew how to get to North Carolina. But the waitress only looked at her like she had sprouted asparagus from her head and asked the cashier who asked the cook who asked the cop sitting at the counter. He made a call on his radio and suggested she hop the Amtrak train in Washington, D.C. Harriet had been to the capital once in her life, and that had been on a school field trip in the sixth grade and at a time when security was not the huge issue it was today. After a round of hearty thank-yous, Harriet boarded a bus to Union Station, where she'd snag a train for North Carolina.

Washington Union Station was the most incredible place Harriet had ever seen. For a second she thought she might have taken a wrong turn and ended up in Europe outside a palace. The place was huge, so huge she had to grab a map to find her way around. It was like its own city, complete with shops and restaurants. It was here that Harriet decided to purchase jeans.

The station was more like a big mall. She checked a large, lighted directory and found her way to Chico's on the mezzanine level. It took the better part of half an hour, but Harriet finally settled on a pair of light blue denim jeans that just barely reached her ankles. The important thing was that they fit comfortably around her middle.

"Thank you very much," she said to the young saleswoman. She seemed a bit jaded for being only around thirty, Harriet thought. Then again she must see millions of people pass through the station every day. It was old hat to her. But for Harriet, purchasing jeans at a train station was something extraordinary and unique. On her way back to the train platform Harriet was delighted when she found a Godiva Chocolatier on the concourse level. She would have to tell Martha.

Harriet had a one-hour wait before the Crescent train was scheduled to leave the station at 6:30 p.m. This did not make her happy. She was starting to feel tired and was anxious to settle into a comfy train seat and rest. Harriet found a store that sold magazines. She purchased two postcards, one with a picture of the Washington Union Station and another with a picture of the National Aquarium.

"Martha will love this," she said, looking at the Union Station postcard. "She'll be so impressed that I am here and finding my way around."

Harriet decided to send the National Aquarium postcard to Henry and Prudence. She found a bench to sit on and wrote out her postcards. First to Henry. She wrote:

I was here for a little while. Enjoyed my stay. Saw many fish. I'm on my way. Kiss Humphrey for me.

Love, Mother.

Next she wrote to Martha.

*I thought you would enjoy seeing this. The picture doesn't do
it justice. A person could live here. It has everything you need.
Spectacular.*

Love, Harriet.

She dropped the cards in a mailbox. On her way to the platform she came across a souvenir shop where she was able to find a set of salt and pepper shakers in the shape of the Washington Monument and the White House. The Monument was the pepper. From there it was a short walk to her platform where she found another bench closer to the trains. She took her journal from her tote and for some odd reason remembered her feet. "I need sneakers. I wonder if I have time to buy a pair of sneakers."

She still had about a half an hour before the train.

"Excuse me," she said to a young woman who reminded her a bit of Lacy.

"Yeah?" the girl said.

"Is there a store nearby where I can buy some sneakers? I mean there must be, there's every kind of store here, but I don't want to waste time."

"Don't know."

This young woman no longer reminded her of Lacy. Oh well. It was probably not such a good idea to take the chance on missing her train anyway. She had seen enough of Maryland and was anxious to get to North Carolina. According to her ticket she would arrive in Greensboro at a little past midnight, late but doable.

* * *

Henry clipped the lead onto Humphrey's collar. "Come on. Maybe a walk will help clear my head enough to write."

Henry had been sitting at his desk since six o'clock in the morning trying to write what he hoped would be the final three chapters of his novel. It was now nearly three o'clock, and he had only written a dozen words. They were good words but still only a dozen.

Humphrey pulled slightly away as they made their way down the street aiming for his favorite bush.

"Okay, okay," Henry said. "You'll make it." Henry paused when Humphrey sniffed around the bush.

"Go on," Henry said, "do your business." Then Henry said, "Good boy, Humphrey. Maybe we should stop by Mrs. Caldwell's. She usually has pie."

Mrs. Caldwell had been the first person on the block to greet Henry and Prudence when they moved into the neighborhood. Henry liked her right off the bat. Prudence said it was because she was a bit like his mother. Maybe so.

"Well, hello there, Henry," Mrs. Caldwell said as she pushed open the screen door. "What brings you by this afternoon and . . . oh my, who's your friend?" Mrs. Caldwell appeared younger than his mother, but Henry still figured her to be in her sixties. She was tall and skinny with short gray hair. She wore fashionable bluish glasses, which almost matched her bluish hair, and white jeans and a yellow blouse.

"Good afternoon, Mrs. Caldwell. This is Humphrey. He belongs to my mother."

Mrs. Caldwell pushed the door open and allowed Henry and Humphrey inside.

"It's okay," Henry said. "He can sit outside."

"Nonsense," Mrs. Caldwell said. "I love doggies."

"Are you sure? He smells a bit."

Henry followed Mrs. Caldwell into her kitchen, a delightful, comfortable country kitchen with cherry-decorated curtains and lots of cabinets with glass windows in the doors. Her colorful dishes and cups were arranged so artistically.

Henry spied what looked like a homemade apple pie on the counter. His stomach grumbled.

"That pie looks great," he said. "Just like my mother used to make."

"Used to make," Mrs. Caldwell said as she grabbed two

white plates from a cabinet. "You mean she doesn't make them anymore?"

Henry dropped Humphrey's leash on the floor.

"Oh, no, she still makes pies, but for the people back home and when we visit, of course. Yours just reminded me."

"I see, well, then, I'll cut you a nice big piece."

"But she's moving here . . . she's on her way — kind of."

"Really. That will be so nice for her and you."

Henry took the pie from Mrs. Caldwell. "Thank you. If she ever gets here."

"What does that mean, dear? I'm a little slow on the draw."

"Oh, nothing really. She seems to be taking her time travel-ing cross-country. When she said she was taking the bus, Pru-dence and I thought she meant she was taking Greyhound, but I'm pretty sure she's decided to take the regular bus, the locals all the way. And anything else she might need, a donkey for all I know. She has no plan. No schedule to keep."

Mrs. Caldwell busted into such a loud laugh that she startled Henry and nearly made him choke on a slice of apple.

Humphrey yowled and wagged his tail. He spun around three times and yowled once more.

"Why is my mother's wild trip across the country funny?" Henry asked. He felt a little hurt.

"It's not only funny," Mrs. Caldwell said, "it's genius."

"Genius?"

Mrs. Caldwell chewed and swallowed, all the time looking straight at Henry. He thought she was sizing him up or something. "Yes, dear, did she *want* to move?"

Henry shook his head. "I . . . I suppose. She's coming."

"Seems to be taking her time."

"Ahhh, so you think this is her way of . . ."

"Avoiding the inevitable. Feeling young again? Making one last stand?"

"Oh, gee, I never looked at it that way. So maybe I should just let her do it her way? She did say she wanted to see the country."

"Well, then, she knows what she's doing. She's a grown woman. She'll ask for help if she needs it."

"I'm worried she'll get lost or meet with some unsavory individuals."

"She might. But that could all be part of the adventure. I admire her."

Henry finished his pie. "Thank you, Mrs. Caldwell. Maybe I need to look at this from her perspective." He scraped the side of the fork across the plate, getting the last of the cinnamony apple goodness.

Mrs. Caldwell sliced a second piece for Henry. "Here you go. Now, tell me what else is on your mind."

Humphrey made a noise. He wagged his tail. He even twirled around and chased his tail just for good measure.

"Would Humphrey like some pie?" asked Mrs. Caldwell. "Or is that not allowed?"

"I can't see a problem with pie. My mom feeds him donuts."

"Your mother sounds like a woman I can be friends with," Mrs. Caldwell said as she gave Humphrey some pie. She looked into Henry's eyes and said, "I'm glad we talked about your mother, but I get the feeling your heart is still heavy. You want to tell me?"

Henry swallowed. "Writer's block."

Mrs. Caldwell smiled. "Don't know much about writer's block, but if it's anything like constipation, well, that I know about."

Henry laughed. "As a matter of fact, there are similarities."

"Well, it just seems to me, dear," Mrs. Caldwell continued, "that the best thing for you to do is go back to your desk and start writing. Even if you don't write what you like I suspect the good words will find their way out. Sitting here with me — as delightful as that is — won't get that book written."

"I know. You're right." Henry eyed the remaining pie in the tin.

Mrs. Caldwell laughed. "Oh, go on, take the rest of the pie.

Maybe it'll help you figure out your story or whatever you writerly types do."

"You sure?" Henry said. "I mean, I don't want to take the last of your pie."

Mrs. Caldwell grabbed a box of plastic wrap from a drawer. "Yes, you do. And that's okay. I always have pie."

Henry and Humphrey said their good-byes to Mrs. Caldwell.

"Come on, Humphrey," Henry said with a tug on the leash. "Let's go home. I think I have an idea that will work for my ending."

Humphrey barked and looked up at Henry as if to say, "I believe in you too."

Henry leaned down and patted his side. "You're a good dog."

Chapter 9

AROUND 9:00 P.M. THE CRESCENT LINE TRAIN PULLED INTO
the Charlottesville, Virginia, station. Harriet especially enjoyed
the sensation and sound of the train slowing down as the driver
blew the horns. It was like they wanted the whole world to know
that they had arrived. Harriet was beginning to develop a fond-
ness for train stations and was starting to feel like a veteran train
traveler, like maybe she should even get some sort of badge for her
adventuring. She decided to take the time to visit the ladies room
—fortunately she didn't need to get off the train.

The bathroom on the train was nicer than the one at the Baltimore Station—cleaner, brighter, and smelled a whole lot better.
A bit like lilacs. But on her way back to her seat, the evening took
a more interesting turn. She noticed the young woman she saw
earlier at Union Station. She was sitting with her head against the
window, and if Harriet was correct she had been crying.

Harriet immediately asked forgiveness for jumping to conclu-
sions about her earlier that day. She had obviously mistaken her for
a surly, young ... well, Harriet would never actually use the word.

"Hello," Harriet said. "I remember you from the station."

The young woman looked up at Harriet.

"I still don't know about sneakers," she said.

"No, that's okay. I couldn't help but notice you've been crying."

The woman looked away, out the window. But Harriet could still see her reflection in the glass thanks to the train lighting.

Harriet sat in the seat next to her. "Now listen. I might have only had one son and not much experience with girls — unless you include my daughter-in-law. But I can always tell when someone's been crying."

The woman sighed. "Please, leave me alone."

"I will, I will," Harriet said. "But I want you to know I'm a good listener. At least that's what Martha, she's my friend back home — in Philly — said. I'm going to California because my son and his wife said ... oh dear, I'm rambling."

That was when the young woman smiled. "Do you always do this ... tell your life story to strangers?"

Harriet let go a slight chuckle. "Only the nice ones."

The young woman smiled.

"How old are you, dear?" Harriet asked.

"Twenty-three."

"What a great age. You have your whole life ahead of you. And I suppose you have a name. I'm Mrs. Beamer. Mrs. Harriet Beamer."

"Tess."

"Tess. A very pleasant name."

"I suppose," Tess said with a sniffle.

"And it suits you just fine. Anyhoo, where you headed?"

Tess shook her head and then leaned against the window. "Home."

"Home? Why, I would think that would make you happy. Isn't that what Dorothy said, 'There's no place like home'?"

"Not exactly. I ... I should be on my way to Bermuda."

"Bermuda? Well, honey, if that's where you're going, you are definitely on the wrong train."

Just then the train started to move, and the man who was originally sitting next to Tess returned. He stood, looking annoyed.

"Excuse me," he said, "but I think you're in my seat."

Harriet looked up. He was tall, stocky, and wearing a three-piece suit with the tie loosened and crooked.

"Oh dear, I want to keep talking to Tess. You can take my seat. It's just over there." She pointed. "It's a window."

The man looked from Harriet to Tess and then back again. "Fine. Just let me get my magazine. Uh, you're sitting—"

Harriet moved to the side and reached under her bottom. "I'm sorry. I sat on your *Time*." She handed it to the man. "You're a nice man."

The man snatched it and made his way down the aisle toward Harriet's seat.

"Now, where were we? Oh, yes, Bermuda ..."

Tess continued to peer out the window, making Harriet feel that perhaps it would be best if she went back to her seat. She still had quite a ways to go before Greensboro.

"Okay, dear," Harriet said. "Sometimes you just don't feel like talking. I can certainly understand that. I'll just go back to my seat and send old Crooked Tie back."

Tess turned back to Harriet. "I'm sorry. It's ... it's just that I should be on my ... my—" Tess busted into a flood of tears —"honeymoon."

"Oh dear, oh dear me," Harriet said. She grabbed Tess's hand and patted it. "What in the world happened?"

"Gordon, that's my fiancé's—ex-fiancé's—name, he ... he left me, stranded, at the church."

"You mean he just left?" Harriet felt her dander rising but knew that keeping her cool was important under this kind of circumstance.

"No. He never showed up. We held up the ceremony for two hours ... two hours!"

"This is just so awful," Harriet said. She continued to tap Tess's hand. "Are you sure something didn't happen? I mean considering the circumstances, maybe he was in a car wreck or ... something."

"My daddy called all the hospitals, the police and ..."

"I'm sorry. It would have been better to have a broken and bleeding fiancé lying in a ditch than no fiancé at all."

Tess cried a bit harder and wiped her eyes on a balled-up napkin she had been clutching. Harriet managed to get a closer look at it. It was yellow and had the words *Tess and Gordon* printed on one side. She sighed.

"Everybody just sat there—waiting and waiting. My Aunt Irene did her best to entertain, but she can only juggle for just so long, and then Uncle Cyrus sang a duet with the pastor; they sang *My Girl*, and it was terrible, and then my maid of honor, Kicky—Kicky Strassmeyer—told a few jokes; they were pretty funny and then ..."

Harriet patted Tess's hand a smidge harder. "I think I understand."

"I'm sorry. I babble when—" she snuffed back tears and snot—"when I'm upset."

"Well, if you don't mind me asking, how come you're traveling alone?" Harriet needed to take a deep breath. Speaking to strangers about such personal matters was not something she did on a regular basis ... or ever, really. But there was something about being on the train that made it possible to poke her head out of the shell.

"I just wanted to. Dad and Mom went on ahead. They'll meet me at the station, I suppose, even though I'd rather ... I'd rather just—"

Harriet put her hand up. "Now listen here, if you are about to say the word *die*, I am going to have to tell you a thing or two. You have your whole life to look forward to. Twenty-three, well, you're barely out of diapers."

Tess smiled. "But why would Gordon do that?"

"Now that I'm sure I can't answer with any amount of certainty, although I have heard that cold feet can get pretty frosty. I'm sure that's just what it is. He'll be back the second he realizes what a fool he's been."

"But he would have called or texted me. It's not like Gordon."

Tess reached under her thigh and produced her cell phone. "Nothing. Not one text from him."

Harriet gazed out the window at the lights on the track and the lights through the trees whizzing past faster than anything. "This train is moving awful fast now. We must be on a nice straight track. But I'm sure there's going to be a curve coming up soon, and the conductor will have to slow down to get safely around."

Harriet stopped patting Tess's hands and turned her face toward her. "Just like life, don't you think? We have times when we move fast, all seems like smooth sailing, then God throws us a curve and we got to slow down, way down sometimes. I think this is just a curve in your track, sweetie. It's gonna get straighter again."

* * *

Henry ripped lettuce while Prudence formed hamburgers for the grill.

"I'm glad you're home this evening," Henry said. "We can celebrate."

Prudence rinsed her hands and dried them on a soft yellow towel. "Celebrate? Did you hear from your mother?"

"No, no, I wrote some words today. Good words. Humphrey and I went to visit Mrs. Caldwell, and she helped me ... well, along with her apple pie."

Prudence smiled into Henry's eyes. "I'm proud of you. Maybe you should be working then and not ripping lettuce into tiny pieces. Here, let me do that."

Henry looked into the bowl of lettuce. "Oh, yeah, look at that. I was distracted. Thinking about my novel."

"That, believe it or not, is the best news I've heard all day."

"The case not going well?"

Prudence sliced a tomato. "We hit a snag."

"I'm sorry, Pru. But you always win, you know."

"I know, I know, but this time ... I'm not so sure."

That was when Henry's cell phone jingled.

"I'll go get these burgers on the grill," Prudence said. "I bet it's your mother."

She was right. Henry pulled his cell from his pants pocket.

"Mother," he said. "Where are you?"

"Oh, Henry," Harriet said. "Must you start every conversation with that line?"

"Okay, okay, how are you, Mom?"

"That's better. I'm fine. How are you . . . and Prudence?"

"We're fine."

"Humphrey?"

"He's fine too, Mom. I think he made a friend. A very tall and elegant white poodle."

"Oh, goodie, I was hoping he'd meet some friends. Poor thing though, all he can do is look." She chuckled.

"Mom. Where are you?"

Humphrey ambled into the kitchen. Humphrey danced a little jig around Henry's feet.

"Mother, will you say hello to your dog?"

"Certainly. Put him on."

Henry held the phone inside one of Humphrey's long, floppy ears. "Say hello to Mommy."

Humphrey only sat on his hunches looking up at Henry with soft, sad eyes.

"Go on, say hello."

Henry took the phone. "He's not talking, Mother. You say something to him." He held the phone to Humphrey's ear again.

"Hello, Humphrey. Harriet misses you."

Humphrey took a breath and howled.

"Oh, dear Lord," Henry said, "the dog is talking to her."

"I'll see you soon. Now put Henry back on."

"Now where are you?" Henry said into the phone as Humphrey tried his best to get his attention.

"I'm on a train in Virginia, on my way to Greensboro, North

81

Carolina. I'm still just tickled to pieces that I can make a telephone call on a train. Your daddy would be so amazed."

"Yes, it is amazing, but Mom, Greensboro? That's still a very long way from here. Are you—" Henry stopped. "That's good Mom. Maybe you'll find some nice salt and pepper shakers."

"Really? You mean you're okay with this now? I mean I did make it all the way to Virginia by myself. You changed your tune all of a sudden."

"Let's just say a friend helped me understand a little better."

"That's nice dear—for both our sakes."

"It doesn't mean I won't worry about you."

"That's okay, you can worry like the fussbudget you are, but not too much."

"Do you know where you'll be staying?"

"Oh, not yet. But I'm sure I'll find a nice place." Harriet said. "My fancy new Droid phone has all the places to stay inside of it somehow, the internet I suppose."

"You got a Droid? Mother I'm jealous. I can't get one yet."

"Henry, would you mind if we hung up now? I'm kind of tired; it's been a long day, and I feel a little headachy."

"Okay, get some rest tonight and keep in touch."

Henry looked at his phone. "How come she gets a Droid?"

"Was that your mother?" Prudence said when she returned to the kitchen.

"Yep. She's in Virginia."

"Virginia. Did she say what part?"

"No, but she's on her way to Greensboro. She's making progress."

Prudence smiled. "I'm proud of her. A seventy-two-year-old woman traveling all alone across the country collecting salt and pepper shakers as she goes."

Henry laughed. "It is kind of funny. I just worry, you know. She's . . . she's my mom."

Prudence smirked. "I know but—"

"But what?"

"Oh, sometimes I still get upset about my own parents and wish—"

Henry took Prudence in his arms. "I know. What your mother did was hurtful, but your Dad did a great job raising you alone."

"I don't even know if she's still alive. I mean she'd be the same age as your mother."

"Maybe we can try and find her someday."

Prudence kissed Henry. "Maybe. But listen, I'm proud of you too, for taking the high road and trusting Harriet."

"I have to, Pru. I owe her after what I did—selling the business and being a writer when she wanted me to follow—"

"But you had to follow your heart. I'm sure she understands. Maybe now more than ever. Or maybe that's what she'll figure out along the way."

Prudence scraped the sliced tomatoes into the salad bowl.

Henry looked at her for a second. "You know, Pru, I've been thinking about something else too. Maybe we should tell her about, you know, what happened . . ."

Prudence looked away a moment and then back at Henry. "I wish you wouldn't keep bringing this up. I don't want to talk about it—not even to your mother. I'm not ready."

"But Pru," Henry said. His voiced turned tender. He touched her cheek. "We lost our babies. You need to talk about it —someday."

Prudence nestled her head into Henry's shoulder. "I'm not ready. I know I keep saying that but . . . but it still stings too much."

Henry lifted Prudence's chin. "I know."

Prudence stepped away and picked up a small stack of mail.

"I'll get the burgers," Henry said. "But I think we're gonna have to when she gets here. She really wants a grandchild and—" Henry moved closer to Prudence and wrapped his arms around her waist. "Maybe if she knew we lost two babies last year, she won't be so . . . so vocal about wanting grandchildren."

* * *

Harriet's train pulled into the J. Douglas Galyon Depot in Greensboro, North Carolina, around midnight. Although she enjoyed the ride she decided she was through with trains for a while and that the local bus would suit her fine for a bit.

She had been writing to Max when she arrived.

Maybe I'm more useful than I thought, Max. Tess seemed really interested in what I had to say. I think God was the real conductor on this train.

She closed her book and tucked it into her tote as she waited until most of the people had gotten up, grabbed their luggage, and made their way out of the train. After a few minutes the herd thinned. She glanced over in time to see Tess looking at her cell phone, with a smile as wide as a crescent moon stretched across her face.

"You were right, Mrs. Beamer. Gordon just texted me." Tess showed her the phone. Harriet read the words. "Forgive me. I love you."

"Well, see there," Harriet said. "It was just a case of cold feet, icy cold feet, but dear heart, do Mrs. Beamer a favor and have a long talk with that man before you say I do — preferably with a member of the clergy nearby."

"Oh, don't you worry, Mrs. Beamer. I love Gordon. And I want to marry him, but we are going to have that talk first."

"Good girl." Harriet smiled.

Once she was off the train, Harriet noticed a warm sensation inside that she hadn't felt in a very long time. Maybe this was how it felt to thaw out. For the first time in a long time, Harriet wondered if perhaps God really did have his hand on her, nudging her along.

The Galyon Depot was not nearly as grand as the Union Station in Washington. Harriet didn't think she'd ever get over that place. But the Depot was still grand, with high ceilings and pillars.

After a brief conversation with a station representative, Harriet learned that buses left regularly throughout the day for Winston-Salem, but she thought for right now the best idea was to find a hotel for the night. She chose the closest, the Biltmore Greensboro Hotel, a historic hotel only a few blocks from the Depot.

Harriet lugged her suitcase through the hotel lobby door and let go a huge breath. Although she would never admit it she was a little nervous walking to the hotel at night. The lobby was large with high ceilings and reminded Harriet of pictures of a gentleman's club with dark wood and leather, not that she'd ever been to one. She saw pictures. A large portrait of a young man in Colonial garb hung near the fireplace.

The man at the front desk was kind and spoke softly, so softly Harriet had a little trouble understanding him. But he showed her to a nice room on the second floor. It was called the Traveler and was especially designed for people just passing through.

Harriet felt annoyed although not surprised about how tired she was. She wanted to talk to Martha, but it was far too late. As the yawns caught up with her, she charged her phone and fell asleep.

Chapter 10

THE NEXT MORNING HARRIET BOARDED THE 10:00 PIEDmont Express Bus to Winston-Salem. She carried a large cup of coffee and an orange-cranberry scone, which she had to tuck inside her tote bag on account of lugging her suitcase.

The big black bus was comfortable, with lots of legroom and large windows that went nearly from the roof to the ground and made Harriet a little nervous, like she could fall out.

"I can't wait to get to Winston-Salem," she said to the woman sitting next to her. "It sounds like such a nice town. But I've been through quite a few — they're all the same, yet different, you know?"

The woman, a tall, skinny thing with close-cropped hair and round glasses, looked into Harriet's eyes. "You a traveler? Kind of a travelin' grandma?"

"Yep, was on the train awhile yesterday. I'm glad to be on the bus now. I like trains, but with buses you get to see more of the towns and cities." She glanced out the window. "See, over there, that's the biggest weeping willow tree I have ever seen."

"That's true, that's true. I been taking the bus ever since I got my license taken away from me."

Harriet's stomach made a little flip-flop. "Why was that?"

"DUI," the woman said. "But it wasn't my fault. I had to drive the car that night."

"I'm sure you did, dear. My name is Mrs. Beamer. Harriet Beamer."

The woman reached out her hand from around the grocery bag she clutched. "Thomasina, but ever'body call me Tommy. You can call me Tommy too."

"Okay, Tommy. It's nice to meet you."

"I only got two more stops before mine. Then I'm home and I can see my little girl. The social worker said she'd bring Maize by me tonight."

Harriet swallowed. "That's nice. I'm on my way to where my son lives."

"So you got family somewheres too."

Harriet let go a soft chuckle. "Sure do. Grass Valley, California."

"California? Why, Mrs. Beamer, you a long way off from there."

"I know. I'm taking the long way home."

"You rightly are." Tommy glanced out the window and then back at Harriet. "You mean to tell me you be taking the bus the whole way there? The whole, long way?"

"Yep. Just taking my time. Seeing some sights before I die."

"The dickens you say. Now that's a trip I wish I could take, but I don't think my parole officer would let me do that. Not just now anyway."

Harriet smiled but had to admit to herself that she was beginning to feel a bit nervous even though she did not want to judge Tommy based on one small conversation. Harriet peered into Tommy's huge, crystal eyes.

"You have the bluest, sweetest eyes," Harriet said. "Very pretty."

"Pretty? You think I'm pretty?"

"I do."

Tommy sniffed. "Not generally the way I get described."

The bus lurched as it went over a bump. "Turbulence on buses too," Harriet said.

Tommy laughed. "Well, this is my stop. Glad I met you, Mrs. Beamer."

"I'm glad I met you, Thomasina. Such a pretty woman. You tell people they need to call you Thomasina from now on."

Tommy smiled as she stood. The dark circles under her eyes became apparent in the odd lighting of the bus. "You have fun. I hope you find your family."

"I will. They're waiting for me."

Harriet remembered her scone. She reached into her tote and retrieved the small white bag. The scone had begun to disintegrate from being crammed, but Harriet didn't mind. She had never eaten out of a bag before and kind of enjoyed it.

*   *   *

A little past 11:00 a.m., Harriet's bus pulled into the Winston-Salem station.

"Last stop," the driver called. "Everybody out of the pool."

Harriet had the impression he said that every time.

This time she was the first one off the bus. The station wasn't anything spectacular, more like a big, covered driveway in a downtown sort of place. The first thing she noticed besides all the pigeons was the chill in the air. It was like the temperature had dropped thirty degrees. She dug her sweater out of her tote and buttoned it on. Before she left the station Harriet had snagged some pamphlets, and from the look of things, Winston-Salem seemed like a great place to do some sightseeing. Besides she wanted an extended rest period.

"Now," she said out loud, "first I should find a place to spend the night. A base of operations." She spotted a cab driver leaning against his yellow car.

"Excuse me," Harriet said, "but can you tell me where I could find a nice hotel close by."

"Close by here," the cabbie said. "Um, let me think." He pulled at his chin. "I guess you could go on down to the Marriott. It's not far, not even a mile. You can walk it."

Walk. That sounded good to Harriet after sitting on the bus for an hour. "Thank you, can you give me directions?"

"Sure thing. Just go on down Liberty Street here until you reach Fifth. Turn left on Cherry Street and you'll see it. Big, tall building."

Harriet checked that everything was still safely tucked into her tote bag and set off down Liberty Street. She liked the sound of that. Liberty Street. Her rolling suitcase got snagged on some uneven pavement, and it toppled to the side a few times.

"Geeze, the center of gravity on these things must be off," she said adjusting the bag.

* * *

After checking in, Harriet grabbed a quick lunch of a cheeseburger and French fries in the hotel restaurant. And that was when Harriet discovered the hotel had an indoor pool.

"Oh, yes, ma'am," said her server. "The hotel has many recreational offerings. The pool is open, and so is the fitness room."

"Fitness room? Oh, dear me, no, I'm not much for lifting weights and such."

The waiter smiled. "There's more than weights. Perhaps a walk on the treadmill."

"Treadmill? Honey, why would I want to walk in place when I can walk and actually see something outside?"

"Oh, I'm sorry. I didn't mean to—"

Harriet raised her hand. "No, I'm sorry. The pool sounds nice. As a matter of fact, I think I will sit by the pool for a while." Although she hadn't packed a bathing suit, just the thought of lazing poolside in the afternoon seemed as if it might be a nice change of pace from traveling. She went to her room and grabbed her journal. "I think I might write a nice long letter to Max." Harriet sat

89

on the bed and let a few tears slip down her cheeks. Grief was an odd sort of bird that flitted around in the background most of the time, but every so often, the bird would come to settle on Harriet's shoulder. And at those times Harriet, like so many others, had no choice but to acknowledge its presence with tears.

She thought about calling Grass Valley first. Maybe hearing Henry's voice would help, or even if she could hear Humphrey bark or whine. How she wished for just a second she had a nice, warm glazed donut to offer him.

But she was just a little too teary-eyed and didn't want to worry Henry, so for solace she opened her wallet and looked at her picture of Max. He was a handsome man — tall with blond hair and bright blue eyes and one dimple in his right cheek. The picture was taken just two days before what would be their last Christmas together. He wore a Santa hat and had a crazy grin on his face. Next she looked at the picture of Humphrey she carried right next to Max's. It was taken at last year's church picnic. Humphrey held an entire hamburger in his mouth. She touched the picture with her fingertips. "I miss you. But I'm coming." And for the first time since boarding the first bus back in Pennsylvania, Harriet thought maybe, just maybe, she should just get it over with and fly to California.

She snuffed back her tears and opened her Moleskine. Dropped her seeing glasses, put on her cheaters and wrote:

Dear Max, grief is like my tote bag. I carry it everywhere I go.

Her eyes felt heavy, and the next thing Harriet knew she woke in a darkened room. The sun had already set, but she took her journal anyway and headed for the pool. The area was nice. Big and spacious with a glass roof that made it possible for Harriet to look out into the night sky. It was too bad that the city lights obscured the sky. Harriet thought the stars would have been spectacular if she could only see them. She settled on a lounge chair and sighed as she opened her notebook and reread what she had just written. Then wrote:

I'm sorry, honey. I must have been tired. I feel asleep. You'll never believe where I'm at — poolside at a hotel in Winston-Salem, North Carolina. It's an indoor pool with a glass ceiling. I can see the moon — a little bit — it's not full, and I can only see a couple of stars. Remember how we enjoyed heading out sometimes, late at night, to kiss in the warmth of the Milky Way? I want to do that again; well, don't get nervous — not the kissing part, unless it was with you. But I want to see stars. Millions of them poured out by the gallons and gallons.

She stopped writing and thought a moment. Then she wrote,

But Max, the most exciting thing is ... well, taking place inside my heart. I had been thinking about my life and do you know — I never accomplished anything. Not really. Oh, I raised a good son. I was a good church lady, but I never did anything. I never even tried, but now I am; I'm finally doing something spectacular. At least it is to me.

She stopped writing again. But then hurried to write,

Oh dear, did I just write that?

She closed her journal and closed her eyes. When she opened them it was nearly midnight and a man was standing over her.

"I'm sorry to disturb you, but the pool is closing."

Harriet shook her head. "Oh, dear me. I'm sorry. I fell asleep."

"Happens all the time," the man said.

Harriet stood. "Thank you. I'll just be going to my room." She looked at the young man. "You remind me of Henry."

"Henry?"

"My son. He's a writer — working on his second novel — I think it's number two. He's not famous — well, not yet. I'm on my way to see him."

"That's nice."

Harriet stared for another few seconds. "Well, good evening, Hen—"

"Phillip, ma'am, my name is Phillip."

She noticed his name badge. "Yes, of course. Thank you, Phillip."

Harriet had chosen a king guest room for the night. It was large with beautiful white linens, a huge bathroom, and of course a flat screen TV bigger than her dining room table. So after taking a shower and changing into a nightgown, Harriet made herself comfy in the large bed. She clicked on the TV and surfed until she landed on a Bette Davis movie—*Now Voyager*. One of her all-time favorites.

Just as Bette and Paul Henreid were about to kiss for the first time, her phone jingled. She was glad it did because it helped her not get all misty-eyed.

"Hello," Harriet said with her eyes on the TV.

"Harriet, it's me. Martha. I know it's late, but you know me —a night owl. I was hoping you were still up."

"Oh, Martha, how nice. How are you?"

"Just fine. There's a big storm here, thunder, lightning. Where are you?"

"Winston-Salem, North Carolina. And yes, I'm still awake."

"How's it going?"

"Fine. It's going fine. But for a minute today I thought maybe I should just get on a plane and fly to Grass Valley."

"Maybe you should."

"Nah, I was just missing Max and Humphrey. Hold on a second, will ya, Martha. Bette Davis is about to—"

"Who? Bette Davis? Harriet, what's going on?"

"A movie, Martha. I'm watching a movie." Harriet set the phone down on the bed. A half hour later she picked it up. Martha had hung up.

"Oh dear. I'll call her back tomorrow."

* * *

Tomorrow arrived and Harriet woke to the sound of rain splatting against the windows. Thunder rumbled overhead and a crack of lightning illuminated the room. She looked at the clock. "Ten after seven."

Harriet dressed. She chose a pullover shirt and the blue capris she had packed. Her new jeans needed washing, so she folded them tightly and shoved them into the suitcase. She would rather have worn the jeans and now wished she had bought two pair, but the capris would have to do until she could purchase another pair of jeans and sneakers. Most definitely sneakers. Her leather shoes had become almost impossible to wear. And even though her ankle was fully healed, it still ached from time to time — especially when it rained.

Harriet finished brushing her hair and teeth. She packed away everything she had taken out of her suitcase and tote and then made her way to the hotel lobby. First things first. Harriet desperately needed a pair of sneakers. She found the concierge desk, but he wasn't there.

Harriet waited and waited until her stomach grumbled and she decided that breakfast was in order. The hotel restaurant was just the place. She ordered a hearty breakfast on account of today was a big traveling day. She wanted to make it clear across North Carolina in search of wide-open skies and stars.

The server brought her a plate of scrambled eggs, grits, toast, and a cup of fresh fruit consisting of strawberries, blueberries, cantaloupe, and watermelon.

"This looks lovely," she said. "But could I have a little whipped cream on my fruit, please?"

"Of course," her server said, taking the fruit cup.

"Thank you."

Harriet liked the look of her server. A tall, graceful young woman who in Harriet's estimation was working hard for some reason—maybe she was putting herself through school, maybe she was a single mom trying to support her family. Harriet's imagination had a tendency to run away with her. It would be best to ask.

The waitress returned with Harriet's fruit. The large white mountain of whipped cream made Harriet and the server smile.

"Ah, looks great," Harriet said.

"Thank you. My name is Grace, if you need anything else."

"I knew it," Harriet said. "I was just telling myself that you are a graceful young woman."

The woman looked away.

"Oh, don't be shy," Harriet said. "I know a hard worker when I see one. And one with your grace and style and sweetness. Well, it's just such a welcome commodity these days."

"Thank you, ma'am," Grace said.

"Your momma knew what she was doing when she named you. If I took a guess I'd say you're a dancer."

Grace smiled so wide Harriet thought her face might crack. "Yes, I am. I'm a ballet dancer. At least I'm trying to be. Trouble is, grace and style, ballet, don't pay the bills, no matter how hard I practice."

Harriet swallowed the little bit of egg she held in her mouth. "No kidding. Well, that's just the sweetest thing. I love the ballet."

"I'm dancing in *Swan Lake* tonight in a recital at my school. I'd love for you to come. We're raising money to get the troupe to Spain."

"Really? Spain? Well, I don't know if I can make it tonight. I'm traveling clear across North Carolina on my way to California. But I'll see what I can do."

Harriet finished her meal, and Grace returned with the check. "Thank you," Grace said. "Have a nice trip."

"You're welcome, dear." Harriet left a sizable tip and a note.

"Dear Grace. Dance your heart away. Have fun in Spain."

* * *

Henry sat at his desk before dawn, Humphrey at his feet. He had been unable to sleep as he wrestled with his story.

"Apparently, Humphrey, the muse has left the building."

Humphrey whined.

"I know, I know," Henry said. "It's not about inspiration. It's about perspiration. But I can't think of a single word, and the book is due to the editor in one month. Why is it that every time I write a new book I completely forget how to do it?"

Humphrey yowled.

"Want to go for a walk?"

Humphrey didn't budge. "Humphrey, old man," Henry said, "I know it's early and you'd rather sleep, but I think the early morning air might do me some good."

The dog still did not move.

"Okay, you win." Henry stared at the screen and read the words out loud. " 'Cash never could shoot straight. He'd rather sling words than bullets.' " Henry hung his head. "Oh, for crying out loud, it's awful."

Humphrey hid his face under his ears.

"I know. I know. But what can I do? I have to at least turn in the manuscript. But I wanted it to be good, and this" — he pushed the keyboard away — "is garbage."

Prudence walked into Henry's study, carrying a cup of coffee and yawning. "Henry Beamer. If you toss one more keyboard on the floor and break it I'll — "

"Pru, I'm sorry. I'm just so frustrated. I lost Cash's motivation for returning to Turtle Creek. There's nothing for him. He lost everything. Why should he go back?"

"Give him a reason. It's fiction, honey, make it up. You have the power." She wrapped her arms around his neck and kissed his cheek. " 'He'd rather sling words . . .'? Henry, did you really write that?"

Henry tried to shield the screen. "I know. It's awful."

"Everybody has a reason to go home. You need to figure that out for Cash. There has to be something for him in Turtle Creek."

Henry shook his head. "I don't know. Nothing works."

"You'll get it." Prudence patted his shoulder. "Any word from your mother yesterday?"

"No, not at all. Maybe I'll call her."

"Later. Spend some more time with Cash. Ask him. He'll tell you."

* * *

After breakfast Harriet found the concierge at his desk. He was an older gentleman, older than Harriet—and that made her smile. So far she had been meeting mostly young people, but it was a pleasure to meet someone from her generation.

"Can I help you?" the concierge said.

"I certainly hope so. I am in terrible need of a pair of sneakers. Can you point me in the direction of a shoe store? I could check my Droid, but it's hard to tell a store from just its name."

"Oh, I know what you mean. Those newfangled contraptions are a good thing I suppose, but sometimes a person just needs a personal recommendation."

"You are so right, even though so far Amelia hasn't steered me wrong."

"Is she your daughter?"

Harriet smiled and felt her eyes crinkle at the corners. "No, no, she's my GPS. I named her that."

"Oh, oh, of course. Well, let me tell you now there's a store at Loehmann's Plaza. About a five-minute drive. It's called the Pic'n Pay—good selection, good prices."

"Oh, I don't have a car. Can I take a bus there?"

"Certainly, just grab the local right out in front of the hotel and tell the driver you want to go to the Pic'n Pay. He'll get you there."

"Pic'n Pay. Sounds good."

Before going outside Harriet opened her suitcase and found the

96

rain poncho she had packed just in case. She slipped the bright yellow poncho over her head and secured the hood with a snap. She waited outside under the cover of the hotel portico. The poncho only covered her down to her knees but that was good enough. The rain still fell hard, but she kind of liked it, even though she thought she must look like a big yellow duck waddling down the street. She liked the sound, the smell, the rush of people on their way to heaven knows where. She thought about buying an umbrella, but it would just be one more thing to pack or carry, and she had all she could handle. And she only had to wait a few minutes before the bus pulled up. Harriet stepped on and bounced her suitcase up the steps. "Could you let me off at the Loehmann's Plaza stop," she said.

"Third stop," the driver said. "Third stop."

Harriet plopped down next to a very wet man wearing a pale blue jacket. He had perfectly round glasses, a bald head, and seemed to be reading a newspaper.

"Morning," Harriet said.

The man flicked his paper.

"Okay, then. I won't disturb you."

Three stops later Harriet found herself on the street looking around for the Pic'n Pay. She didn't see it. Oh dear. Where was it? It was supposed to be right here. She started down the street dodging puddles and drops the best she could until she remembered that Amelia could probably help. She was getting better and quicker at working the GPS. The more she did it the easier it became.

A few seconds later Harriet had the exact location of the shoe store. It was only two blocks away. One left turn and a quick right and she was there. She set off, with a determined stride sticking close to the buildings to avoid being splashed by passing vehicles. She found the store and stared at the CLOSED sign.

"Oh, for crying out loud," she said. "Of course. Stores don't open until ten o'clock most of the time." She spied a coffee shop across the street, and to get out of the rain and warm up, Harriet headed for the shop. It was a place called Chelsee's Coffee Shop with a blue and white striped awning over the storefront in a picturesque row of red brick buildings.

Harriet pulled open the door, and the aroma of freshly ground coffee wafted past her. She loved the smell of coffee. She slipped off the poncho and hung it on a coatrack with five or six other rain coats and slickers. She wished she'd thought to bring galoshes as well. She saw a seat at a small table near the window. A woman wearing a flowery apron indicated that she should choose any seat. It was a good seat with a view of the restaurant and the street. Harriet watched the rain splatter on the sidewalk. It seemed to be coming down in droves now. The drops pummeled the street and obscured her view.

She glanced around the small shop. It was busy but not what she would call crowded. She saw young people, older people, and one very old man sitting by himself with a book and a pot of tea on his table. He wore a long braid that reminded Harriet of a braided horse's tail.

"Welcome to Chelsee's," said the woman in the flowery apron. "I'm Chelsee."

"Thank you," Harriet said. "So this is your place?"

"Lock, stock, and barrel."

"It's very sweet."

"What can I get for you?" Chelsee asked. "We have some really nice blueberry muffins and rhubarb scones."

"Oh, rhubarb scones? I never heard of such a thing. Yes. Bring me a rhubarb scone and a cup of coffee. I've been dying for a good cup."

"We brew the best. All free trade. All delicious."

"Thank you. And would you happen to know when the Pic'n Pay opens?"

"Ten o'clock."

The woman walked away and Harriet couldn't help but make

eye contact with the old man with the tea. She waved. He waved. And the next thing she knew, he was sitting at her table.

"Goodness," Harriet said. "I—"

"Did you want to be alone?"

"No. Well, not exactly. I was going to write in my journal. But I'll talk to you."

The man reached his hand across the table. "David Prancing Elk."

Harriet came extremely close to letting go a laugh but instead she only said, "Really?"

David Prancing Elk smiled. "Yes. I'm a member of the Cherokee Indian Nation."

"No kidding?" Harriet could not hide her exuberance. Her heart did a little flip-flop. "I . . . I never met a real live Indian before—sorry, Native American."

"No problem. I don't remember seeing you in Chelsee's before."

"First time here. First time in North Carolina. I'm traveling to California. Just passing through as they say."

David looked into Harriet's eyes. He was attractive with a long nose and dark brown eyes, almost the color of the distressed wood tables in the café. "Alone? You're traveling alone?"

Harriet smiled. She didn't know how to answer. So far she had only met good people, but she could never know for sure. And right now she had no reason to fear David Prancing Elk, but still she answered with caution. "Not exactly. My son is with me."

"Oh, is he here? In the shop?"

Harriet shook her head. "Not at the moment."

Chelsee returned with Harriet's scone and coffee. "Hey, David," she said, placing the plate and coffee on Harriet's table. "You always spot the newbies."

"Yes. But I think my new friend here is a little nervous about meeting a real live Indian."

Chelsee laughed. "Don't let David worry you. He's a huggy bear. One of the truly nice guys left in this world."

A wave of relief washed over Harriet, even as a huge clap of thunder shook the tiny café and startled her. For the next hour she and David talked about everything from books to politics to stars.

"My Max and I used to venture out — sometimes in the wee hours of the morning — and hunt for stars. 'Course we only stayed in the backyard, but we had a good view."

"If you're heading west and want to see some stars," David said, "you might want to stop at Maggie Valley."

"Maggie Valley. That sounds so nice. Is it in North Carolina?"

David Prancing Elk nodded. "Yes. In the Smoky Mountains."

"Smoky Mountains? Oh dear, I hadn't thought about needing to cross mountains."

David smiled again and then sipped his tea. "Best place I know to see stars."

"I wonder why it's called Maggie Valley. I mean was there a real Maggie at one time?"

"Yes," David said, "it was named for the daughter of Maggie Valley's first postmaster in 1890."

"It is a sweet place," Chelsee said. "Lots of quaint shops, and the Great Smoky Mountains are something to behold."

Harriet glanced out the window at a little past 10:30. The rain had stopped and the sun was beginning to peek out from behind swift-moving gray clouds.

"Then that's my next stop. I hope I can get there from here." She looked David Prancing Elk in the eye. "But, oh, I was heading for Gatlinburg, Tennessee. There's ... something I want to see there."

"Gatlinburg is just on the other side of the mountains," David said. "The Cherokee people will get there. No problem."

"They will? That's terribly nice of them."

"Just program your GPS and set off," David said. "I'm sure your son can help you."

Harriet smiled. "To be honest, my son's in California, Grass Valley — speaking of valleys — and I'm traveling by bus. Alone."

"Greyhound? I'm sure there's a route close by."

"No, not Greyhound, just plain old local buses and a train now and again, and I suspect whatever means of transportation I can find."

David slapped his knee. "Harriet Beamer, I don't believe it. I don't think I've ever met a woman crossing the country by local transportation. Why in the world are you taking on such an adventure?"

"You might say I'm taking the long way home." Tears welled in her eyes. "I thought I'd like to see the country first, and this seemed like the right time."

"I've traveled all over this country. It is beautiful. We are so blessed to live here."

"Oh, that's so sweet," Harriet said.

David Prancing Elk took Harriet's hands in his and looked into her eyes. "And speaking of being blessed, may I leave you with a Cherokee prayer before you leave?"

"Oh my, yes," Harriet said. "I think it would be an honor."

David Prancing Elk took both her hands and said, "May the warm winds of heaven blow gently on your house. May the Great Spirit bless all who enter there. May your moccasins make happy tracks in many snows. And may the rainbow always touch your shoulder."

Harriet smiled and pushed damp hair out of her eyes. "Thank you, David Prancing Elk. I don't think I will ever forget you."

Chapter 11

AFTER A SURPRISINGLY QUICK STOP AT THE PIC'N PAY, Harriet left wearing a pair of bright red Converse high-tops. She thought they were just magnificent and made her feel young and hip. The rain had stopped, and Harriet shoved her poncho into the suitcase. The sun now shone bright and steam rose from the black asphalt street. She boarded the local bus near the Wake Forest Medical Center. Once again she made certain the driver knew her destination. For some reason Harriet still felt concerned that she would miss her stop.

"I'm on my way to the mall," Harriet said. "The Hanes Mall."

"Second stop," the driver said.

"Oh, thank you very much."

Harriet sat near the front of the bus next to a woman who appeared to be about the same age, wearing odd-shaped black glasses that came to a point and a red scarf around her neck. She didn't seem friendly — not one iota, in Harriet's estimation, as the woman stared at Harriet's feet. So Harriet decided to use the fourteen-minute drive to update her journal to Max.

She wrote about meeting David Prancing Elk and what a joy it was to eat scones and drink coffee at Chelsee's Café. She wrote,

Oh, Max, I met an Indian. A real live Indian named David

102

Prancing Elk. He's a full-blooded Cherokee. He was spectacular and kind and has sent me on my new journey to Maggie Valley. I can't wait to get there. I love having new adventures and—

She stopped writing and gazed out the window—

speaking of adventures, I left a hefty tip for a ballerina waitress so she can go to Spain. It felt good to do that, Max. I mean, was that really me? I know you'd never approve but it warmed my heart.

The woman next to her sneezed.

"Bless you," Harriet said.

The woman only made a noise and turned toward the window. Harriet returned to her letter.

David said I would be able to see a million stars in just one inch of sky. And he said I'd even see shooting stars this time of year. Can you imagine it, Max, a waterfall of shooting stars— that's what David said.

I have met so many people. Some nice and some either not so nice or with troubles. I wish I could help them all.

Twelve minutes later Harriet climbed off the bus near the mall. A spare pair of jeans was her first order of business. The mall was pretty typical. This one, even though it was in North Carolina, could have been in any state.

After a quick check at the directory board, Harriet made her way to the Gap, where she picked out a pair of jeans that fit well but were a tiny bit snug around the waist. She hoped she wouldn't regret her decision but elastic waistbands were not an option at the Gap.

Farther down the mall Harriet sat on a comfortable green stool and retied her Chuck Taylors. That was when she saw she was wearing a pair of knee-high stockings with more runs in them than Max had after eating refried beans long after their prime. She went into the nearby Lady Foot Locker shop.

"Um, excuse me," Harriet said, trying to get the salesgirl's attention, but she seemed more concerned with whatever or whoever she was texting at the moment.

"Excuse me," Harriet said a little louder. "But could you help me, please?"

The girl wearing a black and white striped referee's shirt looked up. Harriet did not appreciate the smirk. "Just a moment." She went back to her phone.

"Now listen," Harriet said, hopping on one foot toward the girl, "I am a paying customer. Your boyfriend or whoever can wait. I need a pair of socks to wear with my sneakers. Does this store carry socks?"

The girl smashed a few buttons, which Harriet was certain spelled something malicious about her, closed her phone, and left it on the counter.

"Thank you," Harriet said. "I have to catch another bus in less than an hour."

"Uh-huh," the girl said and handed her a bag of white crew socks. "These okay?"

Harriet took the socks and hopped back to her seat. She tried on the socks. She liked them well enough and slipped her sneakers back on and tied them with nice neat bows. Perfect.

An hour later Harriet emerged from the mall with her new clothes and a set of salt and pepper shakers she picked up at Williams-Sonoma. They weren't exactly souvenirs, but she liked the crank-operated set with a front-loading chute. They would remind her of Winston-Salem. And more importantly she could say she got them herself.

She jammed her new jeans and the bag of socks into the suitcase and set off for the bus stop. But she was too late. She missed her connection. Another was not arriving for an hour. She felt disappointed for a few seconds and then decided to use the time to find a place to ship the shakers. Amelia pointed straightaway to the UPS store in the mall. So off she went, dragging her suitcase with her tote on her shoulder back to the mall. She sent her shakers on to Henry and Prudence.

After snagging a Cinnabon she headed back to the bus stop.

And there she sat on a bench, waiting for the bus, eating a Cinnabon with a plastic fork, and looking forward to what the rest of the day might hold—at least until she finished her treat and consulted with Amelia. She checked the directions list and discovered she would soon need to cross into the next county—that was always difficult on public transit. According to Amelia and the bus schedule she held, this bus would only take her so far and she needed to travel into Catawba County. Thanks to her next bus driver Harriet learned that the Greenway Public Transit system would take her clear to Hickory, North Carolina, where she could spend the night.

* * *

Henry had finally started to feel like a writer again. He did as Prudence suggested and took a long walk with Cash and Humphrey to talk things over. Along the way he discovered that Cash was unwilling to go home until he was certain his family—what was left of it—really needed him . . . and forgave him. Henry thought you could never really be too sure about forgiveness, not right away.

Humphrey, who was just pleased as punch to get outside on such a nice spring day, got to visit with Maxine, his poodle crush. Maxine was in her yard, a spacious half acre of grass and roses with enough chew toys to last Humphrey a year. Henry paused near Maxine's fence and scribbled some notes on a small, yellow legal pad.

After allowing Humphrey and Maxine to sniff at each other, Henry stuffed his notebook into his pocket, tugged the leash, and off they went. Humphrey looked behind him. Maxine had already scampered off.

"Come on, Humphrey. Let's go home. I think I'm ready to tackle the ending now."

When they got back, Prudence was in the living room with her laptop on her lap and a stack of pages at her feet.

Henry unhooked Humphrey, who went immediately into the kitchen for a drink.

"Pru," Henry said. "I got it. I figured out my ending. Well, more than that. I might need to do some extensive revision. But I have it now."

Prudence looked up. "That's wonderful, honey."

"Do you mind if I work?"

Prudence laughed. "Look at me, Henry. I'm not exactly lazing about on a Saturday morning. So, no problem. I'll meet you later after I muddle through these briefs."

Henry leaned down and kissed Prudence's neck. "In the bedroom," he whispered, "I'll help you with your briefs."

Prudence let go a sigh. "That is getting so old. The pun, not the sex."

"I'll say. See you later."

Henry went to his office. It was a nice room with many windows and bright white walls and dark furniture with masculine lines that made him feel like Hemingway — especially since they installed the ceiling fan.

Humphrey was already in his spot under the desk, snoring loudly.

Henry sat at his desk, adjusted everything that needed adjusting, including the way the pens were situated in the pen cup, and began to type. The sound of the clicking keys made him smile at his manuscript for the first time in more than a month. He had written about 250 words when the cell jingled. It was Harriet.

"Mother, where are you?"

"Is that all you can ask? Honestly, Henry, it's the first thing out of your mouth every time I call."

"I'm sorry, Mom. I just don't know what else to ask you."

"Now, dear, don't get worried. But I am pulling up to the Greenway Transit Center in Hickory, North Carolina, on my way to—"

"To where?"

"On my way to Grass Valley, of course."

"Mother, you're in North Carolina."

"Yes, I know. Hold on a sec, I need to get off the bus. Thanks for the ride, Louis."

"Louis. Who is Louis?" Henry asked.

"The bus driver, Henry. What's the matter with you?"

"Oh, of course. It must be late there. Will you be able to get a room for the night?"

"Certainly. I have a room at a B&B. I called from the bus— isn't that amazing? Making reservations as you travel. I love technology. Who says you can't teach an old bird new tricks? How's Humphrey?"

"He's fine. Snoring at the moment."

"What a good boy. Give him a kiss for me and tell Prudence I said hello."

"Mom," Henry said. "Be careful. Call me if you need anything —like a ride or an airplane ticket."

"Silly boy. I'm fine. I can usually find a bus. If not, then a taxicab or train or a trolley. But, Henry, I've been having the best time. I met an Indian, I mean a Native American Cherokee, at a coffee shop. Chelsee's coffee shop."

"Cherokee. Are you sure?"

"Yes. Of course I am. He was the nicest man."

"I think that's marvelous, Mom."

"He was. He told me about Maggie Valley. That's my next stop."

"Maggie Valley. It sounds nice."

"What's marvelous?" It was Prudence walking into the office. Humphrey woke.

"It's Mom on the phone. She met an Indian."

"What? Where? Is she on some reservation somewhere?"

"At a coffee shop," Henry said. He put his finger in the air indicating Prudence should hold on.

Henry spoke into the phone. "I'm going to put you on speaker so Prudence can hear."

Henry sat the phone on his desk. "Say hello to Pru, Mom."

"Hello, Prudence. How are you, dear?"

"I'm fine, Mother. But did I hear correctly? Henry said you met an Indian."

"It's true. At Chelsee's Coffee Shop in Winston-Salem."

"Are you still there?" Prudence asked.

"Oh, no. I just got off the bus at the transit center in Hickory."

"Okay, mother. Be safe," Prudence said.

Henry took the phone off speaker.

"Are you feeling okay, Mom? Taking your medicine?" Henry asked. "How's that ankle?"

"It's fine. Much better since I bought my nifty new high top sneakers. And my Droid sounds an alarm to remind me to take my pill."

"Ask her when we should expect her?" Prudence said.

"Do you know when we should be expecting you?" Henry asked.

"I don't know," Harriet said. "I'll be in touch. But right now I want to get to the B&B. They're holding my room. Oh, my goodness gracious, Prudence. Did you hear me? I said I'm on my way to a B&B. It's all so exciting."

Chapter 12

AFTER A SHORT CAB RIDE HARRIET STOOD IN FRONT OF THE Inn at Hickory outside of Hickory, North Carolina. When she had made the reservation, she'd also made arrangements for someone to meet her at the front door even though it was getting late.

The house, a Georgian colonial built in 1908, sat on a large corner lot like a big mother hen. A white picket fence surrounded the property, with a long sidewalk that led to a red door, almost the color of her sneakers. Black shutters hung on either side of the many windows, while the rest of the house was painted eggshell white.

A lovely woman named Dana and a large yellow Labrador retriever named Peach Melba, Melba for short, greeted Harriet.

"What a good puppy," Harriet said as she patted Melba's side and head.

"Puppy?" Dana said. "She weighs almost seventy-five pounds."

"I love doggies," Harriet said. "Makes me miss my Humphrey. He's an enlarged basset hound."

"Enlarged?"

"Yeah, in other words, fat. So fat his tummy almost drags along the ground."

Dana smiled. "I reserved the Baker Room for you. I hope you like it. Breakfast is at any time."

Harriet followed Dana up a wide oak staircase with a solid handrail and gorgeous pin-top balusters. "It's just down the hall," Dana said. "Third door. It's our largest room. Hope you don't mind, but it was all we had."

"Oh, I'm certain it will be just fine. This is such a beautiful home."

"Thank you," Dana said.

Dana pushed open the dark green door, and Harriet stood at the threshold. The view took her breath away. She let go of her suitcase and stood wordless for a long minute. But then she turned to Dana and said, "It's wonderful."

Harriet walked inside. A large queen-size Victorian bed stood in the middle of the room. A comfy chair stood nearby.

"The bathroom's just over there," Dana said. "Call if you need anything. Have a peaceful night."

"Thank you."

The first thing Harriet did was empty the contents of her tote bag onto the bed. She found her phone charger and plugged it in. Next she visited the bathroom; then she sat on the bed. It was soft and luxurious. She grabbed her notebook from the pile, and after a wide yawn she clicked her pen and began to write.

My dearest Max, tonight I think I might have discovered Paradise. It's called the Inn at Hickory. I've never been surrounded by so much luxury, and you know what? I think I like it—for a change. But I think I will always find the most luxury at home—wherever that is. Even at Henry's, I suppose.

Harriet sighed and reread her words. Then she added,

I loved every second of our time together on earth, Max, but I hope you won't mind if I enjoy life without you now. Oh, being active at church was nice and making silly bets with anyone

willing to play along was fun, but something is stirring inside me
— it feels ... well, a little like Henry's first kick, only this one I
felt in my soul, not my tummy.

She closed her book and let go a second deep yawn. Traveling alone was fine. Harriet had no regrets, but there were times, especially at night, when she felt alone — even with the whole country within a bus ride or two.

She opened her book.

I can hardly believe it's me sometimes, wearing jeans,
working a Droid phone, finding my way across the country.
Quick, I better pinch myself.

Harriet filled the tub, a fancy claw-footed thing with a white cloth curtain that went all the way around. A bottle of bubbles sat on a small shelf in the bathroom. She pulled the stopper. "Um, hyacinth." She dropped a small amount of the purple pearly liquid into the water and watched the luxurious bubbles form and build almost to overflowing. The perfume of the bubbles permeated the room. She wished she could light some candles for ambience, but that was probably not allowed in this historic building. She couldn't blame them. Harriet would not have allowed candles either.

* * *

Humphrey woke Henry the next morning with a yowl. Henry rolled over and checked the clock. It was early — only five o'clock.

"Ah, Humphrey," Henry said. "I told you. We like to sleep late on Sunday."

Humphrey yowled.

"You better let him out," Prudence said with her head under the pillow. "Or you're cleaning it up."

"Okay, okay." Henry pulled on his robe. "Come on, old man."

Humphrey yowled — but low.

111

Humphrey made it to the front door before Henry. Henry opened the door. "Go on. And hurry up. I want to go back to bed."

Humphrey did his best. He sniffed around the lilac bushes and then the fence until he finally settled on his usual morning spot—the birdbath in the backyard. Humphrey trotted back to the front of the house, up the two small steps, and into the house. Humphrey went upstairs as quickly as his stubby little legs could carry him. No Henry. Finally Humphrey found Henry sitting at his desk typing furiously. Henry's fingers continued to dance across the keyboard. "I got it, Humphrey, my friend, while I was standing at the door waiting for you. I had a thought, like a flash of lightning. You just might be my muse—you're a muse hound."

Humphrey closed his eyes and went back to sleep while Henry typed furiously.

* * *

Harriet woke to the sound of clock chimes. She counted them, eight.

"Eight o'clock already. But how can I be sure? Maybe I missed a chime or two."

She looked at her phone. She had missed a chime. It was nine o'clock.

Harriet stretched and yawned and snuggled a bit deeper into the bed. She had such a restful night she didn't want it to end, and she had not slept that late in ... well, in thirty-five years. "I must find out what kind of mattress this is."

But as much as she wanted to stay asleep, she thought it better to rise and shine and plan her day. It being Sunday brought its own complications. Buses ran on alternate schedules for one thing. And she did like to attend church. But in a strange town? Would it seem a little odd?

She pulled out her flowery dress, which she had laundered in Winston-Salem. But it was terribly wrinkled from being balled up inside her suitcase. Fortunately, Harriet located an iron and ironing board in a closet in the hallway. Unfortunately, it toppled out of the narrow closet and nearly banged her head when she opened the door.

She brushed her teeth and did her morning routine. Then she pulled on her dress and made her way down an impressive old staircase with intricate carvings into the dining room, where she found a sterling silver coffeepot sitting like a queen on a mahogany sideboard. Beside it was a tray overflowing with fresh fruit and croissants and jams and jellies. The sun gleamed through the sheer curtains and instantly made Harriet feel like a grand lady of the south. Melba lay on a doggie bed, snoring like a teamster. Harriet suppressed the urge to pet her. Doing so would have made her miss Humphrey too much.

Harriet filled a delicate vine-rimmed china cup with coffee, which smelled strong yet smooth and somehow tropical. She poured in a splash of cream and watched it swirl and mix into the most delightful shade of brown. The smell alone was enough to ignite her brain cells.

She stood with her coffee and peered out one of the floor-to-ceiling windows. The town was quiet — almost too quiet. Not a single car drove down the street, and she saw only one family, dressed in their Sunday best, walking down the street.

Dana came in and greeted her. "Good morning, Harriet. Sleep well?"

"Oh dear, yes. I slept so well I didn't want to wake up."

"That's good. I see you found the coffee okay. Help yourself to any of the fruit and sweets. And would you like a hot breakfast?"

"Thank you, that is very kind of you. But isn't all this breakfast?"

Dana smiled. "Not exactly. We also prepare a hot breakfast. Are you hungry?"

Harriet touched her stomach. "I sure am — as a bear after three months in a cave. And I must say this coffee. It's spectacular. I don't think it's your regular Chock Full o'Nuts."

Dana smiled. "No. It's from Madagascar. Now what would you like—just name it. My husband Chef Chaz is a marvelous chef."

"Oh my, I've never ordered breakfast to be prepared by a chef. I would love scrambled eggs, toast, and bacon. Is that possible?"

"Of course. I'll bring it out when it's ready."

"That's fine. I'll be right here."

"There's a newspaper if you care to read one."

"No, no, I enjoy the view out the window."

"Perhaps a hummingbird will flitter by."

"Hummingbirds. Oh, I do love them."

Dana quoted,

> Within my Garden, rides a bird
> Upon a single Wheel—
> Whose spokes a dizzy Music make
> As 'twere a travelling Mill.

"Emily Dickinson," Harriet said. "You know her?"

"One of my best friends."

Harriet let go a big sigh. She had certainly chosen the best place for a layover.

Melba roused and joined Harriet at the window. Sitting on his haunches he reached Harriet's thigh. She patted Melba's head. "It's a beautiful morning, even if it is a little overcast."

With her coffee in hand, Harriet wandered around the room and then into the living room. She liked the portrait of a stern-looking young woman over the mantel. Harriet pulled her phone from her dress pocket. *I have to tell Henry about this place.* But remembering the time difference she decided it would be better to wait to call.

* * *

Henry typed so fast he thought his fingers might fly off. "I can't believe it, Humphrey. I got this idea, and it turned out to be the right one. What the story needed was a great explosion."

Humphrey opened his eyes.

"Yep. I set the boarding house on fire. And Cash had no choice but to face down his fears. He had to save someone — his daughter or his friend. Trouble is, saving the friend was a sure thing. His daughter? Well, they both would have died."

Prudence padded into the office carrying a cup of coffee. "You are up early for a Sunday."

"I was inspired. That crazy dog got me up, and while I was standing there I got an idea."

Prudence leaned over Henry's shoulder. "I'm happy for you, honey. Keep working. I'll make some breakfast."

Henry kept working. The words came quickly — not all of them keepers but good enough to keep him moving forward — until his phone jingled.

"Drat." He looked at the screen. *Mom.*

"Double drat." For a second he thought he should ignore it, but ... "She could be in trouble."

"Mom," Henry said.

"Henry, I'm in the most marvelous place. A B&B — that means bed-and-breakfast."

"That's nice," Henry said without thinking.

"How are you, dear?" Harriet asked.

"I'm fine, Mom. Is that why you called?"

"Well, I thought you'd care when your mother is happy."

"Sorry, Mom. I'm working and I'm a little distracted."

"On your novel?"

"Yes. On my novel. It's going well."

"I'm very proud of you, Henry."

Henry paused and breathed deeply. "Really?"

"I really am. I ... guess I'm learning how important it is for you to follow your heart."

"Thank you, Mom. And … I guess I'm starting to see how important this crazy trip is for you."

* * *

Harriet locked her phone and dropped it into her pocket, just as Dana entered the parlor. "Harriet. Breakfast is on the table if you're ready."

The table was set so nice in Harriet's estimation that she hated to even sit and use the napkin—a bright yellow one with white trim. Even Martha would have been impressed with the flower arrangement.

"So tell me, Harriet," said Dana as she set a plate of toast, bacon, and eggs in front of her. "Where are you traveling to?"

"Grass Valley, California."

"California?" Dana looked surprised. "That's a long way."

"Yep. Clear across the country. I started in Philadelphia. Right now I'm headed for Maggie Valley."

"Oh, Maggie Valley," Dana said. "A lovely place. Chaz and I have visited. The Smoky Mountains are breathtaking." She fiddled with the flowers.

"My Indian, excuse me, Native American friend, David Prancing Elk, I met him in Winston-Salem, said I would enjoy it."

"You will. But … Harriet, if you don't mind me asking, how are you getting there? Didn't you call us from the bus? Are you going to the Greyhound station?"

"Not sure yet. I've been following my instincts—mostly—and Amelia—my Droid phone, and maybe my heart a little."

Dana chuckled. "That's amazing. But … why? Why not just take Greyhound or the train?"

"Why not?" She buttered her toast. "I decided to take the scenic route home and see as much of the country as I could. And I've already seen so much. And I really want to do this. I want to accomplish something … something big."

Dana smiled as she refilled Harriet's cup then settled in for a chat. "But if Grass Valley is home then—"

Harriet pulled her coffee cup from her lips. "No, no. My home was in Bryn Mawr, Pennsylvania. Lived there my whole life."

Harriet told Dana the whole story, about the bet, the broken ankle, and her decision to travel across the country very, very slowly.

When she was finished, Harriet saw that she had told her story not only to Dana but to Chef Chaz and a honeymooning couple who had come in while she was talking. They all found it interesting and even a little amusing.

"But aren't you afraid?" asked the young bride. "A woman your ... well, your age?"

"Nope. Not really. I just plan to stay out of the seedy parts of the world. Except, well, I did feel a little scared in Greensboro when my train got in after midnight."

"Wow. I'd hate to travel alone," the young woman said with a glance at her brand-new husband. "I'd get so lost."

"What are you traveling with?" asked the young woman's husband. "A backpack?"

"Oh dear, no. A backpack would break my back. I have my tote bag and my wheely suitcase. And my fancy GPS Droid, which I'm still learning to use."

They talked gadgets for a few minutes, the groom giving her some handy tips for her Droid. Harriet sat there soaking in the admiration and interest of the people assembled around the large dining room table.

When the honeymooners left, Dana offered, "Chaz and I can help you figure out some buses from here. Are you leaving today?"

"Well, since it's Sunday, I kind of thought I'd like to attend a church service if it's not too late and there's a church nearby. Give my traveling bones a rest."

"There's a Presbyterian Church just down the road. I believe the service begins at eleven."

"Presbyterian? That's perfect." Harriet glanced at the clock on the mantel. "I guess I have time. But . . . on second thought maybe I can spend time with God just poking around town. Does that make sense?"

"Perfect sense. Where would you like to go?"

Harriet shrugged. "I don't have the foggiest notion, sweetie pie. What's around here?"

Chaz poured a cup of coffee and mixed a large amount of cream into it. He took a sip and considered Harriet's question. She thought he was conjuring up something amazing from the gleam in his eye.

"It seems you like the B&B well enough," he said.

"Oh my, yes. I think the inn is spectacular. As a matter of fact I was writing to Max just last night and—"

"Max?" Dana asked.

"Oh dear. He's my dead husband."

"And you're writing him letters?" Chaz's watery blue eyes grew a little larger.

"Yes. Ever since I started my adventure I've been keeping a journal of my travels and . . ." She looked away a moment. "It just seemed natural to write to Max. Makes the writing easier somehow—since I am not much of a writer. Not like my son."

Dana pulled her coffee cup from her lips. "Your son is an author?"

"Yes. His name is Henry Beamer. He's still trying to finish his second novel. Having a hard time from what I can tell. He's been on a deadline with it, and I think that's making him a little . . ." She twirled her finger around her ear.

Chaz laughed. "Imagine that. Writing a whole book. I have trouble writing out the grocery list."

"I am proud of him. He must get his sensitive writer soul from my sister. She became a nun. Imagine that. Haven't spoken to her in years—vows of silence and all. I could never do anything like that—Rosaline was always the—" She stopped talking. "I'm sorry. Don't know what made me think of her. Anyhoo, did I tell you how much I love your place?"

Chaz smiled and brought the subject back to the trip.

"You're my hero," Dana said. "And between us, I don't get the feeling it's time for you to settle anywhere."

Harriet felt her face warm. "If Henry and Prudence decide to have children," Harriet said, "then I'll settle. I want to be a Nana in the worst way."

"I'm sure it will happen," Dana said.

Harriet sipped the last of her coffee. "But you know what?" She bit the corner of a piece of toast. "I think church sounds better than sightseeing."

Chef Chaz returned to the dining room with a tray of pastries. "Well, okay, but only if I can't tempt you to stay and enjoy some sweets."

"Oh, they look scrumptious." Harriet touched her stomach. "But I think I'm better off walking to church." She glanced at Dana. "If it's close enough."

"Yes," Dana said. "Like I said, the service starts at eleven. It's just ten-thirty now."

"Can I get there in time?"

"It's about a mile — other guests have walked it in about twenty minutes."

"Oh, I should get a move on."

"Can I drive you?" Dana asked. "I would be happy too."

Harriet glanced out the window at the gorgeous summer day. She felt slight aches in her knees but the idea of a walk sounded good.

"Thank you, dear, but I think I'll walk."

"You can't miss it. Big stone building with gray roofs and a sweet bell tower."

Chapter 13

HENRY, STILL IN HIS PAJAMAS, WHICH WERE A PAIR OF Christmas boxers and a T-shirt with the words *Nittany Lions* on it, was in his office typing when Prudence, in running shorts and a T-shirt entered. Humphrey lay at Henry's feet with his head resting against the leg of the desk.

"Are you going to church?" Prudence asked.

Henry shushed her. "I'm sorry. I just need to get this thought on paper."

"Paper," Prudence said. "Don't you mean screen?"

"Screen, paper. It's still black on white and—" He hung his head and stopped talking. "Darn. I lost my—"

"I'm so sorry, Henry. I'll leave you alone. But are you going?"

"Do you mind if I stayed home and worked? I think I'm really on to something. Cash just discovered that he killed his own daughter in the fire. And—"

"Oh no," Prudence said. "That's terrible."

"I know. But it's what the story needed . . . listen, can you leave me to work, please?"

"Coffee?"

"Yes. And bring the pot."

Prudence adjusted the blinds on the office window before she went to the kitchen. "A little light on the subject."

"It's not easy being a writer," Henry said as he rubbed the dog's belly with his bare feet. "Interruptions are the bane of the author's life. I will never get that thought back. Ever." Then he readjusted the blinds to his liking.

Humphrey rolled onto his side as a beam of warm sunshine filtered into the room.

Henry managed to get a few more words onto the screen before Prudence returned with the coffee. She placed a Rattan tray with a pot, a cup, and a small cream pitcher on the table next to his desk where Henry held stacks and stacks of pages and notebooks. She had no choice but to put the tray on top of the stacks.

"I need to get dressed for church. I have to go this morning. Nursery duty."

Henry swallowed. "Nursery? How'd you get roped into that?"

"Roped is right," Prudence said. She poured his coffee. "Mrs. Sternwell cornered me two weeks ago and complained about Misty Frothman not being able to be there today and . . . well, she practically begged me to do it."

"Uhm, but, Prudence, are you sure you're ready? I'm surprised you agreed this time."

She shook her head and sighed. "I don't know. I'm hoping there aren't any infants today."

Henry sipped his coffee. "Maybe I should go, after all—just in case."

"No, it's fine. I kind of . . . need to do this."

"Okay, well, I hope you don't get thrown up on." He smiled, trying to lighten the situation.

"Throw up? You mean that happens? In church?"

"Been known to. My mother used to come home with vomit on her dress."

"Well, I won't wear the Vera Wang this morning."

"Jeans and sweatshirt will do it."

"With my darling new sandals? No, I'll dress."

Henry put his cup down and went back to typing. He could

sense Prudence staring at him like he was about to explode, and she wanted to catch the very moment.

"Henry," she said. "Are you sure you're not ... disappointed?"

"Disappointed?" He continued to type. "What? That you're going to church?"

"No. That I don't want ... I'm not ready to have a baby?"

Henry shook his head. "Another baby, you mean. And no, I'm okay. We have time. It's my mother you have to worry about. When she gets out here — if she gets out here — she'll have stuff to say, I'm sure, in her own delicate, sweet way, of course. Which is why we should maybe tell her about — "

Prudence put her index finger on Henry's lips. "It's private. We're the only ones who need to know."

"Okay." Henry kissed her. "See you after church."

* * *

Harriet returned to the inn from her visit to the First Presbyterian Church. Dana had picked her up in a blue minivan about 12:30. The ride home was sweet and peaceful as they passed houses that reminded Harriet of back home — split-levels and ranches nestled on lots with grassy lawns and trees still in spring flower.

"It was a very nice service," Harriet said. "Isn't it funny how God can find you anywhere, anytime? The pastor spoke from Ephesians, the first chapter. About how we were created to be the praise of God's glory."

"Uh-huh," Dana said. "That's important to you?"

"It certainly is — something I've been thinking about. I wonder if I am sometimes."

"If you are ... what?"

"To the praise of his glory, dear. Lately I'm wondering if I'm living with that in mind ... if I've ever lived with that in mind."

"Guess I'm not sure what it means."

"Well, it's a lot to figure out. For me it just makes me want to be sure the things I do and say matter, no matter how small or seemingly insignificant. Like my sister Rosaline, I guess. She works for God. Now that matters — big time."

Dana coughed. "Sorry, but of course your words matter. The things you do are important."

Harriet looked over at Dana. "I suppose so. But I want to feel God's pleasure — absolutely and for certain before I die. Just like that missionary Eric Liddell."

"Is that what you're hoping to get out of this trip?"

Harriet nodded, smiled, and looked at the passing lawns. "Well, yes, that and ... and a sense of accomplishment — doing something from start to finish."

Dana pulled into the driveway and parked the minivan. "I'm sure you will. Maybe you already have and you just didn't know it."

Harriet patted Dana's hand while it was still on the wheel. "Oh, I'll know it when I feel it. But maybe that's why I'm so anxious for Henry and Prudence to have a baby. I felt God's pleasure at times when Henry was young — you know, when I was raising him. I'm sure you know what I mean. I certainly did something from start to finish then." She laughed. "But now I'm doing something even more courageous that's mine — alone."

Dana looked away from Harriet. "Chaz and I never had children."

"Oh dear," Harriet said as a flush of embarrassment swept over her. "I'm sorry. I just thought with a house so large and this ... this what do you call it? Minivan?"

"It's okay. The Lord just hasn't seen fit to bless us that way. But we are blessed in so many others."

Harriet touched her hand. "I know you have blessed me."

Dana smiled. "But I think I know what you mean. I feel joyful when I take care of folks like you, Harriet. Now why don't you go take a rest? I'll call you when lunch is ready. Chaz always makes something spectacular for Sunday lunch. We serve it a little later and make it the main meal of the day. On Sundays our B&B becomes a BLT."

"BLT?"

"Breakfast, lunch, and talking. We tend to sit around gabbing the afternoon away."

Harriet climbed out of the van. "I can't wait."

She went to her room and promptly called Martha to tell her all about church and the inn.

"It's been spectacular. You would have loved the church. Very nice, inviting folks."

"Oh, Harriet," Martha said, her voice getting soft. "At first I thought what you were doing was crazy and I was worried about you, but now I think I might be a little jealous."

"You can make this trip too. Just do it."

"I just might," Martha said. "Maybe we could go together. Wouldn't that be fun?"

* * *

Lunch was served at 2:00 p.m. Harriet had changed out of her flowery dress and put on her new jeans and a green blouse with her red Chucks. The other guests had still not arrived, although she saw the honeymoon couple in the front parlor. They seemed to be quarreling.

"I hope you don't mind that I didn't dress for the fancy lunch," Harriet said as she sat at the table.

"Of course not," Dana said. "It's fine for us, but ... well, don't get upset, but Chaz did something."

"What?" Harriet said.

"It's just that Chaz invited his friend Sterling Harrison to join us."

Harriet opened her napkin and slid it across her lap. "Now, Dana dear, I hope you aren't trying to set me up on a date."

"No, nothing like that. Sterling is a reporter for the local paper here. Chaz was so enamored with your story he thought Sterling might like to interview you for a feature article."

Harriet felt her heart rate jump to the speed of a startled squirrel. "What? Really, but ... but I don't know if I want to be in the paper. I mean I'm just taking a trip is all. A very slow trip across the country. I'm far from newsworthy."

That was when Chaz and a tall man with a close-kept, grayish beard walked into the room. Chaz carried a tray with several fruit cups on it. "That's just it," Chaz said. "Sterling thinks your story will make a great human-interest piece."

Harriet sipped and swallowed her water. "Really? Me? I'm just little old Harriet Beamer from Pennsylvania. Not like I saved anyone's life or anything."

Sterling sat across from Harriet. Dana placed the fruit cups at the settings. The other guests in the house, an older couple visiting relatives, joined them.

Dana introduced the older couple to Harriet and the young honeymooners. "This is Steve and Laura Grant," she said. The couple waved and sat at the table.

"It's nice to meet you," Harriet said.

"So tell me, Harriet, how did your odyssey begin?" Sterling asked.

"Odyssey?" she said. "I wouldn't exactly call it that. It's just a trip, maybe an adventure. Leastways that's what I've been calling it. An adventure. A woman my age doesn't get many adventures."

Sterling pulled out a small recorder from his shirt pocket. "I hope you don't mind me recording this. It's less distracting than writing it all down on one of those reporter's notebooks."

"Reporter?" Laura asked.

"Oh, I'm sorry," Dana said. And she explained all about Harriet.

"I think that's marvelous," Laura said. "Just marvelous. More power to you, sister." And she raised her water glass to Harriet.

"Thank you." Harriet smiled. "You should try it sometime." She looked at Steve. He didn't appear to be the adventuring type.

"So Harriet," Sterling said, "may I ask your age?"

Harriet looked him square in the eye. She pushed her glasses onto her nose and said, "Seventy-two, no . . . seventy-two and a half."

Harriet looked around the table. All eyes were glued to her like flies to sticky paper.

"You look much younger," Laura said.

Harriet beamed. "Thank you."

Sterling adjusted his chair and smiled at Harriet. His smile made her feel more at ease. "Now please, tell me your story—from the beginning."

"Well, if you can imagine, a broken ankle—*my* broken ankle —started the whole thing. My daughter-in-law, Prudence, insisted it was broken, and I really didn't think it was—or at least I didn't want to believe it. I thought it was a sprain, but the way Humphrey was acting, I shoulda known it was something bad."

"Humphrey?" Sterling said.

"Oh, my dog. He's a basset hound. I miss him. I sent him on ahead to Henry and Prudence. On the plane."

"Oh, okay," Sterling said. "I guess it would have been impossible to bring him."

Harriet chuckled. "Oh, heavens to Betsy, Son, that would have been impossible. It's hard enough pulling my wheely suitcase around what with bumpy pavements and potholes everywhere. And did you know you can't bring a dog on the Greyhound? Now isn't that just a wee bit ironic?"

The guests laughed.

"Anyhoo," Harriet continued. "Prudence suggested this silly bet, and I lost."

"Sounds like a sucker's bet," Chaz said.

"It sure was," Harriet said.

"What were the stakes?" Sterling asked. "A trip across the country? Seems to me that would be a bet you'd *want* to lose."

"No, it was a little more involved than that. I put my house on the line. If it was broken—my ankle, not the house—then I had to sell the house and move to Grass Valley. Now, I knew it was a sucker's bet, but I did it anyway. And now here I am traveling across the country by any means of public transportation I can find."

* * *

At half past noon, Prudence returned from church. Henry heard the front door slam. Humphrey's ears perked and then returned to their usual flop-sidedness.

"Is that you, honey?" Henry called, knowing full well that it was Prudence's slam.

"Of course it is," she called.

"Something go wrong, sweetness? You get puked on?"

"No," she said, walking into the office. "Worse."

Henry looked at her. He noticed the pretty rose-colored jacket she had worn to church was missing, and her silk shirt had a spot the size of a pie tin on it. "Uh-oh, what happened?"

"Little Larry Lintballer, or whatever his name is, happened."

"Lindenmuth," Henry said.

"Yes. I had to change his diaper and just as I was about to secure the new one ... well, he ..."

Henry laughed. Humphrey whined.

"It's not funny. This is an expensive blouse, and it's ... it's ruined. Completely and totally ruined. I should sue. I can do that you know. I *am* a lawyer."

Henry stood and let Prudence rest her head on his shoulder. "I'm sure Rysa can get the stain out. She can clean anything."

"You think? I love this blouse."

"Yes. But are you really upset that you got peed on?"

Prudence looked away from Henry. "I guess ... I guess it made me miss ... something."

Henry wrapped his arms around her. "It will happen for us again. You'll get peed on by our own baby."

Prudence managed a laugh and pulled away from Henry. "Okay. I'm going to get changed."

"Fine," Henry said. "I didn't realize the time. I'm sure Humphrey could use a break."

Humphrey got to his feet.

"Okay. How about lunch? I'm starved," Henry said before Prudence left the room.

"Good idea. Want to go out? It's such a nice day. How 'bout Thai?"

"Sure," Henry said. "Thai not?" He smiled.

Prudence smiled. Humphrey yowled.

"I better get the dog outside before we go," Henry said. "And by the way, I haven't seen Sandra Day all day."

"She's hiding. Been hiding since the dog came to live with us."

"Be nice, Pru, he's your dog-in-law."

Prudence sighed and headed into the living room. "He's a hound."

* * *

Two hours and one scrumptious meal later, Harriet had finished answering all of Sterling's questions. Steve and Laura had long since left the table.

"It's been an arduous trip for Steve," Laura had said. "So we'll just say our good-byes."

Harriet had the distinct impression that Laura would have liked to stay and hear the rest of her story.

"And now here I am," Harriet said. "I hope to reach Maggie Valley tomorrow."

Sterling clicked off his recorder. "This is great stuff," he said. "I'm going to go straight home and write it up. I'm sure it will run in Wednesday's *About Town* section."

"About town?" Harriet said. "I'll be long gone by Wednesday."

"I'll make sure you have our contact info," Dana said. "And

when you get to Grass Valley, be in touch and I'll send you the paper."

"That will be spectacular," Harriet said. She yawned. "What time is it?"

"A little past six," Chaz said.

"Really?" Harriet said. "Well, I think I'll go to my room and write to Max or read. I have a long road tomorrow."

"Breakfast?" Dana said.

"I'm not sure of the time," Harriet said. "I should get the local bus to, well, I'm not sure where. I need to work around bus times."

"No trouble," Chaz said. "I can check the local routes online for you and let you know in the morning."

"That would be great. Amelia's a big help. Couldn't have done it without her."

Sterling laughed. "That's great. My readers are going to love this story. I wouldn't doubt it if it goes viral."

"Viral?" Harriet said.

"Yeah, that's right," Chaz said. "Stories can spread like a virus sometimes thanks to the internet. One news agency picks it up and then another and before you know it . . . Harriet Beamer is a national sensation."

Harriet had to sit back down. "Oh, for crying out loud, I don't think I want to be a national sensation."

"Don't worry about it. You won't have to do anything," Sterling said. "But before we say goodnight, I would like a picture or two."

Harriet stood. "Picture? But I look a fright. Maybe I could just slip into my dress again."

"Actually," Sterling said, "I think you look great in your jeans and red high-tops. In fact, maybe you could get your tote bag and suitcase and I'll take the picture of you all ready to set out on the next leg of your . . . your—"

"Adventure," Harriet said. "Okay. I'll just get my bags."

Harriet returned to her room. She snagged her bag, took a

quick peek at herself in the mirror, brushed her hair, and went back to the dining room.

"Just stand near the door, the front door," Sterling said. "Maybe put one hand on the knob and hold the suitcase with the other." Sterling stepped back and then said, "What's that on your suitcase? A bumper sticker?"

Harriet let go a chuckle. "Yes. My friend Martha gave it to me. Imagine that, California or Bust. She's a riot."

"Well, turn it toward me so the camera can see it."

Harriet stood with her shoulders back and her head high. She felt a wash of pride sweep through her as she smiled. Sterling snapped three pictures and then took a couple of Harriet with Dana, Chaz, and Melba.

"Please send me a copy of the picture when you send the article," Harriet said. "One with Melba."

"I will," Dana said. "And I think if it's okay with you, I might just have the article framed and hang it on the wall there. You're going to be famous, Harriet Beamer."

"Famous? Oh, I sincerely hope not. That wasn't in my plans. I just wanted to collect salt and pepper shakers and see some of the country."

"Oh, that's right," Dana said. "Chaz, go get Harriet—"

"What?" Harriet said.

"He has a set of shakers for you. They're antique and ... well he wants you to have them."

"Oh my," Harriet said. "That's so precious of him. Thank you."

"Want me to mail them for you, Harriet?"

"Yes, that would be perfect. Why, I believe I'm leaving my own little trail of bread crumbs ... I mean, salt and pepper shakers."

Chaz returned with a set of Porcelain shakers in the shape of boy and girl bakers. Pepper had a red chef's hat with two holes in it and salt wore a white hat with two holes.

"These are lovely," Harriet said. "I'd say circa 1958. Probably made in the United States." She turned one over. "Yep, here's the stamp."

"That's incredible," Chaz said.

"You can tell a lot about a generation by the salt and pepper shakers they used. They tell society's story."

Chapter 14

AFTER ANOTHER LONG SOAK IN THE TUB TO EASE HER TIRED
muscles, Harriet slipped into her fuzzy pink nightgown, which she
had rolled into a ball and shoved into the corner of her suitcase to
force it to fit. She plugged in the charger, then retrieved her journal
from the tote and sat down on the bed to write.

*Dear Max, a reporter fellow came by the bed-and-breakfast
to write my story. I could hardly believe it. But it's true. Dana,
she's the proprietress of this wonderful establishment, claims
I will be famous. But, Max, that's not why I took this trip. I
don't want to be famous. When I started out, I wanted to see the
country. I wanted to get my own dang salt and pepper shakers.
But I must admit it's turning out to be more. I only wish I had
done it ten years ago, there might have been some real time to
dream. Am I too old to dream—like Grace, the ballerina I
met. Or ... or even Henry? I finally forgive him for selling your
business. Beamers Beams was your dream.*

She closed her Moleskine and tucked it back into her tote. She
let her fingers grasp the book for a second or two longer. How she
missed her Max. That was when she decided to call Martha, even
though she had just spoken to her a little while ago.

"Martha," she said, "you will not believe it." And then she proceeded to tell Martha all about the newspaperman.

"No kidding?" Martha said. "Wow. So you're like a celebrity in the small town. Make sure they send you a copy of the article."

"I will. It was so weird though, answering all those questions. He said the story could go viral. But I doubt it. I mean who cares about me and my adventure?"

"Probably no one," Martha said. "Look, I'm just glad you're still breathing and haven't busted a leg climbing in and out of buses yet. Now that's the real news."

"You're right about that," Harriet said. "And it's the strangest thing. I haven't fallen down once. It's like that last fall from grace straightened me out."

"Don't jinx yourself, Harriet."

"Now, you know I don't believe in that sort of mumbo jumbo. Anyhoo, tomorrow I'm planning on going to Maggie Valley. My Indian, excuse me, Native American friend, David Prancing Elk, told me it was one of the finest places to stargaze. I hope he's right. I hope the Cherokee take kindly to a middle-aged woman traipsing across the country."

Martha laughed. "Leave it to you, Harriet. You'll be one of them before you're through. An honorary member of the Chero-kee Nation."

"Do they do such things?"

"I don't know. Just be careful, and thanks for the postcard. That station is gorgeous. Make sure you send me some from Maggie Valley."

"Oh, I will. I hope they have some with stars on them."

"Harriet," Martha said. "I need to tell you something."

"Oh dear, what is it?"

"I'm proud of you."

Harriet swallowed. "Really? Why?"

"Why? Look at what you're doing. Look at the people you're meeting. Harriet, you might not want to admit this, but I do believe you're starting to find God's pleasure along with your salt and pepper shakers. Remember when we talked about that?"

"I think about it every day, and you know what, Martha? You're right. Why six months ago I would have never spoken to the people I am — like Thomasina — she was a woman on the bus. Drug addict, I think, and a mommy on her way to see her child. I just wouldn't have had the nerve."

"Really? I'm so proud of you. But you're right. A few months ago you would have been nice to her, smiled but . . ."

"I wonder if I would have encouraged her the way I did." Harriet had to take a breath and swipe a tear that rolled down her cheek. "I wonder why it took me so long to . . . well, to be the person God wanted me to be. I kept myself cooped up in the house. I didn't even know there was more to me than cookies and bingo."

"The point is you're doing it now."

"I sure am, Martha. But I better catch some Z's. Big travel day tomorrow."

"Goodnight, Harriet. I think I can sleep now also."

"Goodnight, Martha. I love you."

* * *

The next morning, Harriet sat down to breakfast at around 7:30 with Dana and Chaz. The innkeepers had peculiar smiles on their faces — this made Harriet a little nervous. Chaz was quick to tell Harriet what he had discovered about traveling to Maggie Valley.

"The trouble with local transportation," he said, "is that once you travel out of the city limits, making a connection is almost impossible."

"I've noticed that," Harriet said. "I've had to take a train or two."

"Well, here's the thing," Chaz said. "To reach Maggie Valley, you'd need to find your way through several small towns, most of which have no public transit other than buses for people with disabilities."

"Oh dear," Harriet said over the most scrumptious eggs Benedict she'd ever eaten — actually it was the *first* eggs Benedict she'd ever eaten. "How will I get to Maggie Valley?"

"Wait until you hear," Dana said. "Chaz has worked the whole thing out for you."

"Now it's your choice, Harriet, you can grab the Greyhound—"

Harriet shook her head. "No. I am determined to do this my way, but if I can't get a local bus I guess I'll need a taxi."

"Not necessarily," Chaz said, his eyes twinkling like stardust. "Here's what you're going to do—thanks to Sterling."

"Sterling?"

"Yes, he stayed awhile after you went to bed last night, and we couldn't help talking about your trip. We spent more than an hour online trying to get things figured out when Sterling got this brilliant idea."

Dana refreshed everyone's coffee. "Sterling can pull strings when strings need pulling."

"And these strings weren't even that hard to pull to enlist the aid of some A.T."

By now, Harriet's excitement level had heightened along with her heart rate. She attempted to surreptitiously take her pulse. "A.T.?" she said, trying to hide her concern.

"Yep," Chaz said, "alternate transportation."

Harriet pushed her plate away. Her stomach had gotten wobbly. Although the cherry pastry did look inviting. "Maybe just one pastry," she said, looking at Dana.

"Of course." Dana handed one over.

"Here's what you need to do," Chaz said. "You can take the local Greenway bus as far west as it will take you—I believe it's the Ashfield Apartment complex. When you get there my friend, Milford—"

"Milford?" Harriet raised her brow.

"That's right," Dana said, "and don't ever call him Millie. Most folks call him Ford."

"Anyway," Chaz said, "Ford will meet you at the stop. You'll know him because he'll be driving what looks like a cop car. It's not really a cop car—not anymore. Ford is retired, but he likes to drive the car. He's a big bear of a man—used to play football."

Harriet swallowed a bitter cherry and winced.

"Ford is going to drive you to the Foothills Regional Airport—"

"What are you talking about? Airport? I am not getting on an airplane and flying to Grass Valley."

Dana grabbed Harriet's hand. "No, no, not a plane. A helicopter."

Harriet's stomach roiled like a blender puréeing a banana. "No, I am not getting in or on or whatever a helicopter."

"Just to Asheville," Chaz said. "From there, you'll be on your own to get to Maggie Valley."

"A helicopter?" Harriet felt tears well in her eyes. "You sure it's the only way?"

"No," Chaz said, "but it's the only way we could come up with."

"How long is the ride? I mean, how long will I be up there with those egg beaters going *whop whop whop?*" She twirled her finger in the air.

"Not sure, but I don't think very long. It's not that far to Asheville. Come on, Harriet. You're a brave woman."

"Brave. Maybe. Stupid? Most definitely. I wonder what Henry will say."

* * *

Harriet boarded the Greenway bus to the Ashfield Apartment complex. It was a nice modern bus, mostly white with lovely green trim. Very clean. In fact the cleanest bus Harriet had ridden since she boarded the first bus to West Chester, Pennsylvania.

She chose a window seat. She nestled back into the vinyl, which was very comfortable for the short ride. But she couldn't help but feel just a wee bit nervous about the notion of taking a helicopter ride. She thought about writing to Max about it, but that was when a middle-aged man wearing a three-piece suit plopped into the seat next to her. He did not appear happy. He rested his mahogany-colored briefcase on his lap. He drummed on it nervously. Harriet's imagination often ran away from her. And so she wasn't surprised when she had concocted an entire short story about the man in the gray suit carrying a bomb on board the bus.

Harriet stared at him, the briefcase, and at his fingers nervously *drum drum drumming* as the bus rolled along the busy city street. She tried to pry her eyes away and look out the window like any good passenger would. But no, she kept getting drawn back to his fingers, which were long and thin and unexpectedly well manicured. A detail she thought could be important should there be a blast and she needed to inform the police of her observations. She also noted the paisley tie he wore — green and yellow swirls. It was ugly.

Harriet pulled her phone from her pack. Now that Chaz had planned her route there was no need to bother Amelia about it. But it was handy in case she needed to call 911.

Bump. The bus lurched and the man leaned into her for half a second. Harriet jumped a little. "Excuse me," he said and went back to his drumming. That was when Harriet noticed his shoes. One brown, the other black. Either he was color blind or had gotten dressed in the dark — or worse, he checked himself out of the hospital and really was a mad bomber.

"Excuse me," Harriet said. "But are you okay? You seem a bit nervous."

The man glared at her as if to say, "Not your business."

"Just asking," Harriet said. "It pains me to see a fellow human being in distress, and that incessant finger drumming is an indication that you just might have something on your mind."

The man stopped drumming and looked at his hands. "Sorry."

"You can drum," Harriet said. "If it helps."

"Quit smoking," he said. "I really want a cigarette. That's why I ride the bus. Keeps me from smoking."

"Good idea," Harriet said. "Well, I will pray for you. I will pray that you can lick that nasty habit. What's your name?"

He looked at her. Then looked past her out the window. "William."

"Okay, William. I mean it. I will remember you in my prayers."

The man stood at the next red light. "My stop. Thanks."

A few minutes later the bus came to a stop in a residential neighborhood of ranch homes with wide, spacious yards. She stepped off the bus and looked around for Milford. When she didn't see anything that resembled a cop car, Harriet's knees began to shake. "Oh dear, Milford." And for the first time since all this started Harriet was frightened.

"What if it was a joke?"

She looked around and saw cars parked in driveways and a woman hanging wash on the line. She looked okay. Next she saw a man tooling down the street on an old bike. She walked a few paces and saw the apartment complex. A couple red brick buildings with white pillars in the front. She saw window air conditioners and bushes, but no Milford in a cop car. That was when she realized she didn't even know his last name. And then all of sudden she heard a siren come whooping and hollering down the street. She jumped.

But lo and behold the car, an old brown and white Crown Victoria, pulled up with lights and sirens blaring. The passenger door opened. "You Harriet?"

Harriet leaned down and looked into the car. A man her own age, wearing a red and green flannel shirt with hair so gray it was nearly white and large aviator-style glasses, looked back. He smiled and exposed a set of teeth more yellow than Harriet's corn bread.

"Are . . . are you Milford?"

"Hot diggity," he said. "The one and only. Climb aboard. You're about to take the ride of your life."

138

Chapter 15

HENRY AND HUMPHREY WERE SITTING ON THE BACK PORCH early that morning. It had started to rain, and Henry was not in the mood to walk Humphrey between the drops. And he liked the screened-in porch in the springtime. A chance to watch the grass grow and the flowers bloom. Humphrey liked it too. Except Humphrey still had a kind of sad look about him—if it was possible for him to look any sadder.

"Cheer up, old man, let's give Harriet a call."

Humphrey, who had been lying like a fat, brown wrinkled puddle of a dog, perked up. At least Henry thought he had perked.

Henry tapped his mother's picture and waited. "Let's put her on speaker."

Humphrey pried himself from the porch floor and ambled close to Henry. He sat and rested his chin on Henry's knee, looking up at him over his wiry eyebrows. Henry patted his head. "I know you miss her."

"Hello, Henry?" It was Harriet.

"Yes, Mother, of course it's Henry."

"Well, I'm sorry, it's a little loud in this police car."

"Police car?"

Humphrey whined.

"Why are you in a police car? Are you okay?"

139

"I'm fine. On my way to the helicopter."

"Helicopter? I don't understand. What happened to buses?"

"Can't always—"

The connection was dropped.

"Did you hear that, Humphrey? Mom is on her way to a helicopter in a police car. Oh, this is getting out of hand." He dropped the phone into his shirt pocket. "I hope everything is all right."

Humphrey danced and trotted to the screen door.

"Okay, but please just pee. I don't feel like picking up poop right now. I have to figure out where my mother is and why she's in a police car heading for a helicopter."

Humphrey yowled and dashed into the yard. He sniffed near the lilac.

* * *

Harriet closed her phone just as Milford hit a bump in the road. She bounced.

"Reception isn't too good out here," Ford said.

"Oh, it's not the reception. I just didn't want to talk to Henry about the helicopter. I think I might have told him too much already."

"Will he worry?"

"Oh, dear me, he will worry about this like a wart on a sore butt—sorry."

Ford laughed. "No problem. We should be out to the airport in about nine minutes."

"Are you sure you can drive a helicopter?"

"Flew 'em in Viet Nam. 'Course those hellies were a might bigger than Crazy Jane."

"Crazy Jane?"

"That's what I named my copter. Practically built her myself from spare parts."

Harriet smiled. Her stomach gurgled. She looked out the window at the telephone poles passing up and down, up and down, and trees and houses whizzing by at near breakneck speed.

"Nothing like the open road," Ford said. "They like to build airports where it ain't too populated. Noise pollution and all."

Harriet looked at her new friend. She had to consider him a friend. It made her feel better to consider him a long lost brother and not some psychotic fiend.

"That's nice," she said. "I suppose Crazy Jane is . . . seaworthy, or should I say, skyworthy?"

"That she is. Flies like the wind, smooth and comfy."

Harriet peered out the window some more. She would have liked to keep staring at Ford—he was so . . . interesting, but she didn't want to appear rude.

"So Sterling tells me you're heading to Grass Valley, California—taking the long way."

"That's right."

"I got to admire a woman like you. I don't think Francine—that's my wife of thirty-seven years—would have the nerve. She can barely take the bus to the shopping mall without getting lost."

"Well, there is a knack to it. And I guess you need a certain amount of determination." She adjusted her tote bag at her feet.

"I suppose you might be right. Francine seldom goes anywhere—'cept to play bridge with the girls and down to bingo on Thursday nights."

Harriet looked out at the world whizzing by. "You know, Milford, you really need to encourage her to do more. Get out. See the world. Have a dream. Accomplish something."

Ford looked over at her. "But how?"

"Ask. Ask her what she wants to do."

"She does have a birthday comin' up."

"You should take her someplace nice, maybe in your helicopter. And ask her then; encourage her to reach for the stars."

"Won't go up in it. She doesn't trust ol' Milford."

Harriet swallowed. "Does she have a reason not to trust you?"

141

"Nah. My goodness, cheese and crackers, Harriet, but that woman is afraid of her own shadow. She's just as happy staying home. Leastways I think so."

"I still think you should take her out this year. Someplace real special. Maybe spend the night at Chaz's inn. And trust me, she'll be glad you asked her about her dreams."

"Now that sounds like a right fine idea."

"And you better help her. Hold her hand through whatever she says because I'll come back here and thump your gums if you don't."

Ford laughed. "Yes, ma'am." He blew air out his nose and said, "Well, here we are. The airport. My whirlybird is parked out yonder."

Milford pulled off the asphalt road and drove over bare, flat ground, over rocks and bumps, which made Harriet feel a little queasy.

"How . . . far to your whirlybird?"

"There she is." Milford screeched to a stop, dirt kicking up around the car. "Ain't she a sight for sore eyes?"

Harriet looked through the windshield at what she figured must be a helicopter. It looked more like a big blue and white shark. It had a wide propeller blade on top, which to Harriet seemed twenty feet long, and a small set of blades on the back.

"Crazy Jane, here we come."

"Can I pay you?" Harriet asked. "We didn't discuss that."

"Hot diggity," Milford said. "I'd be insulted if you tried to pay me. I'm just happy to be part of the adventure, Harriet. Part of the adventure."

Harriet climbed out of the cop car.

"Come on. Don't be afraid. She's a good bird."

"Okay." Harriet sucked a deep breath but coughed it out when dust got stuck in her throat. "Here goes nothing."

Ford helped Harriet climb into the front seat. He secured her suitcase into the back with a bungee cord attached to a thick metal handle and then tucked her tote bag into a small space behind her seat. "Now buckle up." He slammed the door shut with a clang. Harriet felt like she was in a tuna can from the sound it made. Her nerves were a touch rattled. "Courage, girl. You can do this."

Then she watched him run around to the other side and climb in. After he buckled himself Harriet tapped his shoulder. "I'm not sure about this, Mil — I mean Ford."

"Chicken? You getting chicken?" He fussed with some dials and pedals.

"Maybe. Maybe a little. I mean the bus is one thing, but being off the road, in the air, in a helicopter?"

"Speak now. I'll take you back to the bus station, but the only way you'll get to Asheville is on a charter bus or the Greyhound."

Harriet sucked a deep breath. "Okay. Let's go."

"Good." Ford placed a set of headphones on Harriet's head.

"What? I don't want to listen to music," she said louder than normal.

Ford smiled. "No. It's so we can talk." He pointed to the microphone. "It gets loud up there."

A dizzy spell caught Harriet off guard. But she tightened her knees and straightened her back. Determination. Then she said a quick prayer. "Dear Lord. Let this thing fly. Get us there in one piece. Amen."

"Everybody prays," Ford said. "It's the darnedest thing. Guess it's true what they say."

"What's that?"

"No atheists in a helicopter."

Within minutes the whirlybird engine started up and Harriet could hear the rotation of the blades above her head. The craft rattled and rumbled, and then the next thing she knew they had lifted off the ground as slow and easy as spring pollen in a light wind burst.

Harriet opened her eyes. "This isn't so bad."

143

Ford laughed. Then he reached under his seat and pulled out a cigar.

"You aren't going to light that, are you?" Harriet said, her brow arched.

Ford shook his head as he fidgeted with knobs and the joystick. "Nah. Just like to chew on 'em."

Harriet started to relax. The rumble and jostling of the helicopter settled down, and they were sailing smoothly through the air.

"The view is spectacular," Harriet said. "I never knew the earth was so green and blue and orange."

"Hot diggity," Ford said. "There ain't nothing like being five thousand feet in the air looking down on home. Gives you a whole new perspective. That road down there is State Route 70. We'll pretty much follow her into Asheville."

"It looks like a line drawn by a pencil," Harriet said.

"We're passing over Black Mountain. That over there is Lake Tomahawk. Not very big lake. But still, there she is."

"Thank you," Harriet said. "For taking me this way. I never would have believed in a million years I'd ride in a helicopter. Wait'll Martha hears about this."

"Martha?"

"My friend back in Philly. Right now I miss her more than anything and wish she was here in this contraption with me looking down on the world."

"We'll be coming up on the Blue Ridge Parkway soon. Now that's a pretty drive. Right through mountains."

"Which mountains?"

"Why, the Appalachian Mountains, of course. Runs for about 470 miles. Some of the most beautiful terrain you'll ever set eyes on."

"I'd like to see that."

"Yeah, unfortunately I'm only cleared to take you into Asheville. Maybe some other time."

Harriet looked out the window. "One day, maybe."

"Okay now," Ford said. "That over there is the airport. I'll be bringing Crazy Jane in for a landing over there."

"In that little driveway?"

"It's not so little. Keep an eye out—it comes up pretty quick."

Harriet sat back in the seat and adjusted her headset microphone. "That was a very fast ride."

"Yep. Traveling is easy when you have the right equipment. I still don't get why you're doing this on public buses and what have you."

"Like I tell everyone, I'm taking the scenic way to California. And this is about as scenic as it's gotten."

"Excuse me a sec," Ford said. "I got to let them know we're here." Ford fiddled with knobs and then spoke into the radio. Then he turned back to Harriet. "That's what Sterling told me. I'm very impressed, Harriet Beamer. Very impressed." His cigar still teetered in the corner of his mouth.

Harriet nodded. "Thank you, Ford."

"Well, you really are something else. A woman your age traversing the country the way you are—going up in an old helicopter with the likes of me—sheesh. Well, like my granddaughter says—" he raised a thumbs up—"you go, girl!"

"Uh-oh," she said. "There's a man with a flag."

"Yep, he'll guide Crazy Jane in, like fitting a shoe on a foot."

Seconds later the helicopter was on the ground. The man with the flag rushed over with his head bent down. "Go on, now," Ford said. "Herbie will help you out and get you to the terminal."

"But I thought you were coming."

"Nah, I got to get back to town. Things to do. But it was a pleasure, Harriet. A real honor to fly with you." He saluted her.

Harriet saluted back. Herbie reached inside and unbuckled her belt and then lifted the phones off her head.

"Have a safe trip home, Ford," Harriet said. "Thank you."

Ford nodded. Harriet jumped out of the helicopter and held her head down against the wind created by the whirling blades.

145

She and Herbie, who carried her belongings like they were foot-balls or toddlers, ran back toward the building, where they stood and watched Milford take off.

"What a sweet man," Harriet said.

"When he's sober."

Harriet swallowed. Her eyes grew wide as she looked at Herbie.

"Sterling told me to help you get wherever you needed to go," Herbie said.

"Um." Harriet adjusted her tote bag. "I guess if you could tell me where I could catch the bus into town that would be great."

"Easy peasy. Just through those doors, and then wind your way around to the front of the terminal. I believe someone there will help you find the bus stop."

"Thanks," Harriet said. "And I suppose there's a . . . restroom inside."

"Sure thing. Just look for the signs."

Once inside the building, which looked pretty much like every other terminal she'd visited, drab walls, scuffed floors, TV screens with information everywhere she looked, she wandered down the wide passage until she found the ladies room. And none too soon. Age had its weaknesses.

Chapter 16

THE ASHEVILLE REGIONAL AIRPORT WAS SMALL, OR AT least that's what Harriet thought, having not been in many airports. She walked around a little outside, trying to regain her land legs before making her way over to a skycap and inquiring about the local bus.

"Oh, yes, ma'am," he said. "You just go back out these doors, turn to your right, and walk about a block, block and a half, and you'll see the sign for Route 6. She'll take you on into the city."

"Thank you," Harriet said. She reached into her pocket and pulled out a five-dollar bill. "Thanks again."

The skycap smiled. "You have a good day now, y'hear?"

Harriet reset her wheels, pulled her tote over her shoulder, and set off back outside. She had no trouble finding the stop, and just a few minutes later the 1:55 to the Asheville Terminal Center pulled up. It was a long white bus, albeit a grimy, sooty bus with a wide red stripe that reached all the way around. Harriet and three other passengers climbed aboard after seventeen people climbed off.

Fortunately the bus was pretty much empty now except for an old woman in the back. Harriet chose a seat near the front. She sat down with a thud and finally allowed herself to feel relieved she was out of that helicopter.

"Now, I wonder if I should call Henry," she said to the window.

But she thought better of it and decided to wait until later. She had thought she'd try to make it all the way to Maggie Valley, but given the time, Harriet decided to spend the night in Asheville.

"Excuse me," she called to the driver, a young woman who looked friendly enough. "Can you tell me the name of a nice restaurant near the transit center?"

"Tupelo Honey Café on College Street; that's what I like." She never took her eyes off the road but continued talking. "Real nice place, good people, great food."

"Does this bus go there?"

"Sorry. You need to get on the Route 15 to Patton, and then it's an easy walk around the corner."

"Thank you. The Route 15."

The bus pulled into the transit center, a mostly nondescript building lacking any nuance or charm. The bus pulled alongside a portico with large green pillars supporting a roof. Folks were sitting on benches or leaning against the pillars waiting. Probably for the next bus. *The next bus.* Harriet thought that sounded almost like a philosophy for life. Sometimes she felt like she was always waiting for the next bus, and not only since she left Philadelphia but at other times. Waiting until the next bus came along to set her on a different route. Like when she got pregnant with Henry or adopted Humphrey or got married or buried Max. They were all buses taking her in a new direction.

Harriet de-bused. She liked that term. It made her feel like a professional. She went inside the smallish building and located the Route 15 schedule and map just inside the terminal building. Unfortunately, the next bus that would take her close to Patton Avenue wasn't due until 4:00 and it was only a little past three.

So Harriet found an empty bench and sat. She grabbed her cell phone and remembered that she had turned it off before she got into Crazy Jane. "Oh dear, I bet Henry is frantic."

She turned it on and sure enough, she had six new voicemails waiting for her. "Oh dear, I hate getting messages. I know they're all from Henry, so I'll just call."

She tapped his picture.

"Now, Henry, don't be mad, but I had to turn the phone off while I was riding in the helicopter," she said the instant he said hello.

"Mom," Henry said. "Where are you now? Are you okay?"

"I'm still in North Carolina, dear. Decided to spend the night here."

"Where in North Carolina?"

"Asheville. But, Henry, I would like to ask you a question. Do you think I'm . . . I'm still useful?"

"Useful?"

"Yes. Do I still matter, or have I used up all my purpose?"

There was a long pause and Harriet felt fidgety. "I'm sorry, Henry, I shouldn't have asked that."

"Mom, I—"

"Sorry, Henry there's my next bus." She closed her phone. Of course she still had a few minutes to wait, but it felt uncomfortable to talk about personal things with Henry—even long distance. The air was cool for a late spring afternoon, and Harriet enjoyed it. She would much rather be cool than too hot. She observed the people around her and marveled that most of them were young and hip looking. She liked that. Hip kids made her smile and remember her own youth.

Next Harriet got out her journal and pen. She crossed her legs and admired her bright red sneakers again. She never, ever thought she could love a pair of shoes as much as she loved her Converse. Change was good.

Dear Max, you will not believe what I did today. I rode in
a helicopter named Crazy Jane with a Viet Nam vet named
Milford. At first I was scared to death, but then I managed to
sit back and relax. I figured if God was going to call me home

*in a fiery crash, I might as well enjoy the view. I'm writing
this entry under a portico at the transit center in Asheville,
North Carolina, on my way to Maggie Valley, also in North
Carolina. I can't wait to get there. David Prancing Elk made it
sound spectacular. I'll be sure to wink at a star for you. I hope
I see some meteors. Remember how we thought shooting stars
were expressly for us, from God at times. Like, I was thinking,
when we lost the baby. You took me out that night, and we saw
a shooting star. It cut through the sky like a diamond-studded
knife. We prayed for another baby that night and two years later
Henry was born, under a shooting star.*

She leaned her head back against the brick wall and remembered the night Henry came into the world. They saw a shooting
star on the way to the hospital.

Harriet swiped at the tear that fell onto her page. "I miss you,
Max."

She closed her book and set it in its pouch in her tote bag. Harriet sat and listened to the sounds around her, snippets of conversation, birds singing. There were nests in the portico roof.
Sparrows, Harriet thought.

But then, just as she started to feel relaxed, she heard a scuffle
and a scream behind her. She turned and saw a young man yank
the handbag away from an older woman, older than she. The
woman screamed as the hoodlum in dark jeans and white T-shirt
hurdled one of the benches and came running with the handbag
toward her.

Thinking fast, Harriet rolled her suitcase just in time to trip
the thief. He crashed to the ground with a thud and a cry. Harriet
raised her tote bag and sent it crashing down onto the boy. He hollered and cursed as Harriet continued to assail him with her tote.

"What. Is. Wrong. With. You?" she said with each glancing
blow. Her bottle of blood-pressure medicine skittered out of the
bag along with two gel pens and a canister of deodorant.

"Stop it, Lady," the kid hollered. "Stop hitting me."

Harriet looked at the boy. She noticed his bright blue eyes. "Ah, you're not a criminal. You're just a baby."

The old woman, along with several other passersby gathered around. One of the group held a camera.

The young lady with the camera—actually a cell phone—moved closer to Harriet. "This is going on my YouTube channel," she said. "I got the whole thing—from the first whack with that big purse."

A middle-aged man joined the scene and knelt with his knee in the boy's back. "You're a real hero, lady. That was incredible."

It took a moment before Harriet realized she was smiling into the girl's camera.

"Thank you. Thank you so much," said the crime victim. She leaned down and reclaimed her purse. "My ... my life's savings are in here."

Harriet smiled at her. "I'm glad I was here at the right time."

That was when two police officers approached and started asking questions. One of the officers helped the perpetrator up and handcuffed him. And what happened after that happened so quickly Harriet hardly had time to think. There were so many questions. A backup patrol car arrived on the scene and out jumped two more officers. They took Harriet's vital statistics— her name, address, cell phone number, and such, while the original cops tended to the victim.

"You're a true hero," Officer Trotter said.

Harriet felt her face warm. "I just did what anyone would do." Then she glared at the young man. "And you! You should be ashamed. What would your mother think of you stealing purses from women?"

The boy, who couldn't have been much older than sixteen, didn't say a word.

That was when the small crowd applauded.

"Oh my goodness," Harriet said. "But I don't deserve this. I was just on my way to California minding my own beeswax when

I saw him. I think I acted on instinct. I'm just thankful he wasn't any bigger. He's just a kid."

The woman videoing the whole thing stopped for a moment and said, "I'll get this uploaded right away. It's gonna be all over the place. Eighty-year-old woman nabs purse snatcher on her way to California."

"Seventy-two, dear," Harriet said.

"What?"

"I'm only seventy-two."

The police officers led the perpetrator away. The crowd thinned, and Harriet sat with a thud onto the bench. Her heart pounded like a drum in the hands of a two-year-old. She needed to catch her breath. "Glory be. Thank you, Lord, for getting me through that one and for letting me nab that hoodlum."

The victim approached Harriet. She opened her purse and removed a thin bank envelope. "I want to reward you," she said as she offered Harriet a twenty-dollar bill. "It's not much but—"

Harriet waved the money away. "Oh, gracious no. I refuse to accept any reward. You hang on to your money."

The woman smiled so wide her upper plate dropped. She quickly corrected the situation. "Thank you. I'm on my way to live with my son. He's meeting me at the station."

"Oh, that's a good thing." Harriet patted the woman's hand. "I am too. Going to live with my son, only I'm taking the long way."

In all the commotion Harriet missed the first bus and had to wait for the next. But that was fine with her—gave her a chance to settle down after the ordeal. The next bus pulled up soon enough and Harriet once again lugged her suitcase up the steps with a bump, bump, bump that seemed to annoy the driver.

"Come on, Lady, I don't got all day."

"I'm quite sorry, young man," Harriet said as she paid her fare. "But it's getting heavier and heavier." She took the first seat she saw and barely had room for her suitcase. It must have been a older bus, she decided, not as much leg room as the new ones.

Fifteen minutes later her stop came up on Patton Avenue. She moved to the front. "Can you direct me to the Tupelo Honey Café?" she asked the driver. "If it's not too much of a bother."

"Just over on College Street," he said without even glancing in her direction. "Next street over, sort of, you'll find it."

"Thank you."

Harriet stood a moment. It seemed a nice part of town, artsy and earthy like she'd expect to see flower children and hippies strolling about. But mostly she saw young folk, many on cell phones, others carrying cups of coffee and yakking up a storm with friends. All on their way to someplace.

She spotted a small boutique called Aunt Clementine and went inside. It was old with creaky floors. She saw all kinds of jewelry, large brooches and earrings with bright stones in them, and specialty clothing, like a pair of vintage stone martens still with their tails and eyes. She touched the soft fur. Why would anyone want to wear dead weasels around their shoulders? But Harriet did not see a single salt and pepper shaker so she bought the martens.

Next she moved on to a used bookstore. The smell was musty and bookish with a bit of cigarette thrown in. She loved wandering through the dark stacks looking at all the used books. She enjoyed picking out the ones that had cracked spines and dog-eared pages. She figured those were the ones that got read. The others were like brand-new and probably never read or, at the very most, never finished. She finally settled on a copy of *Pride and Prejudice*. "I always wanted to read this," she told the clerk. "And now I think I will."

"You'll love it," the clerk said. "Austen is my favorite."

"I've heard that from other people. My son — he's a writer — says she's great."

"Oh, what's he written?"

Harriet felt a wash of pride. "He's written one novel — a Western. It's called *Ride the Wild Wind*. Why a Western, I don't know.

He's just finishing up his new book, and then I believe it will be sent out to the bookstores next year."

"That's great," the clerk said with a bit of disbelief.

Finally, Harriet found her way to the Tupelo Honey Café, a lovely storefront restaurant nestled amid other stores and businesses. It had a green awning and tables and chairs assembled outside on the walkway. She thought about taking a seat outside, but when a chilly wind, chillier than before, kicked up, she went inside.

A hostess showed her to a seat. "Enjoy your dinner."

Harriet looked at the menu. Everything sounded so good. Too good. She was half-starved. Being on the road left little time to eat. And Harriet liked to eat, even though Doctor Nancy was always on her about watching her carbs. Harriet swallowed and set the menu down as a most terrible thought crossed her mind. Moving to Grass Valley would mean needing to find a new doctor. Oh dear, another reason she should have called off the silly bet when she had the chance.

After a few minutes Harriet settled on the meat loaf, mostly because she liked the name: Not Your Mama's Meat Loaf, and it came with from-scratch mac 'n' cheese. It sounded perfectly comforting on such a long and occasionally harrowing day. She thought about the purse snatching and winced. She could have gotten hurt, but in the heat of the moment there was not time to think.

Harriet liked the Tupelo Honey Café. There were black and white photos scattered about the walls of people and places, and the décor reminded her of an old-fashioned tearoom. The kind she used to visit with her mother so very long ago. Lush potted and hanging plants added to the earthiness of the place. Harriet breathed in the ambience and felt her shoulders relax for the first time all day.

Her server came by. "My name is Sheretha. I'll take your drink order, and can I start you off with an appetizer?" she asked.

"Oh, no, not today. I think I'd like the meat loaf, though—it sounds scrumptious."

"It is," the server said. "The best in town."

"And iced tea," Harriet added. "Not sweet." Her phone jingled. "I'm sorry."

"No problem. I'll be right back with your tea," the server said and walked off toward the kitchen.

"Hello," Harriet said.

"It's me, Martha."

"Martha," Harriet tried to whisper. "How are you? Everything okay?"

"Everything is fine by me, how's by you?"

"Oh, Martha, I just had the most unusual day. I flew in a helicopter." That was when she noticed the couple next to her look over. "But let me call you later when I get to my room. It will be more private, less nosey, I mean noisy."

"Helicopter? I got to hear this. Now, you better call me later."

Harriet closed her phone. In a few minutes, her iced tea arrived, followed not too much later by the main dish. Harriet finished every bite of her meat loaf. It truly was the best she had ever eaten. She told the server so when she came to get her plate. "This was the best meal I've had since I left Hickory, and the meal I had in Hickory was the best since, well, since I cooked for myself back in Philadelphia."

"Are you traveling?" Sheretha asked.

"I sure am, on my way to California."

"No kidding?" Sheretha said. "Cool."

"Thanks. It's been real . . . cool."

"Here's your check, whenever you're ready," Sheretha said.

"Sheretha," Harriet said signing the statement. "I was wondering, do you know of a nice hotel around here?"

Sheretha pondered a moment. "If I was going to stay somewhere tonight, I'd see if I could get a room at the White Gate Inn. Pretty expensive and ritzy, but I hear it is the best. Very luxurious."

"Luxurious. I could do with some luxury."

"'Course I could never afford it, what with being a single mom with three kids. My goodness. But I do work hard."

"The White Gate Inn."

"Yep. You better call first in case they don't have a room available."

"Thanks," Harriet said.

After paying her bill and leaving Sheretha a ridiculously large tip, Harriet called the inn, and much to her delight they had two rooms available for the night. Harriet booked the Emily Dickinson room. She couldn't have been more thrilled. The only trouble was getting there. The inn wasn't that far from the restaurant, but there was no bus going that way, and now it was nearly night, and she was tired. She didn't want to walk.

Harriet called a cab. She stood outside the restaurant and waited. The air was cool but not cold, and smelled of the city — a mixture of exhaust and food smells. Cars whizzed past, bikers with headlights rode by, but mostly Harriet enjoyed watching the people. She thought there were a lot of people out on a weekday evening.

The cab pulled close to the curb, and Harriet climbed into the back. "Hello," she said. "I'd like to go to the White Gate Inn please."

"Okeydokey," said the driver.

Harriet checked the face on the license with the face in the rearview. "Robert," she said. "That's a nice name."

"Thank you," he said.

The ride to White Gate took only a few minutes, and before she knew it, Harriet had passed through a white picket fence and was walking up a flower-lined walkway to the entrance.

Harriet stood for a moment and breathed deeply. The house was spectacular, with red clapboard siding surrounded by gardens on sloping hills. Harriet was certain she heard a waterfall nearby.

She rang the bell and was met by Ralph, one of the owners.

"Welcome," he said. "You must be Harriet Beamer."

Harriet smiled. "I am."

"Well, I couldn't miss you. You're famous."

Harriet stepped through the threshold. "Famous? You must mean another Harriet Beamer."

Ralph shook his head. "Aren't you the Harriet who is traveling across the country using public transportation?"

Harriet smiled. "I guess so, but . . . how did you know?"

"You made the *Asheville Citizen-Times*, honey. At least their website."

"Oh dear. Really?" She looked around at the spectacular parlor. Her eyes landed on a beautiful oil painting above the fireplace mantel. "I love that," she said, hoping to avoid any more talk about her celebrity.

"That, my dear, is called *A Still Wind Blows*. It was painted by Elizabeth Versace."

Ralph checked Harriet in. "The Emily Dickinson suite. You'll just love it. It's one of my favorite rooms."

"Emily Dickinson is my favorite poet."

"Ohh, well then, this is the perfect room for you. It's just so . . . so Emily."

They climbed an elegant stairwell. The room was a couple of doors down on the right. He showed her inside.

"Oh my goodness gracious," Harriet said. She stood still a moment, barely able to catch her breath. "It's . . . it's gorgeous."

"Thank you," Ralph said as he parked her suitcase near the bed. "I think you'll find everything to your satisfaction, but if you should need anything, anything at all, please call the front desk."

"Thank you."

"Have a sweet night," Ralph said as he closed the door.

Harriet dropped her tote on the floor. The room was spectacular. There was a four-poster bed with a lovely rose-covered comforter. A small writing desk sat in the corner surrounded by large windows with blinds, not curtains, so Harriet could enjoy the budding trees outside. The living room section of the suite had a fireplace and chairs and a sofa. Harriet thought she could live there with no problem. The windows looked out over lush gardens. Harriet remembered a bit of Emily: "The lovely flowers embarrass me. They make me regret I am not a bee ..."

She sat on the chair in the sitting room, kicked off her sneakers, and yawned with her whole body. This had to be the most relaxing place in the world.

Harriet checked her phone and decided it would be best to charge it while she called Martha and talked to her with the cord dangling. She still owed her an explanation about the helicopter. Even though it was late she figured it would be okay. Martha was a night owl. She often stayed up late working on her stained glass.

"Martha," she said, "it was ... spectacular. A little scary but still—"

"I don't believe it," Martha said. "You actually rode in a helicopter. Did it have doors? You know some of them don't have doors."

"Yes, this one had doors, and Milford, he was the pilot, was ever so sweet. A little rough around the edges but still quite sweet. I saw North Carolina from a mile in the sky. It was—"

"Spectacular," Martha said. "I would have been scared half to death. Airplanes are one thing but—"

"You would have done it if it was the only way to get where you needed to go. I have trouble finding a bus sometimes once I get out of the city limits. As a matter of fact I have no clue how I'll ride into Maggie Valley. But you know what, Martha, I'm learning to trust God in ways I never had to. He always comes through even if it is a wild helicopter ride."

"That's great, Harriet. I never heard you speak like this. Oh, you always had the God stuff down, but now it's different. Your voice is different."

"This time it's ... personal," Harriet said. "You know what I mean?"

"I think so."

"I guess it's like I can actually feel God's—"

"Pleasure?"

"Um, not exactly. More like God's big, giant hand on my back. He keeps nudging me to take the next bus. To get to the finish line."

"Speaking of which, are you sure a bus won't get you into Maggie Valley?"

"I'm not sure. I'll ask the innkeepers in the morning. Maybe they'll have an idea."

* * *

Henry heard Prudence pull into the driveway. He stood at the door and waited for her to climb out of her little BMW, grab her briefcase, adjust her skirt, and walk up the path.

"How was your day?" he asked and then kissed her.

"Good. We had a good day. No, a great day. I made mincemeat of their star witness. You should have seen me."

"That's nice, dear."

Prudence dropped her briefcase in the foyer and removed her shoes, which she set neatly on the tile. "Iced tea?"

"Sure thing," Henry said. "Be right back."

Henry and Humphrey headed for the kitchen. Humphrey lapped water from his bowl as Henry poured tea into a tall, skinny tumbler. "Maybe a Lorna Doone to go with it. Might help," Henry said.

Humphrey barked. Henry tossed him a cookie, which he very much appreciated. Henry sat in the green wing chair across from Prudence and watched her sip her iced tea.

"You have something to tell me," Prudence said. "Is it your mother? Is she okay?"

"Yes, and yes, she's fine. A little crazy maybe, but fine."

Prudence sipped her tea. "So tell me."

"It's so funny, Pru," Henry said with a chuckle. "She called from a police car on the way to a helicopter."

"Police car, helicopter?"

"That's what I said. But I didn't get to ask anything because the call was dropped."

"Did she call back?"

"Yeah, about two hours later. She hitched a ride with a retired police officer—a Viet Nam vet. Then he gave her a ride to Asheville, North Carolina, in his helicopter."

"Wow, she's really traveling every which way."

"Is that all you can say? My seventy-two-year-old mother in a helicopter!"

"She's safe, right?"

"Yes, but . . . oh, it's useless."

"Now you're getting it."

Humphrey toddled near Prudence. She patted his head. "It's okay, boy. She'll get here."

Henry sighed and changed the subject. "I had a good day too. I'm making progress on the novel. I'm really excited about it. Whoever thought that setting a boarding house on fire would make all the difference in the world. I raised the stakes and gave Cash a reason to live all in one blaze of glory. It was spectacular, Pru. I loved writing the fire scene."

"Oh, honey, I'm very happy for you."

Prudence stood. "You know what? I'm hungry. I had no lunch."

"Got just the thing," Henry said. "Shish kebob."

"Now, that sounds delightful. I'd like to shower and change first."

"Plenty of time," Henry said. "Haven't even made them yet."

Chapter 17

THE NEXT MORNING HARRIET ENJOYED A DELICIOUS THREE-course breakfast in the white-paneled dining room. Peaches, pears, and pineapples baked in a brown-sugar sherry sauce, followed by a mushroom tarragon soufflé, and then cinnamon maple caramel pecan rolls for dessert. She had a grand view of the B&B gardens as she ate. Afterward she went out to the gardens to sit on a bench and write to Max.

> *Dear Max, today I am in Asheville, North Carolina, at a B&B. We always talked about going to one, remember? I wish we had found the time. I would have liked to come to this one with you. I slept in the Emily Dickinson room—it was flowery and comfortable. And Max, yesterday I captured a purse snatcher. I seem to be finding muscles I never knew I had. This morning I need to find a way to Maggie Valley. Remember those stars I wrote to you about? I'm on my way to find them. Maybe even tonight.*

She closed her book, tucked it into her tote, then wandered the garden for a while, enjoying the soothing trickle of the waterfalls. She then returned to her room to read more Jane Austen. Might as well take advantage of her luxurious surroundings while she could.

As the noon checkout time neared, she felt ready to move on.

Ralph had told her the night before that if she needed anything, anything at all she should ask. "I hope he knows a way to Maggie Valley." She repacked her suitcase yet again. This time she crammed her jammies into a zippered pocket along with socks. She tucked Jane Austen into her tote, took one last look around her room, and headed down the stairs.

Ralph was at the front desk—if that's what it was called. It was really an old oak desk in the parlor. A computer monitor was the only thing that made it look businesslike.

"Excuse me," Harriet said. "But I was hoping you could give me some information. How would I get to Maggie Valley from here? I'd like to use a bus, but I don't believe a bus, or even several buses, will get me there. I was hoping you might have a suggestion."

"Um, that is a tough one." Ralph banged on the keyboard. "You're right, you can't get there from here. What about renting a car?"

Harriet took a deep breath and let it out slowly. "Oh, fiddlesticks. I don't know. I was hoping I wouldn't have to resort to a car. I might as well drive the whole way—you know. And if that's the case, then I could just get on a Greyhound or a plane, and I already rode in a helicopter to get here."

Ralph laughed. "Helicopter? You are a hoot, darling."

A guest who was sitting on the sofa reading the paper spoke up. "What about a charter bus?"

Ralph snapped his fingers. "Yes, charter. Maggie Valley has all those casinos. Ever heard of a casino bus?"

Harriet felt her eyes grow as big as poker chips. "I have. Why, the bus leaves every single day to Atlantic City from right outside that little strip mall not far from my home in Pennsylvania. But I never rode on one."

"Well, Pennsylvania isn't the only state with casino buses. The casino makes a mint off of old people—sorry—some old people spending their Social Security checks."

"And they give you ten bucks or so in quarters and coupons for free food," the guest added.

"Hot diggity dog," Harriet said. "Where do I catch the casino bus?"

Ralph tapped a few words into his computer. "Lookee here, the High Roller Express leaves from the Catholic church just down the street. You can walk there."

"Does it give a time schedule?" Harriet asked.

"Sure does. One is scheduled to leave at 4:30."

Harriet looked at the grandfather clock in the corner of the room. "That's over four hours away. What can I do till then?"

"You're welcome to stay in your room till two, then relax in the gardens or living room," Ralph said. "I imagine you get tired from all the travel, and this is a good spot to relax."

"That's for sure," Harriet said. "That's what I'll do. Thank you."

The afternoon passed quickly, and soon Harriet found herself back on the road. The walk to Saint Dorothy's Catholic Church was easy, down tree-lined streets and past flower-filled yards. And the instant she turned the corner onto Christ Our Lord Drive she saw the church. It was a huge palace of a place with high spires and a large neon sign that read WELCOME HOME TO SAINT DOT'S. She strolled a little further toward the back of the church and saw a line of mostly older women standing along the curb. They seemed to be laughing and yakking and generally having a good time as they waited for the bus. Each wore a bright purple fanny pack that indicated to Harriet that this was definitely some kind of casino club.

Harriet paused a moment as she adjusted her pack and built up enough nerve to join the group. She felt odd crashing a group of women who seemed so familiar with each other. They probably traveled together all the time to the casino, maybe even every day. One woman wore one of those green poker-player visors that Harriet had seen in movies. Harriet didn't want to intrude. But if she wanted to get to Maggie Valley it was her only option.

"Hello," she said with a wave.

A couple of the women looked over at her. "Hello," said the older looking of the two. She was short with short gray hair except for a funky purple streak. She wore glasses and a pair of orange clam diggers with white Keds.

"I was wondering if I could ride along with you all today."

Orange Clam Digger Lady smiled over the top of her glasses. "Of course, honey. The more the merrier. This your first time? You a member of St. Dots?"

"Yes. I mean no, I'm not a member of St. Dots, and yes, this is my first time — here. But ... I was just looking for a ride ... to Maggie Valley. If that's okay with — " But she never got to finish her sentence. For the first time in Harriet's life she was recognized — and not by someone who'd known her for a long time.

"Are you that woman?" asked another woman making her way toward Harriet with all the determination of a baseball manager making his way to the third base umpire. Her fanny pack bounced up and down with each stride.

Harriet swallowed and tried to smile. "Well, I don't know. Which woman?"

"The one on the news this morning. You're the woman. You're the woman who beat the snot out of that punk." She laughed heartily.

"Oh dear," Harriet said. "How in the world could you know that? And he wasn't a punk. He was just a kid who needs some direction. Maybe he should join the military when he's of age."

"Hey," called Orange Clam Digger Lady, "we got us a celebrity on board. The woman who nabbed the purse snatcher. It was on the news. They showed the YouTube video."

"No kidding, Christine," said the woman who first recognized her. "She's riding with us to the Maggie Valley casinos." With that a small roar of applause went up.

Harriet adjusted her glasses and smiled. "If it's okay."

"Okay?" said Clam Digger. "We are honored to have you."

"Hey," said the woman standing with Clam Digger, "does this mean we're like celebrities too . . . by association?"

"I'm not a celebrity or a hero. I just tripped him with my suitcase. Any one of you would have done the same."

"But we didn't," Clam Digger said. "What's your name?"

"Harriet Beamer."

The bus pulled up, a short white and red bus with the words POKER EXPRESS painted on the side. The door opened and everyone filed in. It was driven by a man who looked about a hundred and ten years old. He wore a black cowboy hat, huge aviator sunglasses, and had more wrinkles than the prunes Harriet ate at breakfast.

Christine grabbed Harriet's suitcase handle. "Let me help with you that. Imagine lugging this clear across the country. You must be tired."

Clam Digger pulled Harriet's arm. "Come on, sit with me."

"Is he a safe driver?" Harriet whispered.

"Clarence? Sure. He just spent too many summers in the sun."

Harriet was invited to sit next to everyone. All she could hear was, "Over here, Harriet, sit with me." But in the end she chose to sit next to Orange Clam Digger Lady. The others seemed put-out, but it didn't take long for everyone to cheer up once the bus got moving.

"How long is the ride?" Harriet asked.

"About forty-five minutes, give or take. My name is Muriel, by the way. I don't think we introduced ourselves properly."

"Nice to meet you," Harriet said. "My name is — " then she stopped herself and smiled. "But you already know my name."

"Have you seen the video?" Muriel asked.

Harriet shook her head.

"Is that a Droid phone I saw you looking at?"

Harriet nodded.

"You can see it right on your phone."

"No. Really? How?"

Muriel tapped Harriet's phone and typed a few letters. The next thing Harriet knew she was watching herself beating the snot, as Muriel had said, out of that young man. She felt a little embarrassed but also a little excited. Especially when she saw the victim's face. She looked so relieved. Harriet said a quick silent prayer for her and the hoodlum.

The phone made the rounds of the bus as Harriet and Muriel talked.

"So what brings you to the Poker Express?" Muriel asked.

Harriet took a breath and told her the story once again.

"Did you hear this, Patsy?" Muriel knocked on the seat in front of her. "Harriet says she's traveling across the country on buses because she lost a bet. Ain't that ... what do they call it, ironic?"

Patsy turned as best she could, craning her neck over the seat back.

"It sure is. And now here I am on my way to Maggie Valley to see some stars."

"Stars," Muriel said. "You won't see many stars there."

"Really? But David Prancing Elk said that Maggie Valley had some great stargazing sights."

Muriel glanced at Patsy and then back at Harriet. "You mean real stars. The kind in the sky. I thought you meant movie stars. Then in that case, you might see some."

"I hope so," Harriet said. "I love to see stars. Makes me feel like ... like ... well, like I really do live on a planet and that there's other things out there."

"You mean like UFOs," Patsy said. "Aliens."

Harriet laughed. "No. Not aliens. God, something bigger than all of us."

"Oh, yeah, in that case I see what you mean," Muriel said. "I believe in God. I just don't think he believes in me. If he did, I'd go home a winner for sure tonight."

"Not necessarily. God isn't a slot machine."

"That's for sure, Harriet. Don't I know it!"

The bus pulled onto the main interstate. Route 40 Harriet read. The road traveled past large clumps of trees and dense forest. "It's pretty," she said. "Look at all those evergreens."

"The scenery," Muriel said. "Yep, it sure is. But I'll tell you this much. I'll enjoy it loads more on the way back if I win some money, you know."

Harriet expected Muriel to slap her on the back, and she winced preemptively, but the slap never came.

"How 'bout you, Harriet?" Patsy asked. "Gonna gamble while you're there?"

Harriet laughed. "Nah, I'd probably lose my shirt. And I don't have that many spare shirts in here." She patted her suitcase.

The women laughed.

"Harriet," Patsy said. "You're a card. Just an absolute card. And I say, keep busing. Keep busing until you *want* to go home."

"That's right," Muriel said. "You're in charge of your own destiny. You can go anywhere you want."

"Oh, I don't know about that," Harriet said. "This crick in my back and the aches in my knees tell me otherwise. But I will admit that even though I like what I'm doing, there's part of me that's ready to settle now."

Patsy leaned as close as she could toward Harriet. "I think you're an inspiration to postmenopausal, empty-nesting, got-nothing-to-do-but-scrub-toilets women everywhere."

"Hear! Hear!" came the cheer from the rest of the ladies on the bus. Even the two lone gentlemen raised their fists in solidarity. "You go, Harriet," called one.

About an hour later the bus pulled into the Harrah's Casino parking lot. It was surrounded by trees with the spectacular Smoky Mountains as a backdrop. That afternoon there were low-lying clouds that threatened rain. Harriet looked into the sky hoping that the clouds would be gone by nighttime. Stargazing was her number one reason for putting the trip on hold for a day or two.

"Are there really Indians here?" Harriet asked Muriel.

"Indians? Sure, but you came to gamble, right? They have their own casinos up in the hills, like Tribal Bingo."

"Yes," Harriet said as she stood. "I would like to meet some Ind—I guess I should say Native Americans."

"Then you've come to the right place. Cherokee Indians."

Once everyone was off the bus, Harriet tried to break away from the group. "I think I'll just walk a little first," she said. "Thanks for taking me along."

"Really?" Patsy said. "Aren't you coming in? Play some slots. Takes your mind off your troubles."

"I don't have any troubles. I think I'll just take in the sights."

Muriel hugged Harriet. "I know you won't believe this, but you got me thinking that maybe I can do more than ride the bus to play the slots. Maybe I can do more with my life—even if I am over seventy." She laughed.

Harriet looked into her eyes. "I know you can, Muriel. Just do it. Remember what they say: All those who wander are not lost. Although I do wonder how I'll travel next . . ."

"You just wait here," Patsy said, patting Harriet's shoulder. "The Cherokee have their own bus system. Takes you all over Maggie Valley, including the visitor's center."

"Really," Harriet said. "You mean it? How . . . wonderful."

"Yep, should be one along soon."

Muriel and Patsy headed into the casino.

"Good luck," Harriet called.

Not much later a smallish white bus, with a scene of Native Americans painted on the side, pulled up to the curb. The door opened, and several people, looking rather touristy in Harriet's estimation, got off and headed directly to the casino.

Harriet climbed the three steps inside. "Do you stop at the visitor's center?" she asked the driver. A woman with short black hair and a huge smile answered, "Yes, ma'am; welcome aboard." She wore ecru khakis and a maroon golf shirt with the Cherokee Transit insignia over the breast pocket.

Harriet fumbled with her wallet but eventually dropped a dollar into the fare box. She chose a seat by herself and enjoyed the short ride. The driver stopped just outside the Welcome Center. "Thank you very much," Harriet said on her way out of the bus. Her suitcase bumped down the two steps, landed on its side outside.

The visitor's center was a log structure set on a wooded lot. It had a gray roof and not many windows. It was warm looking and inviting. Harriet walked up the long ramp she knew was for wheelchairs. Inside, Harriet looked through the usual racks of brochures and maps, but she didn't see any that advertised stargazing. So she thought it best to ask the clerk behind the counter. She stood in a short line and counted nine other people in the center.

"Excuse me," Harriet said to the young woman behind the counter, "but this is my first visit to this part of the country, and I was told that Maggie Valley is one of the best places to go stargazing. Can you direct me to a specific place?"

"Stars?" the woman, whose name tag read Felicia, asked. She looked at Harriet like she had sprouted onions out the top of her head. "You might see a star or two down at the casino but not so many. Someone said they saw that celebrity-chef woman, Paula Dean, down there the other day, but she wasn't a hundred percent certain."

Harriet chuckled. "No, no, I don't mean celebrities. I mean real stars, the kind in the sky. You know, twinkle twinkle little star. Goodness, doesn't anybody look at the sky these days?"

"Oh," the girl said, "you mean real stars. I don't know of any place in particular, but I know a lot of people talk about how good the camping is up the mountain. Maybe you can see stars from there."

"I don't think I'm much for mountain climbing or camping," Harriet said. "I just thought there might be a nice, dark spot where I could look into the sky and see some stars. Where I come from it's a rare thing to see a lot of stars. Not like when I was a kid.

169

David Prancing Elk—I met him back in—in, oh dear, I don't even remember which town—I've been through so many, said Maggie Valley was the best place to find stars."

"Maybe someone else would have a better idea," said Felicia. "Try the Village if it was an Indian who told you to come here in the first place."

"Village?"

"The Oconaluftee Indian Village. It's not far from here."

"Thank you," Harriet said. But her heart sank. She thought for sure someone in the visitor's center would know where she could stargaze. She thought Maggie Valley would be chock-full of places where she could just sit or stand or even lie on her back on a blanket on the grass and watch the night sky.

Feeling a little disappointed Harriet left the visitor's center.

Chapter 18

HARRIET DID NOT HAVE A CLUE WHERE TO GO. THE TOWN looked friendly enough, but her aching back, the imposing dark clouds, and the evening closing in made her mood go from good to decidedly grumpy as she stood there looking at the Smoky Mountains and wondering what in the world she had done even taking the trip.

But she didn't wallow in self-pity for very long and decided her first order of business would be to find a place to stay. She walked on, pulling her suitcase, seeming to hit every pebble and crack in the walkways. She had passed several small motels on the bus ride from the casino, and if she had to, she could walk to any one of them. It might be nice to spend a night in some place more local than a fancy bed and breakfast. Still she found a bench, sat down with a thud, and sighed deeply. Her heart was set on stargazing, and now it looked like it might not happen.

Harriet opened the town map she snagged at the visitor's center. Yep, the Meadowlark Motel should be right over there, about two blocks. No problem. She pulled up the handle of her suitcase and was about to set off when a man came out of the visitor's center and approached her. He wore jeans and cowboy boots and sported a long ponytail.

"Excuse me," he said, "but are you who I think you are?"

171

Harriet jumped about a mile when he came near. "That depends. Who do you think I am?"

The man smiled. "The woman from the news. The crime-fighter YouTube sensation. You pack a mean tote bag."

Harriet sucked a deep breath and felt a little more at ease but still remained cautious. "Yes," she said and started to turn away.

Just then a woman came out of the visitor's center.

"Look, honey," the man said, "it's that woman who saved that poor woman's purse. Remember, we saw it on the news?"

The woman, who appeared only a year or two younger than the man, cracked a wide, white-toothed smile. "Harriet Beamer? You're Harriet Beamer?"

"I am." More relief washed over her.

The woman held out her hand. "It is such an honor to meet you. You're a real hero."

"Hero? Me? I wish people would stop saying that. It's embarrassing. I didn't even know what I was doing until about the third swing."

The man laughed. "Well, you are a hero. Not many women your age would take such a chance. And is the report correct — are you traveling to California?"

"I sure am. Going to live with my son and his wife. But I'm taking my time and whatever it takes — some buses, trains, taxis, a casino bus, and oh, a helicopter."

The man laughed. "That's a riot. Have you had dinner yet? Pamela and I would love for you to join us. By the way, my name is Hank."

"We sure would," Pamela said. "It'd be an honor."

"Well, I was just going to check into a motel, but I suppose I should eat dinner. My stomach is starting to rumble."

"What would you like to eat?" asked Hank. "There's several good restaurants."

"Oh, I don't know," Harriet said. "You seem to know the town pretty well?"

"You name it," Pamela said. "How about a steak? A big juicy steak. There's a great place right across the street." She pointed to a rustic-looking restaurant made from log timbers. The sign read J. ARTHUR'S.

"I think you'll enjoy it there," Pamela said. "The steaks are the best."

"Sounds good," Harriet said.

Hank took hold of Harriet's suitcase, and the three crossed the street. J. Arthur's was rustic, sort of like a log cabin with maroon awnings and a long front porch with hanging baskets of flowers. Harriet especially liked the stone fireplace chimney.

The hostess led them to a nice table, near a window. Harriet was pleased because she could gaze out at the mountains, which to her looked like a line of party hats sticking up from the horizon.

"I usually have lunch," Harriet said. "But I had a huge break-fast at my B&B, so I haven't felt hungry till now."

"Well, you just order whatever you like," Hank said. "It's our treat."

"Oh no, I can't let you pay for my meal. As a matter of fact, you've been so kind to me I'd like to pay. I am, after all, what you call a rich widow."

Pamela smiled at Frank. "Well, if you insist."

"I do."

Pamela pointed to Harriet's menu. "Have the prime rib. It's slow-roasted and succulent. Cuts like butter."

Harriet let her seeing glasses drop around her neck and slipped on her readers. "That's better. Prime rib? Sounds good. And maybe with the French fries. I love French fries."

The server, a man about forty years old with short blond hair and light-blue glasses approached their table and smiled. He spoke with the deepest Southern drawl Harriet had heard since she started her trip. He introduced himself and named the specials, but truthfully, all Harriet could understand was something about French onion soup.

After the small group ordered their meals the conversation continued. Mostly they talked about Harriet's trip and why she was doing it. She explained the best she could, but Harriet was getting a little tired of talking about it to tell the truth. It never occurred to her that she would need to tell her story so often and thought for a moment to find a way to travel incognito. And besides, that evening, she really just wanted to settle down and go star hunting. But as the meal seemed to drag into a nearly two-hour gab fest, Harriet decided she might as well relax and enjoy the company.

The check arrived after a scrumptious brownie ice cream dessert. Harriet got her credit card from her wallet and tapped it slightly on the edge of the table as she waited for the waiter to return.

Pamela put a hand to her temple. "Oh dear, Harriet," she said. "I'm getting one of my migraines. Why don't you give me your card, and I'll just go find our waiter so Hank and I can get back to the hotel and you can get to yours."

"Good idea," Hank said. He turned to Harriet. "She gets terrible headaches. Best to let her take charge when one's coming on. She'll get the bill settled, and we can go."

"Oh, but, that's fine, why don't you two just —"

But in that moment, Pamela grabbed Harriet's card and started toward the front of the restaurant. Then Hank stood. "Excuse me. I just need to use the restroom." And he headed toward the front of the restaurant.

Harriet suddenly felt like her head was spinning. Something was not right. She could feel it in her bones. Just then Harriet noticed the restrooms were in the opposite direction. Her stomach went wobbly. Her heart palpitated, and she thought for a moment she would pass out when she realized what just happened. She scrambled to her feet, knocking a glass of water to the floor with a crash.

"*Stop them,*" she hollered. "Pamela and Hank, those two. They took my credit card."

She dashed as quickly as she could, tripping on the leg of a chair and hurling herself to the ground. She lay face down and started to sob. "They got my credit card."

Several patrons rushed to her rescue and helped her up.

"Come on, sweetheart," her server said. "Sit down. Are you hurt?"

Tears poured as Harriet sat on the very chair she tripped over. "Oh dear, I am so clumsy. I was doing so well until those . . . rats stole my . . . card." She sobbed harder. "And all my money. How will I—"

"It's okay, dear," said a woman about her age. "The police are on their way, and you should call the bank and cancel your card right away."

"Yes," said the man sitting with the woman. "Call your bank immediately, and let them know what happened."

"Oh dear," Harriet said, tears still streaming down her cheeks. "All my money. It's all on the card."

Harriet looked back toward her table. "Oh dear, my tote bag. It's way over there. My phone is in it. They could spend all my money."

The manager, who introduced himself as Sandy, came by. "No, they won't," he said. "Look!"

Harriet looked up and saw three strong men, three strong Cherokee Indians walking toward her. Two of them were holding the arms of Pamela and Hank.

"These the two?" one of the men said. "We ran them down. The lady here is fast as a jackal. Had to tackle her myself."

Pamela tried to yank her arm away but couldn't.

"I told you we needed a table closer to the exit," Hank said. "Last time I let you run a job."

"Yes, that's them," Harriet said through tears. "You terrible people." Harriet fought the urge to pound Hank's chest. "You terrible, terrible people. I bet Pamela isn't even your real name."

"Oh, can it, lady," Pamela said. "You rich people think ya own the whole world, traveling around like ... like some teenager. Not a care in the world."

"I have cares," Harriet said. "And I'm sorry you have to resort to crime, committing felonies. You should be ashamed of yourselves. And after I told you all about Henry and Humphrey and my salt and pepper shakers."

The entire restaurant began to chatter and call expletives and words at the criminal couple. One of the Cherokees gave Harriet her credit card back.

"The police are on their way," Sandy said.

The three men dragged the couple out of the restaurant to a round of applause.

Harriet took a deep breath and settled back in the chair. "Phew. That was close." Her heart still raced, but the tears had stopped. "I ... I feel so ..."

"Violated?" said a woman sitting nearby. "Those people had no right."

The police arrived within a couple of minutes.

"What happened, ma'am?" asked a strikingly tall and beautiful policewoman. "Are you okay? Should we call the EMTs?"

"Oh, no, no," Harriet said. "I'm okay. Just a little shaken." And then she proceeded to tell the officers the story. They took notes, then apologized for the situation but assured Harriet that Pamela and Hank, if that was their real names, would never bother her again. She just had to sign some paperwork, leave her contact information, and her part was finished.

After the officers left, the three Cherokee men approached Harriet. "We'd like to drive you to your hotel."

"Hotel? Oh dear, I haven't even got a place for the night. Everything happened so fast. I didn't even bother to make a reservation."

"Reservation." The men laughed.

"Oh, I didn't mean—"

"We know. But why don't you come and stay with us in the village. You will be our honored guest."

"Really? You won't try and steal my credit card?"

They laughed.

"These are some good people," Sandy said. "I've known Ricky and Little Feather my whole life. They'll take good care of you."

"Okay, then," Harriet said. "Let's go."

She tucked her credit card into her wallet and zipped it up tightly in her tote. "Do you have a place I can ... freshen up in the village?" She straightened her glasses and then pulled her tote up onto her shoulders. "I must look a fright."

But just as they reached the door Harriet stopped. "Oh, I haven't paid the bill."

"No, it's taken care of," Sandy said. "You just enjoy the rest of your stay in Maggie Valley."

* * *

An hour later Harriet was sitting comfortably on a sofa that had been draped with a red and yellow wooly blanket in her new friend Ricky's home. His wife, Shawna, brought Harriet blackberry tea and gave her a pair of comfortable moccasins for her tired feet. Ricky's home felt like being inside a log cabin. He lived outside the Oconaluftee Village in a small community of mostly Cherokee.

"Henry," Harriet said into her phone. "I'm surprised I get service out here," she whispered as an aside to Shawna.

"Where are you now?" Henry asked.

"Oh, you won't believe it. I am on an Indian reservation. My new friend Ricky and his wife, Shawna, said they were going to take me sightseeing tomorrow and then someplace to see the stars."

"Stars," Henry said. "You mean like Doris Day?"

"Oh, geeze!" Harriet said. "People just don't get it. No, Henry, I mean real stars. Ricky said the Arietids meteor shower is spectacular this time of year."

"Oh, that's nice."

"Are you okay?" It was Prudence's voice.

"She must have grabbed the phone from Henry," Harriet whispered.

Prudence said, "I had a worry thought about you."

"I'm fine, Prudence. Why do you ask? Don't I sound fine?" For a second Harriet thought the events of the evening — her run-in with those two-bit criminals — might have made it out to California.

"Yes," Prudence said. "You sound okay. But I . . . I . . ."

"Oh, well, now that you bring it up, I did have a harrowing evening," Harriet said. "But really I'm safe with my new Indian friends; they really don't mind being called that here in North Carolina. I'll be on the road again in a day or so."

"What happened?" Prudence asked. "Are you hurt?"

"No, well, just a couple of bruises on my knee. I thought I was having dinner with a nice couple I met at the visitor's center, but it turned out they just wanted to steal my credit card."

"Oh no," Prudence said. "Did you call the bank?"

"Well, hold on, dear; three nice men captured them, and they're in jail now. I got my card back. So all is well."

"I'm sorry," Prudence said. "Henry was worried something like this would happen."

"Oh, he's just being a worrywart. I'm fine, and even if they did get my card, they couldn't have done much with it. Amateurs."

Prudence laughed. "Okay, Mother. But make sure you stay in touch."

"Okay. Can I speak with Henry now?"

"Oh, he can hear you," Prudence said. "I put you on speaker when you were talking about your run-in."

Harriet smiled when Shawna handed her a cup of tea. "How's Humphrey?" she said into the phone.

"He's fine," Henry said. "He misses you. But Mom, are you sure you're okay? I don't like the idea of you traveling alone, and now . . . well, now that you were mugged, maybe you should let me come get you."

178

"No, I'm fine. Maybe a little tired, but I really am having the time of my life. And that whole mugging thing was just a . . . just a speed bump on the highway of my adventure."

"Mother, leave the writing to me, and please, please call me anytime you want to be rescued."

"Oh, pish, Henry! I don't need rescuing. Now give Humphrey a scratch behind the ears for me. I'll talk to you soon."

Harriet clicked off.

"Phew. That's over."

"They love you," Ricky said.

"Oh, I know that. I just don't want them to worry." She waved her hand like she was brushing the thought away. "But I'm glad I told them before it gets on YouTube or something."

Shawna showed Harriet to her room. "The bathroom is just down the hall. Ricky already put your suitcase on the bed."

"Thank you," Harriet said. "But I was wondering, would it be too much trouble to ask to use your washer and dryer? I'm afraid that suitcase is just chock-full of dirty traveling clothes."

"Oh, certainly. Best thing about the house is that the laundry is on the second floor. No need to schlep clothes up and down steps."

"Thank you. You've been very kind."

Harriet sorted through her clothes and got a small load washing. Then she sat on the bed and wrote to Max while her clothes finished spinning. She'd make sure they were in the dryer before falling asleep.

Dear, dear Max, you will never believe where I am or what
happened to me. I am spending the night on an Indian
reservation. A real Cherokee Nation reservation with my new
friends Ricky and Shawna Blakely. They are the kindest people.
But I need to tell you something. I don't want you to worry, but
two sophisticated criminals mugged me tonight. They tried to
steal my credit card. I was so scared, but the men wrestled them
to the ground, and they're in jail now. So I'm okay. I was scared,

but I'm okay. Tomorrow we're going sightseeing and then to a place in the Blue Ridge Parkway to go stargazing. I can't wait.

Harriet stopped writing and sighed as she looked out the window.

I'll say a wish on a shooting star. But I know it can't come true. Not on earth anyway. Goodnight, honey. I love you and miss you every second of every day.

Harriet turned off the light and settled in. The bed was soft and deep and cozy, maybe a little too soft, but it felt good to be in a bed that didn't smell like a hotel or even lilacs. Ricky and Shawna's home was solid and peaceful and smelled of wood smoke and homemade jams.

Harriet rolled her wedding rings around her finger and fell asleep with the stars smiling down at her through the window.

Chapter 19

THE NEXT DAY HARRIET HAD A WONDERFUL TIME TOURING Cherokee and Maggie Valley with her new friends. They stopped at nearly every little curiosity shop, and much to Harriet's delight she was able to purchase several salt and pepper shakers, most with a Native American theme — drums, teepees, an Indian chief and his wife kissing. She bought others that were more reminiscent of the Smoky Mountains — a wooden pair with a decal that read: THE GREAT SMOKY MOUNTAINS, trees, and bunnies. She sent them off to Prudence from the Cherokee Welcome Center.

"But I can hardly wait to see the Salt and Pepper Shaker Museum in Gatlinburg," she told Shawna. "I never would have believed such a place existed. But it does. And I'll be the only one in my club chapter to see it."

The three friends walked farther down the main drag. "I never knew there was such a place," Ricky said.

"I did," Shawna said. "It's just over the mountains. Near the winery."

"Really?" Ricky said. "That's kind of cool. Well, you can visit it tomorrow."

Harriet sighed. "If I can figure out how in the heck to get over the mountains."

For lunch Ricky suggested a local hamburger joint, where they discussed the next leg of Harriet's journey: the Salt and Pepper Shaker Museum.

"But how in heaven's name will I get over the mountains to Gatlinburg?" she asked Ricky. "It never occurred to me there'd be mountains to climb on this trip." Harriet could hardly look at her menu with thoughts of the mountains in her mind.

"There's always mountains to climb," Ricky said, "and you have nothing to worry about. The Eastern Band of the Cherokee Nation has their own public transit system. They'll get you into Gatlinburg."

Harriet was elated. "Yes, I think I rode on one of their buses after I got off the casino bus at Harrah's."

"That's right," Ricky said.

"You mean they'll get me over the Smoky Mountains?" Harriet sucked Coke through a straw.

"No problem," Ricky said. "It's only about an hour or so ride and they even stop at one of the lookouts so you can take pictures of the view over the Smoky Mountains. Quite a sight."

"Really?" Harriet was amazed. "I can't believe it. I thought it would be a lot harder to get clear across the country just taking whatever local transportation I could find. But who would have thought the Cherokee Indians would have their own buses? Wait till I tell Martha."

After lunch the three new friends wandered around Cherokee, where Harriet got to see an actual tribal dance. She especially loved the sounds of the drums and the colors. Even the small children participated, and Harriet enjoyed that most of all.

But it was the evening that brought the most happiness to Harriet. She rode with Ricky and Shawna along the Blue Ridge Parkway as the sun headed toward the western mountains. Even in Ricky's pickup truck the ride was gentle and peaceful as they climbed the Smokies.

"Where're we headed?" Harriet asked about twenty minutes into the ride.

"A spectacular place called Craggy Gardens."

"Craggy Gardens? What a funny name."

"It's a beautiful spot," Shawna said. "We'll stop at the visitor's center first, and then it's an easy hike—"

"Hike?" Harriet said. "Oh dear me, I didn't know we'd have to hike."

"It's easy," Ricky said. "One of the easiest in the mountains. We'll stop at the grassy summit."

"Will we see stars?"

"Millions of them," Shawna said. "Star trails this time of year."

Ricky parked the truck near the visitor's center and after a quick bathroom break the three set out down a well-marked, well-lit path lined with rhododendrons that were just beginning to bloom.

"It is gorgeous," Harriet said. She almost felt overwhelmed. "I never even thought I would see such a place. And here I am as old as I am, hiking like a twenty-year-old kid. Just hope this old ticker can take it."

"Oh," Shawna said. "Is there a problem?"

Harriet took another two steps. "Oh, no. I'm fit as a fiddle."

The grassy summit was wide and green. Ricky set out a large woven blanket. Shawna opened her backpack and set out containers of fresh fruit—watermelon, honeydew, blueberries, nuts, and a large loaf of bread with cheese.

Harriet sat on the blanket and breathed deeply. "The air is thin up here. My head feels a little funny."

Shawna handed her a water bottle. "Keep drinking. Best thing for the elevation, and eat something also."

* * *

Soon Harriet was enjoying the sunset over the Smoky Mountains. Ribbons of gold, yellow, orange, and purple stretched as far as she could see and reminded Harriet of a Jell-O parfait. The sky turned black quickly, and before she knew it the stars blinked into place. Harriet had never seen a sky so big.

"It goes on forever," she said. "I've never seen so many stars, like billions of pinpricks in a velvet fabric."

"Keep watching," Ricky said. "It's early yet, but we might catch a meteor shower."

Harriet swooned at the notion of witnessing meteors cutting their paths toward the earth.

"Did you know the Bible says that God calls each star by name and sets them in their place every night?" Harriet said.

Ricky leaned back as though he were catching moon rays. "I know. Isn't that incredible. To think that God knows each and every star. How is that even possible?"

Harriet looked out at the star field. "All things are possible with God."

It didn't take long before a couple white, dusty streaks shot across the dome of the sky, seeming to come from the horizon and streak the sky like chalk.

"Oh my goodness," Harriet said. "David Prancing Elk was right, I have never seen anything more beautiful than this. The sky is so dark it's almost purple, the meteors are so fast and bright it's like ... like I'm really on a planet, spinning through space. I hope there are more."

But then, as a few wispy clouds floated past, Harriet thought she could see Max's face. He was smiling. She swiped at tears and smiled as the meteors rained down.

"Are you crying?" Shawna asked.

Harriet sat up. "Oh, it's ... it's just so spectacular. And I just can't help but think about my Max. I miss him so much, but I think these stars might have just blinked his blessing on me and my little adventure." She wiped her eyes and blew her nose.

Chapter 20

THE NEXT MORNING HARRIET DECIDED IT WAS TIME TO
leave Maggie Valley. She packed her suitcase. The stone martens
were a little bulky, but she managed to squeeze them inside. She
loved it here and told Ricky and Shawna she'd like to come for a
real vacation someday. But it was time to move on.

"I really want to get to the museum. I'm so excited."

"Our door is always open," Shawna said. But then she laughed
and pointed at Harriet's suitcase. "Your luggage has a tail."

Harriet looked down and sure enough one the marten tails was
sticking out. She shrugged. "Maybe I should leave it and see if
anyone else notices."

Ricky drove her to the visitor's center.

There were about a dozen people already waiting for the bus
when Harriet arrived, most of them tourists on their way to Gatlinburg. None of them seemed to pay her much attention. Which
was fine with her. She was just as glad not to be recognized as the
Old Lady Avenger. After all, there were better things in life to be
remembered for than beating up a thug.

The bus pulled up, and Harriet said good-bye to Ricky and
Shawna.

"Thank you," she said. "This has been the best part of my trip
so far."

Ricky smiled into her eyes. "May the warm winds of heaven blow softly on your home," he said, holding both of Harriet's hands and looking deep in her eyes.

"And may the Good Lord make his face to shine upon you," Harriet said.

Ricky kissed her cheek first, and then Shawna. Harriet climbed aboard the bus.

"Hi," she said, recognizing that the driver was the same one from before. Harriet found a window seat toward the middle of the small bus. She managed to tuck both her tote and her suitcase in front of her. Seconds later, a large woman flopped down next to her and let go a groan. Harriet smiled and then looked out the window.

The bus traveled along the Blue Ridge Parkway climbing, climbing the mountains. Harriet enjoyed the view until her stomach started to feel a little wobbly.

"Oh, goodness," Harriet said, "but I'm feeling a little funny."

Fortunately, the woman sitting next to her offered her a bottled water, also a product of the Cherokee Nation.

"It's the altitude, honey," the woman said. "You'll get used to it. When we stop at five thousand feet you can get out and throw up if you havta. You do look a mite green around the gills."

"Throw up? I ... I don't think so." Harriet sipped the water and prayed she wouldn't vomit. "I felt this way last night but it passed."

"Good, you'll be fine. Just keep hydrated."

Harriet smiled and gazed out the window. The view transcended anything she ever imagined.

The woman offered Harriet her hand. "Name's Delores."

Harriet nodded. "Nice to meet you. I'm Harriet Beamer."

At five thousand feet the driver pulled into a parking area and announced that they were now at Newfound Gap and the passengers could get out and enjoy the view.

Harriet was the last one off the bus as she prayed her stomach would settle. Her legs were wobbly, and for a moment she felt concerned she might pass out. But she didn't. She locked her knees and looked out at the mountains. They were so high they were in the clouds. An experience Harriet had no idea she would ever witness.

"It takes my breath away," Harriet said.

"Long as it didn't take your lunch away," said her seatmate. "Some folks really do throw up along the way. But they are just so eager to get to Gatlinburg. Most are on their way to Dollywood, you know, the Dolly Parton amusement park. Not me, I just go for the ride. Never get tired of the view. I prefer to spend my money at the casino. How 'bout you, honey?"

Harriet swallowed and tried to answer, but frankly, she was a bundle of nerves and really wanted to get off the mountain. She could hardly speak.

"Huh, what's the matter, dearie? You scared or something?"

Harriet nodded and then sipped her water.

"Ha, you're too young to be scared of a little height. The Great Spirit, he'll watch over you. Always does for me. We'll be on the other side in about thirty minutes."

"Thank you," Harriet said. "I'm on my way to the Salt and Pepper Shaker Museum."

"Wee doggies, really? You really want to see that place?"

"Yep."

"Then prepare to leave in a daze, dearie. I went in there once —awhile ago. Out of curiosity. It's pretty boring if you ask me. I mean, why would anyone be that interested in salt and pepper shakers? It's stupid."

"Oh, I'm sure I'll enjoy it. I'm a collector. It's a pretty big hobby."

The woman sputtered something Harriet couldn't make out.

About half an hour later the bus rolled into Gatlinburg. It stopped at the third stoplight in town, and Harriet had never been so happy to get on solid ground. Even the helicopter ride was easier than that bus ride over the mountains.

187

"I just don't get it," she said to Dolores. "It never occurred to me I would be afraid of the mountains. I wasn't the other night when we went to Craggy Gardens."

"Craggy Gardens. That is weird; it's higher than the lookout. Craggy Gardens, dearie. That's a long way."

"I suppose. I think maybe I'll just find a spot to sit. Maybe it was because I was in a car or it was night and I just didn't notice it."

"Or you're just getting sick," Delores said. "See you on the return trip, maybe. And hey, sorry about the crack I made — about the salt and pepper shakers."

Harriet shook her head as her brain started to clear. "Don't worry. Not everyone understands about shakers. And no, I'm not going back. I'm on my way to California."

"California?" Delores laughed. Her voice was like crinkled cellophane. "You sure are getting there the hard way. What'd you do? Lose a bet?"

Harriet laughed as best she could. "Yep. Lost a bet."

* * *

At the Gatlinburg Welcome Center, Harriet learned she could take the trolley just about anywhere in downtown Gatlinburg and Pigeon Forge. She could even trolley out to the Salt and Pepper Shaker Museum. But the trolley was nothing like what she expected. Back home the trolleys ran on rails, not wheels.

When the trolley pulled up at her stop she felt elated. It was the cutest darn thing she had ever seen, reminding her of Mister Rogers' Neighborhood Trolley. The trolley was gorgeous and shiny and clean, red on the bottom, beige in the middle where the arched windows were, and with a green roof. She thought the trolleys kind of accented the mountain backdrop. She climbed aboard, paid her quarter, and off she went toward Brookside Boulevard and the Salt and Pepper Shaker Museum.

Fortunately, her stomach settled down after she drank a Coke. At the next stop a woman boarded and plopped down next to her.

"Hi," Harriet said.

The woman chose to ignore her, and that was okay. Harriet was more interested in taking in the sights of the adorable town. It was like stepping into a new world, so quaint and easygoing. Not anything like Philadelphia or Baltimore or even Winston-Salem. She thought about calling Martha, but her stop was just a few minutes away.

"I'm going to the Salt and Pepper Shaker Museum," she said after the silence got to be too much.

Still, the woman only grunted and turned away. Then she got off at the next stop without so much as a glance in Harriet's direction.

"Oh, well, not everybody can be hospitable. Probably a local who doesn't like us tourists invading her town."

Harriet's trolley stopped only a few hundred yards from the museum, an easy walk, and fortunately, the weather was nice for mid-June. She was getting a little weary of dragging her suitcase everywhere she went, but she had no choice; so, giving it a hearty tug, off she went toward Nirvana—The Salt and Pepper Shaker Museum. The air smelled clean and fresh like a million dryer sheets were wafting in the low winds. She could still see the mountains in the distance, and it made her feel like she was in a bowl of some sorts, contained by hills. That made her feel secure.

And then she saw it—her own private heaven, the Graceland of shakers. The mother lode.

For a minute she just stood outside the museum and breathed deeply, almost too excited to go in. She had no idea what wonders of salt-and-pepper-shaker design awaited her. That was when she noticed that her suitcase still had its tail. "Why not," she said. Harriet unzipped the case and retrieved the stone martens, which she draped around her shoulders, making her feel rather regal and fancy. "Only the best for a visit to the museum."

She entered the rustic building and was immediately smitten. She could hardly catch her breath. Rows and rows and rows of salt and pepper shakers. Most of them were inside glass display cases with lights inside—all set against dark walls. She walked slowly and took in the sights. She saw old and new, wooden and plastic, novelty and golden shakers from Italy. She saw the biggest pepper mill, which was forty-eight inches tall, as well as the tiniest salt shaker, which measured about a half an inch and was crafted from silver.

But of the twenty thousand sets displayed, Harriet most enjoyed the whimsical ones. She saw nodders, which made her laugh—the kind that bobbed back and forth in their holder. She held a plastic lawn mower from the fifties, which you could push to make the shakers move up and down like pistons. There were bench sitters and kissers, holiday and celebrity shakers. She couldn't decide on a favorite. There was no need. Harriet could love them all. But the real thrill came when she met Andrea, the owner, who told Harriet all about her collection that started from a single pepper mill.

As it turned out, Andrea was an archaeologist who told Harriet that salt and pepper shakers made an excellent anthropological statement.

"You can really learn a lot about the culture of the time," she said, "by the characters, the shapes, the materials used. Salt and pepper shakers tell a story."

"That's what I keep telling people," Harriet said, delighted that she had finally met someone of like mind. "A thousand years from now when someone unearths a Mickey Mouse salt shaker they'll know what was important to us."

Andrea patted Harriet on the shoulder. "Always nice to meet an enthusiast."

Harriet needed to catch her breath again.

"I like to think of them as a little bit of sculpture on everyone's dinner table."

Andrea smiled. "Yes. Yes."

"I have about three thousand in my collection," Harriet said.

"I shipped them to California. Maybe I should start a museum in Grass Valley."

"That would be terrific," Andrea said.

"And I am a past president of Shake It Up, one of the largest salt-and-pepper-shaker clubs in Pennsylvania. Wait until I tell them."

Harriet walked through the exhibit seven more times. But before she left she was sure to purchase a few sets as souvenirs of her most amazing day. She bought ten — a nice number.

"Now, I better get these sent straightaway," she said. Harriet managed to cram her bundle into her tote bag.

* * *

Henry and Humphrey were just about to leave for a late morning walk when the mail truck pulled up to the curb.

"Got a package for you, Henry," called June, the postal carrier.

"Oh, good," Henry said, taking the package. "This one's from Hickory, North Carolina. Probably more salt and pepper shakers from my mom."

"Salt and pepper shakers?" June said. "Why the fascination?"

"I don't know," Henry said, "but my mother has been obsessed with them for . . . for as long as I can remember. Now she's collecting them from all over the country. Everywhere she stops. She's on a trip right now."

"Really, that's fantastic. Wish my mother would do something like that. She just sits around our house all day and complains or argues with my father."

"Oh dear," Henry said, holding the package under his arm. "When you think about it, I guess salt and pepper shakers aren't so bad. She's on her way to live with us."

"At least she has a hobby. Believe me, you'll be happy she's still out there doing stuff, you know, involved in life, not just sitting on the porch waiting to die."

"Thanks," Henry said. "See you later."

He waved as the truck moved down the street.

"How many salt and pepper shakers can one woman collect?" he asked Humphrey. "But I suppose the driver is right. It's better she's happy." He opened the garage and stared at the boxes, not only of salt and pepper shakers but also some books and household furnishings and clothes — mostly winter stuff Harriet had sent ahead. Dozens of them in all sizes and shapes taking up Prudence's parking spot.

"But then again, we might have to make a change. Store these things somewhere else."

Humphrey howled. Then he lay down and yawned.

* * *

Harriet clambered aboard the trolley with her treasures and a full and satisfied heart after her visit to the museum.

"Can you let me off near a UPS place or a post office?" she asked the driver.

"Sure thing," the woman driver said. "Final stop, the Welcome Center. They have a post office inside."

"That's great." Harriet sat on the seat and yawned. "Seems the trip is catching up with me," she said to the man next to her. He had the window seat.

He only nodded.

"I just came from the Salt and Pepper Shaker Museum. Thought I'd died and gone to heaven. My goodness, almost twenty thousand sets there; 'course some were singles, but still, can you imagine that many salt and pepper shakers in one place? Wait till I tell my club members. I bought a few."

Harriet was tired but knew she still had a long way to go. She also knew it was time she checked in with Henry and Martha. So she made plans that right after she mailed her package she'd find a coffee shop, take a rest, and make her calls. After that she would have to figure out her next destination. She hadn't needed Amelia in a little while, but now she had the awful feeling she was on her own again.

The man at the Welcome Center post office was very nice and helped Harriet pack her shakers in bubble wrap. "They'll be nice and snug," he said. She insured them just in case. After all, Harriet had finally seen the museum. "I don't know why, but these ones are more ... more important than all the others."

On her way to find a restaurant, Harriet wandered into a shop. It had many souvenirs—even shakers, but for the first time in her life, she wasn't interested. Instead, her eyes fell on something else. A line of baby articles and clothing. She couldn't help herself and went to investigate. Her favorite item was a small yellow bib with a silhouette of the Smoky Mountains. Under it were the words "My Nana Climbed a Mountain for Me," embroidered in green thread.

Harriet's heart sped. "It's perfect. I have to purchase this. I ... I'll just give it to them when the time is right."

* * *

Harriet mostly enjoyed her lunch, a salad and a hamburger at a little joint called Bunny's Luncheonette. It was quaint and old-fashioned, with a counter and spinny stools bolted to a black and white checkered linoleum floor. She sat at a booth, Formica with a little personal-size juke box attached to it. She thought that was just swell but was too tired to play music and was thinking it might be a good idea to spend the night in Gatlinburg.

Her waitress, a short bleached blonde with ten pounds of eye makeup, dropped the check on her table.

"Excuse me," Harriet said. "But ... I was wondering if you might be able to suggest a nice motel or a B&B for the night."

The waitress crossed her arms and looked disgustedly at Harriet.

"There's the Wander Inn not too far from here, but I wouldn't recommend it. Heard they got a case of bed bugs."

Harriet winced. "Ew. No thank you."

The waitress tapped her pencil on her order pad. "I heard some folks in here talkin' the other day 'bout Carr's Cottages. They seemed to like it well enough."

"Carr's Cottages. It sounds nice. Do you know how I can get there?"

The server looked at Harriet and started to laugh. "Honey. I just take orders. I am not no GPS."

"Oh, I'm sorry. I just thought—"

"Nope. But someone else might know."

Harriet snapped her fingers. "Amelia. She'll tell me." Harriet rooted around in her tote for her phone.

"You ain't gonna tell me you got Amelia in that bag, are you?"

"Actually, yes, I do." She pulled out the phone. "My GPS. She'll tell me."

Chapter 21

AND AMELIA DID — FIGURE IT OUT, THAT IS. THE PIGEON Forge Trolley got her within walking distance of Carr's Northside Cottages and Motel. Nestled within a scenic view of trees and a creek, the motel was a lovely two-level building. Harriet was able to get a room on the first floor, which made her happy since the only way to the second level of rooms was via steps, and she just wasn't up for climbing stairs. Her room had one queen-size bed and opened out into a rustic backyard.

"It's perfect," she said as she flopped onto the bed. "Peaceful." But since she still owed Henry a call she tapped his number and said, "Hello, Son."

"Mom. Where are you now? We've been worried. We just heard about that incident with the purse thief. How come you didn't tell us?"

"Oh dear," Harriet said. "I was hoping you wouldn't find out."

"Of course we did. Those kinds of stories often make the news. An old ... older woman taking down a thug. It's priceless. People love it. I just never thought my own mother would be one of the ... older women." Henry sounded a bit frantic. "I watched the YouTube a couple of times. Mom, you know you could have gotten hurt."

Harriet sighed. "I know that ... now. But at the time I didn't think. I acted. I'm just glad that kid didn't have a gun — and Henry, he was just a kid. I hope he gets help. I pray for him now."

They were both silent a moment.

"You know what, Mom? I'm kind of proud of you," Henry said. "I'm not saying I condone what you did, but you still got spunk. It made me remember the time you went to school and let Mrs. Stark have it for accusing me of cheating. You never did take any guff."

"You were innocent, Son. I had to back you up. Just like I am now."

"What do you mean?"

"I . . . I want to tell you that I'm proud of you being a writer and helping Prudence follow her dreams even if . . . it doesn't include grandchildren."

Harriet could hear Henry take a deep breath.

"Henry?"

"I'm here, Mom. It's just . . . just . . . oh, nothing. I want to help you achieve your dream—even if all I can do is hang on to the other end of the phone."

"That's plenty. But I hardly call seeing the Salt and Pepper Shaker Museum a dream."

"But it is. And you did that. What's next?"

Harriet thought a second or two. "I don't know. A woman my age shouldn't have too many dreams—"

"Nonsense. You're not too old to have dreams."

"And besides, you and Prudence aren't interested in—"

"Mom. Let's not go there."

"You're right. Well, I best be going, Son. I love you, and I really am looking forward to seeing you—now."

That was when she remembered she wanted to call Martha, but the giant yawn that bubbled up inside of her made her forget about it for the moment.

* * *

Harriet locked her phone screen but unlocked it just a second later. She needed to figure out her next destination. According to the map, it seemed to make sense for her to reach Saint Louis where she could grab a train for a long bit of the trip. But fortunately there were a lot of miles between Pigeon Forge and Saint Louis. She still had plenty of places yet to discover, and that, after all, was the point of the trip. Saint Louis would still be there in a day or two. Henry and Prudence would still be waiting. And Humphrey would still enjoy a glazed donut from time to time. Amelia routed her from the Gatlinburg/Pigeon Forge area into Knoxville and from there into Nashville.

Harriet sighed. Nashville. She was never what you would call a fan of country music, but the idea of visiting the Grand Ole Opry excited her. She had been hearing about it ever since she was young. She especially remembered seeing television specials with Minnie Pearl, the woman with the funny straw hat with the white tag displaying the price of $1.98 dangling off the brim.

"Minnie always said, 'How-w-w-dee!'" Harriet spoke the words aloud, forgetting for a second that Humphrey wasn't there to talk to.

That afternoon she found a nice restaurant called the Whole Earth Grocery Café nearby. It was a vegetarian place. Harriet enjoyed a nice cheeseburger from time to time, but thought it might be kind of interesting to eat vegetarian for a change—long as there weren't any tomatoes. Harriet hated tomatoes, although she didn't mind tomato sauce.

The small café was a combination grocery store and eatery. She found it delightful and sat at one of the round tables in the front of the establishment.

She ordered the Veggie Wrap and enjoyed it very much, although—and she would never tell the waitress—she still preferred burgers.

* * *

After a restful night at Carr's, Harriet decided to tackle the next leg of her journey. She spoke with a man named Houston she met on the motel porch. They sat together on the porch in the warm mountain air. Houston said he was a businessman visiting from Texas. Harriet made certain not to chuckle at the irony.

"That's right," he said, "I drive nearly 50,000 miles a year."

"No kidding," Harriet said. "Well, I don't need to get that far. I just need to find my way to Knoxville, and I'm finding that a little difficult."

Houston scratched under his hat. "Well, seems to me, you might be in a pickle. No public transportation that I know of gonna take you that far."

Harriet's spirits sank. "There must be a way. A shuttle bus or a ..."

"I know," Houston said. "A pretty woman like yourself should ride in luxury. Why not hire a limousine service. It's not even an hour's drive to Knoxville from here, straight up Route 441. Shouldn't be a problem."

"You mean one of them long cars with the TVs and wet bars inside?"

"I sure do, ma'am. I'm certain the proprietor of this fine establishment will be able to help you find a car."

* * *

Around noon that day, a long, shiny black limousine pulled up in front of the hotel. Harriet nearly swooned when she saw a tall, dashing young man step out of the driver's side. He wore a well-pressed black suit, bright white shirt, and red bow tie. He stood near the door and held a sign that read "HARRIET BEAMER" in big black letters.

"Oh my goodness gracious, I feel like a celebrity," Harriet said. She waved to the driver.

Houston waited with Harriet until the driver approached. "Ready, ma'am? Is this your bag?"

Harriet couldn't contain a nervous giggle. "Why, why, yes, young man. It is."

198

The driver looked at Houston. "Will you be joining us, Mr. Pike?"

Houston touched the rim of his hat. "No, sir. But you take good care of this little lady. She's a personal friend of mine. You drive real nice and slow."

Harriet looked up at Houston. "Now how does he know your name?"

The driver took hold of Harriet's suitcase. Lifted it like it was made from paper maché.

"Everybody knows Houston Pike," said the driver. "He's one of the richest men in the country."

"Well, thump my gums, you didn't tell me."

Houston smiled. "This ride is my gift. And like I said—" He looked at the driver—"nice and easy wins the race."

"Yes, sir."

Then Houston handed the driver a wad of money.

Harriet rode off in style toward Knoxville, Tennessee.

* * *

Houston was, of course, correct. It was a pretty short trip into Knoxville. Harriet enjoyed the comfortable limo even if the driver was pretty much silent the whole way. It gave her an opportunity to write to Max.

My Dear Max, I am writing from a limousine. I've never been inside a car like this—not even at a funeral. You know we chose to ride in our own cars the day we buried you. Anyhoo, I will admit that I'm starting to feel a tad weary, must be all the excitement. But I'm not ready to call it quits—not by a long shot. I set out to see the country, buy some new shakers for my collection, and arrive in Grass Valley on my own terms. I figure that might be a way to show Henry and Prudence that I don't need to be put out to pasture just yet.

Harriet looked out the tinted windows at the scenery rushing past. It was hard to make out much more than trees and telephone poles. She went back to her letter.

> *Have I told you lately how proud I am of Henry? Oh, I was pretty ticked when he wanted to quit Beamer's Beams and Buildings, but now it's okay. We raised a writer, Max. A man of letters.*

Then she drew a little smiley face.

She also consulted Amelia and instructed the driver to take her to the Knoxville Greyhound bus terminal. She'd catch a bus to Nashville from there. It would be her first Greyhound, even though she had hoped she wouldn't have to resort to that. But if Harriet learned anything on her journey it was that sometimes the road of life throws you a curve you weren't expecting.

Kyle, the limo driver, pulled up in front of the bus station, and Harriet had to admit, as he helped her bring her bag inside, it was not the prettiest place on earth . . . and nothing like the spectacular train stations she had visited.

But she also learned that the next bus to Nashville didn't leave until 5:30 that afternoon.

"Oh dear, Kyle," she said. "What does a person do in Knoxville, Tennessee, for five hours?"

Kyle shrugged. "I don't know, Ma'am, maybe get some lunch, read a book. How about visiting a museum?"

Harriet looked around. She didn't see any museums right off.

"Thank you, Kyle," she said. "I'm sure Amelia will help me find some attractions." But actually Harriet didn't want Kyle to leave. Her stomach wobbled a bit with nerves. It was nothing she could put her finger on, but for some reason this day, being alone in a strange city for five hours made her anxious. She had never wished so hard that Humphrey was by her side.

Harriet watched Kyle pull away from the curb. He honked the horn and waved from the window. And there she stood in her red high-tops and blue denim jeans, wearing her stone martens and clutching her flowery tote like it was a life preserver.

Harriet took a deep breath, checked her Greyhound ticket again to be certain she was right about the time, and set off down the street with a big sigh. But a couple of blocks down the road she spotted one of the most interesting buildings she had seen in her travels. It stood on the corner and was kind of an eclectic mish-mash of architectural styles—Queen Anne Victorian but with a splash of Gothic Revival and Romanesque. She rested a moment and looked at it. PATRICK SULLIVAN'S SALOON. She liked the turret and dome and the red and yellow colors, and decided she had to go inside.

And that was no disappointment, although it was dark and subdued. But then again it was a saloon and, as she found out from a waiter, a onetime brothel and meeting place for characters like Billy the Kid.

Harriet ordered lunch and coffee and spent the better part of two hours in the saloon. She read Jane Austen and wrote to Max. She called Martha, who wasn't home, and tried to wait out the time before her bus.

She wandered around Knoxville, being certain to keep close to the bus station, so when it was finally time to leave, she was more than ready to get on board. The time spent was pleasant enough. At 5:30 Harriet boarded what she figured might have been a newer bus, with comfortable seats and video monitors. And the best part? Her luggage had a place in an actual luggage compartment, not at her feet or over her head. Although she did keep her tote bag with her.

The ride from Knoxville to Nashville took almost four hours thanks to some traffic woes, so Harriet didn't arrive until close to 11:00 that night. Fortunately, she consulted Amelia along the way and located a hotel very close to the terminal. She also arranged for a cab to pick her up on account of the late hour. So when the bus pulled into the station, which was little more that a one-level bright

201

blue building in the center of a parking lot, Harriet felt relieved to see the taxi parked and waiting to take her to the Best Western.

* * *

As she entered the room, she said, "Oh, this is lovely," to the young man from the front counter, who had offered to carry her luggage. He placed her suitcase on a small table. "Just right for me."

Harriet yawned and stretched. Her neck had developed a crick on the bus ride, and all she wanted to do was sleep. So she plugged in her phone, changed into her jammies, and made a mental note to find a washing machine in the morning. No clean socks. But she was so plum tuckered out that she fell fast asleep thinking about visiting the Grand Ole Opry in the morning.

But Harriet slept and slept and slept like a rock. As a matter of fact, she slept nearly the entire day away and never made it to the Opry. She woke once or twice before lunch to use the bathroom, but the thought of finding her way to the Opry was too much. She was exhausted from traveling, she figured, and ended up sleeping the day away. Not even a phone call to Henry or Martha until she was set to embark on the next leg of her journey.

"Martha," she said as she zipped her suitcase. Harriet had discovered the speaker button on her hotel-room phone. "I tried to call yesterday but you weren't home."

"Oh, yes, well, I had to see the doctor."

"Doctor? Are you okay?"

"I think so. You know doctors, always wanting to take tests."

"Tests? For what?"

"It's nothing. Just some blood work."

Harriet took the phone off speaker and brought it to her ear. "Now you'd tell me if something is really wrong, right?"

There was a short lull in the conversation. "Yes, of course. Now tell me where you are and where you're headed."

"I'm in Nashville and—"

"The Grand Ole Opry. I've always wanted to visit."

"I never made it. I was just so dang tired I slept nearly the whole day away. I'm getting set to leave town now."

"You slept through your visit to Nashville?"

"I did. But that's okay. I feel so much better now that I've had the rest."

"So what's your next stop?"

"I want to get into Kentucky today and it's already nearly 1:30. Amelia is taking me through Saint Louis. I could probably bus the whole way, but I think I'll make a stop or two. I'd like to see some of that Kentucky blue grass more close up."

After saying good-bye to Martha, Harriet did something she had only thought about. She closed her eyes and pointed to the map of Kentucky as it was displayed on her phone and said, "Wherever my finger lands, that's where I'll go."

She opened her eyes, and the closest town to the tip of her index finger was Hopkinsville, Kentucky. "Sounds good to me." The only problem was that there was no mass transit that would get her there, even though it was only about seventy miles away. Fortunately the hotel desk clerk was able to arrange an airport shuttle bus to pick her up and drop her off at the Best Western in Hopkinsville.

The ride to Hopkinsville, Kentucky, reminded her of Pennsylvania in many ways with its lush green lawns and rolling hills dotted with clumps of trees and azaleas. Harriet loved to watch the azaleas bloom in the springtime. And seeing them here made her miss her old house.

* * *

After saying good-bye to the shuttle driver — she never did get his name — Harriet had an urge for pie. Even though her stomach grumbled, she wasn't really hungry for lunch — just pie. Harriet toted her stuff down the street until she found a coffee shop called Aunt Fran's. It was small and cute and full of gingham, red and white checked. A tall, skinny woman who introduced herself as

Bunny brought her to her seat. A small table in the middle of the room with an unlit votive candle in the center.

"Excuse me a second," Bunny said, "but how come you look familiar to me?"

Harriet shook her head and sat down with her suitcase tucked next to her. She plopped her tote bag on the empty seat next to her.

"That tote," the waitress said. "I know I seen it somewhere. I always notice fashions and such seeing how my daughter, Ginger, is working in fashion. But I got to say that bag don't look like it just walked off the pages of *Vogue* magazine."

Harriet felt her eyebrows lift. "Coffee would be great." She glanced at her bag. "It's nice enough for travel."

That was when the waitress snapped her fingers. "That's where I'd seen you b'fore, honey. You're that woman that beat up that punk. The one taking the trip across America. You clocked that punk but good with that bag. I like to watch them YouTube videos. Better than TV."

The waitress called toward the kitchen. "Hey, Marty. We got us a celebrity right here at Aunt Fran's Pie Shop."

Harriet felt all the eyes in the little shop turn toward her.

"You go, girl," called someone from the back of the restaurant.

"I wouldn't want to tangle with you," said another voice.

Harriet felt her face warm. "Please. I just came in for pie."

"Oh, yeah," her server said. "Let me get your coffee, and I'll tell you what—coffee—all you can drink—it's on the house."

"Thank you," Harriet said, looking at the menu.

"Can we get a picture?" asked a woman who was walking toward her, leading a teenager with ponytails and braces. Harriet assumed she was the woman's daughter. The girl looked completely mortified.

"Only if your daughter really wants one," Harriet said.

"Now, don't you worry about Juliet. She always looks like that, all sourpussed and wrinkled. It's the age."

Harriet looked into Juliet's eyes. "Do you want your picture taken, Sweetie?"

Juliet shook her head.

"Then how 'bout if we take one with just your mama? You take it okay?"

That seemed all right. Juliet took the camera from her mother and snapped some shots. First with Juliet's mother and then with Harriet and practically everyone in the shop.

"Don't you just love those cameras they stick in phones?" Bunny said. "Can do practically anything with the shots. But mostly they sit inside my phone till I delete them."

Harriet winked at Juliet.

After the impromptu photo session Harriet returned to her seat. "And do you have pie?"

"Do we have pie?" the waitress said. "Hey Marty, do we have pie?"

Harriet heard a boisterous laugh.

"Honey," Bunny said, "you're in Aunt Fran's. Nobody does pie like Fran."

"Oh, good. I have been dying for a slice of rhubarb pie."

"Comin' up." Bunny elbowed Harriet's shoulder.

It didn't take long for her pie and meal to arrive. Harriet was hungry. The sandwich was homey and good, the coffee strong. She got up for just a minute to use the restroom. When she returned she found a second slice of rhubarb pie at her place.

"That's on Aunt Fran," Bunny said. "She's in the back and shyer than a groundhog in December. She's so old she went to the prom with Moses and as ornery as a mule."

Harriet smiled. There was something appealing about being a kind of minor celebrity. And Harriet liked the little coffee shop well enough that she took her time and basked in the hospitality of the owners and patrons. But when she saw what she thought was a local news station truck pull up outside, she wondered if she should make tracks or not.

But there wasn't time. Before she knew it, a reporter carrying a microphone with a long thick cord that reached clear back to the news van approached her.

"Harriet Beamer," the reporter said, "my name is Tracy Endicott with the local news station. Bunny called and told us you were here. Mind if we ask a few questions?"

Harriet wiped her lips with the pretty pink paper napkin she held on her lap. "I guess not."

"It's not often we get celebrities through town, and I thought folks might like to see how you're doing and how your trip is coming along. How does it feel?"

"Oh, it feels okay," Harriet said as she wiped rhubarb from her shirt. "But really, I'm not so important. I'm just taking a little trip."

"Little?" Bunny called. "You're traveling clear 'cross the country. Know how many women wish they had the guts to just up and run like you?"

"But that's just it. I'm not running," Harriet said. "I thought I was running by taking the slow route, but now I know I'm on my way to do just what God wants me to do."

Tracy smiled and signaled to Bunny to refrain from blurting out anymore. Bunny went back to wiping tables. But Harriet could see her listening in. It was fine with Harriet.

"But most of all," Harriet said, "I like meeting so many dear folks, like Bunny." The cameraman swung his camera in her direction. Harriet thought Bunny would absolutely die from excitement. She pulled herself up, stuck her rather ample bosom out, pushed a free hand through her long orange hair, and smiled into the camera like she was movie star.

"Will this be on the news this evening?" Harriet asked.

"It sure will," Tracy said. "And on the AP wire. It'll be all over the country by morning."

"And YouTube by afternoon," Bunny said.

"Oh dear, not another YouTube."

"What's your next stop?" Tracy asked.

"I'm not sure; Amelia, my GPS, has me routed through to Saint Louis, but I might make a stop here or there, or I should say *from* here to there in one conveyance or another."

That was when a big, burly man, wearing a sleeveless denim jacket over a long-sleeved shirt with a picture of a motorcycle on it, approached Harriet.

"Hey, lady," he said.

He was quickly followed by a woman wearing a leather jacket. "Have some manners, Snake."

"Pardon us, ma'am," she said, "but we couldn't help overhear you with that reporter and all. Well, ma'am, we'd love for you to ride with us. Can take you as far as Collinsville; that's in Illinois, but it's only a stone's throw to Saint Louis, if you want."

Harriet swallowed and looked around.

"That's a great idea," Bunny said. "On account of it ain't easy to catch buses across Kentucky. Not unless you went Greyhound."

"Oh, I don't want to take another Greyhound," Harriet said. "So far, from what I've seen, this looks like a pretty part of the country, sort of reminds me of home. I'd like to see more."

"Then ride with us," the woman in the leather said. "You can ride in Snake's sidecar."

"Sidecar? But I don't even know Snake or you well enough to be —"

"Well, where are our manners," the woman said. "My name is Pearl. Pearl Abscot, and this is my husband Snake. We're Hogs."

"Hogs?" Snake was a bit overweight with a Santa Claus paunch, but Harriet wouldn't call him a hog.

"Harley-Davidson motorcycle owners," Pearl said. "HOG is one of those ... what do you call 'em ... acronyms for Harley-Davidson Owners Group. It's our club."

"Ah, go on along with them," Bunny said. "I've known Pearl and Snake goin' on umpteen years now. They'll get you close to Saint Louis real easy. Be fun too."

"But I don't know . . . motorcycles? I've never ridden one. Aren't they a little dangerous?"

"Nah, they aren't dangerous—it's the other people on the road that's dangerous. Just sit back in my sidecar and feel the wind in your face and enjoy the scenery."

"You can use my extra helmet," Pearl said. "Come on, whaddaya say? We'd consider it an honor to be part of the great Harriet Beamer Beat 'Em Up Road Trip."

"Is that what they're calling it?" Harriet said.

"Nah, I just made that up," Pearl said.

"Look, why don't you just think on it a few more minutes while Pearl and me finish up our lunch." Snake looked at Pearl. "We'll have you in Collinsville, Illinois, by suppertime, maybe a little before depending on if we make any stops."

"And look." Pearl said. "You want to stop and catch a bus at any time, just holler."

"Okay," Harriet said. "Maybe if I could sit here and think a minute."

Bunny freshened Harriet's coffee. "Really, honey. You got nothin' to worry about. Snake and Pearl are top drawer. They'll take good care of you."

Another voice chimed in. "I can vouch for Snake."

Harriet turned her head. The voice belonged to a tall, skinny police officer, holding a motorcycle helmet and wearing knee-high black boots.

"You can?" Harriet said.

"Sure thing, ma'am. Snake and Pearl are all right."

Harriet thought about what happened in Maggie Valley with those two awful crooks. And, of course, the purse snatching. It didn't seem possible that she could have such terrible fortune three times in a row?

"And believe you me, buses ain't the way to go in these parts."

"What about the train?"

"Nope. No train runs through this part of the world either.

208

And you got to cross over the Ohio River up there. No bus I know of does that except the Greyhound, and I heard you say you don't want to ride Greyhound. Seems to me you got no choice."

Harriet thought about what Henry and Prudence would say about her riding on a motorcycle. Henry would flip his lid. But when all was said and done, even if she died today in a fiery crash, she figured she'd lived a good, full life. If it was her time to go she might as well go in the sidecar of a Harley-Davidson.

"Well, okay, let's ... ride." She looked at the police officer. "Will you be a dear and call my son — his name is Henry — and let him know I'm okay." She scribbled his number on a napkin. "I'd tell him myself, but I think he might get a little upset about me riding a motorcycle. I fell off the Carousel horse at Playtown Park three times when he was a boy. And with the incident last Christmas, this might just be too much."

"You take good care of yourself, honey," Bunny said. "Now here's another slice of pie. I wrapped it to go. Blueberry this time."

Harriet smiled. "Thank you, Bunny. It was sure nice meeting you."

"I wish I could do what you're doing."

"You can. It doesn't take much. A little money. A GPS. And the willingness to see the world and the people in it — maybe in ways you hadn't expected."

Harriet opened her suitcase and slid the pie inside right after she removed her stone martens and draped them around her neck.

"If I'm gonna ride, I may as well ride in style."

Chapter 22

"AIN'T SHE GORGEOUS," SNAKE SAID, REFERRING TO HIS BIKE and not his wife as Harriet had thought at first.

Harriet stared at the motorcycle with the attached sidecar. The bike was large and looked heavy. It had nice shiny bright yellow paint and black trim. It reminded Harriet of a large bumblebee. The sidecar was also bright yellow and looked a little like half of a torpedo, sliced lengthwise. The seat seemed okay, vinyl with some rips in the seat but plenty of legroom. And she was happy it had its own little windshield. She didn't want to get bugs in her teeth.

"She's a 1997 Road King. Custom paint."

"She's very pretty," Harriet said.

"Climb in," Pearl said. "Snake won't bite you. I think there's room for your cute little tote bag but, honey—" she directed her voice to Snake—"You better tie her suitcase down on the back."

"You are asking me to climb into that ... that side bucket?"

"Sidecar," Snake said. "Closest thing to flying without leaving the ground."

"And you're sure I don't have to worry about it falling off on the highway with me in it."

"No, ma'am," Snake said. "She's a worthy machine."

"Snake hasn't lost a passenger yet," Pearl said. She gave the big lug a punch in the shoulder. "And he ain't planning to." Then she kissed his cheek. "See you on the road."

Pearl gave Harriet a helmet. "Now just put this on, sweetie, and climb in. We'll be on the road in no time. You are gonna love the wind in your hair and the scenery whizzing past. There ain't nothing else like it."

Harriet took a deep breath and plunked the helmet onto her head. It felt big, but when Pearl snapped it under her chin, it was snug enough.

"Now don't you just look adorable," Pearl said. "Them foxes are so elegant."

Harriet smiled and then stuffed her tote into the sidecar and watched Snake lash her suitcase to the back of the bike. Good and tight.

Harriet settled her rump down into the seat. The vinyl was hot for a second or two. And the next thing she knew Snake had started the engine and yelled, "Geronimo!" And off they went down the country road toward Saint Louis — she hoped.

* * *

Henry stared at the computer screen, shaking his head. "It's dreck. I write dreck." Then he pulled a copy of *The Sun Also Rises* from the bookshelf. He leaned down and patted Humphrey. "Sometimes it helps to read some Hemingway — not that I'm Hemingway. But I need some inspiration."

Humphrey opened his formerly closed and resting eyelids. He looked up at Henry.

"It's like I completely lost control of Cash," Henry said. "I don't really know him anymore. Not like I used to. He's off doing things that . . . that I never thought he would do."

Henry carried his book onto the porch, followed closely by Humphrey. "Maybe I'll call Mother."

Humphrey howled.

"She should be making her way into Kentucky by now." He

211

directed his words to Humphrey. "You know, old man, I wonder if I keep asking her if I should go get her because I don't want to finish the book—avoidance."

Humphrey glared at Henry.

Henry reached into his pocket to retrieve the phone, but it jingled just as he did. "Maybe that's her."

"Henry Beamer?" said a deep voice on the other end.

"Yes. Who's calling?"

"This is Officer Valquez of the Hopkinsville, Kentucky, police department. Now this is not an emergency call, but—"

Henry had to sit down. His heart pounded.

Humphrey sidled next to him and rested his head on Henry's knees.

"Your mother asked me to call you and tell you she's doing fine," the officer said. "I was down at the luncheonette while the TV crew was there talking to your mother."

"TV crew? Not again."

"Well, now, yes, yes, sir, the news people were out there reporting on your mother's little trip when she started talking about her next destination."

"Uh-huh. Is she okay?"

"Yes. Yes, sir, as far as I know your mama's just fine. Leastways she looked fine when she took off with Pearl and Snake on that motorcycle. She was wearing a helmet and all."

Henry swallowed. "Motorcycle? My mother does not know how to drive a motorcycle. Wait a minute—did you say Snake?"

"Yes sir, Snake—he's a nice fella, and, well, now she wasn't exactly driving it. She was riding in Snake's sidecar."

"Snake's sidecar? What in the heck are you talking about? What is Snake's sidecar? Some kind of traveling show?"

"No, no, Snake . . . now, that ain't his real name."

"Really?"

"No, his name is Louis DuPree. He's a preacher fella, has a

little church just outside of Slaughters. Nicest guy you'd ever—
but he does like to ride his Harley."

Henry felt a little better until Officer Valquez continued
talking.

"Yes, sir, Mr. Dupree and his wife, Pearl, they got quite a following in these parts, especially when they do all the rattlesnake
handling during their services, woo hee, but it's quite a show.
That's why they call him Snake. If it don't make a believer out of
you, nothin' will."

"Oh, good grief, my mother is traveling with a band of snake
handlers."

"Kind of, but I thought you'd want to know. They'll take good
care of her."

"Yes, of course. Did they say where they were headed?"

"I believe it's Collinsville, Illinois, or nearby there anyway.
About a four-hour drive from here. They'll be there a little after
suppertime I imagine, even if they stop for a bite. But you never
know with the DuPrees. They can get sidetracked."

"Thank you," Henry said. And he closed the phone.

"I don't believe this, Humphrey. Your mother is gallivanting
across Kentucky on a motorcycle with a snake-handling minister.
Maybe I should have stayed in Dad's business. Least then she'd
be safe at home."

Humphrey lay at Henry's feet. He rolled onto his side, giving
Henry an invitation to scratch.

"She's gonna be okay," Henry said, trying to convince himself
also. Henry took a breath. "But what if something happens? What
if she falls out of that thing? You know she used to fall off the
merry-go-round at Playtown Park."

* * *

By the time Snake, Harriet, and Pearl pulled onto the main highway, Route 64 headed toward Saint Louis, according to the sign
she saw, Harriet had already decided that this would be the last

213

time she rode in a sidecar. Her tote bag took up most of her feet space. She felt a bit dizzy as they whizzed past trees and houses. She also had a little trouble keeping her furs on. The wind was stronger than she thought it would be. And watching the telephone poles go past one ... after ... the ... other—the wires somehow following the terrain of the road with all its ups and downs —made her stomach churn. She thought this was all very strange considering she was not one prone to carsickness.

Pearl rode next to her at some points but hung behind Snake for most of the time. Harriet's sidecar had a little sideview mirror, and she could see the other motorcyclists following closely. Her knees started to ache on account of being kind of bunched up toward her chest. And to top it off, she had to use the ladies room. Unlike the local bus, where she could get off at the next stop and find a restaurant, or the train, where she could use the train toilet, she wasn't even sure if she could get Snake's attention to ask him to please pull into a rest stop.

She liked Snake and couldn't help but wonder why he had such a dreadful name. She liked Pearl's name well enough. It made her think of the ocean. Now there was a positive about moving to California. She'd be near the ocean—or would she? That was when it occurred to her that she really had no idea where exactly Grass Valley was in relation to ... to anything.

Soon enough Snake pulled off the main road and stopped at a red light. He leaned over toward Harriet. "Figure we can use a pit stop," he said very loudly. "We're about halfway to Collinsville."

Harriet smiled and nodded even though she wasn't one hundred percent sure of what he said. She looked in her mirror just to make sure Pearl was still there, but unfortunately one of her foxtails flew across her face, nearly whipped her glasses off and momentarily blinded her.

She regained her composure in time to see the light change, and Snake sped off until they reached a little diner that flashed the name RED'S in bright blue, which made Harriet wonder for a second. But no matter, she was just glad to get to a bathroom. And from the looks of Pearl, she was happy too.

Red's was nice. It was cozy, not very big, with a line of booths on one side and a counter on the next. Signs hung above the kitchen window with the diner's not-so-expansive menu.

"Excuse me," Harriet said, "but I need—"

"Right over there," Snake said, pointing toward a sign shaped like a finger pointing to the left with the words LADIES and GENTS burned into it.

"Thank you," Harriet said.

Snake smiled and headed toward a booth. The others took booths also. Harriet met up with Pearl in the bathroom.

"Snake ain't his real name," Pearl said. "He's Pastor Louis DuPree."

Harriet looked at Pearl in the mirror as she washed her hands. The rust stains had painted themselves in the resemblance of two hearts. "What? Snake is a pastor? You mean a bona fide pastor?"

"Sure 'nuff. A good one too."

"Then why does he call himself Snake of all things?"

"That will take a little explaining. But mostly it's because the nickname puts folks at ease. Says he can nab folks by the heart quicker when they don't know his true identity. He's kind of like a superhero in that respect."

Harriet and Pearl slid into the booth across from Snake.

"Now listen, Snake," Harriet said. "I want this to be on me —for everyone. Even those guys. Whatever you want."

Snake smiled, his eyes softening into two light blue gems. "Why thank you, Harriet. Much obliged."

Harriet said all she wanted was toast and coffee.

"Oh, my, my, my," Snake said. "Is that all you're having? Red's is famous for their meat loaf. Have more than pie. We still have a couple hours on the road."

"Well, okay," Harriet said, "but my stomach was feeling a little queasy."

"Then you probably need to eat," Pearl said. "I'll have the meat loaf too."

"That makes three," Snake said.

Harriet laughed. "It must be good. I just hope it settles okay."

"'Course it will," Pearl said. "And besides, you need your strength, traveling all over the countryside by yourself."

Snake and Pearl locked eyes for a second. It made Harriet just a trifle nervous given her encounter in Maggie Valley. It was the same kind of look shared by Pamela and Hank.

A waitress wearing a white dress and a red apron approached the table. "You all ready?"

"Meat loaf all around," Snake said.

The waitress wrote on her order book. "Drinks?"

"Coffee, I do believe," Snake said.

"And water," Harriet added.

"Thank you, I'll be right back with your drinks," the waitress said after she scribbled their order.

"She's not the usual waitress," Pearl whispered. "Donna must be out today." She turned toward the kitchen. "Don't see her anywhere."

"I hope she's okay," Snake said.

"Me too," Pearl said. "She was looking a little pale when we were in before."

"Let's just eat and get back on the road. I need to be at the church by 7:30 tonight."

"Church?" Harriet asked. "Is that where you're headed? Church?"

"That's right," Snake said. "We have a meeting tonight."

Harriet peered into his eyes. "Well, that brings me to a question. How come you're called Snake — if you don't mind my asking? And why would any self-respecting church have a pastor named Snake?"

Snake laughed so hard he shot water out his nose. "That's just my street name."

"Ah, fiddlesticks," Harriet said. "I'm getting duped again. Are you gonna do something, because just so you know, I bought a canister of mace in Maggie Valley, and I am NOT afraid to use it." She lied.

Pearl grabbed Harriet's hand. "No, no, it's true. We have a church in Slaughters. The Apostolic Church of Moses in the Wilderness."

"Really? Well, that's just wonderful. I knew I had a feeling about you. So you all believe in Jesus and God and the Holy Spirit and getting saved and—"

"Yep," Louis said. "We sure do. They call me Snake because I often preach while handling snakes."

Harriet choked on her water. "What? I don't get it. Like in a zoo show? You know when the snake people hold snakes while they teach about them?"

"No, no. Rattlers," Pearl said. "Poisonous rattlers. They dance with them."

Harriet gasped until an image of two snakes entwined in a waltz made her smile. "But . . . but why on earth would you do such a thing?"

"Mark 16," Snake said. " 'They will pick up snakes with their hands; and when they drink deadly poison, it will not hurt them at all; they will place their hands on sick people, and they will get well.' "

Harriet sat spellbound, so much so that when her meat loaf came she grew very quiet and had to ponder all of what she just heard. She knocked the tiny bits of onion floating around the gravy onto the side of her plate. Pearl attempted to lighten things up.

"We didn't mean to upset you," she said. "It's not like he carries snakes in his saddlebags."

"That's good," Harriet said. "I . . . I mean you folks can do what you want, but I am not holding a snake. I hate them."

"And you should, darlin'," Snake said. "Snakes are the devil's disguise."

"That's why we're heading to Collinsville in Missouri," Pearl said. "We're attending a revival service."

"Oh, okay," Harriet said, still stirring her gravy. "Will there be snakes?"

Snake smiled. And then patted Harriet's hand. "Yep."

On the outside she was smiling and calm. But inside she experienced a little bit of trepidation and gas.

Chapter 23

HARRIET, SNAKE, AND PEARL PULLED INTO COLLINSVILLE, Illinois, just a little past 5:00 p.m. — just like they said. Although grateful to be out of the sidecar, she was going to miss Snake and Pearl. They stopped right out front of a small white clapboard church. The only way Harriet could tell it was a church was by the pointy steeple and the rundown sign out front that read: HAPPY TIMES GOSPEL PREACHING CHURCH.

"This is where the revival is?" Harriet said. "In that little bitty church?"

"It might be small in stature, but it's mighty powerful and big in the Holy Spirit," Snake said. "Want to join us?"

Harriet felt her eyebrows arch like a gothic cathedral. She had been intrigued by the snake-handling preacher, but to actually join a service . . . well she wasn't too sure.

"Oh, I . . . I don't know. I've never — "

"Come on," Pearl said. "You'll be blessed."

Harriet nodded, and the next thing she knew she was sitting in a wooden folding chair inside. It was warm, with air as thick as wool. Dozens of people filed in as three men, including Snake, stood at the front. A large woman wearing a large brimmed hat banged on the piano as a man in a white shirt plucked a banjo. Harriet saw another woman, younger than most, shaking a tambourine as folks started singing without even being told which hymn. They stood and joined hands and sang and swayed back and forth. Some danced in circles with their heads thrust back like they were in a trance of some sort. Harriet could not understand how any of this had anything to do with Jesus even though folks were shouting his name and saying praises.

Harriet noticed a particularly fat woman near the front go out into the aisle. She tossed her head back and swirled around, uttering words Harriet couldn't understand. She swayed and sang in the strange language until all of sudden, as though she had been shot from behind, she dropped to the floor. She was quickly ministered to by two men in white shirts and dark pants. They dabbed her forehead and helped her to her seat as she called, "Thank you, Jesus. Thank you."

Harriet swallowed and looked at Pearl who was singing and swaying with the others. Harriet couldn't help but feel a touch nervous, but at the same time she felt a wash of peace, a peace that passed her understanding. She didn't want to leave, but at the same time she didn't know how to act. Her heart raced and then slowed as she closed her eyes and tried to move while what she could only believe was the Holy Spirit led.

But when Snake and the other two men reached into a box and pulled out rattlesnakes Harriet wanted to cry and run from that place. But she couldn't. She watched as Snake raised the rattler above his head. "They shall pick up vipers," he shouted. "And not be hurt." He danced and shouted, danced in circles as the music swelled. Snake then took a second snake from the cardboard box and draped it around his neck. Harriet was beginning to feel a bit dizzy from the heat and the excitement. Then a young woman reached into the box. She couldn't have been more than seventeen. She held the snake and kept saying, "Praise Jesus. Praise Jesus." She danced also until she lowered the snake back into the box. She shouted something Harriet couldn't make out, and then she started to writhe and jerk on the floor.

"Is she all right?" Harriet asked Pearl. "It looks like a fit of epilepsy."

Pearl laughed as she continued clapping. "No, no, she's fine. She's been slain."

"Slain? But—" Harriet didn't know what to say except, "My little old Presbyterian heart can't take this. I better leave."

Pearl nodded. Harriet made her way into the aisle as Snake approached. He held both her hands and prayed in the midst of the seeming chaos, asking God to give her extreme traveling grace. At least that's what Harriet thought he said. It was so loud.

Pearl walked out with Harriet where the air was cool and misty.

She sat on a small green bench on the church lawn and took a deep breath. What she really wanted to do was cry. What she just experienced was strange and overwhelming. "That was ... was something." Harriet didn't know exactly what to say. "I never saw anything like it." She fanned herself with a bus schedule she pulled from her tote.

Pearl patted her shoulder. "Guess we should have told you, but it's a little tough to explain. We leave it up to the Holy Spirit."

"No, no. I'm glad I went. But I hope you don't mind if I don't stay for the whole service." She puffed and fanned. "And for right now I need to check with Amelia to figure out where to go next."

"I would imagine," Pearl said, "that the best thing would be to get to a big city like Saint Louis and go from there."

"Yes, I am heading there but—"

"But it's been a long day. Maybe you should spend the night in Collinsville and then catch the express into Saint Louis in the morning—and from there? Well, you'll figure it out, but I'm thinking it might be a good idea to train right into Kansas City, Missouri, it's right on the border. I know the Amtrak goes there, not sure about the locals."

Harriet yawned as she looked around at the street. Other than music and the rattle of the tambourines drifting through the windows of the small church, Harriet figured no one really knew what was happening inside. Not that it was a bad thing—just different.

"That sounds like a plan. I need a rest. No offense but riding in a sidecar is not the most gentle ride. I think my rump felt every bump. I got knocked around like a teacup in a UPS truck. I'm looking forward to a comfortable bed."

"Now, I'm sure that fancy phone of yours will help you find a hotel and then maybe a taxi to get you to a motel. Doubtful that the buses are still running," Pearl said. "May God bless you and make his face shine upon you."

Harriet pulled out her Moleskine and read David Prancing Elk's Indian blessing aloud: "And may the warm winds of heaven blow softly upon your house. May the Great Spirit bless all who enter there. May your moccasins make happy tracks in many snows, and may the rainbow always touch your shoulder."

"That was so sweet," Pearl said.

"I learned it from a Cherokee Indian in North Carolina. I haven't got it memorized yet."

"God has his hand on you, Harriet," Pearl said. "He didn't set you on this journey without a purpose."

And right at that moment Harriet felt a wave of peace and relief wash over her like a warm summer shower. It was like daisies had bloomed in her heart and she had a brand-new reason to keep going. For the first time since she started the whole thing, she knew beyond a doubt that someone out there, along the bus routes, needed her—or she needed them. Or at least that's what she decided to believe.

* * *

Humphrey was not feeling well, not well at all, according to Henry. It had been a week and a half since he'd come to California, so it seemed natural that he would miss Harriet terribly. That afternoon, while Henry typed feverishly on his manuscript, Humphrey lay at his feet letting go an occasional whimper or whine.

222

"I know, old man," Henry said, leaning back in his black office chair. "But she's okay. She'll get here. God is watching over her." Then he leaned down and patted Humphrey's head. "But do you really understand?"

Humphrey looked up, rolled onto his side, and let his tongue loll out.

"I think she'll be here before the week is out." Henry yawned and stretched and then went back to his work. But that only lasted a few seconds.

"Hey, whaddaya say we call her?"

Humphrey scrambled to his feet, danced a jig, and barked twice. Two loud, happy barks.

"Okay, okay." Henry opened his phone and tapped Harriet's picture. He waited. And waited, and then the phone went to voice-mail. He sighed. "Mom, it's me. I'm just calling to see how you're doing and where you are. Call me back."

He closed his phone.

Humphrey, his red eyes drooping, looked up at Henry. He lay back down. This time on his belly and rested his head on his paws.

"Don't be sad, Humphrey. She'll get here safe and sound." Henry swallowed as he pictured his mother squashed into a motorcycle sidecar. "I hope."

Henry went back to his work. He wrote:

> *Cash waited outside Polly's house for the better part of an hour. He wanted desperately to see her. To make love to her and then hold her in his arms forever and ever. He wanted to tell her he's sorry. Sorry for it all. Sorry that ... the fire even happened. Sorry it was his doing. But how could he ever expect Polly to forgive him?*

Henry kept writing and writing, losing all track of time. His words were free now for some reason. He could feel Cash's pain. He could even feel Polly's pain. He cried, but only a little because he didn't want Humphrey to see him. The last time he had cried was when his father died, and he'd held on to Harriet so tightly that he could feel her breaking apart, breaking apart right in his arms. And now he wanted Cash to hold Polly like that, to forgive him for killing Madeline. But why? Why would anyone forgive a murderer?

Henry hung his head and then looked at the picture of Prudence on his desk. It was taken back east in Cape May during the tulip festival. She was smiling so wide he thought she might break. He lightly touched her image. "I love you, Pru. I really do." That was when he knew what he wanted. He was ready. Ready to try again. Ready to have another child.

"I never told Harriet," he said to Humphrey, "but losing those babies was so hard on Prudence. We were so happy the second time—well, we were happy both times, but the second seemed different. Prudence said it felt different." He leaned down and patted Humphrey's head. "She carried him the longest, almost ten weeks when ... well, we never told Mom. We wanted to surprise her when we visited and Prudence had a big baby bump." He sniffed back his tears.

* * *

Because of a convention in town the DoubleTree Hotel in Collinsville only had one king-size room available. Harriet took it without batting an eyelash. Her joints ached, her head ached, and if she had to pull her suitcase one more block she'd scream. All she wanted to do was take a shower, get into her jammies, and relax.

She didn't even care that all she had was a ten-dollar bill to tip the bellman.

She took off her sneakers first, visited the bathroom, and then opened her suitcase. And that's when she saw it. The blueberry pie that Bunny gave her back at Aunt Fran's had exploded.

"Oh, for crying out loud," Harriet said. She pulled the paper plate covered with aluminum foil out of the bag. Blueberry had been squeezed out onto her best nightgown. "This must have happened on the motorcycle ride." She remembered the way Snake bungee corded the case down on the back of his bike. "This is bad." She found blueberry goo on her underwear, her new crew socks, and some even managed to slip down into the bottom of the case and stain her pink capris.

She didn't know whether to laugh or cry. What she did know was that she didn't have the energy or the time for either. This catastrophe was better handled post haste.

"No. I . . . I have to find the laundry."

She worked fast and pulled out all her clothes. Separating what had met with unfortunate blueberry surprise and what had survived unscathed. She held up her capris. "This will never come out —not in a hotel laundry anyway."

She put all the soiled clothing into the bathtub to rinse and then hurried to the phone. She called the front desk.

"Oh, hello, dear. I've had a bit of a blueberry-pie disaster. Is there a laundry available for the guests?"

"Yes, ma'am. But did you say blueberry disaster? In the room?"

"Oh, no, not exactly. In my suitcase."

Harriet heard the desk clerk chuckle.

"Well, I guess it is a little funny. But right now I need to wash my clothes."

She hung up and returned to the mess. "Oh dear. I might have to buy new clothes."

Harriet bundled her clothes into one of the large, fluffy hotel towels, dropped her phone in her pocket, and made her way to the laundry. It was a nice room with five washing machines and five dryers with a table in between. The hotel provided laundry soap, and she even found stain pretreatment spray, which she used most happily.

Then she stood there. What now?

A woman with her own bundle of laundry walked into the room. Harriet watched her get the machine started and then leave the room.

"There see," she said out loud. "I guess it's all right to just leave while they wash."

On the elevator she even said to a man standing with her, "And so what if someone steals my clothes? I'll buy new stuff and I doubt the blueberry stains will come out anyway."

The man looked at her like she had sprung a leak in her brain pan. He got off at the next floor.

Back in her room Harriet finished wiping out her suitcase and ordered room service. Expensive room service. But Harriet didn't mind. She ordered dinner—pasta and salad and iced tea. Something light but wholesome. She had been cramming down the carbs lately, and her tummy felt it; and given the late hour, she didn't want to sleep on a heavy meal. Even after a hot shower, while waiting for room service, her body ached. She noticed a couple of bruises on her legs that she didn't remember getting and a large purple bruise on her right bicep. But nothing was broken. That was the important thing. She had to slip into a pair of capris and the only top that didn't have blueberry on it since her nightgown was in the wash. She sat on the bed and unlocked her phone.

Harriet saw that she missed a call from Henry, but called Martha first.

"Now, you are not going to believe what I did this evening," Harriet said.

"Oh ... I'll believe anything at this point," Martha said.

"You know how I love pie, but let me tell you this—never pack blueberry pie in your suitcase."

Martha laughed. "What happened?"

"It was a disaster," Harriet said, and then she related the whole messy story.

"That's funny," Martha said. "But at least it wasn't a total loss."

"I'm just glad I sent the bib on to the kids. I was gonna pack it."

"Bib?"

"Oh, I found a cute bib while I was in the Smoky Mountains."

226

"Now Harriet, you still aren't bugging them about—"

"No, no. I'll keep it till they're ready."

"Good girl. Now tell me what else you're doing."

"Hold on, room service is here."

Harriet put Martha on speaker while she ate.

"I went to a snake-handling revival meeting in a tiny church with a preacher named Snake and his wife, Pearl."

"Snake handling? What in the world?"

"It was just the most amazing thing I have ever seen. It just showed me the power of the Holy Spirit in a way I never knew possible. These people danced with rattlesnakes, Martha, living rattlesnakes. The people, young women too, danced and sang in words I never heard before."

"Oh my goodness," Martha said. "Were you scared?"

"A little at first, but then I felt calm and . . . hot mostly. It was hot in there."

"Well, where are you now?"

Harriet looked around the luxury accommodations. She felt a twinge of shame that surprised her. "Well it's a far cry from where I was last night. I'm in a king room at the DoubleTree in Collinsville, Illinois—almost to Saint Louis."

"It sounds fabulous."

"It is, but you know, isn't it funny how God can show up in such a ramshackle place as that tiny church? I mean I felt him there, but here in all this luxury, well, it's not the same."

"God is with you in the hotel too," Martha said.

"Oh, I know, but it's different. Those people tonight felt God's pleasure and have seen his glory in ways we only talk about."

Harriet yawned deeply. "Oh dear, Martha, it's almost eleven o'clock. I think I need to get to bed. I have to be on the road early."

"Are you getting tired of traveling?" Martha asked.

Harriet had to think a moment "I'm not sure. Maybe. But I suspect it will look brighter in the morning. Especially after I get my clothing figured out, and speaking of which, I better go put them in the dryer."

* * *

The next morning, after deciding she could live with purple crew socks, Harriet boarded the 7:30 a.m. Collinsville Express to downtown Saint Louis. She paid her fare, took her seat, and winced. The bus had a peculiar odor that was not pleasant. And it was warmish inside, even though the weather outside was not particularly hot.

"Excuse me," she said to the woman sitting in the seat in front of her once she got her luggage settled. But the woman didn't respond. Harriet called again. "Excuse me." This time she tapped her shoulder. The woman turned around. Her brow wrinkled at Harriet.

Harriet asked, "How long will it take to get to downtown? I need to go to the train station."

The woman pointed to her ears and shook her head.

"Oh dear me, I am so sorry. I had no idea. You're ... you're deaf." Harriet's stomach did a flip-flop from embarrassment.

The woman, who was about Harriet's age, smiled and started to sign something that Harriet could not decipher. She made a mental note to learn American Sign Language just in case something like this ever happened again. It seemed only right.

Harriet apologized as best she could.

* * *

Twenty minutes later the bus rolled across the Mississippi River into Missouri. The sight was spectacular. She had never seen a river so big, so wide, or so busy. She thought there were hundreds of ships on it. But when she spied the Gateway Arch, it nearly stopped her heart. She had heard of the arch and knew they called it the Gateway to the West and all, and perhaps it was that notion that excited her. She was now officially on her way West.

228

The Collinsville Express bus pulled into the ultra modern-looking Gateway Station. The terminal was a big place, with every amenity a traveler could want or expect. There were counters for Amtrak, Greyhound, the MetroLink, and places to call for taxi cabs and limos. It was quite the busy transportation hub. The floors were shiny and clean. She saw two men working floor polishers, and other workers were picking up trash and emptying trash cans. There were kids with backpacks and older people pulling their luggage along. It was a far cry from the rural towns she had just been through. Just looking made her feel harried.

Just outside the doors she could still see the Gateway Arch. She knew people took elevator rides all the way to the top, but she had enough excitement last night and decided that was one adventure she should pass up.

After a brief discussion with a ticket clerk, Harriet decided to take the train into Kansas City. A nice, peaceful train ride sounded nice.

Harriet bought her ticket. She had about an hour to explore before her train arrived. She found a place to buy coffee, postcards, and a copy of *Better Homes and Gardens*, and a book called *The Edge of Grace* by some woman named Christa Allan because it sounded interesting.

Then she found a bench and sat. Her feet were tired, her back ached — probably from riding in the sidecar for so many hours — and she was definitely developing another headache. She took off her glasses and rubbed her eyes. She checked her phone and remembered that Henry had called. She fumbled around with the phone for a bit but finally got into her voicemail and listened to his message.

"Ahhh, he sounds good. I'm starting to look forward to seeing him." That made her feel a trifle bit better. Harriet opened her notebook.

My dear, dear Max, I would have written last night, but I was

*pooped. You won't believe what I witnessed, a snake-handling
revival service. I say "witness" because I didn't participate,
you'll be happy to know. I could only watch and be amazed as
those folks grabbed snakes, sometimes two and three at a time,
and lofted them above their heads and then danced a jig with
them. Not one of them got bit.*

She went back and crossed her t's and then took a breath. She
could still hear the banjo and see the people dancing in her mind.

*Max, you would have whisked me right out of that place.
But you know, I'm glad I stayed. I'm glad I saw the Holy Spirit
moving like that. I think. I don't know how else to explain it.
All I can say is that watching those people dance around with
poisonous snakes was a sight to behold. It made me believe that
if they can do the Charleston with rattlers around their necks
then I could keep going. I figure I'm about half way to Grass
Valley as it is. Right now I am in Saint Louis waiting for the
9:15 train to take me to Kansas City, Missouri.*

Harriet heard her train called.

Time to go, honey. I'll write soon.

The train, the Missouri River Runner, was long and comfortable. She found her seat with no problem, thanks to the nice conductor. He took her ticket and helped her settle in by placing her
suitcase in the overhead compartment. He had a nice, reassuring
smile. Harriet dropped her tote at her feet and leaned back in the
wide comfortable seat. She had upgraded to business class even
though she saw precious little difference between coach and what
she had now. Maybe a bit more legroom.

Chapter 24

HARRIET SETTLED INTO HER SEAT TO ENJOY THE RIDE. THE scenery was lovely. She might have even dozed a little because before she knew it the train was slowing down for a stop at Kirkwood. It wasn't a long stop. Harriet watched people move about on the platform. Everyone always has someplace to go.

Soon the train moved along slowly again and then gained speed as it traveled through some very beautiful countryside.

"This is Missouri wine country," said the conductor.

"Wine country?" She never knew Missouri had wine.

A little while later the conductor made certain that folks knew they had just passed the infamous spot where Jesses James pulled his first train robbery. Harriet was unimpressed. Didn't look like much more than a plot of brush-covered, dry land with a small stream running through it. But still, how many people can say they passed the spot of a famous train robbery?

And then right on schedule at 2:55 p.m. the River Runner pulled into the Kansas City station. She grabbed her tote bag but needed help from a nice, tall young man who snagged her suitcase from an overhead bin.

* * *

Henry was quiet over dinner. He had made a nice meal: steak, salad, even a chocolate mousse dessert. Prudence lit candles and seemed in a good mood.

"Are you okay?" she asked as Henry pushed lettuce around his plate.

"Uh-huh." He looked across the table at Prudence. "No. Actually."

"Is it your mother? Did something happen."

"No. She's fine. Having the time of her life. It's me . . . us."

"Us?" Prudence placed her fork on her plate, crossed her arms, and sat back in the chair. "What about us?"

"I want a baby."

Prudence sucked all the air out of the dining room and then stood. She walked into the living room. Humphrey, who had been sleeping under the dining room table, followed her. "Pru," Henry called. "I think it's time. Can't we just discuss it?"

"But . . . what if I lose another child? I couldn't take that."

"What if you don't? Seems more likely you won't. The doctor said miscarriages are not uncommon the first time or the second time. There's things the doctors can check for. Remember? That's what your doctor said. I thought she was very positive."

"But . . . my career. I'm about to be named to the city council and—"

"You can still do all that. Listen, my novel is going well. There'll be more books. I'll get a real job if I need too. You can still be a lawyer. I'll be Mister Mom. Come on, Pru. Ready?"

Prudence sat on the sofa. "I don't know. I'm scared. I can't go through that again."

"I was thinking, it might be weird but with my mother here it could help. A built-in babysitter. Maybe you can keep working."

"Your mother *will* be happy," Prudence said. "But . . . I don't know."

"Will you just consider it?"

"Okay. I'll think and pray about it." She looked away for a second. "If God still cares about it."

Henry cracked a slow smile. "That's all I ask. And of course God cares."

Henry's phone chimed.

"That's Mother now," Henry said.

"How can you tell? Your phone's in your pants."

"I changed the ring for her. Should I answer it or—"

"Yes, go ahead."

"Mom," Henry said. He wanted to ask her where she was but remembered what she said before.

"I'm in Kansas City, Missouri."

"Okay, you're getting closer." Henry couldn't keep his eyes off Prudence. She seemed to be crying. "Listen, Mom, I'm glad you're okay. Any idea when you'll get here?"

"Not sure. Henry, I'm having such a good time, but I got to tell you, riding in a motorcycle sidecar—"

"I heard about that," Henry said.

"Oh, goody, then that nice officer called you."

"Yes, he did, but listen Mom, I need to get off the phone. Prudence needs me."

"Oh, okay, Son, tell her hi for me, okay?"

Henry closed his phone and dropped it into his pants pocket. "It's nothing. Mom hitched a ride with a motorcycle-riding preacher, that's all. I haven't had the chance to tell you yet."

Prudence shook her head. "Well, I'll say this much, our baby will have the most exciting grandma."

"So it's yes, we can try?"

Prudence closed her eyes and leaned back in the sofa. "I didn't say that. Not yet."

"Okay, honey. What do you say we finish dinner?"

* * *

The Kansas City station reminded Harriet a little of the Baltimore Union Station. Much smaller but it still boasted high ceilings and huge rounded windows that could have worked just as well in a

233

cathedral. She pulled her suitcase along the clean, shiny floor, pausing long enough to look at the arrival and departures board. Harriet would need to decide on a next destination. On the train she had found an Amtrak route map and looked it over, but having never been any farther West than Pittsburgh for a funeral, Harriet really had no clue. There were still many cities between Kansas City and Grass Valley.

After a conversation with a young man behind the ticket counter, Harriet scheduled her next stop—Dodge City, Kansas. Sure, it was further south than she wanted, but the ticket person had said, "Ever been to Dodge City?"

"You mean as in Wyatt Earp, Doc Holliday, and all those famous cowboys? I have cowboy salt and pepper shakers; one set's the shape of a boot. The salt and pepper comes out the toes."

"Yep. That's what I'm meanin'. You could go there for a day or two. Maybe see the sights and then get back on the train and be on your way to Grass Valley once again."

"Well, it sounds wonderful, young man."

"Should I make it for Dodge City?"

"Yep, Dodge City here I come." Of course Harriet had no idea that going to Dodge City would put her off course.

The young man, whose name tag read PHILIP, smiled. "You have a little bit of a wait. The train doesn't leave until 10:45 tonight. It gets into Dodge at 5:25 tomorrow morning."

"What?" Harriet said. "But, that means I'll be spending the night on the train."

"Well, sure. That's not a problem is it? The trains are quite comfortable."

"Oh, I know. But it's just that ... well, I guess that will be okay." Harriet pulled her seeing glasses off and slipped on her cheaters to get a better look at the ticket. "It does say the train arrives in Dodge at 5:25 in the morning." Harriet felt her heart race just a little. "But, no matter. I wanted to see the country. I wanted an adventure."

"Good for you," Philip said. "You can go see some sights around town or get something to eat. Be back at the platform by 10:30."

Harriet glanced at one of the clocks in the station. She had nearly seven hours to wait. And that sounded fine — time enough to call Martha or read her new book or see some sights or sit and do nothing.

"Thank you, Philip."

"You're welcome. They call KC the city of fountains. You could take a tour."

"Fountains?"

"Yep, there are over two hundred fountains in Kansas City. A walking tour might be nice."

Harriet looked at the young man. "A walking tour of fountains? Well, who doesn't like a good fountain?"

She flung her foxtail across her shoulders. "I'm off to see the fountains."

* * *

Henry watched the FedEx driver pull up out front of the house.

"Oh no, more shakers."

The driver hopped out of the truck carrying three small packages.

"It'd be easier if she just combined these," she said.

"That's my mom."

Henry signed for the boxes, and this time instead of just putting them in the garage with the others, he sat down on the front porch and opened them. "You know, Humphrey, I never did get what Mom sees in these things."

Humphrey let go a low grumbly growl and flopped near Henry.

Henry removed a set of shakers shaped like teepees, a set of kissing Indians, and a set emblazoned with the words BLUE RIDGE PARKWAY on them.

"Look," Henry said showing the set to Humphrey. "She's

235

been on the Blue Ridge Parkway, which means she had to cross the Smoky Mountains. How in the world did she manage that? I mean she is seventy-two years old. Okay, not ancient but still."

Henry examined the next box. Instead of being addressed to himself or Prudence, it was addressed to "Harriet Beamer in care of Henry Beamer." "That's odd," Henry said. "I guess I shouldn't open it but—" He couldn't resist and discovered not only a set of shakers shaped like Mr. and Mrs. Santa Claus, but he also found something he was not expecting—a baby bib with a picture of the Smoky Mountains that read, "My Nana Climbed a Mountain for Me."

His heart raced and then he let go a long sigh. "Mom. This is—"

But he couldn't really think of anything to say except, "I can't be angry, Humphrey. It's her business. I shouldn't have opened it."

Henry held the small yellow bib. "Wishful thinking, I suppose ... Nana. For both of us."

* * *

Although she might have had some trepidation about sleeping on the train, Harriet's concerns were quickly gone when she saw her room—or more accurately her roomette. It was lovely in her opinion, even if it was a bit cramped. But what could you expect on a train?

Harriet discovered quickly how to make the two facing seats into one bed. There was an overhead berth as well, but Harriet liked the lower option better.

"Not climbing up there," she said looking at herself in the small mirror on the closet door. "You look a fright."

But it was late and after touring the fountains of Kansas City for most of the day she figured she deserved to look a little disheveled.

Harriet settled in, took a shower—an experience she would most certainly remember. Her first traveling shower experience.

It wasn't too bad. The water was just barely hot enough but still it soothed her tired muscles. She changed into her PJs and by then it was nearly 11:30. Late just about everywhere. She thought about calling Martha knowing she'd more than likely be awake but that night she thought it might be better to sleep considering how early she would need to rise the next morning.

So she set her alarm on her phone for 4:30 in the morning—giving herself plenty of time to get ready for the day ahead. After making her bed up with sheets and a blue blanket and finding the pillow—which was stuffed into the closet—she lay down for what she hoped would be a peaceful sleep, and that's when it struck—insomnia or something close. She closed her eyes. They popped back open. The motion of the train—which she hoped would lull her to sleep was troublesome. Every few seconds it seemed to lurch side to side instead of rocking gently.

"Oh dear, I really need to sleep. Please, Jesus, help me to sleep so I can have energy for tomorrow."

Harriet stayed awake for the next several minutes. It was like she just could not shut her brain off. She saw flashes of salt and pepper shakers, snakes being lifted toward heaven, trees whizzing past at breakneck speed, numerous cups of coffee and stars. It was like the trip came rushing back in one fell swoop. She shook her head. "Sleep, Harriet. Just go to sleep."

A few hours later she heard the music of her alarm. Shaking herself from what turned out to be a deep sleep, and searching her brain to remember that she had spent the night on a train, she grabbed her phone, pulled out the charger, and swiped the alarm off.

* * *

The Dodge City Amtrak Station was nothing like any other train station she had visited. It was more of a stop than a station and, according to a sign Harriet read, was a former two-story brick Santa Fe Railway depot built in 1898. Now it was covered with rust-color stucco and had light bumpy bricks around the foundation. The platform was the same rust color, and there was no one there to help with bags or give out information. "Kind of like a ghost station," Harriet said to no one. "Especially so early in the morning. Guess folks in town are not what you would call early risers."

She felt a little anxious standing on the platform. It was lit well enough, but the sounds of crickets and what she thought could have been a coyote's howl unnerved her.

Fortunately, Amelia was able to map several restaurants nearby, and nearly all right on Wyatt Earp Boulevard. She pulled up the handle of her suitcase, adjusted her tote so it was as comfortable as possible, but frankly, Harriet's shoulders were beginning to complain. And she set off in the direction of Kate's Coffee House.

* * *

"Are you going to work all night?" Prudence said as she entered Henry's office. "It's almost ten o'clock."

Henry stretched and leaned back in his chair. "No. I guess this is as good as any place to stop."

"Any word from Mom?"

"In a way." Henry stood and pushed his chair toward the desk. Humphrey whimpered. "More salt and pepper shakers arrived." He took a breath and was just about to tell her about the bib when he thought better of it. "She picked them up in the Smoky Mountains." He took Prudence's hand, and they walked to the kitchen.

"You know," Henry said. "I kind of admire her. I've never seen the Smoky Mountains or ridden in a sidecar or visited a salt-and-pepper-shaker museum."

Prudence chuckled as she opened a jar of strawberry jam. "Want toast?"

"No, I'm going for ice cream." He pulled open the freezer door. "Moose tracks."

"She is brave," Prudence said, "but I'll still feel better when she's here — safe and sound."

Henry dug into the ice cream. "Have you been thinking . . . praying — I mean besides with me?"

Prudence's toast popped. "About having a baby?"

"Uh-huh."

"Sure. How can I not think about it? But every time I do, I remember and — "

"Will you see the doctor at least?"

Prudence slathered the bread with jam. "Okay. It can't hurt to talk. I'll call in the morning."

Henry felt a wide smile stretch across his face.

Chapter 25

AFTER A HEARTY BREAKFAST OF DELICIOUS COFFEE, FRUIT, A cinnamon roll, bacon, and eggs Harriet decided to walk down Wyatt Earp Boulevard and see the sights. The weather was great. Expected warm temperatures and blue skies. She found the main drag easily enough and visited several of the little shops and even managed to find three sets of shakers she could not live without. Next she found herself outside of the Dodge City Jail, watching a gunfight reenactment between a sheriff and some kind of desperado. She laughed at the jail sign that read BUILT AROUND 1868. It was little more than a concrete shack with one cell. It had bars on the door, no windows, and best of all, she was able to get a picture taken of her behind bars. She found someone who helped her text it to Henry.

She walked further on through the town and learned some history as she passed the general store and another saloon. She learned that a good buffalo hunter could make $100 a day in the 1800s. She passed statues of famous cowboys, including Bat Masterson and Wyatt Earp, and was quite surprised by a stagecoach whipping past. She bought several postcards for Henry, figuring he might use them as research. By noon she was tired of walking and needed a rest — since she was still lugging her suitcase, Harriet needed to take several breaks. She found a green bench advertising a place called the Long Branch Saloon. She sat and yawned, and that was when a man about the size and stature of a beanpole plopped down next to her.

"Never wanted to come in the first place," he said.

"Excuse me?"

"Nothing. Just ready to go home." He smiled at her, and Harriet felt more at ease. He then reached into his pocket and pulled out a paperback book. It was a Western from the looks of the cover —a cowboy, a horse, and enough tumbleweeds to dam the Ohio River. The man started to read and never looked Harriet's way again.

Harriet pulled out her Moleskine and wrote:

Dear Max, looks like people really do enjoy Western novels. I must tell Henry.

Next on her agenda was to figure out how she could get out of Dodge; she had seen enough. The Long Branch Saloon, which she realized was sitting right smack dab across from her in a small strip of stores, looked inviting.

She sat at a table with a red and white gingham tablecloth and ordered a cup of coffee and a slice of apple pie. As she was eating she noticed a sign on a stage. It was old-timey writing with curlicues and flourishes. It read, MISS KITTY'S CANCAN REVIEW. FIRST SHOW — HIGH NOON.

"That sounds like fun. I've never seen a cancan," she said to her waiter.

"Miss Kitty is pretty amazing. Show starts in less than a half hour."

She had just ordered a cherry Coke and French fries when a curtain opened on the stage and a group of dance-hall girls came out onto the stage, dancing what Harriet thought must be the cancan. They danced by lifting their skirts and kicking out their legs, just like Harriet had seen in the movies, nothing too provocative. There were children in the restaurant. She enjoyed the show so much she asked her waiter if there was any way she could meet the woman they introduced as Miss Kitty Bloom of Dodge City. She seemed to be the star of the show. Kitty was dressed in a period costume with black lace-up boots and a bright blue satin dress with a black bustier top that had more ruffles in it than a meringue. Her dress had puffy sleeves, and she wore a matching hat with a long black feather. Harriet thought she was spectacular and wanted to tell her. And she looked quite a bit older than the cancan saloon girls. Harriet admired that.

Twenty minutes went past, and Harriet was about to give up on meeting Miss Kitty Bloom when she saw a woman approach her table.

"Howdy," she said. "I understand you wanted to meet me."

Well, Harriet had never been so thrilled. It was Miss Kitty Bloom standing right there in front of her.

"I just had to tell you how much I enjoyed the show," Harriet said. "Especially when you sang and shot the pistols in the air."

"Thank you," Kitty said. "Most folks just come in here to wet their whistle. Not sure if anyone pays attention. That's why I'm taking the show on the road."

"On the road?" Harriet said.

"Yep. I'm taking me and the girls up to Pueblo . . . that's in Colorado. I got an offer to do the show for fourteen nights up there. It was an offer too good to resist. Besides, I really need to get out of this armpit of a town."

"Oh, I think it's rather nice. I like the whole Western thing. I saw a gunfight and got my picture taken in jail. I sent it to my son and daughter-in-law. They'll get a kick out of it."

"That's nice. Well, if there's nothing else—"

"No, I just wanted to make your acquaintance. I'm just gonna sit awhile and figure out my next plan of action."

"Plan of action?" Miss Kitty sat at Harriet's table. "What do you mean?"

"I'm traveling to Grass Valley, California. I stopped here on account of the nice Amtrak ticket man said it was a nice place. But now I have to find my way to Denver, Colorado."

"Goodness gracious, girl," Miss Kitty said. "You got some . . . well, let's say *nerve*."

"Not really. The bus drivers and train conductors do the work. I just have to find my way to them."

"But still—"

That was when a waiter walked up behind Kitty. "Excuse me, but I just had to ask. Are you the woman in the video? The one who beat up the purse snatcher?"

Harriet swallowed and nodded. "You mean that's still making the rounds?"

"Wait just a cotton-pickin' minute," Miss Kitty said. "You mean we got us a celebrity?"

"No, no," Harriet said, "I just did what anyone would do. I couldn't let that hooligan steal that old woman's purse."

The waiter laughed as he refilled Harriet's water glass.

"Well, now," Harriet said. "She was older than me. I'm only seventy-two."

"You're as young as you feel," Miss Kitty said.

"That's true, but I am starting to feel a little bedraggled. It's been a long trip. And I still have miles to go before I sleep."

"Robert Frost," said Miss Kitty.

Harriet smiled. "I don't suppose you know anything about public transportation around here. I could take the train, but . . . well, I see so much of the country on the bus."

"Well now, I have an idea if you're game." Miss Kitty laughed so hard the table shook.

"The girls and me are taking the Beeline Express now that it stops in Dodge."

"Beeline Express?"

"Yep, take us clear to Pueblo. Ain't that a stroke of good luck?"

"Yes, yes, it is. Can anyone ride this Beeline?"

"Sure. You interested?"

243

"Well, yes, leastways I'd be heading west," Harriet said. She liked the way Miss Kitty made eye contact. Harriet could tell she was warm and sensitive and wound up telling her the entire story. Miss Kitty stayed glued to every word.

"Harriet," Miss Kitty said when she finished her story, "I would be honored if you rode along with me and the girls."

"Really. I can travel with you and the cancan dancers?"

"Sure cancan." She smiled. "I have one more show in about twenty minutes, and then I'm blowing this joint. Well, not until tomorrow mornin', but yeah, I'm outta here."

"Getting out of Dodge," Harriet said.

"Now there's one I haven't heard." Miss Kitty winked.

Harriet looked over at the stage. "Boy, I wish —" Before she could finish her sentence one of the dancing girls interrupted them.

"Miss Kitty," she said, "it's Betty. She sprained her ankle in the last show and says she can't go on."

Miss Kitty shook her head. "Geeze, okay, call the doc, and we'll just have to do it without her."

"Okay, Miss Kitty."

Miss Kitty looked at Harriet. "What were you saying?"

Harriet's heart raced. "Oh, well, I was just gonna say I wish I could do what you do ... up there swishing your skirts around like that."

"Want to do it?"

"What? Really?"

"Come on, I'll hook you up with a costume. We have room in the line now. What do you say? You'll be doing me a favor. DottyJo will teach you the steps in no time. And what you don't know — you fake. Believe me, no one will know the difference."

* * *

Harriet fit into the saloon dancer outfit with no trouble at all. DottyJo zipped her right into it and then pinned a large black flower in Harriet's hair. Her costume had a pink skirt and a bright blue bustier with ruffles. Harriet saw herself in the standing mirror. She looked like she had just stepped out of a movie set.

DottyJo looked Harriet up and down. "You are one gorgeous dancer. Now come on, I'll teach you the steps."

"Are you sure you can? I am not much of a dancer. Never was."

"Nothin' to it, honey, just follow along and kick as high as you can. Swish your skirt like you're puttin' out a fire."

"Okay," Harriet said, her heart all aflutter.

She practiced for a few minutes until Miss Kitty called them all to the stage. "Let's go, girls. One more show, then it's on to the bright lights and the big time."

Harriet heard the music swell as she and the girls lined up on stage. The curtain opened and Miss Kitty began to sing as the girls stood still with their arms interlocked. Harriet was the last dancer on the left. Then as Miss Kitty sang, the music grew faster, and all of a sudden she and the other dancers were moving around so fast Harriet needed to catch her breath. They kicked their legs high and swished their skirts. Harriet could hardly believe she was on stage dancing the cancan in Dodge City. But she was. And when the show ended and the audience applauded, Harriet's heart swelled with the music.

"This was one of the best days of my life," she told Kitty backstage. "Thank you so much for letting me do it."

"You're a natural," DottyJo said, "a born dancer."

Harriet felt her face flush. "No. Just this once is fine with me." She huffed and puffed. "Maybe I am getting too old for adventure."

* * *

After a restful night at the Comfort Inn near the Boot Hill Casino, Harriet met Miss Kitty and the girls at the saloon. The six girls, including Betty, who was leaning on crutches, were huddled in a circle with their luggage off to the side.

Miss Kitty stood a few yards from them looking over a clipboard.

"Morning, Miss Kitty," Harriet said. "Thank you again for yesterday."

"No problem, honey. I'm the one who should be thanking you."

The bus pulled up to the curb. It was big. Red on the top, gray in the middle, and blue on the bottom. But the paint was so slick and shiny Harriet decided it was the prettiest bus so far. It had large tinted windows. There was a fun red, blue, yellow, and orange logo on the side that said BEELINE with a picture of a yellow-and-black bee raring to go.

"Let's go, girls," Miss Kitty called.

The girls grabbed their bags by the extension handles and pulled them to the bus, where the driver piled them into a luggage compartment like fish in a sardine can. Kitty waited with her clipboard until each of the girls boarded the bus. The driver helped Betty board. Harriet and Miss Kitty followed.

"Hey," Betty said, "you were pretty good last night. But don't get any ideas, sweetie." Then she smiled.

Harriet laughed. "Don't you worry about that. These tired legs are only interested in getting to California now."

The bus driver pulled away from the curb and Harriet was off to Pueblo, Colorado, with Miss Kitty and the western showgirls.

Chapter 26

HENRY OPENED THE WEDNESDAY PAPER, BUT HIS MIND wasn't really on the news. His thoughts kept shifting between Cash and Turtle Creek and wishing Prudence would decide about having a baby. "I'm almost forty," he told Humphrey, who was sitting at his feet, poised for a treat. "I want to be able to play ball with him—"

Humphrey barked.

"Or her." Henry snagged a bag of dog treats from the end table. "Here you go. Enjoy."

Humphrey happily chewed on a leathery strip of beef.

Henry found the sports pages. He still followed the Phillies. Prudence padded her way down the steps. "Morning," she called as she made a beeline into the kitchen.

"Coffee's on," Henry called.

She waved on her way past.

Henry's phone chimed. "It's Mom," he said.

"Hi, Mom."

"Henry. Henry can you hear me? The connection isn't very good."

"Mom? Yes, Mom, I can hear you. Sort of."

"Henry, it's me, Mom. I'm calling from ... someplace. We stopped at a McDonald's. I ordered a Big Mac and a Coke and fries."

247

"That's good, Mom. Which McDonald's?"

"Hold on, I'll ask Miss Kitty."

"Lamar," Harriet said a few seconds later. "Lamar, Colorado. "On our way to Pueblo."

"Who is Miss Kitty?" Henry asked.

"A saloon-hall dancer. I suppose that's what she is. In any event, she's a sweet lady I met in Dodge City."

"Dodge City? Really, Mom? You mean like in the Westerns?"

"That's right. And Henry, people really do like this cowboy stuff."

Henry swallowed. "Did you just approve of what I'm doing?"

"Didn't Prudence show you the picture of me I sent . . . I mean texted her yesterday?"

"No, she didn't. But she got in from Sacramento late." It was hard to know if his mother heard his question or not.

"Well ask her to show you." By now Harriet was shouting. "Listen son, I got to go. Just wanted to check on you."

"Mom, I opened one of your packages. The one you self-addressed."

"You what?"

"I opened the package. I found the bib. Mom you really shouldn't — there's something you should know."

"What's that dear?"

The connection was dropped just as Henry looked up and saw Prudence.

* * *

The dance troupe and Harriet filed onto the bus, and the driver pulled out onto the flat highway once again heading for Pueblo.

"Not so sure what I'll do once I get there," Harriet told Miss Kitty. "Probably spend the night for sure."

"You'll figure it out, Harriet Beamer. Look how far you've come. How many buses do you figure you've taken?"

"I lost count after twenty-one but that includes trains, a helicopter, a trolley, and a motorcycle sidecar."

"You're one incredible broad," Miss Kitty said. "You knock my socks clear off my feet. I wish I had your guts."

"Nah, it's not about that. It's about—well, I'm not sure. I think it's about following a dream. You see, all my life things just happened *to* me—you know I just let things happen. Max made all the decisions. Henry sold Max's business. Other people sent me salt and pepper shakers from all over the world—"

"And you just wanted to get your own dang salt and pepper shakers," Miss Kitty said.

"That's right. I'm seventy-two years old, don't have many good years left. I needed to dance the cancan and get my own shakers. Be . . . well, be the person I think God intended me to be." Harriet looked out her window. "Yeah, it was time to step out on my own. I needed to do . . . to do something."

Miss Kitty took Harriet's hand. "You're an inspiration."

"You sure are," DottyJo said from the seat in front. "I ain't never gettin' stuck in a rut." She turned around and looked into Harriet's eyes. "I'm gonna carve my own path."

"Just make sure it's the right path," Harriet said. "I'm not saying you won't get lost a time or two. But just do Mrs. Beamer a favor and take the time to have dreams."

Ninety minutes later, the bus pulled into the Pueblo Transit Center, a long, kind of nondescript, pinkish building. Harriet didn't think it was as impressive as some of the other transit centers she had visited. She thought for a second as the driver brought the bus around back and parked his rig. But the saddest part of the more than five-hour trip from Dodge City was saying good-bye to Miss Kitty. Miss Kitty stood on the pavement with the girls, checking her clipboard as the driver unloaded their suitcases.

"I hate to leave you," Harriet said.

"I know, I know," Miss Kitty said. "But you look me up sometime. I have a feeling this won't be your last trip."

Harriet laughed as she hiked her now very heavy tote bag onto her shoulder with a grunt. "I don't know. These old bones and muscles might not be up to another cross-country jaunt."

"Old? After all that dancing you did yesterday? Why Harriet Beamer, you are not old. You're just getting started. Your life is your own now."

"Um, maybe," Harriet said as they walked toward the street. Two taxis were waiting for the dance troupe. She had never thought about her life being her own. It always seemed to belong to others, family, friends and most importantly, God.

"Can we drop you anywhere?"

"Well, I made a reservation at the Marriott. I don't think it's far from here, and I think I'll hoof it."

"Long as you're sure."

Harriet leaned into the cab. "Thank you, Miss Kitty," Harriet said as they hugged. "I had so much fun."

"Now you look me up some time, and by the way, my real name is Francine Lipshutz."

Harriet laughed. "I much prefer Miss Kitty."

* * *

Harriet settled into her room at the Marriott around 3:45 that afternoon. It wasn't until she sat on the bed that she realized how pooped she was from the long Beeline Express ride, although she did enjoy talking to Miss Kitty. She removed her sneakers and let go a huge sigh.

"You look terrible," she said to her reflection in the mirror. "Your hair is a fright and ... oh my goodness, where are your cheaters?" Harriet always wore her reading glasses around her neck. "Now what did I do with them?"

She dumped the contents of her tote bag onto the bed and rifled through it. No glasses. Next she searched her suitcase, but no cigar. The glasses were gone. She looked at herself in the mirror again. "Now you need to buy a new pair. I just hope they carry them in the hotel store. I really don't feel like going out."

So after a shower and locating the guest laundry, Harriet visited a store in the hotel. Fortunately they carried the reading glasses. She tried on several pair until finally settling on a pair with a zebra print frame. "These will do."

By the time she made it back to her room after finishing up her laundry it was nearing six o'clock — dinnertime — again. "I don't think I used to eat so often at home," she said. "Must be traveling. It gives me an appetite."

According to the information she found on the credenza in her room the hotel had two restaurants, one in the bar and the other . . . well, same name, Charley B's, but not a bar. When she arrived in the lobby she gathered a couple of brochures to read while dining. The first one she looked at caught her eye and even sent a chill whizzing down her spine. It was for the Royal Gorge Bridge and Park. The gorge dropped a thousand feet straight down into the Arkansas River. The sight itself was amazing, but the thought of crossing the gorge made her a little bit nauseated. The bridge looked scary enough, but when she saw that it could be crossed by an aerial tram ride she felt dizzy. Imagine that, suspended a thousand feet over a river on a cable!

Her phone rang just as her waiter brought her cheeseburger.

She looked at her phone. Henry's home number. "Hi, honey," she said, expecting Henry. But it was Prudence.

"It's Prudence, Harriet."

"Oh, Prudence. How are you, dear?"

"Henry showed me the bib, Harriet. You had no right to — "

"Hold on a second, Prudence. First of all Henry should not have opened my mail and secondly — "

"How could you do this? Having a child is between Henry and me."

"I never said it wasn't. I didn't intend for — "

Harriet thought she heard Prudence sniff like she'd been crying.

"Are you all right, dear?" Harriet asked.

"Mom, it's Henry. I'm sorry. But the bib ... well it ... it—"

"It what, Henry? I wasn't going to give it to you until the time was right. That's why I sent it addressed to me."

"Mom, there's something you should, know."

Harriet swallowed. "What is it?"

"Pru and I ... we've lost two babies already. Miscarriages."

Harriet felt like she had been punched in the stomach. Tears welled at the corners of her eyes. "Oh, honey, I'm ... why didn't you tell me? And here I've been going off on you two, trying to put pressure on you to have a—I'm sorry."

"You didn't know. We were having a hard time with the whole pregnancy thing. We didn't tell you because we didn't want to get your hopes up or make you worry."

"Oh, Henry, I feel awful. Put Prudence back on please. If she wants."

Harriet waited a long minute. She heard them talking but couldn't make out what they were saying. But in that long minute, Harriet needed to choke back tears of her own to stay strong for Henry and Prudence.

"Hello, Mom?"

"I'm so sorry, dear. I was wrong to put pressure on you. I thought you were putting your career first, waiting until things took off. Forgive me for hurting you. I promise I won't mention it again."

"Thank you."

There was a long pause between them until Harriet said, "But, Prudence, honey. I really do understand. And I want you to know that I'm here for you, or I will be there for you soon—but—" she needed to sniff back a tear—"only if you want."

"Thanks, Mom. But, I'm okay ... really. I just need time."

Harriet heard a little shuffle on the other end.

"Mom?" It was Henry.

"Henry, I'm very sorry for giving you such a hard time about having kids and about selling Dad's business and running off to write books. I know you needed to follow your heart, and I'm sorry if my nagging made it hard for you to tell me about your babies."

"I know, Mom. Let's just start fresh when you get here," Henry said.

"Okay, Son. And please tell Prudence I never meant for her to see the bib."

Harriet clicked off her phone and sighed. Poor Prudence. Poor Henry.

The conversation made Harriet lose her appetite. But she knew she needed to eat to keep up her strength. She still had a long way to travel. She chewed a French fry as she looked at the picture of the aerial tram on the table.

"I wonder . . . do I dare?"

Harriet finished her pie and headed for the front desk. She was greeted by a nice tall man in his late fifties. He wore a large gerbera daisy in his lapel.

"I like your flower," Harriet said.

"Well, thank you, honey. I just love my gerberas."

"I was wondering" — Harriet pointed to the tram — "can you tell me how I can get there from here? I don't have a car. I'm taking buses — well, mostly buses the whole way across the country."

The concierge looked at Harriet for a long second or two. "Royal Gorge. Um, that could be a bit of a sticky wicket. Although — " he tapped his finger against his temple — "I did hear about a new shuttle service that's taking folks clear up to Salida, and Cañon City is halfway there. In the middle. Maybe they stop. I'll call and let you know in the morning. Would that be okay?"

"Thank you," Harriet said. "I'll be in my room for the rest of the night."

Back in her room, Harriet changed into her blueberry-stained nightgown and slipped into bed. She yawned twice before reaching for her notebook.

Dear Max, I'm in Colorado and I just received news. Painful news. I suppose I shouldn't have sent that bib, but I never meant—

She sighed and leaned her head into the pillows. Tears threatened. She squeezed them back and returned to her letter.

I never meant to hurt Henry or Prudence. I just wanted to be a grandma. But Max, Henry told me that Prudence had two miscarriages. No wonder she's not anxious to try again. That kind of loss is at its worse, unspeakable. Why would she want to experience it again? I'm glad I know now and believe you me, I will never bring it up again.

She went back and underlined the word *never*.

* * *

Henry found Prudence on the back deck, sipping iced tea and staring out over the garden. She looked sad.

"What's wrong?" Henry asked.

Prudence turned toward him. "Oh, I'm just thinking."

Henry moved closer and put his arms around her waist. "About ... a baby?"

She pulled away from him. "No ... well, not exactly. Not just ... that. Your mother, also. And about being on the council—everything, I suppose."

"Well, look, you needn't think about babies anymore. I'm sorry this happened. I'm sorry about my mother. My mother's sorry about the whole thing. She would never—"

Prudence pulled the tumbler from her mouth. "I know. It's just that maybe ... maybe it's a sign of some sort. Maybe it is time to—"

Henry smiled and said, "Really?"

"To seriously consider the possibility."

"Good enough."

Prudence kissed Henry. "I need some more time to pray and think."

"Okay. I love you, Pru."

Humphrey trotted onto the deck and sniffed the air. He lay down at Prudence's feet and let go a contented sigh.

"That silly dog. Sometimes I think he can read minds."

Chapter 27

THE SHUTTLE BUS PULLED UP TO THE HOTEL AT JUST PAST noon. Harriet had already had her lunch and was feeling pretty good. She said good-bye to the concierge and climbed aboard the small, van-like bus.

"Hello," she said to the driver. "Thanks for the lift."

"No problem."

Harriet sat next to a woman wearing a brightly colored jacket with horses on it. She wore a cowboy hat and boots.

"Howdy," Harriet said.

"Hi," the woman said.

Harriet immediately sized her up as a nontalker. She'd met quite a few nontalkers on her journey. And that was fine with her. To each his own, she figured, but it was nice when she got a talker, since Harriet enjoyed a good conversation. The bus was practically full. Harriet counted only two empty seats. She felt sad, though, when she noticed that one of the people was blind, even though she knew she wasn't supposed to feel sad for people who were differently abled. The woman wore dark glasses and carried one of those red-tipped white canes. But the more Harriet looked, the more she realized that everyone on the bus, except her and the cowgirl next to her, was blind, with the exception of two sighted people who were issuing instructions and directions to the group.

"Well, lookee there," Harriet said to the cowgirl, "all these folks are learning how to ride the bus. Must be hard when you can't see. Something the rest of us take for granted, I suppose."

Less than an hour later the shuttle stopped in Cañon City, not far from the Royal Gorge Park. It stopped at a Walmart on Route 50, which made Harriet smile. She enjoyed seeing the RVs in the parking lot because she had heard that sometimes people camp out at the Walmarts.

The woman instructor asked Harriet and the cowgirl if they wouldn't mind debusing ahead of her group.

"No problem," Cowgirl said.

"Anything I can do to help?" Harriet asked.

"No," the woman said rather sternly, "they can do it all by themselves."

Of course, Harriet had not intended any insult. She genuinely wanted to help if she could. Having never been blind, she didn't quite understand how it worked.

Just to see, Harriet closed her eyes as she made her way to the front of the bus. She tripped over two sets of feet sticking in the aisle and crashed into the driver. Harriet looked back in time to catch a nasty look from the instructors. "I . . . I didn't mean anything by it."

Harriet got off as fast as she could and walked down the street as quickly as her achy legs would carry her. To her dismay, Harriet discovered that Cañon City was one of those towns that did not have a local bus service. She found this out from the clerk in Walmart. Harriet had gone in to escape the blind group she had inadvertently insulted and decided to purchase new socks. Unfortunately, as she stood in line she noticed the same group making their way around the store, learning to make purchases with the aid of their instructors. Harriet hid in shame.

The only way she was going to make it to the park was in a taxicab. She didn't really want to, but she had no choice. That was before she had a scathingly brilliant idea. She had stopped in the Walmart snack area when she heard a family discussing their plans to visit the Royal Gorge Bridge and Park. She thought long and hard about whether she should try to horn in on their vacation, but she would rather hitchhike the nine miles than take an uncomfortable taxi ride.

So she brazened herself up enough to ask if she could ride along with them. At first they were confused, then amused, then they finally agreed. She followed the family — a mom, a dad, a son, and a daughter — back to the parking lot. When they stopped next to a large Winnebago, Harriet felt a smile about as wide as the gorge stretch across her face.

"You mean I get to ride inside that?"

The father nodded. "Yes, ma'am. You'll be fine in the back with Sissy and Trevor."

She assumed Sissy and Trevor were the children and not the two Chihuahuas she saw yapping when Howard, the father, opened the door. "Come on, kids. Let's go see the gorge." He tried to sound upbeat, but Harriet had the distinct impression the children could not have cared less about this family vacation.

Harriet, on the other hand, loved the RV and settled into a fairly comfortable seat.

"My goodness," she said to the sullen teenager, Sissy, who obviously did not like Harriet being in her space and preferred to sulk in the corner with earbuds stuffed into her ear canals. "It's like a little house . . . a little rolling house."

Sissy rolled her eyes. Harriet smiled. "Don't fret, deary, puberty doesn't last forever. You'll become nice again."

Sissy's younger brother, Trevor, laughed. Harriet shifted in the vinyl seat, which was supposed to look like leather, facing Trevor. He just kind of glared at her like she was a sideshow amusement. This made Harriet feel terribly awkward and for some reason aware of her nose, which Trevor stared at like he was waiting for it to explode or something. Harriet resisted the urge to scratch it until Trevor turned away when Howard hit a bump in the road.

Fortunately the drive was short, and Howard pulled the huge rig into the park. They had designated spots for campers.

Harriet thanked them kindly, handed Howard twenty dollars for gas, then went on her merry way in search of the tram. She was trying hard not to actually look at the view, considering it was a thousand feet straight down into the Arkansas River. She went to the visitor's center, purchased her ticket, and looked around the souvenir shop. She was thrilled to find salt and pepper shakers shaped like the tram car.

She ventured outdoors, where the air was crisp and warm-ish but certainly not hot. The sky was blue. Light, wispy clouds floated past like lacy parasols. What disturbed her was that there were actually clouds below her and next to her in the gorge, between the two rims. She tried not to think about it and made her way to the tram loading dock. The dock was attached to a little brown shack carved into the rocks.

"Yep. That looks safe. If only Prudence were here. She'd have so much to say."

She fell in line, being the ninth person to board the tram. Everyone seemed excited except one lady, about her age, who kept saying, "Oh, Lord! Oh, Lord, protect us. Don't let the cable snap."

Harriet was happy the woman was surrounded by her family. She heard her son say, "But, Mom, it's what you wanted for your sixtieth birthday, to travel across the gorge on the tram. And here we are."

Harriet willed her knees not to shake, even though she thought about grabbing the nervous woman by the hand and running away with her. Harriet had never been fond of heights, but this? This was ridiculous! Crossing the mountains by bus had been one thing, but crossing a gorge locked inside a flaming red tram car was something entirely different. She could now see the bottom of the gorge between the clouds. "It's gorge-eous," she said aloud, hoping to get a reaction from someone. But folks seemed just too intent on staying alive as they crossed.

The line began to move and just as she was about to step aboard the red dragon, Harriet's tote bag slipped from her shoulder and knocked another, rather short passenger in the head, who turned suddenly and inadvertently slapped the birthday lady's butt, which made her jump, nearly starting a domino chain of people.

"I'm sorry," Harriet said, "I tripped on . . . something and that made my pack—"

"It's okay," hollered someone, "just keep moving."

Harriet moved to the front of the tram car and sucked in a deep breath. It was small and enclosed with windows all around. She stood close to the tram operator, an older man who looked like he might have been dealing with some indigestion. Harriet certainly knew she was. Nervous situations always made her gassy. She hoped she wouldn't have to expel any gas in the close quarters. But then, someone else beat her to it. She didn't feel so alone.

Why did I do this? Harriet thought as she looked out the window. The view was spectacular, but it made her feel dizzy. And what good was a spectacular view if you were too dizzy to enjoy it?

"I'm dizzy," she said.

The operator looked at her. "Want to get off? Speak now because once she goes I can't bring her back. You won't be the first."

"Oh, good Lord . . . ," Harriet heard the birthday woman say.

"No, no, I told Prudence I'm doing it, and I am going to do it. Cast off, Gilligan."

The operator didn't find that amusing. He spoke into a microphone. "Closed and ready."

The car lurched and then bobbled, and then—weeeeee—they were out over the gorge, suspended by two cables that looked like threads to Harriet. She closed her eyes. Opened her eyes. Closed them again. Until, she started to feel okay, like she had gotten her tram legs. The ride was smooth, even though she felt like she was walking a tightrope. She was in the sky, eye level with clouds. She could see the river so far below it looked like it had been drawn with crayon. This is what it must be like to be a bird, an eagle. She thought about the Scripture that reminded her that she could soar like an eagle, and now here she was doing exactly that. Well, not soaring maybe; the tram didn't move at breakneck speed.

About halfway across, the family riding the train burst into a chorus of "Happy Birthday." Harriet joined in and remarked how it made the passage that much easier. The birthday girl burst into tears. "Oh, Lord, oh, Lord."

The tram docked on the other side. The doors opened, and Harriet had never seen a group of people move faster to get out of anything in her life. She was the last one off. The operator stayed to reload.

"Would you do me a favor?" she asked the operator before she got off. "Take my picture in this tram contraption so I can show it to Prudence and prove I really rode it."

Chapter 28

AFTER THE RIDE ACROSS ROYAL GORGE, HARRIET NEARLY lost her resolve to make it all the way to Grass Valley, California, by taking public transportation. She considered hitching rides with motorcycle-driving preachers and a family in an RV as public transportation, considering that people are the public.

But now, atop this wonderful mountain called Point Sublime, staring down at what amounted to an abyss, Harriet started to cry. There was no bus to take her through this part of Colorado. It was rural and open and fit for a cattle drive and not much else. The towns were few and far between.

Harriet looked at her phone and, for the first time, thought her only recourse was to call Henry and scream, *"Uncle."* And then wait until he came and rescued her. She brushed her fingers over the phone. "What to do. What to do." Her spirits sank as she looked out over the gorge. It was such a magnificent place, but for all its splendor, it lacked bus service.

She checked Amelia once again, just to double-check her bearings. Yep, her next large city destination needed to be Colorado Springs, but how?

"Oh dear. I'll figure it out. I got up this dang fool hill. I can get down."

She thanked God for getting her this far — and safely. She

praised him for such a beautiful place and then checked on the family she rode up the mountain with. Their Winnebago was gone, nothing but a grease spot where it had been parked. She sighed and wandered over to a concession stand and bought two funnel cakes and a Coke. She sat at a picnic table and ate her snack and ruminated on her predicament. From where she sat she had an incredible view of the bridge. She could not even begin to imagine how it was ever constructed between the two rims, crafted as it was into rock and with nothing supporting it underneath. It seemed an engineering impossibility. It was now nearly four o'clock and a warmish wind was whipping around, but she kind of enjoyed it. It made her think of Max and how he loved to fly kites with Henry. She pulled out her notebook and wrote:

Hi, honey, I think I am in one of the most beautiful places on earth. It's called the Royal Gorge Park. And it is just that —royal. I am sitting on the west side now. You won't believe this but I rode the tram, an aerial tram clear across it, over two thousand feet. Yep, one of those little cars suspended from cables like they show in the movies that always snap just as the murderer is about to kill his victim. There was no killer on board, just a birthday girl. The view was spectacular. A river runs down below, a thousand feet down from where I am sitting right this minute. But I imagine you might be able to see from way up in heaven. It made me think about what it means to take a leap of faith. It kind of felt like that when the car left the dock. Suddenly suspended by cables, I had no choice but to trust the driver and those cables. Faith is like that, isn't it, Max? Trusting in that which we cannot see. I think I'm beginning to get that.

Harriet looked around for a second.

But here's the trouble. I can't figure out how to get back down. No buses. There's a train but it only runs at the bottom of the gorge.

Harriet looked out over the rim as two clouds floated past. Tears welled up in her eyes, and she began to cry. But as she did she kind of felt a presence, like someone was staring at her. Oh dear, it was so embarrassing to be caught crying.

"Excuse please," came a deep but definitely female voice. "You okay?"

Harriet turned. The woman was tall and husky with short curly blond hair. She wore blue sunglasses and a felt hat with a feather sticking out of it with the words DON'T JUMP embroidered into the rim and a bright yellow Windbreaker.

Wiping her eyes, Harriet said, "I seem to be stuck. I hitchhiked up here, and now I have no way down, unless I can hitch another ride. My name's Harriet, by the way ... Harriet Beamer."

"My name is Olga, Olga Stanislavsky. Don't worry. You ride with us."

Olga waved to a group of women standing about fifty yards away—all wearing the same bright yellow Windbreakers and felt hats.

"That be my church group over there. We take trip out here sometime. It's most beautiful place on earth, no? Gretchen's made first trip 'cross on the tram. She throw up after, but they say that happens a lot."

"Phew," Harriet said, "I didn't throw up, but I can see why she would."

The rest of the church group ambled over and hovered near Harriet like a band of guardian angels. And if the truth be known, Harriet couldn't imagine being happier seeing angels than she was seeing these ladies.

"*Devojke,*" Olga said, looking at her friends, "this is Harriet, and she needs a ride. We give Harriet ride, no?"

"Of course, yes." They all spoke together.

Olga slapped Harriet on the back. "There. You see, we take you. No problem."

Harriet felt her face warm. "But ... where are you heading?"

264

"We are from Gunnison, about an hour away," Gretchen said. "but ve take you vere you need."

"Would it be much of a bother to take me back to Pueblo? I can get a train or a bus from there."

"No problem," said another voice in the small crowd.

Harriet breathed a huge sigh of relief. "Thank you. Thank you so much."

"Vee go then," Olga said. "On da bus."

Harriet tucked her notebook into her tote and followed the women to the small blue bus with the words SAINT HERMAN OF ALASKA ORTHODOX CHURCH on the side. It looked quite old and rickety.

"Olga is driver," Olga said, tapping her own chest.

Harriet swallowed. "Sounds like fun." Or so she thought.

The bus was rickety and seemed to not have a single working spring left in it. Harriet felt every bump and pothole along the road. And Olga seemed to enjoy taking the twists and curves with abandon.

"Here vee gooo," she would holler just before a curve. And all the women would end up leaning to the left and then to the right.

"It's like being on a roller coaster," Harriet said to Gretchen.

Gretchen laughed. "Yep. But she'll get us home. Does every time."

BUMP!

"What was that?" Harriet asked.

"Who knows," Gretchen said.

Needless to say, Harriet was quite pleased when Olga and everyone else on the bus made it safely back to Pueblo, back to the Walmart from whence she started the day's adventure.

Harriet stood with her suitcase at the front of the bus. She thought for a moment how wonderful it was to have church people, and then she said her good-byes to her new friends.

By now it was nearly dinner time, close to 5:00, and Harriet was bushed, hungry, and even though she knew where she was, geographically speaking, she felt a little lost as she surveyed the town. She found a bench, sat down, and tucked her tote between her feet and parked her suitcase next to her and, for a moment, thought she must look like a runaway or a homeless woman. Not wanting to draw attention to herself, she checked in with her GPS. According to Amelia her best bet was to head for Denver where she could probably catch an Amtrak for a good distance across Colorado.

Unfortunately, according to the Amtrak website, she would need to wait until the next day to catch the Thruway Motorcoach to Denver. No trains ran from Pueblo to Denver. But she discovered she could walk from the Walmart to the Comfort Inn, which was just dandy to Harriet after the harrowing bus ride down the mountain.

*　*　*

That evening, after supper, Henry and Prudence settled down to watch a little TV. "Well," Henry said, "no salt-and-pepper-shaker delivery today."

Prudence tucked her feet under her bottom and snuggled into the sofa next to Henry and Sandra Day the cat. "Really? I bet she chickened out."

"You know," Henry said, "I did a little research earlier, looking at some maps online, and I cannot imagine how on earth she's going to get up or down from the gorge without a car. And she certainly can't rent a car up there. And from what I can tell, there is no public transit—maybe a taxi but I'm not even sure that would work."

"If she said she was going to do it, she did it. I keep telling you, my mother is stubborn like a mule."

Prudence stroked Sandra Day's back. "What's next? Skydiving?"

Henry shrugged. "Who knows, but at least we know she's in Colorado. Almost here."

"I suppose. I just hope she arrives in one piece." Prudence yawned. "I'm sleepy."

Henry flipped through the channels until he landed on a show about how pencils are made. Prudence rested her head on his shoulder. "This is good," she said.

"Have you been thinking . . . ," Henry said, "about a baby?"

Prudence didn't respond right away. "Off and on. I think I'm just scared. I can't go through that again."

"I don't want to go through it again either, but the doctor said—"

"I know what the doctor said." Prudence lifted her head. "Let's just get your mother here in one piece before we decide."

"Okay, we can do that."

Humphrey ambled into the living room. Sandra Day startled, meowed loudly, and took off lickety-split up the stairs.

"That dog," Prudence said.

Henry stroked Prudence's hair. "You know what? Part of me is glad she might have to call for help, but another part of me wants to see her make it."

Chapter 29

AFTER A CONTINENTAL BREAKFAST AT THE COMFORT INN, Harriet boarded the Amtrak Thruway bus toward Denver, Colorado.

She sat on the seat next to a man wearing cowboy garb and who smelled a lot like horses. Harriet rubbed her nose and then quietly moved to another seat. She looked at her phone. Henry had been calling her repeatedly for almost one full day.

"I guess I better call. Next stop." She sighed. "Denver, Colorado." A well of excitement burbled up inside. Denver. The mile-high city. The thought made her excited and nervous. Even the name sounded big.

Harriet watched as several small towns whizzed past, some like images straight out of a spaghetti western, others more suburban, and still other stretches of road with nearly no houses or stores to be seen.

The bus pulled into the Denver transit center, a long blue and white building, which doubled as a Greyhound Bus station. Harriet lingered a moment in her seat as the other passengers disembarked. There was a little bit of a stampede as though they all had connecting trains or buses to catch. And since Harriet had nowhere to go — not immediately anyway — she waited, and as it turned out she was the last to leave the bus.

"Now where?" was Harriet's first thought as she stood on the pavement with her tote and suitcase. It was also when she noticed the tail of one of her foxes was hanging out of the suitcase and was probably the reason she had been receiving some curious looks by passersby. She unzipped the case and stuffed the fox inside. As she looked up she noticed the looming building across the street. The Ritz Carlton Hotel.

She checked the time, although she already knew it was around 1:30 in the afternoon. She also wondered why people always checked the time even when they already knew.

"I am hungry," she told herself. "I'm also tired." She once again felt the pang of traveling alone as she talked to herself, wishing she could have brought Humphrey along. Maybe next time.

Harriet set off across the street to the Ritz. It was a spectacular place, and Harriet was positive it was because of this hotel that we get our word "ritzy". She was also lucky to get a room since there was a convention of ophthalmologists in town.

"Oh, my," Harriet said to the desk clerk. "Let's hope they don't make a spectacle of themselves."

The clerk didn't see the pun.

Harriet laughed out loud when she passed a sign displaying information about the upcoming Ophthalmologist Eye Ball.

Her room was nothing less than amazing in her mind. Kind of golden with yellowish walls and a golden bedspread on the queen-size bed. After the bellman showed her all the amenities — the climate control, the fancy bathroom — and opened the curtains to a grand view of the city and the snowcapped Rocky Mountains, she needed to catch her breath.

"Oh dear," she said, "it's glorious. I can't wait to tell Martha."

After a trip to the bathroom Harriet sat on the bed and felt a little like Cleopatra on her barge with all the gold around her. She called Martha's number.

"Harriet," Martha said, "I was starting to worry about you. Are you okay?"

Harriet could hear the concern in her friend's voice. "Of course I am. I've just been a little busy. I'm sorry I didn't call sooner."

"Well, tell me where you are now."

"Denver. I'm staying at the Ritz Carlton. Can you believe it? Me. Harriet Beamer at the Ritz."

They both laughed.

"I have so much to tell you," Harriet said. "But let me start with the snake handlers."

Chapter 30

HENRY WAS WITHIN TWO WEEKS OF HIS DEADLINE. HE WAS almost finished with his story, although he also knew the book would need work, and he was glad that another set of eyes, another mind would be looking at it. Henry also knew that he must turn in the manuscript on time, not only for the sake of his editor but also for his own. He knew there had to come a time when an artist stopped his work, when he had to say, "Enough."

Henry was pleased that Cash was able to ask forgiveness. But not so pleased that Katherine said nothing, but merely walked away.

Cash held his head low as Katherine walked back inside the hotel to look after her daughter, their daughter. The child he would be denied because of a moment's indiscretion. A moment of unthinking.

The typing was coming faster now, more intense, more focused as Henry neared the end. He could feel it now, all the emotions that rattled around inside Cash, all the feelings that told him to run, start anew, and yet every time Cash started for high ground, he turned back.

"How can he leave them?" Henry said.

Humphrey whined.

Henry took a deep breath and leaned back in his chair. He stretched and yawned and had just settled his fingers onto the keyboard when the phone jingled. It was Harriet's jingle.

"Oh, Mom, I was worried sick over you. Where are you? Are you okay?"

"I'm a little tired, Henry. I'm in Denver, Colorado."

"Denver, well at least that's a city I recognize. How do you like it?"

"I like it just fine, dear. I'm staying at the fanciest hotel I have ever been in."

Henry paused. He liked the notion of his mom surrounded by luxury. "I'm glad. Mom. And I'm glad you're almost here."

"Almost," Harriet said, "but I still have plenty of miles and plenty to see."

"You could just take the train straight across to California from Denver," Henry said looking at his computer screen. He moused down to a section he wanted to reread.

"Oh, I don't know. I'll check with Amelia and decide. But first I'm going to order room service. Fancy-dancy room service. I could go for a donut."

Henry laughed. "Mom. You should order something more healthy. But remember, room service is quite expensive."

"I know, dear. That's the point. Now how are you? How's the book? How is Prudence? Does she really know how sorry I am for butting in?"

"It's almost finished. I think Cash and Katherine are going to reconcile. You know, a happy ending and all, and yes, Pru knows how sorry you are, and you know what Mom?"

"What?"

"She's thinking and praying. Maybe we'll try again."

Harriet smiled and then let go a long sigh. "I knew she would, Son."

"Thanks, Mom. You know, I think that bib got us talking again."

"God doesn't waste a thing, does he?"

"I can't wait to see you," Henry said.

"Now, how is Humphrey? I miss him so much. I wish he was here to share a donut with me. That is, *if* I can get donuts here."

"I bet he'd love to be with you. Crazy dog loves donuts."

With that Humphrey jumped up and danced his usual jig.

"Look, he's dancing," Henry said. "It's like he understands."

"Of course he does. Put him on."

"What?"

"The phone, dear. Put Humphrey on the phone."

Henry held the phone to the dog's ear.

"Hello, Humphrey. Harriet misses you so much."

Humphrey's tail wagged a mile a minute.

"I have donuts. You want some donuts?"

Humphrey barked.

Henry took the phone away from Humphrey.

"Mother, what did you tell him?"

"Now listen, you must go straightaway and get Humphrey two glazed donuts. They must be glazed. Nothing else."

"Mo-om, are you kidding?"

"I never kid about donuts. Now promise me you'll get donuts for Humphrey."

"Okay. I promise."

"Now listen, dear. I'll be there soon. Tell Prudence I ... I love her."

"I will. I think we're anxious for you to finally arrive."

"And you know what, Son? I am too. Oh dear, my stomach is rumbling something fierce."

Henry touched the End button and dropped the phone onto a pile of pages on his desk. "Donuts. That woman and her donuts."

* * *

That evening Harriet enjoyed a scrumptious room-service meal of steak and baked potato. The potato was rather large, and she could only eat part of it. But the steak was like butter in her mouth. She also watched a little TV and caught up on the news and weather. She was heading into some rainy skies across the West. But she rather liked that.

After dinner and a shower and changing into her jammies, Harriet consulted Amelia and Amtrak and, of course, Greyhound. It seemed local bus service was getting sparse. She checked the maps and decided that her best bet was to train into Provo, Utah, and from there she liked the idea of heading up to Salt Lake City. It seemed the obvious choice on account of her liking salt and pepper shakers.

"Now I just bet I can get some nice shakers there," she said as she tapped the Amtrak number.

* * *

The next morning Harriet made her way to the train station via taxi. She needed to be there early as the train left at 8:05 a.m. The weather was warmish, although the sky was darkening and threatening rain. She made certain her rain poncho was in her tote bag just in case.

Inside, the Denver station was sparse, not much in the way of artwork like Harriet had seen in other stations. And the benches reminded her of church pews. She chose a nearly empty bench and sat down to wait for the call to board. It wouldn't be too long. Harriet had come to love the sound of the announcer telling passengers to board the trains. It made her feel so exotic, like she could be a spy. This time out she'd be riding aboard the California Zephyr. She liked the name Zephyr. It meant wind. She'd ride the wind into Utah.

What she didn't expect was the announcement that the train would be nearly an hour late. Apparently there was some kind of problem on the tracks. So she took the time to purchase, fill out, and mail three postcards to Martha. She knew Martha would enjoy the images of the amazing limestone rock formations she had been seeing all over Colorado. Harriet thought they were spectacular also, but Martha, being so artistic, would no doubt value them all the more. She also chose a postcard that featured the Rocky Mountains, seeing how she would be riding right through them on her way into Utah.

But finally, at 8:45, the California Zephyr left Denver for points west, including Provo. The train was cool and comfortable. She again had a window seat and was able to enjoy the sights, mostly brush ground and telephone poles zipping past and the clackety-clack of the train wheels on track. Harriet decided to tell Max about the train.

Dear Max, I'm on the train called the California Zephyr on my way to Provo, Utah. It was the only easy way to go, and to be honest, honey, I need a bit of the easy way right now. My body is tired now. But the good news is that once I reach Provo I can catch some local buses into Salt Lake City. I wonder if there really is a salt lake and if it's anything like the Dead Sea. I'll find out. Anyhoo, the train is passing through some mountains. It's like they carved the rails right into the hills and valleys. The conductor just said we're approaching a place called Castle Gate. He said it used to be a mining town, and Butch Cassidy held up the Pleasant Valley Coal Company here for $7000. Imagine that. I really am in the Old West, honey.

Harriet stopped writing and looked out the window at winding mountainside, the craggy rocks on one side, the trees and shrub and brush on the other. Just a couple of days ago she was suspended a thousand feet in the air looking down, and today it was like she was a thousand feet below looking up, or at least looking out at walls of dirt and rock. She closed her eyes and dozed, but they popped open when the conductor, who was acting more like a tour guide, spoke again.

"We are now approaching Soldier Summit," the conductor said, "with an elevation of seven thousand feet. They say this abandoned town is where a group of Southern soldiers en route to join the Confederate Army were caught in a snowstorm in July 1861."

And then approximately five and three quarter hours after leaving Denver, Harriet detrained at the Provo, Utah, station. It was just about 3:30 in the afternoon. She stood on the platform with her bag at her side. At other stations she had seen taxis lined up like the train cars ready to take her wherever she needed to go. But not here. The station was nothing more than two small shelters, and only one was enclosed. She stood a minute and stretched her arms and legs. There was something about getting off a train that made her wobbly. It always took a few minutes to get her land legs back.

The one thing Harriet did not like about her decision to bus across the country was that at times she was forced to spend the night in a place where she would rather not. But bus schedules being what they were, she had no choice but to spend the night in Provo. She could have stayed on the train all the way to Salt Lake City—but she still had a notion to bus as much as possible.

Harriet checked Amelia for a hotel and a restaurant as usual. It seemed she was often arriving at places around dinner time and wondered if this was part of a grand scheme. She would need to walk just a short distance to University Avenue, the main drag through town where she would find the closest motel. A place called the Rest Inn. It sounded better than it looked, with a rusty red roof that seemed to be sagging in one section and chipped paint everywhere else. But she was so tired she thought she could sleep hanging on a nail.

It was one of those motels that was really a long building of small attached rooms all on the ground level. There was a neon sign that flashed the words REST INN and had a neon bed underneath with flashing Z's. She thought that at least was cute. A man who reminded her of Herman Munster led her to her room. She swore he was wearing a holster. That in itself made Harriet worry.

He unlocked the door and let her in first. It was the smell that struck her first—musty, damp, dank, and dreary were the only adjectives she could come up with. The bed looked lumpy with a gold quilted thing on it that made Harriet wince when she felt it. She decided she would be sleeping on top of the covers that night. And sleeping quickly so she could hightail it out of there the next morning.

Chapter 31

AFTER SETTLING INTO HER ROOM HARRIET SET OUT FOR A late night snack. She found an open coffee shop within a few blocks. It was quaint and pretty inside and smelled of coffee mixed with the aroma of butter and toast and vanilla. She sat at a tall bistro table and ordered a latte, which arrived in a widemouthed porcelain cup. She also happily ate a cranberry scone and ordered two more to go. As she paid, she asked the young woman working the cash register, "Can you tell me where the closest bus stop is?"

"Right outside, across the street."

"Thank you," Harriet said, making a mental note for the next morning. According to Amelia, Harriet would need to take a light rail into the city after a couple of buses. The light rail was called TRAX and was kind of an above-ground subway. And that was fine.

Harriet set off for Salt Lake City the next morning. Once again she had a window seat. The train was not crowded, and she had the entire seat to herself. She passed through downtown Provo. Very city-like with tall buildings and rows of offices. People just about everywhere. She thought it odd how the train could stop in a big town, right on top of a road. She enjoyed the sights and sounds of the train as the gates came down and the lights flashed.

Thirteen stops later she was in the middle of Salt Lake City, not far from the Amtrak Station where she would need to catch a train to get out of Utah and into Nevada. She felt like cheering.

The Salt Lake City train station was not much to look at in her opinion. It was very modular and reminded Harriet of a trailer home. She sat on a bench and considered her next move. She consulted Amelia, who suggested she just stay on the train right into Grass Valley, but no, Harriet was determined to take a bus into Grass Valley. Given how tired she was feeling she decided to head into Reno, Nevada, directly. So she purchased a ticket to Reno.

"Got some time," the ticket agent said. "About eleven hours."

"Oh dear, well, I'll just see some of the sights, then."

But now what? Salt Lake was a huge city. Maybe she would set out to find the lake — if there really was one. She inquired at a small shop, where she purchased five sets of salt and pepper shakers and two salt crystal Christmas ornaments that she had to pack into her suitcase since it was too late to FedEx anything.

As it turned out a salt lake did exist, but it was too far to travel to and Harriet was still feeling a trifle under the weather. Although the weather in Salt Lake City was pleasant enough, about fifty degrees by noon. She still had a crick in her neck and a pain in her back that no amount of acetaminophen squashed. So she waited and wrote to Max:

> Salt Lake City is huge, dear. I think I'll just sit close to the station and wait for the train. What else is there for an old, make that older, woman to do? Oh, dear Max, dear dear Max, if I was twenty years younger I would go out on the town. Remember how we loved the jazz bars, Iggy's especially. We could sit for hours it seemed and listen to the sounds move around the place, and every so often it was as though some of the notes would reach our ears in an unexpected way and surprise us. You liked Coltrane, I remember that. I never told you this, Max, but I couldn't stand his music, but I listened because you loved him so. Oh dear, now why did I bring that up?

Harriet closed her notebook and leaned her back against the cold, stucco wall.

I miss you and John Coltrane.

* * *

Henry and Humphrey started down the street. It was a beautiful northern California day. The sun was finally shining after several days of rain. Humphrey trotted alongside Henry, stopping occasionally to sniff or pee, but he was not quite ready to do what everybody knew he needed to do.

"Come on, old man," Henry said.

Humphrey just kept moving, leading Henry around the corner.

Mrs. Caldwell was in her yard tossing weeds into a bucket. She wore a straw hat and white gardening gloves with green thumbs.

"Morning," Henry said.

"Why, Henry, dear," Mrs. Caldwell said. "I haven't seen you or Humphrey in a while."

"I've been busy."

"On your novel, I hope." She stood from her kneeling position and craned her back. "Oh, to be twenty years younger."

"Yes. I'm nearly finished."

"Care for some pie?" Mrs. Caldwell smiled as she slipped her gloves off and tossed them into the weed bucket. "Come on inside. I have coffee on."

Henry and Humphrey followed her through the back porch and into her bright kitchen. It made Henry feel instantly at peace.

Mrs. Caldwell washed her hands and then sliced into a lemon meringue that already had a slice missing. "Hear from your mother?"

"Uh-hum, she's still out West but getting closer. I worry about her though. Hate that she's traveling alone."

"She'll be fine. She has a cell phone, right?"

"She does but still . . ." Henry swallowed a bite of pie. "Get this.

She rode part of the way in the sidecar of some snake-handling preacher man in Kentucky."

"Get out." Mrs. Caldwell's eye grew wide.

"Nope. It's the truth."

With that Mrs. Caldwell busted into a laugh that Henry was certain could be heard around the neighborhood. "That's wonderful. My goodness, your mother is a riot. I cannot wait to meet her."

Mrs. Caldwell could hardly contain her giggles. "Oh, Henry, I can't tell if you're proud of your mother or upset. Seems to me she is handling things pretty well. She's being quite resourceful, don't you think? You know, Henry, she's a big girl. She'll make it."

"I know."

Mrs. Caldwell sat at the kitchen table. "What's really bothering you?"

"Oh, it's . . . it's silly."

"No, it isn't. Seems like there's another reason you want your mama out here."

"Are you always this perceptive, or is it just me you can see through?"

"Nah, I see through everyone. You don't live as long as me and not learn a few things about human nature." She cut Henry another slice of pie.

"Well, Prudence would skin me alive if she knew I was telling you this, but . . . I guess I was hoping having her here would inspire Prudence to . . ." He looked away. "I shouldn't say. She wouldn't appreciate it."

"That's fine. I don't need to know. But, Henry, dear, you need to be the one to inspire Prudence. Not your mama. Don't put that on her. She's at a time in her life when all she needs to do — should do — is enjoy it as best she can. As she sees fit, don't you think?"

"I guess."

Henry finished his pie. "Thank you — for everything."

"Now go finish that book and let your mother find her own way home."

Harriet boarded the California Zephyr bound ultimately for Emeryville, California, at 11:00 p.m. after spending a rather uneventful day in Salt Lake City. Oh, she enjoyed buying the salt and pepper shakers and seeing some sights but she was thankful to be settling into a comfortable train seat once again. The train didn't arrive in Reno until 8:30 the next morning. She was excited about sleeping on the train again and thought it was the most relaxing way to sleep in the world. It would be kind of like being cradled and rocked in huge arms. But unfortunately Harriet had a terrible night. She slept off and on, but mostly off. It wasn't that the train was uncomfortable. It was just her thoughts keeping her awake. She kept going over all she had seen and done, and now it seemed her adventure would be coming to an end. According to Amelia, Grass Valley was only one hour and thirty-nine minutes from Reno.

But as the sun rose so did her spirits. She was served a lovely breakfast aboard the train — eggs and fruit, toast and potatoes, coffee with real cream. And she remarked to the conductor on his way past how nice the trip had been.

The Reno train station was not so exciting and mostly under-ground — or so it seemed, so when she emerged onto the street and into the brightness of the morning she felt elated. The town was nice. It still had a Western feel to it but also a glitzy appeal with bright lights, tall buildings, and people walking about. But the most spectacular sight of all was the famous Reno Arch. Now Saint Louis had their arch and Harriet thought it was nice, but the huge neon arch that spanned one of the main drags in town nearly made Harriet swoon. She stood gazing upon it. The word RENO so tall and bright and under that the words THE BIGGEST LITTLE CITY IN THE WORLD.

"My goodness. I'm . . . really here." She swiped at unexpected tears. She knew she still had a short leg of the journey left, but as she looked at the Reno Arch she saw perhaps for the first time since leaving Philadelphia that she was in a whole new world.

She also knew that Reno was kind of like Las Vegas, famous for casinos on every corner, and at first she thought she would avoid going inside one. But after a few minutes of walking around town, avoiding the bus ride into Grass Valley and the necessary phone call to Henry, she poked her head inside a casino. Then she let her whole body inside, and my-o-my, but it was the most colorful, brightest place she had ever seen. Even with no windows it was spectacular. She had never seen so much purple and red and blue and yellow in her life. It reminded her of a cartoon come to life.

Then she spotted a man sitting alone on a bright purple bench.

Now the reason he caught her eye was that he seemed to have only one arm and a guitar case at his feet. His sleeve was pinned up at his shoulder and he seemed terribly distraught. Harriet took a deep breath. She said a prayer. "Lord, I just have a feeling I need to talk to that man. So here I go. Protect me, and please don't let him be some kind of psycho." She moved toward him and got within a few feet, thought better of her decision, and turned around. But it was like she had walked into a brick wall. She had no choice but to turn around and talk to the young man who now held his head in his hand.

Harriet sat next to him on the same bench. "Mind if I sit here?" With his head still in his hand he said, "Free country."

"And a big one," she said with a chuckle. She tucked her suitcase to the side of her. "I know. Boy, do I know that." She slapped her knee. "Huge. Huge country with so many things to see and do you could never do them all, not in one lifetime — believe me, I know — " She stopped talking, realizing she had started to babble.

"Uh-huh."

Harriet took a deep breath. She thought it was like talking to a statue, but she had to try again. So she took a breath and dove back into conversation. One-armed man, one-sided conversation. She accepted this for the moment.

"You kind of remind me of my son, Henry. I'm on my way to see him, well, more than that, move in with him and his wife, Prudence."

"Why? Does he have one arm?"

"Excuse me? What?"

"You said I remind you of your son."

"Oh, oh, no, I'm sorry. I hadn't really ... noticed, well lookee there, that sleeve does seem to be a little ... empty." By now Harriet had figured she embarrassed herself so much it didn't really matter if she just kept talking. She had no dignity left.

She took a breath. "No. My Henry has both his arms. Leastways he did the last time I saw him, which was last Christmas when all this—" She stopped talking again. "I babble when I'm nervous. Now look, do you mind if I ask—"

"Birth defect."

Harriet thought about that a second or two. "Defect? Now that is no way to describe yourself. What makes being born with one arm a defect? You were born just how God Almighty intended you to be born, no two ways about it."

"Look, lady, I'm not interested in all that mumbo jumbo. Could you just go away, please?" He picked up a cowboy hat that was on the floor and set it on his head.

"Now, look, I would like nothing more than to go away. I didn't want to sit here in the first place, but I felt a kind of nudge to sit, and here I am. I try to pay attention to certain nudges in life, and besides I'd rather talk to you than spend my money in those rat-blasted machines."

"That's how I lost all mine. Was hoping to ... win."

"Why? Why do you need to win? If you come to these places thinking it will make your life better ... well, that's not the reason you should come."

The man grew a little fidgety.

"That your guitar?" Harriet asked.

"Yep."

Harriet had to think a moment before speaking. Then she couldn't contain it anymore. "Here's the thing, son, I probably got no right asking this, but how on earth do you play the guitar with one arm? If you don't mind me asking."

The man looked away for a second. "I don't. I play with my feet. My bare feet."

Harriet had to hold back a chuckle. The images his words brought to mind were comical, but she managed not to laugh, seeing how if he was telling the truth it would be insulting. "No way. How do you do that?"

"Just do. Been playing that way since I was eight years old when I found my granddaddy's guitar in the toolshed."

"I think that's amazing. Well, if we weren't sitting here with all that noisy casino stuff going on, I'd ask you to play me a tune."

The man laughed. But it was not a happy laugh. More like a derisive laugh. A laugh that told Harriet that this fella had given up playing.

"Been thinking about pawning the guitar for more money so I can play some more."

Harriet nearly gasped. "Now that is the dumbest thing I have ever heard in my life. You are going to pawn your guitar for what, twenty minutes at the slot machine. That's just stupid, if you don't mind me saying."

"Well, I do mind. It's my guitar and my business."

Harriet let her pot simmer down before she spoke again. "That's true. That's very true but, look, I'd rather give you money than let you do that."

"Really?"

"But not to gamble with. You look hungry. I could buy you lunch or dinner or whatever. I can't even tell what time it is. They keep these places dark and windowless on purpose, I suppose. Keep you off center, that's what they do."

"Not hungry. I might just go—"

"Go where?"

285

"To my room."

"You got a room in this fancy hotel?"

"Comped."

Harriet nodded like she understood what that meant.

"Means it's free," said the cowboy. "They give you free rooms when you gamble a lot."

"Uhm. I see. It kind of keeps you spending money in their casino that way."

The cowboy looked away and nodded.

"Will you at least tell me your name?"

"Bernard Weston, but folks call me Buddy. Buddy Weston."

Harriet shook his hand. "Well, it's a pleasure to meet you. My name is Harriet Beamer."

Buddy swallowed and looked out onto the casino floor. "Lady, I'm starting to wonder who's more crazy. Me or you."

"Guess we're both crazy. I just crossed the country on public transportation. And you . . . you're sitting here all dejected for some reason you won't tell me and claim to play your guitar with your feet. I think both stories are crazy."

"I do play. And sing. I'm pretty good too. It's just . . . just that . . . ah, forget it. I got no hope."

"Hope? Of course you have hope. Hope never goes away. It's like a little bird that sits in your soul and just keeps right on singing and singing no matter how bad the storm."

Harriet looked into Buddy's eyes. They were soft and sad and missing something.

That was when Harriet got her dander and her nerve up. "Now, you tell me straight, Buddy Weston, are you planning to do something stupid and insane like kill yourself on account of you can't play your guitar with your feet and make money doing it?"

He stood and made like he was going to leave. "Look, lady, I didn't ask you to help me. I never told you to sit down next to me and start yakking about your stupid son and your stupid trip across the country. You're just a rich old woman trying to tick off her daughter-in-law by taking your idiotic trip. What good is it doing? What good is anything?"

"I only wanted to help."

"You can't. Nobody can."

He grabbed his guitar and vanished into the crowd.

Harriet felt terrible. She stared down at her red sneakers. Maybe Buddy was right. What good was the trip? Was it really necessary?

Harriet opened her notebook.

Oh, Max, I met a young man who I think is fixing to do away with himself. I want to stop him, but I don't know how. Seems to me someone determined to die is going to find a way. I wish I never came here.

Harriet looked toward the lights and sounds of the casino. She heard a couple or three cheers.

I guess all those people are having fun over at the games. But in the real world? A man is trying to end his life. It's not fair. And here I am, almost home and what have I really accomplished? I helped a little along the way. I learned it's okay to dream. I found courage I never knew I had. But when it comes down to a man living or dying I can't make a difference.

She thought about going after Buddy, but he didn't want her help or her friendship. How could she keep a man that bent on self-destruction from doing what he wanted? She looked skyward. "You got me into this. You took me all those miles for this? To not be able to stop him? I know you sent me here . . . now what do I do?"

Harriet looked around at the blinking machines. It seemed of all the places she'd seen, this was the saddest in many ways. It was noisy but not with conversation. It was noisy with noise.

Harriet made her way back to the street. It had grown cold and overcast, just like her mood. She could take the bus and be in Grass Valley before bedtime or she could stay and help Buddy —somehow. If she could find him.

That was when she heard the words of Kitty Bloom just before they said their good-byes in Pueblo. "You go, Harriet, your life is your own."

But then just behind those words, in the back of her mind, she heard a deeper voice say, "No, Harriet, your life is not your own." And at that moment she felt relieved. She was much better off thinking that her life was God's, for him to do with what he wanted, not what she desired. Or thought she did.

She walked a little farther with one eye trained on the buildings, concerned she'd see Buddy about to leap from fifty stories up. But no, he was staying at the casino. Maybe she should go back.

Harriet turned around just as the local bus pulled up. The door opened and three passengers stepped off. It was heading west, just like her. Maybe it was a sign that her journey had come to an end. Harriet looked at the driver, then at the passengers.

"Come on, lady," the driver said, "you getting on?"

"Um, no, I have something else to do."

Harriet pulled out her suitcase handle and made tracks back to the casino talking to herself. "If that Buddy Weston thinks he's going to end it all just because he has one arm and has to play his guitar with his toes and has no singing record deal he's gonna answer to me first. Lord, help me."

She arrived at the casino and looked around. It was a huge place, and Buddy could have been anywhere—including his room, knocking back a bottle of Oxycontin or whatever the younger folks used for pain these days. She went to the hotel front desk and asked them to ring his room.

After a few moments, the desk clerk looked up. "I'm sorry, ma'am, no one is answering."

"I failed." She flopped down on a comfortable chair in the lobby. "Oh, Buddy . . . if you die, it's my fault."

"You lookin' for me?"

Harriet looked up. It was Buddy, and he was still carrying his guitar case.

She jumped up and nearly fell flat when she tripped on her suitcase. "You bet I am looking for you! You had me worried sick. I was afraid you were gonna take pills or jump off the building or hang yourself with your guitar strings."

"I was . . . but not the hanging part. Hard to do with one arm. But I got to thinking about you, and, well, you remind me of my mother, and that made me think about how much she wanted me to sing and play the guitar and make a name for myself." He settled himself into a chair nearby and waved to have her join him.

"I'm glad I found you, Buddy," she said, sinking back into her chair.

"Yeah. My mother was all I had, and . . . now I got nothin'. She kept me from being alone."

"Maybe you could visit her," Harriet said. "You could use some good old-fashioned family time. Home-cooked meal and, frankly, someone to do your laundry, son. What about your mama? Where does she live?"

Buddy glared in Harriet's eyes, making her feel uncomfortable. "Didn't you hear what I said? I said my mother *was* all I had. She . . . died. Breast cancer. She had it bad. I took care of her right up to the end. But I wasn't there the night she . . . she took her last breath. I was out playin' some gig in some rundown two-bit taproom."

"Oh, Buddy. I'm sorry. It's hard. I know. You need someone, though, someone in your life to cheer you on."

"I got you."

"But I'm leaving, probably today. Maybe tomorrow."

"You can't," Buddy said. His voice grew cold and severe. "I won't let you." He grabbed Harriet's wrist.

"Buddy, stop, you're hurting me."

"Just come with me."

"No." Harriet yanked her arm back. Her heart pounded. "Buddy. Stop. People are watching."

"If you keep quiet no one will care. If you scream, I'll . . . I'll do something. Now come with me. And don't holler. I can't stand hollering. And don't cry, neither. My mom cried. I hated to hear it."

Harriet tried to take a breath, but she couldn't. She looked into his eyes. They weren't the same crystal blue eyes she saw earlier. Buddy's desperation frightened her to her core. His eyes weren't like the young purse snatcher.

She wanted to panic and scream, but she couldn't make a sound or a move. The casino was so busy yet no one noticed them. Not even the security guard gave her a second look.

"Don't make a scene," he said through gritted teeth. "Just come with me." He took her arm again. "Keep walking. Out to my truck."

"No. I don't want to go." Tears spilled down Harriet's face. She tried to plead silently to the passersby. But they ignored her. She even heard one man say, "She must have lost big time."

Once they were outside the casino Buddy forced her to a parking lot. "That's my truck over there. The blue one with the gray fender and the Confederate flag."

"Where are you taking me?"

"Shut up!" he said. "Get in."

"No. I won't."

Buddy squeezed tighter. He opened the door and pushed her inside. He climbed in after her. "Don't try and jump out."

For some reason Harriet laughed. "Buddy, you're not serious. You're just troubled. You need help. But I'm not the one to help you."

"I said shut up!"

Buddy pulled the truck onto the highway.

"Where are you taking me?"

"Don't matter. I . . . I don't want to die alone."

"Buddy. No."

Harriet felt the truck accelerate. "Slow down. You're driving too fast. We'll have an accident." She tried to get her phone from her tote but it was down deep.

"What are you doing? Don't try anything."

Buddy jerked the truck onto a dirt driveway that came up suddenly. Dust kicked up all around the cab.

"I know a place. A place where I can . . . I can run this truck off a cliff. I can't die by myself."

"Don't make me watch you. Is that what you want? You couldn't watch your mom die, and now you want me to watch you die? I won't."

"Stop talking. You're . . . you're confusing me." Buddy swerved the truck around a large rock.

Harriet screamed. She couldn't help it. She screamed as loud as she could. She punched Buddy's arm. "Stop this. Stop this right now."

But Buddy kept driving.

Harriet reached for the door handle. She thought she could jump but the truck was moving too fast. Then in a flash she grabbed onto the steering wheel. "No." She pulled hard.

Buddy slammed on the brakes. "What are you doing?"

"Just stop," Harriet said. She forced her voice to be calm, smooth. "You don't have to die because you weren't there for your mother. She understands. I know. You can be a singer, you can live your dream. With God's—" She stopped talking and looked into his eyes. "I could be one of those people who pulls Jesus out of my bag and tells you how much you need him, which, don't get me wrong, you do, but I don't think you want to hear that right now."

Buddy hit the steering wheel with his palms. "Don't tell me about Jesus!" He looked at Harriet and cried. "My mother believed in God and—" He sobbed.

Harriet reached over and pulled the keys from the ignition. "Let me tell you about the snake handlers I rode with," she said as she reached into her bag and clicked 911.

It only took a few minutes for the police to arrive—three squad cars and a paramedic. There was a lot of confusion at first but the next thing Harriet knew, she was standing next to one of the squad cars with a female police officer. The officer was asking questions so fast, or so it seemed, that Harriet could hardly catch her breath.

"Calm down, ma'am, and tell me what happened."

Harriet leaned around the tall woman in time to see Buddy's one arm handcuffed to his belt loop. Two other officers were taking him to another car. She watched as they put him in the backseat.

"That poor man," Harriet said. "I don't think he would have hurt me. He's just so troubled."

"What happened?" the officer repeated.

Harriet took a breath, and that was when unexpected tears began to flow down her cheeks. "Oh dear, I suppose it was a bit unsettling at that."

"Unsettling? You were kidnapped."

"I . . . I know that, dear." Harriet wiped her eyes. And then she told the officer everything that happened. She needed to sniff back tears on a few occasions, but she finally got the whole story out.

"So, you see, I was just trying to help the dear. He just needs his mama, and well, like I said, she's gone now." Harriet looked off toward the cliff. "I think I must have favored her somehow. There was a connection." Her stomach wobbled at the thought that maybe, just maybe Buddy could have driven off it like some wild movie scene—with her in the car. "I'm just so thankful I'm still here for my Henry—no matter what might have gone before or whether they ever give me a grandchild."

Chapter 32

AFTER GIVING HER STATEMENT AT THE POLICE STATION, THE officer told Harriet she was free to go.

"But we may need to speak to you at a later date," she said. "Even though he confessed and was peaceful and all."

"Please take care of him." Harriet's knees still shook as she sat at the table across from the police officer. "I need to get back to the casino. I left my suitcase there. I hope it's still there."

The officer shook her head. "Where did you leave it?"

"Well, when Buddy forced me away, it was in the lobby."

"Oh no. I hope it wasn't stolen."

"Can you call the hotel?"

"Sure."

A few minutes later Harriet went to the restroom and had a little cry. She freshened up with a cold splash of water on her face. She went back to the lobby and waited for the officer. This station was nothing like the one she saw in Dodge. No, this station meant business.

"Good news. They have your suitcase," Officer Wilkes said. "Fortunately some good Samaritan turned it in to the front desk."

"Oh, thank God," Harriet said.

"I'll have one of our officers drive you back to the casino."

Harriet got into the police car and cried. It had been a harrowing day to say the least. A ride on an emotional roller coaster Harriet never wanted to ride again.

"You know, that was pretty brave what you did," Officer Jones said. "That man could have killed you."

Harriet sucked a breath and snuffed back tears. She blew her nose into a tissue. Officer Wilkes gave her a box at the station. "Yes, he could have, but I had the feeling he really just wanted some attention. Someone to get him help."

"He'll get that in jail — if he wants it."

Harriet couldn't help herself. She needed to take another deep breath just to try and slow her heartrate.

"Maybe you should call your son. Freda — I mean Officer Wilkes — said you were traveling alone and had a son."

"I will — a little later. I just got him to relax about the trip and now . . . this."

"But you're okay. That's what's important."

* * *

Harriet was surprised how easily she could make bus connections from Reno, through several smaller towns, and then into California. When she crossed the state line, she turned to her seatmate, an older gentleman with two cigars sticking out of his shirt pocket, and said, "My heart just grew three sizes. You know like the Grinch, only I'm not a Grinch. At first I didn't want to go. But now that I'm here, I do want to be here."

Cigar Man ignored her. But that was okay. Harriet had talked plenty for one day.

At a town called McQueen, Harriet needed to take four buses toward the airport and then transfer to the Green Route to the Truckee bus depot. From there Harriet had no choice but to find her way to the Truckee Amtrak Station and buy a ticket. The Truckee Amtrak Station was cute, or so Harriet thought. She liked the small clapboard building, which was painted bright yellow like a sunflower with brown trim and wooden benches outside. There wasn't much else in the way of amenities, but at least they had a bathroom and a vending machine where she could get a Diet Coke. The only trouble was, when she went to get her ticket, she discovered that the California Zephyr, which had become like a friend to her, was not scheduled to return until around eight o'clock the next morning. Harriet would need to spend the night in Truckee.

Amelia lead her to a lovely little hotel, Mrs. Frank's Inn on Donner Boulevard. She had to think about that a minute as she stood outside the bright purple house turned hotel. It had lovely gingerbread trim around the gables and a pretty little garden chock full of purple and yellow and red flowers. She had to think about the Donner thing she had learned about. It was creepy to think about the Donner Party, the infamous incident way back in 1840 when a group of pioneers became stranded by a blizzard and had to resort to cannibalism to survive. She shuddered at the thought.

Harriet was greeted inside the house by an older woman, who looked to be closing in on eighty.

"Can I help you?" the woman said with a scratchy voice as she sucked on a cigarette and then blew smoke into the air.

"I need a room for the night."

"Yeah?"

"Do you have one? Because I can just find another — " Harriet was in no mood to fuss with anyone.

"No, no I got one. Got 'em all as a matter of fact. We don't see folks usually till fall. Ski weather."

"Oh, well, I'm just on my way to Grass Valley."

"Room 2 — top of the stairs."

Harriet found her room easily enough. It was okay, smelled from mold, though — mold and cigarettes. Her bed was small, not quite a double, some weird size with a mattress so hard she figured you could play tennis on it. But she had no choice but settle in and make Mrs. Frank's Inn her base of operations until morning.

One of the first things she did was call Martha.

"No, I'm serious, Martha," Harriet said into her phone. "The man kidnapped me." Her heart pounded at the thought.

"You're serious. Oh, Harriet. You must have been scared out of your mind."

"Well that's the strange thing," Harriet said. "I was at first, but then, I don't know what came over me. It might have been something I learned from the snake preachers. But I knew that I'd be all right. I kept silently calling on the name of Jesus through the whole ordeal until finally I laughed at him. And that seemed to settle him down."

"Now you really are a hero," Martha said.

"Oh, I just can't hardly believe it's me doing all these things. But I was thinking that for the whole trip and even before that, folks were driving me. I followed. But when I grabbed Buddy's steering wheel and made it go the way I wanted it to, well, I was in charge. Me—the gambling cookie lady from Bryn Mawr."

Harriet thought she could hear Martha's smile. "Anyway," she said. "I'm safe and sound in Truckee in the Sierra Nevada Mountains. I am not making that up, either. That's the name. It's nice, pretty much what you'd imagine a mountain town to be like. And get this, Martha, I'm staying near the famous Donner Pass; you know, you heard about the Donner Party."

"You mean those folks who had to eat—"

"Yep. Weird, huh. Can you imagine?"

"Let's not talk about that. When will you get to Henry's?" Martha asked.

"Tomorrow. I think I'll surprise them and just show up on their doorstep."

Harriet and Martha enjoyed more conversation. Harriet told her she had sent thirty-six boxes of salt and pepper shakers to Grass Valley including her collection from home.

"And I think I'll pick some more up here in Truckee."

Martha laughed. "You're a card, Harriet. A real card."

* * *

Mrs. Franks, the hotel owner, suggested Harriet go to a restaurant called Doilies. "You can get a decent meal there; burgers ain't bad. 'Course I'd stay away from the grizzly guts stew."

"Grizzly guts? Really?"

Mrs. Franks lifted her bushy eyebrows. "Really. And be careful walking around town after dark. Some of the Donner Party are still out looking for livers to eat. Then you'd be stuck here, looking for livers."

Harriet swallowed. "I don't believe in ghosts."

Mrs. Franks' eyebrows rose. "Suit yourself. I'm just saying. Be careful." She sucked her cigarette.

Harriet spent a fitful night in the uncomfortable bed. She kept imagining noises that weren't there, and if that weren't bad enough, a thunderstorm blew in. The lightning lit up her room with scary white light and made shadows dance like ghosts looking for livers to eat. And each rumble of thunder shook her bed, and one time it boomed so close overhead it made her bed move. It took a moment to blame it on the thunder. She thought maybe a ghost had moved it. "Get out," she said. "I need my liver."

But the creepiest part was when the lights went off and Harriet only had her phone to illuminate the dark. She thought she should call Henry and was just about to when her door creaked open and she saw Mrs. Franks in a long striped night shirt and a long tasseled nightcap standing at the threshold with a lantern. At least she prayed it was Mrs. Franks.

"I come to light your lantern, if you need it. No telling how long the lights will be out."

"Sh . . . sure," Harriet said. "Thank you."

"Like to keep the oil lamps just in case."

Mrs. Franks flicked a match on the wall and lit the small lantern. "Won't keep you warm but least you got light. Until the oil runs out."

Mrs. Franks left, and Harriet pulled the cover over her head and sang, "Give me oil in my lamp, keep it burning, burning, burn—" And then *crack*, lightning struck.

Morning, in all its mercy and light, finally came. Harriet dressed quickly without washing or brushing her teeth. She shoved her belongings into her pack and made her way downstairs, paid her bill, said good-bye to Mrs. Franks, and hightailed it to the Truckee Amtrak.

She had a short wait of about an hour so she sat on one of the benches outside. "I'll get coffee on the train." She shivered against the chill air.

"How 'bout that storm last night?" said another waiting passenger.

"It was something," Harriet said, trying to sound brave. "But I like thunderstorms, 'specially in the mountains."

"Me too," the man said. "Except when we lose power like we did last night."

Harriet shivered.

Right on schedule the California Zephyr pulled up. Harriet stood, but as she did she felt a sudden pain, a huge pain right in the middle of her chest. It was like an anvil had fallen onto her chest. She staggered. Couldn't catch her breath. She tried to sit back down, but she stumbled and fell against the building. The pain was horrible, like nothing she had ever felt before. She clutched her chest. Pain shot down her left arm. She saw the conductor running toward her.

"Ma'am, are you all right?" he hollered.

"Don't let them take my liver."

And then everything went black.

* * *

That evening, after supper, Henry and Prudence had settled down to watch a baseball game together. Sandra Day sat on Prudence's lap, while Humphrey lay near Henry's feet.

"Good night for baseball. I just want to catch the news first," Henry said.

"What's wrong with Humphrey?" Prudence asked. "He looks even more depressed than usual. Is he sick?"

Henry patted the dog's head. "Don't know. He's been glum all day. He hasn't eaten much and has just been hanging close to me like a big fat barnacle. Wouldn't even eat the donut Mrs. Caldwell brought him."

Humphrey moaned.

Just then the phone rang.

"Henry Beamer?"

"Yes. Who's calling?"

"This is Hilda Shim at Incline Village Hospital."

Henry's heart nearly stopped. He looked at Prudence. Prudence looked at him.

"Hospital? My mother?"

"Yes, sir. She's been admitted. She had a small heart attack. But she's stable."

"She had a heart attack," Henry said to Prudence.

Humphrey howled.

"Incline Village? Where the heck is that?"

"Near Lake Tahoe."

"Is she all right?"

"She's being admitted to the cardiac care unit."

Henry clicked off his phone. "Come on, we have to go to Lake Tahoe."

"Lake Tahoe?" Prudence slipped on her sneakers. "What about the dog?"

"Should we take him?"

Humphrey perked up and trotted toward the front door. "Look at him. He knew something was wrong," Henry said. "I don't feel right about leaving him here alone. He'll have a nervous breakdown."

Henry and Prudence got into the BMW. Humphrey lay

down in the back. "Set the GPS, Pru," Henry said. "What's the address?"

"Hold on, I have to do a search."

"I'm sorry, I'm just worried."

Henry pulled onto the main street heading toward California Highway 20. "Incline Village?" he said. "Sounds small. Sounds like they won't be able to take good care of her. What if they have to relocate her to a bigger hospital? What if she needs surgery, or a bypass, or a heart transplant?"

"Then we'll go wherever she is. And she won't need surgery or a transplant. Honestly, your mind. Everything is a plot, a story." Prudence patted his hand as it rested on the gearshift. "Don't worry, honey. We'll get to her."

Humphrey whimpered.

* * *

Harriet woke in the presence of two doctors and a nurse. The pain had subsided. She noticed she was hooked up to IVs. "What happened?"

"You had a small heart attack, Harriet," the doctor said. She had a soothing voice and Harriet felt at ease, although a bit nervous.

"Oh, then it wasn't the liver-stealing Donner party."

"What?" The doctor looked at her. She smiled. "Could be the drugs."

"Nothing," Harriet said. "You say it was small? How small? It didn't feel small." She spoke softly. She was so tired and a little dizzy. She pointed to the middle of her chest. "It hurt right here, and then, just like they say in the TV commercial, I felt the pain in my arm."

"That's exactly it. But it was minor. I don't think there is any damage to the heart muscle. But just to be sure I want to keep you overnight."

"Overnight? Do I have to?"

"It's advised. We'll put you on the cardiac unit. We already called your son."

"Oh, why'd you go and do that? Now he'll never let me finish my trip." Harriet took a labored breath.

"Oh, I didn't know you were on a trip. But I wouldn't advise you to continue, Harriet. Maybe your son can come and get you. Take you home from here."

Harriet's spirits sank. "But, but ..."

The doctor patted her hand. "No need to make a decision. Let's get you into a room and settled first. But I really think you should consider letting your son come and drive you home."

Harriet lay her head back into the pillow and closed her eyes. The bright lights in the room disturbed her. "I guess I am pretty tired, after all."

"It's been a long trip," the nurse said.

An hour later Harriet was tucked into a bed on the third floor of the hospital. It was a private room, and she had more bells and whistles attached to her than she could count. She hated hospitals. Hated being sick and was quite frankly angry she even had the stupid heart attack. So when the nurse came in later to take her vitals and help her to the bathroom Harriet asked, "Why did this happen? I am so healthy, little high blood pressure. But otherwise—"

"Hard to know why. Things happen. Sometimes the body has ways of telling you to slow down."

Harriet shook her head. "I feel pretty good right now."

"That's good. The docs take good care of folks here."

"Speaking of here," Harriet said as she adjusted herself and her gown, "where exactly am I?"

"Incline Village Community Hospital."

"Incline Village? Where on God's green earth is that? I was in Truckee."

"Near Lake Tahoe. Not far from Truckee. This is the closest hospital."

"Lake Tahoe? Isn't that a ritzy part of the world? Full of movie stars and such?"

"Sometimes. But to us it's just home. Pretty place. I moved here last year from Grass Valley."

"That's where I'm headed."

"Later. You just get some rest. That sedative will be kicking in any minute. Don't get out of bed yourself. Call me."

Harriet immediately defied the nurse and got up long enough to reach her tote bag. She found her phone, and when she unlocked it she saw two missed calls. One from Henry and one from—she could hardly believe her eyes. It was from Lacy—the young woman who helped her buy the Droid and was so sweet and encouraging.

"How did she get my number?" Then she remembered. She practiced calling Lacy way back in West Chester. She wanted to call her back right away, but she had never felt so tired.

Harriet closed her eyes and tried to sleep, but with all the hospital noises it was pretty hard, even with all the drugs she had been given. On the whole Harriet mistrusted drugs and much preferred a warm toddy over a sleeping pill.

She rang for the nurse and waited impatiently.

"Did you need something?"

"I was wondering, could you send a text for me? I'm not very good and—"

"Well, we're not supposed to use cell phones near the machines but—"

"Can you use it in the lounge or—"

"Okay."

Harriet handed her the phone.

"Sweet," the young nurse said.

"Yes. It is. Please text to the number for Lacy. She's one of the missed calls today. Say, I made it safe and sound. Well, safe anyway. No, don't say that, just say, Harriet made it. Safe and sound. Thank you."

"Okay. I'll be right back. But then the phone gets turned off until you're released."

Harriet pushed her head into the pillow. "I made it, huh, not really." She looked toward the window. "So, hey there, God," she whispered. "What's up with this? Did I do something wrong? I thought you were behind me the whole way, and ... and now it seems like I'm not going to make it even though I just told Lacy I did."

* * *

"You need to take exit 188B," Prudence said.

"188B?" Henry said.

"Yes."

Prudence tapped her phone and waited a moment. "This is Prudence Beamer. I was inquiring about Harriet Beamer, my mother-in-law."

"She's resting comfortably," the nurse said.

Prudence tapped the phone off. "See. She's okay."

"Call her room. I want to talk to her."

"Let her rest. We'll talk when we get there. It's safer."

"Prudence, please. Just call her room."

"I think we should wait. What if she's sleeping? Hearing your voice could excite her."

Henry grew silent. Then a few seconds later he asked, "What exit did you say?"

"188B toward Lake Tahoe."

"Lake Tahoe. It's like she's going backward."

"It was probably closest from Truckee."

"Truckee?"

"Yes, everyone goes to Truckee, it seems."

Forty-five minutes later, Henry pulled into the hospital parking lot. "Come on," he said.

Prudence patted Humphrey's head. "Don't worry. I'm sure she's okay."

The dog whimpered and hid his eyes under his long ears.

Henry and Prudence had no trouble finding his mother's room. He peeked inside first, unsure of what he'd see. The room was dark except for a faint light over her bed and the lights on all the equipment. Henry had not seen so much medical equipment since his father died in a very similar room. He inched closer and stood at her side.

"Hi, Son," Harriet said as she opened her eyes.

Henry leaned over and kissed her cheek. "Hi, Mom. How ya doin?"

Harriet adjusted herself. "I'm fine, honey. Really. Doctor said it was a little heart attack. Nothing to get excited about."

Henry patted her hand. "I love you so much, Mom. I'm so happy to see you."

"I love you too. Now please, bring the back up a bit."

Henry pushed the button on the side of the bed, and the head section rose.

"That's good, Henry. I'm comfy now."

"I'm so sorry this happened, Mom."

Harriet smiled. "Me too. But the doc says I'm doing great. I'll be out tomorrow. I think they're just watching me."

"That's good."

Harriet looked around. "Hi, Prudence."

"Hi, Mom." She leaned down and kissed her cheek. "I'm so happy you're okay. And ... and I'm sorry I got angry about the bib. I was oversensitive."

Harriet smiled. "Oh, it's over now, dear. It was just me doing some wishful thinking."

"I know. But ..."

"Please. Say no more. Now, how's my Humphrey? Did you bring him?"

"He's in the car," Henry said.

"Ah, you mean he's right outside? Go get him. Sneak him in."

"Mom," Henry said. "That breaks all the rules."

"Please. It's late. No one will notice. Carry him like a ba—"
She looked at Prudence. "Sorry."

Prudence kissed Harriet's cheek a second time. "You hold on.
I'll be right back."

"Pru, no," Henry said.

"Shhh."

* * *

Several minutes went by and still no Prudence. "I wonder what
happened," Henry said. "I hope they didn't kick her out of the
hospital."

"She would have called if that happened ... or come back up
without him."

Prudence appeared at the door. She was pushing a baby carriage. She entered the room and quickly closed the door.

"Pru, what the—"

"Shhh, look." She removed the blanket that covered the carriage, and Humphrey poked his head up.

"Humphrey." Harriet burst into tears. "You ... brought him
up here? You really did it."

"Just for you, Mom. I'd do it for no one else. Thought he'd do
you good."

Henry lifted Humphrey out of the carriage. He held him so
Harriet could pet him.

Humphrey whimpered and licked Harriet's cheek. Then he
whimpered some more.

"I'm okay," Harriet said. "Just a mini heart attack. No worries.
Just getting older. The ticker still has plenty of miles to go." She
patted her dog and smiled as he tried to lick her hand.

"Where did you get the carriage?" Henry asked.

"I bought it. From a woman in the lobby. She seemed thrilled
to get the money."

Harriet looked at Prudence. "Thank you, Prudence. But now
you have a baby carriage to store."

The door burst open, and a large nurse with a scowl entered the room. "I thought I smelled a dog. How did you get that animal in here?"

"Oh, don't get so upset," Prudence said. "She hasn't seen him for almost a month. It's . . . therapeutic."

Harriet looked at Prudence in disbelief. "Prudence, you . . . amaze me."

"It's against the rules," the nurse said. "That's what it is. Now, kindly remove that . . . that . . . that beast from these premises."

"No problem, toots," Henry said. "Come, dear, let's get him home." He put Humphrey into the carriage. "We'll see you in the morning, Mom. We'll stay at a motel close by. Get some sleep," he said. Henry wheeled the carriage out with his head held high and Prudence on his arm. Humphrey held his head high also.

* * *

The next morning, the doctor put Harriet through more tests, all of which she passed with flying colors. "I can discharge you today, but . . . I think you should call your son and have him drive you home. No more buses and trains and—"

"Motorcycles?"

"No. Not even a motorcycle, at least for a while. You need to recover."

Harriet's spirits sank again. She failed, or at least that was how it felt. She was so close, yet so far away. "Please, just to Grass Valley."

"From here? Too far. And besides I think it will take more than one bus."

"Probably. Okay, I'll call Henry and tell him to come get me."

The doctor looked at Harriet. "I'm serious. No bus. Straight home and right to bed."

"Fine."

Harriet placed the call in spite of what she was told about cell phone usage. "Come get me. The doctor said I could go home. Straight home."

"Okay, Mom. We'll be there shortly."

"Thank you, dear."

Harriet clicked off her phone. And then clicked it back on. She needed to tell Martha. Martha took the news pretty well, but she made Harriet promise also that she would stay off the bus for a while. Harriet promised.

"But I was so close, Martha."

"I know. And you should feel very pleased with yourself. It's not your fault you had a heart attack."

"Thank you. But do you think it's possible I overdid it?"

"Who's to say. You probably would have had the heart attack at some point."

"I had a good time, Martha. I'd do it again. In a heartbeat. Ha, ha. Well not the part with Buddy, I think."

"I am sooo proud of you," Martha said.

Harriet took a breath. She was still a little shaky and worried whenever she needed a deep breath, like it would cause her heart to stop beating again.

"Martha," she said. "There's something I need to tell you."

"Uh-oh, what did you do now?"

"No, no, nothing like that. I . . . I used to be jealous of you."

"Me? Why?"

"Because you're such a fabulous artist; you dress so young and . . . bohemian. You could make a dead raccoon into a lovely centerpiece if you had to."

"Well, fortunately, I never—"

"That's not the point. I used to wish I could be like you. But now, now I don't have to be like you. I can get along in this world by just being me."

"Well, sure you can. You never had to be like me. I always admired you too. You could listen better than anyone. You have that discerning spirit; it's a gift. And you make better cookies."

307

"But, Martha, the thing is, I think this trip was good for me. And not just me, but . . . some others. And even if that heart attack had killed me, that would have been okay too. I think I made a difference."

"I love you, Harriet," Martha said. "You're my best friend. I'm going to miss you. I miss you already."

"When are you coming for a visit?"

"I don't know. Maybe Christmas."

Harriet felt a gush of tears come on. "Oh, Martha. I . . . I . . ."

"It's okay. You're where God wants you."

Harriet changed into her street clothes. She took her time though as she filtered through some of the mementos she had collected. "It was a good trip."

Then she sat in the visitor's chair and wrote to Max.

Dear Max, this might be my last letter for a while. I guess you know about the heart attack. Well, I would do it all again. I learned so much about people, the country, cowboys and Indians, stars and dolphins and most of all about myself, especially when Buddy, the one-armed country singer . . .

Harriet swallowed. Hard. And then went back to her letter.

. . . tried to take me away. I stood up to him too, Max. It was like a well of strength burbled up inside of me, and I stood my ground until the police arrive. Poor soul. I will pray for him.

The nurse came into the room with her final discharge orders. Harriet signed a couple of pages, looked over two prescriptions that would need to be filled right away, and then sighed. She went back to her letter.

I learned that I'm strong and capable, Max, and I learned that I can get my own dang salt and pepper shakers, to quote a cancan dancer.

* * *

Henry arrived.

"Mom is this all you have?" he asked as he zipped up her suitcase. "This and the tote bag?"

Harriet, who was sitting in a wheel chair, smiled. "Yep. That's all I have. But say, Henry dear, would you please give me my martens. I'd like to wear them."

Henry unzipped the case and found the martens. "Eww, Mom, what in tarnation?"

"They're very classy. Or at least they were back in my generation."

Henry draped the martens around his mother's shoulders. He kissed her cheek. "It never occurred to me that you could make a dead marten look elegant."

That was when a transport boy entered the room. "Ready to go?"

They rode the elevator to the lobby.

"So, tell me, Mom," Henry said when they were alone again, "are you disappointed you didn't finish the trip?"

"No, not really. I may not have made it all the way to Grass Valley, but I accomplished so much. I made it to the places God wanted me to. And that's what's important. I guess what's important is not how you get where you belong, but that you get there."

Henry led her to the car. Humphrey was in the back, dancing and barking to the beat of the band. Harriet was pleased as punch to see him. "I'm coming home, boy."

Prudence got out of the car and came over to hug her. Then she leaned down and whispered in Harriet's ear, "I'm glad you're coming to live with us." They all got in the car. "I hope you continue feeling that way," Harriet said.

"Okay," Henry said. "Let's go, and please, no more of this nonsense."

He pulled away from the curb and drove for close to an hour before Harriet said another word. "Do you really think it was nonsense? My trip?"

Henry glanced at her.

"Well, no, Mom, I didn't mean—"

"Yes, you did. Now, look, Henry. I had a reason to do it. You don't know what happened in all those days and ... and I had a good time—including the snake handlers. The gorge was a little scary, the kidnapping nearly killed me. But that's water under the bridge. And I met some—"

"Kidnapping?" Prudence said.

"Oh, I didn't tell you about how Buddy, the one-armed, foot guitar-playing country singer, took—" She sighed. "Oh dear, it's a long story. I'll tell you when we get home." That was when she saw a sign for Colfax, California. "Henry, point this vehicle in the direction of Colfax. I'm getting out there."

"But, Mom. You can't. The doctor—"

"I don't care what the doctor said. I don't care what you say. Take me to the train station in Colfax."

"The train?"

"Never mind. I know what I'm doing."

Henry obliged much to his dismay. "Fine. Suit yourself. I'd rather do this than see you get upset and have another heart attack. I'll ride with you."

"You will not."

Humphrey barked.

"You tell him, Humphrey. There's donuts in it for you."

Henry parked the BMW and helped his mother out of the car. He helped her with her tote bag, leaving the suitcase in the car. Prudence walked closer.

Harriet smiled. "I'm getting on the bus. According to my GPS"—she looked at Prudence—"I can catch the Gold Country Stage here. Take me right into Grass Valley."

"Are you sure about this?" Prudence asked.

"As sure as I was about my broken ankle."

Then she leaned down and whispered in Harriet's ear. "We'll be following right behind. And I'm glad you're coming to live with us. I can't wait to tell the baby that his Nana climbed a mountain to come be with him."

Harriet looked up. Tears flowed down her cheeks. "What? You're ... you're pregnant?"

Harriet watched Prudence smile at Henry. "Not yet. But we're working on it."

Harriet swiped a tear away from her eye. Then she hugged Humphrey. "Ready to go home, boy?"

Minutes later the bus pulled up. "Okay, Mom, we'll see you at home," Henry said.

Harriet climbed aboard. The driver smiled. "What about him?"

"My son? Nah, he's driving."

"No, the dog."

"Humphrey? But he's not allowed on the—"

"Come on. He's welcome here," said the driver. The other passengers agreed.

Henry helped Humphrey onto the seat next to Harriet. He kissed her cheek and then left the bus. Harriet waved to him and Prudence.

As the bus driver pulled away he hit a pothole just slightly smaller than the Royal Gorge.

"Ahh," Harriet said, "now I know what it means to feel God's pleasure."

Carrying Mason

Joyce Magnin

What does it mean to lay down your life?

Luna has learned an awful lot in her thirteen years — how to skin a rabbit, how to gut
a fish, how to pick the perfect wildflowers
— but it's not enough. When her best friend,
Mason, dies, she decides to honor his memory by moving in with his mentally disabled
mother, Ruby Day. While cooking and cleaning for Ruby Day isn't always easy, everything seems to be going relatively fine — until trouble
arrives in the form of Ruby Day's aunt, who will stop at nothing to
make sure her niece is put away in a mental institution.

Luna is only thirteen. How can she stand up to Ruby Day's aunt?
What would Mason want her to do? And why is saying good-bye so
difficult?

Available in stores and online!

ZONDERVAN®
.com

Share Your Thoughts

With the Author: Your comments will be forwarded to the author when you send them to *zauthor@zondervan.com*.

With Zondervan: Submit your review of this book by writing to *zreview@zondervan.com*.

Free Online Resources at
www.zondervan.com

Zondervan AuthorTracker: Be notified whenever your favorite authors publish new books, go on tour, or post an update about what's happening in their lives at www.zondervan.com/authortracker.

Daily Bible Verses and Devotions: Enrich your life with daily Bible verses or devotions that help you start every morning focused on God. Visit www.zondervan.com/newsletters.

Free Email Publications: Sign up for newsletters on Christian living, academic resources, church ministry, fiction, children's resources, and more. Visit www.zondervan.com/newsletters.

Zondervan Bible Search: Find and compare Bible passages in a variety of translations at www.zondervanbiblesearch.com.

Other Benefits: Register to receive online benefits like coupons and special offers, or to participate in research.

ZONDERVAN®

ZONDERVAN.com/
AUTHORTRACKER
follow your favorite authors